EVIL INTENT

BERNARD TAYLOR

Bestselling Author Of *Charmed Life*

When Jack Forrest and his family move to a beautiful old house in the English countryside, he doesn't expect their newfound happiness to be disturbed by a run-in with one of their neighbors. And just as they are determined to dismiss the encounter as a trivial spat, the first death occurs—the opening episode in a spiraling nightmare of events that threatens them all. Over the following months, Jack can do nothing more than stand and watch as a relentless scourge destroys his family bliss. In a battle between good and evil, Jack desperately tries to combat a supernatural force born of a dark place where justice has no meaning.

"Taylor is capable of making your hair stand on end! Fascinating!"
                                                                 —*Newsday*

EVIL INTENT

BERNARD TAYLOR

Book Margins, Inc.

A BMI Edition

Published by special arrangement with Dorchester Publishing Co., Inc. and Headline Book Publishing Limited, a division of Hodder Headline PLC.

This is for Mary and Brian.

*In acknowledgment of the debt I owe to
M.R. James, without whose talent
this story would not exist.*

Prologue

Mary Hopper pressed the play button on the CD player and the overture to Von Suppé's *Die Schöne Galathée* exploded into the room with all the colour and exuberance of a firework display.

Mary stood for a moment listening, letting the sound sweep over her, then, with the music following, she left the sitting room and moved back into the little cloakroom to finish her work in there. It was almost one o'clock, and she had been cleaning the house since ten that morning. This particular Saturday had a difference, though. Today, before getting busy with the vacuum cleaner and dusters, she had packed up all her school textbooks and papers and put them away in the study. There they would remain for the next two weeks, the duration of the school Easter holidays. As much as she enjoyed her work as a teacher at the primary school in the nearby village of Barfield, she was nevertheless always glad when the long spring break came round. Yesterday afternoon she had said goodbye to her pupils. She would see them nearer the end of the month, she had told them, and in the meantime they should enjoy the holidays and try not to get into any trouble.

She looked around her. The room was just about finished. After giving a final polish to the mirror she hovered for a moment studying her reflection. She saw a woman of thirty-eight years old, of medium height with light brown hair and clear grey eyes. She was reasonably attractive, she observed dispassionately, but not in any way striking. Leaning closer to the glass she brushed a fingertip to the sprinkling of freckles across the bridge of her nose and upper cheeks. Those she could do without, but there was no banishing them now.

Abandoning her cleaning implements for the time being, she moved to the kitchen where she put on the kettle for coffee and made herself a sandwich. While the water heated she sat gazing out. The day was warm, the bright sun high in a cloudless sky. Beyond the window the wide, sun-drenched rear garden reproached her with its growing wildness. Nature was slowly but surely reclaiming it, and if allowed to continue unchecked for much longer would turn it into a jungle. She sighed, remembering it from times past. In her earliest childhood memories it was always a place of beauty and much loved, and indeed it had been so. It had been her mother's consuming passion, and her father's too, after the opera, the first love of his life; when he had not been at work in his study or away taking in some new opera production, he had often worked on the garden. With all the love and care her parents had lavished upon it, though, they had always endeavoured to keep it a natural, growing thing, not like some gardens with their neat, self-

10

conscious, manicured appearance. They had seen themselves as servants of nature, or at least as co-workers; never its masters.

Sitting there while the memories came pouring in, Mary suddenly saw herself a girl once more. And in her memory she runs shrieking and laughing across the sunlit lawn and down the garden path towards the orchard, followed by David, her elder brother, and her tease and torment. Continuing in the melancholy sweet memory she sees her mother and father bending over one of the herbaceous borders, and as she dashes past her father looks up and smiles and groans and asks David, 'For God's sake, can't you leave the girl alone?' But David just yells out some pathetic justification and continues on in pursuit.

The kettle was boiling, bringing her back to the present. She heated the cafetière, measured out the coffee and added the water.

The banal, simplistic thought went through her mind that all the time life brought changes; nothing ever stayed the same. As a child she had never questioned her security, had never dreamed that anything would ever be different. But of course it had all changed. How could it not? Her mother, her father, her brother—they were all gone now. And she herself was different. There had been changes to her own life, not least through a marriage and divorce which had caused emotional wounds that had only recently healed, though, as with all wounds, leaving scars that would remain.

It was after her divorce that she had come back to the village, to live with her widowed father again, and to take up the teaching post at the Barfield primary school. With them both being alone it had seemed the natural and sensible thing to do.

11

When she had poured the coffee she sat on the high stool, sipping from the mug, eating her sandwich and gazing out. Now that spring and the holidays were here she should make an effort to do a little work on the garden, though she doubted that she could make much of an impact on the burgeoning chaos. It was too much to cope with on her own; she'd never be able to bring it back to the way it had been.

A calendar hung on the wall beside the refrigerator, and her eye was drawn to a red-painted circle enclosing the date of Tuesday, 7 August—the day that she and Ruth would be leaving for Italy. Having made their booking just the week before, they'd be picking up their tickets in Reading next Saturday.

'Italy.' She spoke the word aloud, and the sound was magic on her tongue. It would be her first holiday abroad since her marriage when she and Ian had gone to France. That was years ago. It would be wonderful to get away again, and she had no doubt that Ruth would be a fine and agreeable travelling companion. They got on well together, having become firm friends in the two years since Ruth had come to teach at the school. Like herself, Ruth was a divorcée. The trip to Italy, Mary said to herself, was something to look forward to.

Her sandwich finished and her coffee mug empty, she left the kitchen to resume her house-cleaning chores. With the Von Suppé CD replaced by a tape of excerpts from Verdi's *La Traviata*, she carried her cleaning implements upstairs, the overture to the opera rising up through the stairwell. In her bedroom she dusted and polished the dressing table and bedside chest. On the bureau below the window stood a vase holding some white marguerites, now dying.

She was just taking the flowers from the vase when

her glance was attracted by movement from beyond the window. Looking out over the front garden she saw a man appear at the gate.

She froze, and then, quickly recovering, stepped back behind the curtain, at the same time uttering a long drawn-out groan: 'Oh, no-o-o!' Surely not him—not now. Where Callow was concerned she had hoped that it was all finished with. After what had happened at their last meeting she had never expected to see him near the house again. But now here he was, coming back once more to disturb her growing sense of peace.

She remained where she was for a second or two longer, and then carefully moved out from behind the curtain. She had dared to hope that he had merely stopped at the gate for a moment and would soon pass on by, but now as she peeped out she was just in time to see the top of his head pass out of sight beneath the window on his way to the front door. A yard or two behind him came his dog, an old black labrador. She held her breath, and two seconds later, cutting discordantly through the music, came the ringing of the doorbell. For a second the thought went through her mind that if she ignored it he would think she was out. But no, he would hear the music and know she was at home.

Still she waited, while up from below came the sound of Verdi's tragic heroine Violetta singing in wonderment at the revelation of love. '*Ah! forse lui,*' she sang—*Ah! perhaps he is the one!*—though the irony of the sentiment was lost on Mary, preoccupied as she was by her situation. *Perhaps*, sang Violetta, *it is he who has lit within me the burning flame of love* . . . And then there came over the singer's wondering tones the ringing of the doorbell again.

Still Mary stood there, one hand to her mouth, the

other clutching the dead flowers. The sound of the bell came yet again, more piercingly than ever. It rang again, and again, and again, this last time a long, long ring, as if the bell had jammed or the man was keeping his finger on the button.

She did not know what to do. She had been so sure that it was all over and done with between them, but clearly she had been wrong. She would have to finish it now, though; she must, and this time for good and all.

She became aware that water from the stems of the dead marguerites was dripping onto the carpet. She looked helplessly around her for a moment and then jammed the flowers back into the vase. Her heart thudding, she left the room and went down the stairs. As she reached the hall the ring at the doorbell came again. She stopped before the door, took a deep breath, then stretched out her hand and opened it.

The man standing just beyond the step was slim and tall, over six feet, and looked to be aged in his mid-sixties. His pepper-and-salt hair was thick and wiry and cut with a no-nonsense, military precision. The flesh over his nose and cheeks was marbled with a fine red tracery of broken veins, and his wide smile showed long, yellowing teeth. He wore a tweed sports jacket and a collar and tie, and in his buttonhole was a perfect little pink rose. His dog stood beside him.

Mary looked at him coldly, saying nothing, while inwardly she shrank from him.

'Good afternoon, Mary.'

John Callow's voice was full and round, its trained, clear projection giving evidence of his theatrical back-ground. Its unctuous tone had been one of the first things about him that Mary had come so much to loathe.

In answer to his greeting she merely nodded, her mouth set and unsmiling. She would give away nothing that could be construed as encouragement. In the past, at the beginning, she had been a coward, rejecting him with apologies, wanting to let him down lightly. And of course it had only led to his being ever more persistent. It couldn't go on that way, though. If he wouldn't willingly face the facts he must be forced to.

'Yes?' she said. 'What can I do for you?'

'I wasn't sure whether you'd heard the doorbell over the music,' he said.

'I heard it.'

He glanced past her into the hall. The closing aria from act one was soaring out as Violetta passionately sang in favour of freedom and non-commitment. '*Tra viata*,' he observed, adding with a wry smile, 'If you'd been expecting me to call I might well have thought that this was a piece carefully chosen just for my benefit. And that would have been unforgivable. But seeing that you couldn't have known that I was to drop by we'll put it down to coincidence.'

For a moment Mary wondered what he was talking about, and then remembered that it had been that particular opera that had been the cause of the bad feeling between Callow and her father.

Callow, however, gave all the appearance of being unaffected by the memory. With a cocked ear he listened to the music for a moment then gave a nod of approval. 'A beautiful, expressive voice, isn't it?' Then, showing off his knowledge, added: 'It sounds like Cotrubas. Is it?'

Mary didn't answer. She had no intention of being drawn into anything resembling a conversation.

'Ah, well,' he said. 'Beautiful, whoever it is.'

In the drawing room the tape came to an end and she and Callow faced one another in silence while the dog wandered away to sniff around the flowers of the herbaceous border.

'Well,' Callow said after a moment, 'do I find you well? I trust I do.'

She answered with a silent nod.

Giving a fretful little shake of his head he said, 'Mary, you are not—not warm towards me.'

She gave a sigh. 'I have to say I'm somewhat surprised to see you here, to say the least. I thought on the last occasion you called I'd made it very clear to you how things are.'

'You wouldn't accept my flowers,' he said. 'In fact you went so far as to throw them down at my feet.' He shook his head as if in judgement of a badly behaved child. 'Mary, that was not nice. Not nice at all.'

Her heart was thudding against her ribs. 'I told you I didn't want your flowers,' she said. 'I don't ever want flowers from you. I don't want *anything* from you, *ever*.'

'I rather gathered that,' he replied. 'And you'll notice that I haven't brought flowers with me today.'

She said nothing to this, while through her mind flashed pictures of their last meeting when he had thrust the yellow roses into her hand. Although they had been wrapped in paper she could still recall the feel of the thorny stems against her palm. She had protested, holding the flowers out to him, saying that she did not want them. But he had refused to take them back and in her anger and frustration she had hurled them down onto the flags. Before it had happened she would never have imagined herself capable of doing such a thing, but he had driven her to it. Afterwards she had been glad; the violent, dramatic

16

act had left her feeling somehow cleansed. If nothing else, she had thought, such a gesture would have to get through to him; even he would not be able to ignore such a demonstration. But it seemed she had been wrong.

'What is it you want?' she said.

He paused. 'What I want,' he said, 'is to ask you if we can make a new start.'

'I wasn't aware that we'd ever made a start before so I don't see how we could make a new one.'

'Oh,' he said, shaking his head, 'Mary, Mary, so contrary.'

'Mr Callow, I have—'

'Please,' he interrupted, 'John. Call me John. How many times do I have to ask you?'

She said nothing.

He went on, 'We miss you at the operatic group, you know. And we could do with another good mezzo for the chorus. You do know we're doing *The Pearl Fishers*, don't you? Oh, Mary, won't you come and join us again? Even if you don't want to sing we'd be so glad of your artistic talents to help with the sets or in the making of the props.'

As if he had not spoken she said, 'Mr Callow, I can't stand here talking to you. I've got things to do. I've made it as clear to you as I possibly can that there can never be anything between us and for the sake of your own happiness I suggest you accept the fact.'

'Look,' he said quickly, 'I know how it was when your father was alive. You had certain responsibilities. But now that—'

'My father's death has nothing to do with it,' she interrupted coldly. 'My responsibilities towards him had no bearing on anything where you and I are concerned. They never did and they never will.'

'But Mary—'

'Please,' she said, briefly closing her eyes in exasperation, 'try to get it into your head. I have no wish to insult you, but you've got to realize, there can never be anything between us. Never.'

'I don't think you mean that.'

As he smiled his infuriating smile she shook her head in growing despair. Her inclination was simply to close the door, but she knew that such a gesture would not end it.

'Can't I make you understand?' she said. 'I shall never care for you. If you were the last man on earth I would never turn to you. I would never—'

'But I can look after you, Mary,' he broke in. 'I can take care of you.'

'I don't want you to look after me or take care of me,' she said. 'I can take care of myself.'

'Can you?' One of his eyebrows rose slightly. 'Do you really think you can?'

She reached out for the door. 'This isn't getting us anywhere.'

'No, wait,' he said, stepping forward. 'Just a minute.' When she hesitated he added, 'Isn't there something I can do to make you change your mind, to make you think differently about me?'

'Believe me, there's nothing.' She made the tone of her voice as cold as she could. 'And now if you'll excuse me, I must get back to my work.'

'Why are you like this towards me?' he said. 'What have I done to you that you should behave in this way? I know I'm a good bit older than you, but—'

'Your age has nothing to do with it.'

'What is it, then?'

She took a breath. 'It's *you*. It's just *you*. And what's

more I'm tired of being the object of your—your sick obsession.'

'Oh, look at you,' he said. 'Standing there so hard and—and unyielding. I never imagined you could be like this.'

'Well, now you know differently.'

He shrugged. 'I'm learning, it seems. Though it's a hard lesson. But even so, I've never been one to give in easily.'

Nothing she said seemed to get through to him.

'Please,' she said on a little moan, 'go away and don't bother me again. If you do . . .' She let her words trail off.

'If I do you'll what?' he said. 'What will you do?'

'Just—just leave me alone. Don't bother me again. And don't write to me any more either.'

'You didn't read my last letter,' he said sadly.

'I told you I wouldn't.'

'Sending it back to me like that, unopened. Not polite, Mary. Not polite at all.'

'I told you that's what I'd do.'

He put his head on one side. 'Well, no. As a matter of fact you told me you'd burn it. Even more cruel.'

'And I *shall* burn it if you ever write to me again.'

He gazed at her for some moments and then reached into the inside pocket of his jacket. 'As a matter of fact I've got a letter for you here. I wrote it in case you were out.' He held it out to her.

'I don't want it.'

'Please, Mary.'

'I told you, I *don't want it*. I'm not interested in anything you've got to say to me.'

Still he held out the letter.

She gave a groan. 'Oh, God, don't you see what you're doing? Look, we both live in this village. And

19

you're making the situation impossible. It's getting to the point where we shan't both be able to remain here.'

'They're your words.'

'What does that mean?'

'Is this final?' he said, ignoring her question. 'Do you truly mean that you could never, never turn to me? Are you quite certain of that?'

She nodded. 'As the night follows day.'

'Oh, Mary.' He gave a sad shake of his head. 'I had such hopes for us. I thought that once a little time had gone by after your father's death you would see things differently. It seems I was wrong.'

She said nothing. She stood with her lips set, her left hand holding the edge of the door, her other hand against the frame. Stepping forward, he quickly and neatly slipped the envelope down between her palm and the door jamb. She gave a little gasp of anger and exasperation, then grasped the letter and held it back out to him.

'I don't want your letter.'

'Please, read it. I think it might make you change your mind.'

'Nothing will do that. Haven't you heard a word I've been saying?'

He stepped back from the step out of her reach and held up his hand, palm out. 'Just read it.'

'I shan't read it. I told you, I shall burn it. And I mean it this time.'

He smiled. 'Oh, no, Mary, I don't think you'd really go that far.'

'You don't?'

'No, I don't. Shall I tell you what I think? I think that in spite of all your protests there's a part of you—perhaps unacknowledged at the moment—that is not altogether unsympathetic towards me. I'm certain that behind all your protests you're rather curious as to what I've written. Aren't you? I'm quite sure that as soon as I've gone you'll open that envelope to see what I've said.'

'You think so? I told you I shall burn it, and I mean it.'

He shook his head. 'Oh no, I don't think you will.'

'No?' She forced a cold semblance of a smile to her lips. 'Wait there just a moment and you'll see whether I mean it or not.' She turned away, hurrying off in the direction of the kitchen. 'Wait there,' she called over her shoulder. 'Just wait there.'

She was back within a minute carrying a box of matches. On the front doorstep she took out a match, struck it, and put the flame to the corner of the envelope. 'There,' she said. 'Now do you believe me?'

She looked over the flowering flames that began to consume the letter. Callow looked back at her with a slight smile on his face, his expression unreadable. With the flames devouring the paper and threatening to burn her fingers, Mary stepped forward, bent and let the burning remains fall onto the stone path. The last scrap of paper flared, turned dark and curled up. She straightened and faced Callow once more.

'So don't waste your time writing to me again.'

He gazed at her for a moment, gave a slow nod and then glanced down at his watch. 'Five minutes past two,' he observed. He raised his head again, gave her another nod and then turned and walked away. As he made his way along the path the dog moved to join him and trotted along at his heels. Moments later they were passing out through the gate and into the lane.

From the porch Mary watched his departure. When he and the dog had gone from her sight she gingerly picked up the curled and blackened remains of the envelope and its contents and dropped them onto the earth of the herbaceous border. That done, she stepped back into the hall and closed the door. Her heart was still beating fast from the confrontation. But she must put Callow out of her mind, she told herself. All that unpleasant business with him was finished now; she had burnt his letter before his eyes, and he could no longer be in any doubt as to her feelings. And yet—yet he had not behaved in quite the way she had expected. When she had burnt his letter he had looked almost *satisfied*. But no, she told herself impatiently, don't think about him Forget him; relax.

And after a while she was able to put him out of her mind. But then, while tidying up the study a little later, she came across her father's journal. There was no relaxing or forgetting after that.

'And was that it?' Ruth said.

'Yes, that was it.'

'He went? Just like that?'

'Just like that. Quiet as a lamb.'

'And that was last Saturday, you say?'

'Yes, just after two o'clock.' Frowning, Mary added, 'He looked at his watch and remarked on the time. Five minutes past two. God knows why.'

'Who cares?' Ruth said. 'The man's mad. Forget him.'

'I intend to.'

With a little nod of appreciation Ruth said, 'Well, I do admire you for what you did, Mary. I should think he'd get the message now all right.'

'I hope so.' Mary did not sound totally convinced. 'I don't think I could put up with any more scenes like that.'

'I'm sure you couldn't, Ruth said. 'Neither could I. God, what a creep.'

In the restaurant of the Wheatsheaf Inn the two women sat facing one another across a table near a window. Ruth was forty-two years old. She was taller than Mary, and a little more solidly built. She had reddish-brown hair that she kept cut fairly short, and a broad, smooth, good-natured face. Today she was wearing navy slacks and a blue and white check blouse. Mary, dressed a little more formally, wore a cream linen jacket and skirt and a pale lemon blouse. With a sigh, Ruth pushed aside her near-empty plate then took up her glass and drank the last of her wine. When the waitress came to them a moment later they ordered coffee.

The two of them had driven to Reading that morning to collect their tickets from the travel agent. Having done that, they had come to the pub for a relaxed lunch before getting down to the business of shopping.

'Oh,' Mary said with a sigh of pleasure, 'it'll be so good to get away. I can't tell you how much I'm looking forward to it.'

'Me too.' Ruth paused in the act of lighting a cigarette. 'And for two whole weeks.'

From the public bar next door there came over the chatter and the clinking of glass the sound of one of Stevie Wonder's golden oldies. Mary cocked her head to listen as he sang: *I just called to say I love you, I just called to say how much I care*. 'Oh, I love that song,' she said. 'It was the one and only pop record I ever bought after coming out of my twenties. Even Dad suffered it without too much protest.' She looked off into the distance for a moment and gave a little wondering shake of her head. 'It's almost a year now since

Dad died. I can hardly believe that so much time has gone by. The weeks and months go so fast.'

Ruth nodded. 'I know what you mean.' A little pause, and she added, 'But it gets easier, doesn't it?'

'As regards Dad, you mean? Oh, yes, it does. Thank God. Nature is wonderful. She's got it all worked out.'

The waitress appeared with their coffee. When she had gone away again Mary bent and took from the shopping bag beside her chair a number of colourful holiday brochures. Placing them on the table she began to flick through the pages. 'It's so long since I had a holiday,' she said. 'Imagine—Florence, Rome, Milan. I remember so well the holidays we had there when we were children, Mother and Dad and David and I. The museums, the galleries—and always the opera, of course. I should think certain things will have changed a bit by now, though—progress and all the tourism— but I don't care. I'm going to love it, I know.' She gave a sudden little laugh. 'Oh, Ruth, how can we wait?'

Ruth took a sip from her coffee cup. 'We haven't got any choice. But it'll come soon enough. And it's going to be just what we need. People do need holidays. They need to unwind. And you particularly, after all that's happened.'

Mary nodded. 'After Ian and I divorced and I came back to live in Valley Green, Dad was always telling me to get away, have a break. But it's not the same when you have to go off on your own, is it? And I didn't like the idea of leaving him.' She fell suddenly silent, as if all at once preoccupied with some alien thought. Then, shaking herself free of the preoccupation, she lowered her gaze to the brochure before her. 'The eternal city,' she said. 'You know, Ruth, you've got such a treat in store for you.'

'I sincerely hope so.'

'Did you know that Keats died in a little room over-looking the foot of the Spanish Steps?'

'No, I didn't.'

'Yes, in the arms of his friend, Joseph Severn.'

'Were they lovers?'

'No, no. Just good friends, as they say. In fact Keats was getting over a disastrous love affair with a certain young English woman. His friend Joseph Severn was a painter. I read some of his letters—Severn's—written at the time, describing Keats's death. They'd break your heart. When we get to Rome we must go there. See Keats's little room.'

'Oh, absolutely,' Ruth said dryly. 'I can see this trip's going to be a laugh a minute.'

'Oh, don't,' Mary protested. 'You'll love it.'

Ruth chuckled. 'I'm kidding. Of course we'll go to see his room. I don't want to miss a thing. We'll do it all—Keats's house, the Coliseum, the Spanish Steps.'

'And the opera too.'

'Of course. We'll do everything.'

They talked for a while about the coming holiday, and then Mary said: 'You know, I've been thinking—I might sell the house and move away from Valley Green.'

'What? Are you serious? Sell your beautiful house?'

'Yes.'

'And give up teaching?'

'Oh, no, I'd keep on with that. I've got no choice there. No, I just thought I might find a little flat somewhere. Here in Reading maybe, or in Newbury. I don't know. Just so long as it's close enough for me to get to school.' She shrugged. 'It's just an idea.'

'But Mary, you can't sell your house. You've lived there most of your life.'

'I know, but it's too big for me. I don't need all that

space. There's the garden too. I haven't got the talent or the time to look after it. It hasn't been touched in ages, and it needs to be cared for.'

'Are you sure that's the reason? The garden, and the house being too big?'

'Well . . . what else could there be?'

Ruth didn't answer; she had not missed Mary's slight hesitation.

'Oh, I know what you're thinking,' Mary said. 'You're thinking perhaps I'm running away, right? Running away from *him*—*Callow*.'

Ruth still said nothing.

'Well,' Mary said, 'I can't pretend that I relish the idea of bumping into him in the village.'

'Listen, Mary, you mustn't let that creep drive you away. You really mustn't.

'No, I'm not. It's just that . . .' Mary gave a deep sigh, took a drink from her coffee cup then said, avoiding Ruth's eyes, 'You know—just before Dad died he—he was afraid.'

Ruth frowned. 'What are you talking about?'

'My father.'

'I know that. But I don't get it. What's brought this on?'

Mary hesitated. 'I mean it, you know.'

'You mean what?'

'He was afraid.'

'Mary—'

'I'm not kidding, Ruth.'

Ruth gazed at her steadily for a moment. 'Tell me what you mean, Mary. In what way was he afraid? And what was he afraid of?'

Mary was silent for a moment, then: 'He—he thought he was in danger. He believed he was going to be killed.'

'Are you serious?'

'Yes.'

'Oh, dear.' Ruth shook her head sympathetically. 'Poor man.'

'It wasn't something that he was imagining.'

'Oh, but—'

'It was very real to him.'

'How do you know this?'

'I was there with him, wasn't I? I could see what he was like. I wasn't absolutely sure of it before. But I am now.'

'How come? What makes you so sure now?'

'Well—I've got it in his own words.'

'Mary—what are you talking about?'

Mary gazed at her for a second then bent to her bag and brought out a large-format hardcover notebook. She placed it on top of the brochures before her. 'This is his journal,' she said. 'One of them. The last one.'

'Your dad kept a journal?'

'Yes. For as long as I can remember. They're all there at home, going right back.' She looked down at the journal in front of her. 'I only found this one last Saturday, though. It had slipped down behind the others on the shelf.' She laid her hand on the book's cover. 'He wrote in it about being afraid.'

'Oh, Mary . . .' Ruth reached out and touched Mary's hand. 'You should be trying to forget all that. It doesn't do any good to keep dwelling on the past.'

Mary said, as if she had not heard, 'Callow hasn't always lived in Valley Green, you know.'

'Callow? What's Callow got to do with this? What are you talking about?'

'He moved to the village a couple of years before I returned.'

'I think I'm missing something here,' Ruth said as

27

she stubbed out her cigarette. 'I don't understand what your father's got to do with Callow.'

Mary gazed steadily at her. 'It was Callow my father was afraid of. I *know* it was.'

There was concern in Ruth's expression now. 'You think your father was afraid of *Callow*?'

'Yes.'

'But *why*?'

'Because of what Callow might do.'

'I don't get it. What could he do?'

Mary opened her mouth to speak, paused for a moment then said, 'My father felt that Callow was a threat to him. Over those last days it was almost as if—as if he was waiting for something to happen.'

'Waiting for what to happen?'

'I don't pretend to have all the answers,' Mary said, 'but he was afraid because—because Callow had sent him a piece of paper with runes on it.' She touched a finger to the cover of the journal. 'He wrote about them.'

'Runes?' Ruth said. 'You mean like mysterious symbols?'

'Yes.'

Ruth nodded. 'I think I remember reading a story about them once. Don't people use them to tell their fortunes?'

'I don't know about that.' Mary waved the notion away. 'All I know is that Callow sent them to my father. And they got destroyed.'

'Destroyed how?'

'The paper got burnt. I wasn't there when it happened, but Dad wrote about it.' She shook her head. 'You must think I'm nuts.'

'Mary,' Ruth said, 'what I think is that you're possibly getting a few things out of proportion.'

'Imagining things, yes?'

'Well . . .'

'You're thinking that in view of what happened, I'm making things fit the events. Early menopause? Is that it?'

'Oh, come on now. But with your dad dying so suddenly, the way he did—I mean there's no doubt that it must have been the most awful shock for you.'

'Of course it was. But that's nothing to do with what I know. His death hasn't coloured my thoughts, if that's what you're thinking. It hasn't affected my judgement.'

Ruth said nothing. After a moment Mary went on: 'It was Dad who first warned me of Callow.'

'Really?'

'Yes. Soon after I met him at the Operatic Society here in Reading. I remember Dad was quite passionate about it—that I should have nothing to do with him. Not that I wanted to anyway. He made my flesh crawl.'

'I know. Wasn't he the reason you left the company?'

'Yes. Well, he just wouldn't leave me alone. Which was a shame because I really enjoyed being a member. My voice was never good enough to get me a principal's role, but I was very happy in the chorus, or helping with the sets or making the props. It was a lot of fun. Hard work, but good fun. And then he had to spoil it all.'

'He was already a member of the company when you joined, wasn't he?'

'Yes. He'd done two or three productions by then.'

'Did he only *direct* the operas? Or did he sing as well?'

'He always directed and produced. Still does. Well, with all his years in the theatre . . . And the company needed somebody at short notice when the other director died.' She gave a little snort of derision. 'Callow thought he was God's gift to us all.'

'He'd never had that much of a professional career, though, had he? I seem to remember him doing odd parts on television and in a few films, but it was nothing of any importance.'

'No, it wasn't. He'd also done some directing in a few rep theatres, I believe.'

'Is he any good? With the opera group, I mean.'

Mary thought about this. 'Yes, he is, actually. I hate to admit it. Though a couple of his productions have been pretty disastrous. Certainly my father thought so. That's why the two of them never got on.'

'What d'you mean?'

'Well—and this happened before I came back to the village—Dad was asked to write a review of one of Callow's productions for a local paper. He did, and he slammed the man. Not the performers, but the direction and the general interpretation. A production of *La Traviata*, it was. I don't think Callow ever forgave him for it. He certainly never forgot it. I know that Callow created a scene between the two of them once, in the village. Because of Dad's opera review. Apparently he was quite vitriolic.' With a rueful smile she added, 'And wouldn't you know that when he called round at the house last Saturday I had to be playing that particular opera. Great timing, eh?' She fell silent for a few moments, then added, 'I know how it must sound to you, Ruth, my saying that Dad was afraid—but I haven't imagined it. My father, for all his eccentricities, was a very down-to-earth man. And a very smart old man too.'

'Oh, there's no doubt of that.'

'And if you could have seen him over those last days you'd know what I'm talking about. He was like a cat on hot bricks. I know it sounds crazy but, well, it was as if somehow he *knew* he was going to die, and soon, and there was nothing he could do about it.'

'Mary . . .'

'I wouldn't make up such a thing.'

'No, of course you wouldn't, but . . .'

'You know, Dad told me—not long before he died, that if anything should happen to him I should sell up and move away.'

'Did he say why?'

'No.' Mary looked down at the journal. 'But I know why now.' Raising her eyes again she gave a little smile and said, 'It's no good your looking at me like that, Ruth. I'm not making this up. I'm not imagining things. And I don't think Dad was either.'

'How can you be sure?'

'Oh, all kinds of things. For one thing, he talked about his will. And another time he spoke of his funeral, of being buried with my mother.'

'He was an old man, Mary. It's natural for old people to get to thinking about dying. I mean, in the natural order of things, when you get to a certain age death isn't usually that far away. Old people—they want things to be sorted out. It's natural.'

'It's not natural to be the way he was. The way he behaved. He—' She came to a stop.

'Go on.'

Mary's voice was lowered to a hush as she said on a little intake of breath, 'He—he kept a gun.'

'Mary . . .'

'He was ready to use it—on Callow.'

'You can't mean that.'

'I do mean it. He was afraid. He was afraid he was going to die. And he *did* die.'

A little silence fell between them in the midst of the general easy chatter. After a while Ruth said: 'But whatever you fear, Mary—whatever ideas you've got—you can't escape the fact that your father died as the result of an accident. You know that better than anyone else.'

'Well, I know that's the way it looked.'

'It's the way it *was*. It couldn't have been anything else. What else could it have been?'

Mary did not answer.

Ruth said softly, The only alternative is suicide.'

'Well, you can forget that,' Mary said a little heatedly. 'That's the last thing he would have done. No, not suicide. Never.'

'What are you saying, then? If it wasn't suicide, and it wasn't an accident, then it—it would have to be murder.'

Mary remained silent.

'Oh, come on,' Ruth said. 'Anyway, even if Callow did cause your father's death, what possible motive could he have had? A bad review of one of his opera productions isn't enough, or the fact that your father told him to stay away from you.'

'You think not? Some people can be pretty strange. Some people can bear grudges beyond all reason. Callow hated my father, I know that much. For what it's worth, he envied him too. Well—What Dad didn't know about opera wasn't worth knowing.' Absently she lifted her coffee cup, drank from it. 'And at the end, Dad was afraid of him. And his death came just at that time—with him being so very much afraid. Over those last days he hardly set foot outside the house. And that wasn't like him. I'd never seen him like that before. But in spite of all his precautions he died just the same.'

'In an *accident*, Mary.'

Mary said nothing.

'A simple fall.'

'Yes, I know.'

'He fell over your cat, for God's sake.'

'Not *our* cat. I don't know whose cat it was, but it certainly wasn't ours. It was some stray—some old tabby that had come into the house.'

'Even so . . .'

Mary said after a moment, 'I know it doesn't make sense to you. But what I can't get away from is his fear, his *knowing* that something was going to happen.'

Ruth studied her. 'Had there been any contact between them towards the end?'

'Yes—and strangely enough they became quite friendly. Swapping records and tapes and things.'

'Don't take this the wrong way, Mary, but your father—well, he *was* getting on in years.'

'Getting on in years? Oh, I see—you think he might have been going senile.'

Ruth shrugged. 'It does happen, to the brightest of people.'

'I know that.' Mary shook her head. 'No, he wasn't going senile. For God's sake, he was only sixty-nine.'

'No offence, Mary.'

'I'm not offended.' She looked at Ruth in silence for a second then glanced down at the journal lying before her, picked it up and held it out. Ruth made no attempt to take it.

'If you read it,' Mary said, 'you'll know. That I'm not making it all up.'

'I never thought you were. I don't need to read it, Mary.'

'But—'

'I don't need to read it, Mary. And I don't really want to.'

With a sigh, Mary set the journal back on the table before her. Ruth put out a hand and gently touched Mary's wrist.

33

'Mary, listen to me. Whatever's happened in the past, it's over. There's no changing anything now.'

Mary nodded. 'Yes. You're right. Of course you're right.'

'So why don't you give it all up? Forget about it. Get on with your own life. What purpose will it serve to keep going back over everything? All these post-mortems. What good will they do?'

'None at all, I suppose.' She gave an awkward little laugh. 'Perhaps I *am* cracking up.'

'There's nothing the matter with you that a couple of weeks in Italy won't put right.'

'Right.' Mary's smile was bright. 'I should just be looking to the future. I should try to be positive.'

'Be positive, yes.'

Mary nodded. 'Yes.' Taking up the journal she put it in her shopping bag. The gesture signified an ending.

Ruth gave a little nod of approval, then said, changing the subject; 'Now—are you going to have more coffee?'

'Are you going to have another cigarette?'

Ruth lowered her voice. 'I don't think I dare. I've already been getting the fish eye from the woman at the next table.'

'I won't have any more coffee, then.' Mary looked at her watch. 'It's twenty to two. Let's get on, shall we?'

'Fine.' Ruth turned and signalled to the waitress for the bill.

Glancing from the window at the cars moving in the car park, Mary said, 'When we get back from our holiday I'm going to get a new car.'

'Good. It's about time.'

'Though I'm not sure yet what I'll get.' Mary began to gather her things together. 'Some neat, dependable little Japanese job, I expect.'

34

'First a holiday, then a new car. You're splashing out. Where's it all going to end?'

'And I've been thinking—I might apply to study for an Open University degree. Try to get my PhD.'

'Really? There's ambitious for you.'

'I haven't decided yet, but in any case I'd like to take some classes in something or other. Evening classes. Maybe study a new language or something. You want to join me?'

Ruth smiled. 'I'll think about that.'

'You're a coward,' Mary said, laughing. 'But now that I'm alone I intend to do something with my time. Apart from teaching, I mean. I've only got myself to look after now.'

'Right. It won't hurt you to start getting out a little more. Start meeting people. Who knows, you might even meet *somebody*.'

'Mr Right?'

'Why not? Or even Mr Not-so-bad.'

Mary laughed. 'I don't think so, but I suppose anything is possible.'

'You haven't got anything against relationships, have you?'

'No, of course not.' Mary sighed. 'It's just that it so rarely happens. Finding the right one, that is. Mind you, I don't think I'm as fussy as I once was. Get to a certain age and you can't afford to be.' She put her head on one side, considering the matter. 'He wouldn't have to be handsome, or even a Brain of Britain candidate. Just so long as he wasn't covered in tattoos and didn't keep a couple of Rottweilers in his kitchen. And no Disneyworld stickers on the rear window of his car, either. Oh, yes, and he wouldn't say things like, "Today is the first day of the rest of your life", or dot his i's with little circles.'

'Sounds to me like you're pretty fussy,' Ruth said. 'Aren't you expecting rather a lot?'

'Not at all,' Mary laughed. 'I'm not expecting anything.'

When they had settled the bill, they left the pub and set off towards the shops. 'What we were talking about—your getting out and meeting people,' Ruth said, raising her voice over the noise of the traffic. 'You've got relatives, haven't you?'

'I've got a cousin.'

'One cousin? That's the extent of your family?'

'As far as I know. Jack, his name is Jack Forrest. He lives in London with his family.'

They reached the corner of the main street just as the pedestrians' light turned red, and stood side by side waiting as the traffic roared past.

'I haven't seen him since we were children,' Mary added. 'We never kept in touch, though he wrote when Dad died. I'm afraid I never got around to answering his letter. I should have done.'

'It might be good for you to look him up,' Ruth said. 'Catch up on old times.'

Mary shrugged. 'Perhaps I will. I've got his address somewhere. Though I don't know what good it does to start opening old doors. But whatever I do, you can rest assured that I'm not going to just sit around and stagnate.'

'Good for you.'

'And starting with Italy. We can let our hair down.' Mary gave a little laugh. 'There we'll be, two unattached English signoras of mature years. And who can say what handsome young Italians we might fall prey to—if we play our cards right.'

Ruth laughed with her. 'Listen, you're the one with all the experience of Italy. So I shall rely on you for

36

everything, you do realize that?'

'But of course.'

'And you do speak Italian, don't you?'

'*Si! Certo!* I spikka da lingua pretty damn gooda! Listen, when you're brought up on a diet of Verdi and Puccini you get to learn or go under.'

Ruth laughed again, at the same time drawing back a little as a heavy lorry came perilously close. There was no let-up in the traffic. Observing another large truck coming round the bend in the road, she shook her head in disapproval. 'Damned great monsters. They shouldn't be allowed on the streets.' Turning back to Mary she opened her mouth to make a further comment, but her words remained unspoken.

Mary, eyes fixed steadily on the oncoming truck, had let fall the bags she was carrying and was stepping off the pavement. Ruth's scream as she vainly reached out a grasping hand was joined by the cries of other pedestrians and, a moment later, by the screech of the vehicle's brakes.

It was all too late. A second later Mary was struck by the vehicle, the impact tossing her up into the air. Looking like some loose-jointed doll, she fell heavily into the path of an oncoming Ford Escort. Unable to swerve in time to avoid her, its nearside wheels passed over her head with the sound of crumpling paper, sending her blood and brains spraying onto the surface of the road.

As Ruth stood there, stunned into silence and immobility, there came on the air the distant sound of a church clock striking the hour of two.

Chapter One

Pt . . . pt . . . pt. A large black fly, unable to learn that freedom did not lie that way, repeatedly threw itself against the windowpane.

Apart from the sound of the fly's impact on the glass, the house was silent. It would be time soon to go and pick up the children from school. They had to go on as if life were normal, though life as they had known it would never be the same again. And even if they survived and won through, even if at last they got through this terrible nightmare and woke to daylight once more, there could never be more than relief. He would not, he was sure, ever know happiness again.

Pt . . . pt . . . pt . . . The fly wasn't giving up. He turned from the window and glanced about him. Like the rest of the rooms in the house it gave clear evidence of the work that he and Connie had done. They would make it perfect they had said; and they had indeed tried. Their efforts showed in so much—from Connie's carefully chosen colour schemes for the walls and paintwork to the choice of fabrics for the sofa cushions . . . Nothing of it mattered now.

If only, he thought, as he had done so many times, they had never come here. If only they had remained in London. If only . . . You could go on, but it was the most pointless exercise, playing games of ifs and buts, trying to rewrite the past. Yet it was difficult, if not impossible, to avoid doing it. Their coming here had been almost inescapable once the possibility had been in their grasp. Nevertheless he couldn't leave the alternative scenarios alone, and kept returning to them, like a child picking at a scabbed knee. So it was that he kept reliving that first visit, seeking out the signs, the warnings that he had not heeded, the warnings that had been there all the time.

He could remember Connie and himself preparing to set off from Chiswick in the car that September morning. It had been little more than a year and a half ago. Rain had been forecast and up above the rooftops of the row of drab terraced houses the ragged clouds had gathered dark and threatening. The children had wanted to go with them, but Jack and Connie had said no, closing their ears to the resulting pleas and groans. 'We're not going off on a pleasure trip,' Connie had said, at which her mother, Sarah, had remarked, *sotto voce*, 'May God forgive you,' knowing that Connie and Jack were secretly regarding the excursion as just that.

At last, with Joel and his twin sisters Kitty and Lydia standing at their grandmother's side waving them off, Jack and Connie had driven away under the lowering sky.

The rain hadn't held off even as far as the end of the street. Before they reached the corner, it had begun to fall, lightly at first, and then swiftly increasing till it was lashing at the windscreen with such violent fury that the wipers were hardly able to keep it clear. The rain kept up as they left the city behind them and drove along the M4, but began to lessen slightly as they turned off onto one of the roads that wound through the Cotswolds. Then, as they approached the little village of Valley Green, the rain eased still further and then ceased altogether.

As the Citroën topped the brow of a hill, the village lay before them in the valley, looking as neat and compact as some idealized conception dreamed up for a Hollywood film. On an impulse Jack pulled the car to a halt beside the verge and they sat gazing down. Through a gap in the clouds the sun shone, sudden and unexpectedly brilliant. Connie, who had been navigating, clasped her hands over the open map on her knees and leaned forward slightly against the restraining seatbelt. 'So here we are,' she said.

Jack nodded. 'Here we are indeed.'

They drove on down. As they entered the village, he peered about him, while Connie glanced at him from time to time, waiting to see the light of recognition in his face.

'Does it look familiar?' she asked.

He shook his head. 'Not really. Or perhaps just vaguely. It's been a long time, remember.'

As a child he had visited the house of his Uncle Edwin and Aunt Christine, and on occasions had played there in the garden with his cousins, David and Mary. It was all too far in the past now, though. He couldn't even remember in which direction the house lay.

Eventually, after driving around the streets for some minutes, he stopped the car near the post office-cum-general store close by the green and asked directions of an elderly woman who was walking a small terrier. A few minutes later he and Connie were driving on through the village to its eastern side and the entrance to Princes Lane.

For a hundred yards or so Jack drove slowly along the lane, eyes searching the houses on the right. Memory was now returning in little drifts, like scents borne on the wind. Then, at last, with a sighing 'Ah' of recognition and satisfaction, he gave a nod and brought the car to a halt.

'This is it.' He turned to Connie. Her smile showed eager anticipation. Glancing at his watch he saw that it was just after twelve-fifteen. The journey from London had taken just over ninety minutes.

'What do you think?' he asked.

'Impressive.' Connie nodded. 'Very impressive. You never said it was anything like this.'

The house, The Limes, took its name from the two tall lime trees that grew beside the long front path. Standing well apart from the dwellings on either side, the house was a two-storeyed, solid-looking, early Victorian building with a wide central porch and front door flanked by deep bay windows. Part of its white façade—now much in need of a coat of paint—was covered by Virginia creeper, the foliage supplemented near the ground by straggling shrubs that grew about the walls and crowded the shuttered windows.

At the right end of the front garden wall stood double gates that led onto a gravel drive. Jack got out of the car, unlocked the gates with the key given to him by the solicitor and drove the car through onto the drive.

They got out and stood looking around them. The sight of the garden brought back further memories to Jack, and he suddenly had a picture of how it had been all those years ago. 'It was so different then,' he said.

Stretching for thirty yards in front of the house and

round it on either side, the garden had once been a pattern of well-tended lawn marked with herbaceous plots and borders in which grew masses of roses and a colourful variety of other shrubs and flowering plants. All of it now was wildly overgrown. In the beds the roses and everything else had run riot, while the lawn was a jungle of overgrown grass, and nettles and other weeds.

Hitching aside a thorny frond of rambling rose, Jack started off along the path of weed-rimmed flags that led to the front porch. After the rainstorm the scents from the surrounding lush greenery rose strong and fragrant. Reaching the house, they walked up the steps onto the front porch where Jack unlocked and opened the front door. Then, followed closely by Connie, he stepped through into the dusty, shadowed hall. There they stood looking around them and Jack recognized the old coatstand, and on the wall the elegant gilt-edged mirror and the pictures of operatic divas. Touched by memories, the ghosts of familiarity reached out to him and briefly he saw himself as a small boy again, standing there close to his mother's side, the kind and welcoming faces of his aunt and uncle before him.

Taking Connie's hand, he moved to the door on the right. He opened it and they passed through into a shadowed drawing room. Stepping to the windows Jack folded back the wooden shutters, letting the sun pour in and light up the dusty interior. Behind him in the middle of the room Connie stood gazing about her while the newly disturbed motes of dust slowly danced and swam in the shafts of sunlight.

It had been a much lived-in room this, anyone could see. Everything testified to it, from the wear apparent on the old chesterfield sofa and armchairs to the worn padding on the footstool. On either side of the marble fireplace stood a glass-fronted bookcase packed with volumes. On the mantelshelf, the bookcases and the bureau stood delicate bowls and finely modelled porcelain figurines. On the faded walls hung original oil paintings and framed photographs.

Moving on from surveying a painting of a young woman in late-nineteenth-century dress, Connie stopped before an array of photographic portraits of men and women in contemporary dress and theatrical costume.

'My God,' she said, 'I know your uncle's business was the opera, but I didn't realize it was quite such a devouring passion with him.'

The photographs, more than a dozen of them, were of operatic stars of the past and present, most of them inscribed in varying terms of respect and affection to Edwin Maddox. Connie looked at the faces, some of which—Maria Callas, Joan Sutherland and Luciano Pavarotti among them—were instantly recognizable. Those faces that she did not immediately know were identified by their signatures: Renata Tebaldi, Tito Gobbi, Franco Corelli, Maggie Teyte.

'Did he meet them all?' Connie said.

'I shouldn't think there's any doubt,' Jack replied.

Against another wall stood a stereo system with large speakers, and shelves of tapes, CDs and records—long-players and old 78s, nearly all of operatic performances and vocal recitals.

From the sitting room, Jack and Connie went into the old man's study, its lining of shelves crammed with books, files and papers. On his desk lay his typewriter, its plastic covering filmed with dust. On the walls hung more framed photographs: Renata Scotto, Giuseppe Di Stefano, Birgit Nilsson . . .

After lingering there for a while they went back into the hall and from there entered the dining room with its more formal appearance—taking in the large sideboard, and lyre-backed chairs set neatly around a long dining table with a maroon baize covering. On the wall hung oil-painted landscapes and several designs for theatrical costumes. Back in the hall, another door led them into a second reception room, more grandly furnished than the first, and with less evidence of use.

They entered the kitchen next, and Jack stood by while Connie looked over the outdated facilities, opening the cupboards and generally poking about. Then they went upstairs, into the bedrooms. The first one they looked at—with its bed neatly made and more opera stars' photographs on the walls—had clearly been Edwin's. They did not remain there long, but backed out and went into one of the rooms at the rear. This contained nothing but what appeared to be discarded furniture and various items of clutter. The one next to it turned out to be Mary's studio and, seeing it, Jack recalled that, like himself, Mary had studied art before going to work as a teacher. It was a smallish room, with a worktable, easel, and numerous shelves laden with art and crafts materials: paints, brushes, papers, etc.

The bathroom came next, and then Mary's bedroom. Like Edwin's, it looked out over the front garden. It was neat and feminine, with patterned chintzes on the bed and chair cushions. On the walls hung original watercolours and framed prints of French Impressionist landscapes and Victorian domestic scenes. On her bedside table lay a paperback copy of Graves's *I, Claudius*, with a marker in it. Everything was in very neat order, and but for the layer of dust over the surfaces looked as if its owner might return to it at any moment. Feeling rather like intruders, Jack and Connie turned and went back out onto the landing.

As they reached the stairs, Connie, who was leading the way, came to a halt and turned round to face Jack, gazing at him in silence.

'What's the matter?' he said.

'Look,' she said, 'I know what we agreed.'

'What are you talking about?'

'This house.'

'What d'you mean? What about it?'

'Well, we said we'd just go ahead and sell it as soon as we could.'

'Yes? So?'

She said nothing, just eyed him steadily.

He shook his head. 'I know what's going through your mind.'

'Oh, Jack. Do we have to sell it?'

'We don't need two houses, do we? It's hard enough looking after one.'

'That isn't what I mean, and you know it.' She was eyeing him steadily still. 'Do we have to sell it?'

'Obviously you don't think we should.'

'It's such a great place. Think how the children would feel, living here. And it would be the perfect place for you to write, wouldn't it? In a place this size you'd actually be able to get away from everyone else.'

He nodded. 'Obviously. If you couldn't write in a place like this I shouldn't think you could write anywhere. That's what you wanted me to say, isn't it?'

'Something like that.'

As they stood facing one another the light from the window altered, darkening dramatically as clouds obscured the sun once more. Moments later there came the sudden pattering of rain on the pane. Connie stepped to the window and looked out to the rear garden that stretched away, wild and untended, to the orchard. Jack moved to stand beside her, gazing out as the rain came teeming down, lashing the leaves of the Virginia creeper that framed the window, and the foliage beyond.

'Oh, to live out here in the country,' Connie breathed. 'Right away from the city!' She turned, looking back along the landing and down the stairs. 'And with all this space. Oh, Jack, we don't have to sell it, do we?'

'Con,' his tone was all reason, 'we've only just moved in at Chiswick. We've only been there just over a year. The paint we put on is hardly dry.'

'I know, I know.'

'You had your heart set on going there.'

'I had my heart set on leaving Carling Street, is more like it. Anything had to be better than that place.'

Carling Street, or 'that place,' as Connie contemptuously referred to it, was a narrow, crowded street at the wrong end of Streatham. They had bought the little semi-detached house there soon after their marriage. They had never pretended it was perfect but it was handy for their work with both of them teaching in nearby Wandsworth; more significantly, it was all they had been able to afford at the time. With all its drawbacks, however, they had assured themselves that it had possibilities, that it was really just a matter of settling in and that in time they would have it the way they wanted. Of course they had always kept the dream of moving to somewhere better, but the children had come along and Connie had had to give up her work, and so their dreams had receded further and further with each year.

With the passing time it had seemed to them that their immediate environment was crumbling in proportion to their growing desperation. Had there been, when they'd moved in, quite so many dogs yapping away in nearby back yards or wandering about and fouling the pavements? Had there been quite so many half-dismantled cars and motorcycles littering the street? Had there been quite so many parties with their attendant loud music held into the early hours, making sleep impossible? They had not known what to do and had felt trapped. In the end, it was only with Connie's mother pooling her resources with theirs that they had at last managed to get away. And so, some fifteen months before, they had given up the house in Streatham, shaken off the grime of Carling Street, and moved to a relatively quiet street in Chiswick, with pleasant neighbours and a comparatively attractive outlook. And there, Jack had assumed, they would stay.

Giving a sigh, he looked around him, taking in the walls, the ceiling, the woodwork. 'It'd need a hell of a lot of work. And I don't just mean redecorating, either. Although that'd be a big enough job. I don't think they could have had much done to it for a good few years.'

'I don't see that that would be so terrible,' Connie said. 'It might need a little modernizing here and there, but it's sound enough, isn't it?'

Jack nodded. 'Oh, I don't doubt that. But could you really go through that nightmare all over again? I mean, all the business of the removals and having painters and plumbers in and out of the place all the time. Could you put up with all that again so soon?'

'I could if I thought it would be worth it.'

He was silent for a moment, then said, 'A property like this—we'd probably get a good price if we sold it, you know. In spite of the recession. Or we could hang on to it and sell it at a later date, once the market's recovered.'

Connie said nothing.

'Connie,' he said, 'there'll be so much work.'

'You already said that.'

'Well, it's true.'

'So what? We're not decrepit, are we? We're reasonably young and able-bodied. We'd get it done. And besides, that way you'd be sure of having things the way we want them. You move into a place where all the modifications and decorations are newly done and you end up living for years with somebody else's mistakes and compromises.'

He gave a reluctant nod. 'I suppose so. But what about the children's schooling? That's something we'd have to look into.'

'Well, of course. That goes without saying. But they'd have as good a chance here as anywhere. Probably better in many respects. Jack, we could all be so happy here, I know.'

He smiled at her tone now, the pleading expression in her face. 'Connie, don't. *Don't.*'

'I'm also thinking what it would be like to live in a small community, with plenty of space for the children to play in and grow in. That's something they've never had. Oh, I just think this would be ideal for us. All of us. You, me, the children, and Mother too. My God, she'll be in her element licking that garden into shape.'

'Are you kidding? That's a job for a team, not one lone elderly woman.'

She smiled. 'OK, but we don't have to tell her that.'

'You've got all the answers, haven't you?'

'I'm working on it.'

He looked at her with a wry smile then moved to her and took her in his arms. She nestled there, glad to be held. She was thirty-five years old, a year older than he; slim, not quite pretty, but with soft, gentle features, and full dark hair that fell to the collar of her jacket. Standing in the circle of his arms, the top of her head was on a level with his eyes. He was a tall, lean man with a long, narrow face, and fair hair thinning at the crown. Holding her closer he pressed his mouth to her forehead. She lifted her face to him and he looked into her eyes and saw the eagerness and excitement there.

'Oh, Jack,' she said. It could be soe wonderful. And I'm sure we'd never regret it."

'I don't know,' he said. There was no doubt that it was a fine house; he had always been impressed by it—and it could be beautiful, could be perfect for them. Yet there was something about it that disturbed him. 'We've come by it through tragedy,' he said after a moment of silence. 'That bothers me somewhat.'

She drew back a little, looking up at him. 'But every inheritance comes about through death in some way or another, doesn't it?'

'I suppose so.'

'God knows it was terrible, the way your cousin died, but it's over now and, well, people have to get on with their own lives.'

'I know. I know.' He was sure that she would have her way, eventually. He had rarely refused her anything. But also he knew it made sense. It was foolish to allow events that were no concern of theirs to get in the way; to let some half-imagined phantasms cloud his better judgment.

Interrupting his thoughts, Connie drew back from him again. 'It *is ours*, isn't it?'

'This place? Yes, of course. You heard what the solicitor said.'

She nodded. 'I suppose I'm still having difficulty accepting it. I mean, it all happened so fast. I can hardly believe it's true.' She waved a hand, taking in the house. 'I never expected it to be like this.'

Downstairs in the hall, Connie said she wanted to look over the kitchen again. As she left his side Jack hovered for a moment and then wandered away in the direction of the study.

Entering the dusty, crowded room once more he stood and looked around him. The gloomy, rain-dulled light from the window reflected in the pictures on the walls, while the dark wood of the furniture and the rows of dusty books on the shelves gave the place a sombre atmosphere. Moving to the nearest shelves he looked at some of the titles. Most of the books appeared to be concerned with some aspect of grand opera, either the composers or the singers and conductors. On one shelf stood a row of books bearing his uncle's name as their author, among them biographies of Bellini and Puccini. Edwin's keenest affections, it would appear, had been for the Italian composers.

After a moment or two Jack moved to the window and gazed out onto the rain-lashed garden. Its tangled wildness gave it a strange beauty. How different it all was from their neat little patch in Chiswick. Connie was right, of course; the children would love it so, as would Connie's mother. As indeed would he.

He turned to take in the room again. He had never been inside this room during his visits as a child. It had been one of those places that were forbidden, a place in which children did not venture.

He thought back to those earlier times, the days of his childhood. His uncle and his mother had been brother and sister, and up until his twelfth birthday he and his widowed mother had visited the house in

Valley Green at regular intervals. He and David and Mary had become as good friends as was possible under the circumstances and he had enjoyed the visits. But then Jack's mother had died and he, orphaned, had been taken from their small Swindon house to live with his paternal grandmother in Salisbury. Although the distance from Valley Green had not been that great it had served to sever contact with his relatives there, and they had never had occasion to meet again. Once, long after his grandmother had died and he had begun working as a teacher in London, he had visited friends in the West Country, and while there had seen in a local newspaper a photograph of his uncle—widowed by then, he had learned—on the occasion of the publication of a new book. For a while he had toyed with the idea of driving to Valley Green to visit the old man, but he had been hesitant about renewing the acquaintance after so many years and consequently the trip was never made. Not long afterwards Connie had come to teach at the school, and in doing so had changed his life. A year later they had married. He had heard nothing more of his uncle until some seventeen months ago when he had read in a newspaper of the old man's death.

He had sent his condolences to his cousins, but they had not replied. Afterwards he had hardly given them a thought, but then, right out of the blue, less than a month ago a letter had arrived from a firm of Reading solicitors telling him that his cousin Mary was also dead, that she had died in a road accident, intestate, and that he, Jack, was her sole heir. He and Connie had driven to Reading to the solicitors' offices where Jack had learned that his inheritance amounted to The Limes and all its contents, all proceeds from his uncle's writings, and a considerable sum in cash and various stocks and shares. 'But Mary was married,' Jack had said, to which the solicitor replied that she had been divorced some years before her death and that her former husband was therefore not a legal beneficiary. Further, the solicitor added, there had been no issue from the marriage. On Jack asking what had become of his cousin David, the response came that he had died of a heart attack in America several years earlier.

Moving to the desk, Jack pulled out the old leather-padded chair and sat down. Unlike the cheap, flimsy affair he had bought to go in the boxroom in the Chiswick house, his uncle's desk was solid mahogany — and bore the scars of years of industry. Connie was right, of course: this place would be the perfect environment for his own writing. It was what every writer must dream about—a house in a peaceful, beautiful setting, away from the noise of traffic and the bustle of everyday life. He did need the right place in which to work, there was no question of that, and now that the teaching was behind him—for good, he hoped—the need was even more urgent.

In the spring of the previous year, before the move to Chiswick, Jack had written a pilot episode for a TV situation comedy. Called *Fat Chance*, it dealt with the efforts to find happiness of a mature and overweight spinster. The pilot had been taken up by the BBC who had shown their faith by commissioning a further six episodes. Jack had worked on them during the weekends and in the evenings after getting in from school. The work had often proved to be very difficult—there had been many occasions when he had wanted to do nothing other than relax after the day's teaching—but with a deadline hanging over him he had pushed onward, and eventually the whole series had been completed.

Over the summer and autumn the series had been produced, parts of it being filmed on location, but most of it before audiences at the White City studios in west London. Jack, Connie and the children, and Connie's mother Sarah, had been there on each occasion. Much of the humour had gone over the children's heads but they had nevertheless enjoyed the outings, particularly the novelty of going behind the scenes in the studios. The series had been shown this past winter and spring, and although it had been attacked by some critics as sexist and patronizing it had proved a hit with the viewing public and had won a major award into the bargain. On the strength of its success, Jack had been commissioned to write a second series. It was all he had been hoping for.

Now, when the new school term began in September, he would not be in his usual place at the blackboard. He had taken sabbatical leave to finish the second series and, with luck, if it brought the success he was hoping for, he would never have to go back to the classroom again.

Among the books and papers on the desk was a photograph in a silver frame, and he leaned closer to look at the dated image of a young woman with two children, a boy and girl. David and Mary with their mother, his Aunt Christine. All gone now. Seeing the child faces of his cousins he was struck again by the feeling of melancholy he had felt earlier. He brushed the feeling aside.

On one of the shelves over the desk were several large-format hardcover notebooks. He took one down and opened it. The pages inside were covered with writing, in ink, in a scrawled hand. The entries were dated. A journal of sorts, he realized. A great part of the text consisted of notes on various opera productions in connection with Edwin's newspaper reviews and other writings, while further sections dealt with books he had been reading, or other things in which he had an interest. The rest of the contents seemed to be concerned with day-to-day observations—and comments on the garden or on the wildlife in the surrounding fields and woods.

'Found something interesting, have you?'

Connie was standing at his shoulder. He had not heard her come in.

'The old guy kept a journal.' He tapped the page with the back of his hand and then indicated the other volumes on the shelf. 'There're a number of them.'

'And are they good reading?'

'Mostly they're to do with the opera.'

'Oh, you do surprise me,' she said dryly. Leaning forward she took down another of the volumes from the shelf. She opened the notebook at random, looked at the text and began to read aloud:

' "8th February 1964. *Rigoletto* last night at the Garden. Geraint Evans somewhat ill-at-ease in the title role, but what an exquisite Gilda from Anna Moffo making her debut here. Totally enchanting. Solti conducted with his usual drive and drama. But after being much heralded, the event turns out to be something of a curate's egg." ' Glancing down the page Connie added, 'It's not all to do with the opera, though.' She read aloud again: ' "What a moon here tonight. Like something in the tropics." Even notes on the weather.' She closed the book, put it back on the shelf and took down another. 'Here's a later one. From three years ago.' She read: ' "I get so concerned about Mary. She doesn't get out enough. It's not the right life for her, spending all her time with only an eccentric old man for company. Surely she didn't come back here just to hide herself away with me." ' Clicking her tongue, Connie said, 'I feel a bit of a sneak, reading this. And he does sound such a nice old man.' She put the notebook down on the desk and took in Jack's expression. 'What's the matter? Is something wrong?'

He was frowning. 'Something here. Something he's written here.' He shifted his gaze to the date at the top of the page. 'An entry from eight years back . . .'

'What about it?'

'He's talking about a friend of his who died.'

'Oh?'

'In mysterious circumstance.'

'Mysterious circumstances?'

'Those aren't his actual words.'

'What does he say?'

Jack cleared his throat and began to read: ' "I can't stop thinking about poor H. He was adamant that something was about to happen to him, and he was proved right. He said it would happen within days, that on the surface it would appear to be the result of an accident, and that it would arouse no suspicion. When the news of his death came to me I went cold. It was all exactly as he said it would be. When I heard what had happened every word he spoke came back to me. How could he know? But he had made some study of the runes, he said, and there was no mistaking what was happening. It would be the same as with the Simoneaus, he said. In spite of it all, though, I can't believe there can be anything in it. But if H *was* right then that malign force is here, in our midst." '

'Runes? Malign force?' Connie said. 'Can he be serious? What does it mean?'

Jack shrugged. 'Your guess is as good as mine.'

She shook her head. 'Poor old fellow. But there's nothing in it, is there? There can't be. Is he really suggesting that there's some evil power here and that it destroyed one of his friends?'

'So it would seem.'

A silence fell in the room. Connie bent her head and looked into Jack's face.

'Jack?'

'What?'

'Let's not take this too seriously, all right? Let's keep it in perspective.'

'Of course.'

'After all, your uncle himself admitted that he was a bit eccentric, didn't he?' She was studying him. 'You don't believe there's anything in this, do you?'

'No. No, of course not.' After a pause he added, 'But it's a little disturbing. I mean, it looks as if his friend forecast his own death by a supposed accident and then died from a supposed accident only days later.'

Connie was silent for a moment, then she said, 'It's coincidence, that's all. How could it be anything else?'

'No, it can't be. Of course it can't, I realize that.'

'Right.' She reached out, gently took the journal from him, closed it and put it back on the shelf. 'Let's forget all that.'

He nodded, still preoccupied. She looked at him closely for some seconds, then said, 'I can see you writing here, you know. Can't you?'

He smiled now and gave a groan. 'God, you're so subtle.'

'No, really, I mean it. I can see you here finishing the second series of *Fat Chance*—and the third, and the fourth come to that.'

'It gets better.'

'Well, can't you? See yourself working here?'

57

'Yes, I suppose so.'

She stood there for a moment, then glanced out of the window. 'What do you say we start back? The rain's stopped. Let's get going before it comes on again, shall we?'

'We haven't been out into the back garden yet.'

'It'll be too wet. Let's save it for when we come back with Mother and the children.'

'You're truly sold on this place, aren't you?'

'I am.' She gave a deep sigh. 'I can't wait to tell Mum and the children about it. And I can't wait to bring them here. They're going to love it so.' In a sudden, impulsive move she stepped to him and wrapped her arms round his neck. 'I love you, you know that?'

'Do you?'

'Didn't I step in and save you from a life of misery and loneliness?'

'Is that the way you see it?'

'I just tell it like it is. It's the way it was. Doesn't that prove I love you?'

'I suppose it does.' He paused. 'Just don't stop.'

'Never. Don't doubt it.'

'No.' He needn't have asked; her love was one of the few things he could be sure of.

She lowered her arms, releasing him. 'I'll go on out. I want to cut a few of those lovely roses to take back for Mum. I'll see you outside.'

Jack remained sitting there after she had gone from the room. Somehow the questions about their taking over the place seemed to be all settled. And it had all happened so quickly. He gave a mental shrug. Why not, after all?

The twin pedestals of the desk each held three drawers, and idly, one by one, Jack began to pull them open. For the most part their contents were uninteresting, consisting of files and stationery and a hundred and one other accumulated items such as combs, broken pens, tickets, receipts, aspirins, etc. The last drawer he turned to, however, was different. For a start it was locked, though the key was there in the lock. He turned the key, pulled the drawer open, and began to rummage through chequebooks, chequebook stubs, bank statements, old correspondence and other predictable items and then found his hand closing round some hard, weighty, cloth-wrapped object. He brought it out and laid it before him on the desk, then unwrapped it and revealed a revolver. With it was a box of shells. He sat gazing at the weapon in silence.

'Jack?' Through the hall, from the direction of the front door, Connie's voice came to him in the quiet.

He sat there for a moment longer, then carefully wrapped the gun again and replaced it where he had found it. After locking the drawer he put the key in his pocket. As he straightened, Connie's voice came calling him again. He got up from the chair, took one last look at the closed and locked drawer, then up at the journals on the shelf, and then turned and started towards the door.

As he stepped into the hall he saw Connie standing in the open front doorway holding a bunch of pink roses. 'Oh, the scent of these,' she said. As he crossed the hall she added with a breathless little smile, 'Imagine—this being ours. It's hard to believe.' She turned from him, moving out across the porch and stood gazing out. Beyond her the rain dripped from the lime trees onto the sodden foliage beneath, while the unbelievably sweet, lush scents of the garden rose up. 'Oh, Jack,' she said, 'look at it all.'

'Yes,' he said, though all he could see in his mind's eye was the revolver lying in its wrapping of oily cloth.

Bernard Taylor

And then added to the picture came Edwin's voice speaking the words that he had written in his journal: *If H was right then that malign force is here, in our midst* . . . Almost unconsciously Jack raised a hand towards Connie in a gesture of restraint, and opened his mouth to speak, to tell her, *Wait—let's not be hasty about this. Let's give this a little more thought* . . . But he said nothing.

Moments later, as he closed and locked the front door behind him the old man's words were still going through his mind. He straightened, turned and stepped towards Connie, suddenly full of doubt.

'Connie—don't you think—'

'Oh, Jack, *look!*' Her voice cut off his words. She was stepping down onto the path as she spoke, looking over to her left, to the horizon. 'Look, a rainbow.'

As he moved across the porch she turned to face him, giving a soft laugh, light and clear in the rain-washed air. From high up in one of the limes came the singing of a blackbird. 'A rainbow,' she said again. 'It's an omen.' She turned to him, meeting him as he stepped down onto the path. 'It's a sign. For us. From now on everything's going to be just great.'

'Is that right?'

'You can bet on it.' She nodded in affirmation. 'What was it you were going to say just now?'

'Nothing. It wasn't important.'

He took her arm and together they started off along the path towards the car.

Chapter Two

'It's marvellous, isn't it,' Sarah said, glancing from the study window onto the back garden, 'to be able to let the children out without having to bother about traffic or any other such dangers.'

Duster in hand, Connie followed her mother's glance out to where the children, not long back from school, played in the warmth of the late June sun. 'Too true,' she said. 'I was so relieved to leave Streatham, but even in Chiswick I never really relaxed, I realize that now. So often when you live in a town the children are either in the house and under your feet, or outside and on your mind.'

It was Friday afternoon. Jack was absent, having set off that morning in the Citroën to drive into London for a meeting with the producer of the TV series. Following his departure Connie and Sarah had begun the task of dusting off Jack's books and arranging them with Edwin's collection on the newly cleaned shelves.

Side by side at the study window, the two women

stood looking out at the sunlit scene. Connie wore an apron over her blouse and jeans, and Sarah an overall over a blouse and skirt. Like her daughter, Sarah had a slim build, though her features were smaller, neater. A lithe and agile sixty-four, her long hair was still thick, its dark brown only now giving way to encroaching grey. She wore it, as she had done for years now, in two braids, coiled and pinned at the back of her head.

The two women looked very content standing there at the window. All three children were in their view. Eight-year-old Joel, the eldest, was building a make-shift tent over in one corner of the lawn. Its frame was a rickety old clotheshorse supplemented by a few sticks and bits of timber, over the whole of which construction he was in the process of draping an old blanket. The sun, which had brought out the freckles on his nose and upper cheeks, shone brightly on his untidy fair hair. Connie looked with warm amusement at his intent expression as his slightly protruding front teeth chewed his lower lip. On the other side of the lawn the twins, Lydia and Kitty, six, were having a dolls' tea party, sitting on a blanket with their dolls around an assortment of little cups and saucers and other paraphernalia. Almost two weeks had passed now since the move from London, and the children had just completed their first week at their new primary school in Barfield. To Connie's relief they appeared, after their initial fears of the unknown, to be settling in very well.

In the nine months that had passed since the decision to move to Valley Green, much had been accomplished. At the end of April, after periods of near hopelessness, the house in Chiswick, along with some of its furniture, had eventually been sold. While wait-

ing for a buyer Jack and Connie had done their best
to make what alterations to The Limes they had felt
desirable. In the months before the move they had
visited it at every opportunity, clearing and cleaning
and sorting through its contents. Some items they had
sold to dealers, while others had been set aside for
their own use. Then, finally, professional house-
clearers had come in and swiftly and methodically
gone through the house like scavenging ants until it
was picked clean. Afterwards Jack and Connie had
been left with a great deal of good furniture, numerous pictures and ornaments and the major part of Edwin's library.

Early in the spring, with the second TV series com
pleted, Jack had temporarily moved into the house
and, advised by two or three neighbours who were
only too happy to help, had hired the services of local
electricians, painters and plumbers. With new wiring
and new facilities installed in the kitchen and bathroom, things had at last begun to take shape. It had
seemed at times that the house would never be free of
the sound of workmen and the dust and dirt they created, but eventually they were gone, and the furniture
could be placed in its chosen sites. The only sounds
now in the house were those made by its new occupants, who were at last free to relax in it and begin to
settle in. There was still much work to do, but as far
as possible, Jack and Connie had decided, it would be
done by themselves.

Now Sarah left the study and went into the kitchen
where she began to prepare a tray with biscuits and
glasses of Coke. When it was ready she carried it outside. There was no need for her to call the children to
her; even before she had set the tray down on the old
wooden bench they were beside her, small hands

reaching out. 'Easy, easy,' she said, adding with a shake of her head, 'Anybody'd think you hadn't eaten in days.'

Returning to the house she boiled the kettle, then called Connie and together they sat in the kitchen and drank cups of tea. They felt a sense of accomplishment and satisfaction, both enjoying their new surroundings, and not only the house and its environment, but their immediate view of the new sink, stove, refrigerator, dishwasher, washing machine and pristine cupboard units.

When their tea was finished, Sarah announced her intention of leaving Connie to get on in the study alone while she herself went out to the front garden to spend an hour or so tackling the weeds there. After exchanging her skirt for a pair of old slacks she put on her gardening gloves and went outside. It was a beautiful afternoon, the sun shining brightly, with very little humidity in the air.

She had been working there for about an hour when Connie came out to join her. Sarah straightened, wincing and stretching from her exertions as Connie approached along the path. 'It's warm work,' Sarah observed.

Connie was about to reply when her eye was attracted by movement, and looking beyond Sarah's shoulder she saw a large, overweight old black labrador enter at the open gates and meander onto the drive.

'Oh, look,' she said with a smile, 'we've got a visitor. Dark-haired, too—that must be good luck.'

As Sarah turned to follow the direction of Connie's glance, Connie's smile suddenly vanished.

'Oh, no!' she said. 'Look at that!'

Having turned a couple of circles the dog had come

to a halt, and squatted down at the edge of the drive and begun to relieve himself.

'Get off!' Sarah called out, stepping forward and flapping her hands. 'Get away!'

Making no response to the women other than merely to look round at them, the dog carried on with his business. When he had finished he moved back towards the gate and stood there waiting. Sarah took another step forward, yelling to the dog as she did so: 'Get out! Get out, will you! You filthy creature!'

As she spoke a man came in view, walking along the lane. Hearing Sarah's words he came to a stop at the open gate and looked over at her with unconcealed hostility. He was tall and slim, and somewhere in his sixties. He had a long, thin face and wore a tweed jacket and corduroy trousers. On his head he wore a fashionable-looking cap which, Sarah thought, might have looked better on someone forty years younger.

'What's the problem?' he said in a deep, mellifluous voice. 'Something wrong?'

'Well, yes,' Sarah said. 'Since you ask, it's that dog. Is he yours?'

'My dog? What about him? What's he done?'

Uncertain, Sarah turned and looked at Connie who gestured to the mound of steaming faeces on the gravel drive.

'I should think it's obvious,' Connie said. '*There. That's* what he's done.'

'Nonsense,' the man said, frowning, following her pointing finger. 'He wouldn't do that.'

'What d'you mean?' Connie replied. 'We saw him do it. He just wandered in and did it.'

'Did he now?' The man gave a cold little smile. 'Well, well.'

'Yes, he did,' Connie said, then added sharply, 'Did

65

you bring your poop scoop with you?'

'My *what*?'

'Are you going to clean it up?'

'Clean it up?' The man gave a derisive little chuckle as if the idea were of the utmost absurdity.

'It's not a joke,' Connie said, her anger growing. 'It's anything but that. It's disgusting.'

'If it's so disgusting,' he said, 'then I suggest in future you keep your gates closed.'

'That's not the point,' Connie retorted. 'Besides, if we want to leave our gates open that's up to us. Certainly we should be able to do it without getting landed with a mess like that.' She paused. 'Well?'

'Well, what?'

'Are you going to clean it up?'

He made no answer, but glanced at the mess and then back to Connie's angry face.

'If *you* won't,' she said, 'then someone *else* has to, and it's not a job I care to do.'

'I don't know what you're making such a fuss about,' he said. 'Anyway, it's good for the garden.'

'If it's good for the garden,' Connie said, growing still angrier, 'then let him do it on *your* garden. When I want piles of dog crap dumped on my property I'll let you know. Until then, I suggest you keep that disgusting thing on a lead. He's a pest. And a health hazard into the bargain.'

The man's eyes flashed in fury at this, and he looked at her with contempt in the curl of his lip. 'You're new here, aren't you?' he said. 'Well, I'd better tell you that as newcomers you've got a bit to learn.'

'From you?' Sarah broke in heatedly. 'I don't think there's anything we can learn from you. Except perhaps bad manners and a complete lack of consideration for other people!'

'And another thing,' the man said, as if Sarah had not spoken, 'you don't come here telling the villagers how to go on.' He looked down at the dog. 'Come on, Chip, let's leave 'em to it. We've got better things to do than stand around talking about dog shit.' With this he turned and walked on, the dog trotting along at his heels.

Connie and Sarah gazed after him in angry amazement.

'I don't believe it!' Connie hissed, almost shaking with fury. 'What an ill-tempered, ill-mannered old bugger!'

Later on, when Jack got in, Connie told him of the encounter with the man.

'Forget it,' he said.

'But he was so hostile. And yet he was so clearly in the wrong.'

'Then of course he was hostile,' said Jack. 'Guilt turns to hostility. Didn't you know that? It always does. Anyway,' he finished, 'he'll have taken your point. There won't be any further trouble with him, I'm sure.'

The next morning dawned fine and fair again, and while Jack and Connie set off to do some shopping in Reading Sarah prepared to take the children out for a walk. There had been so much to do since their arrival and this would be their first real opportunity to see anything of their new surroundings.

From the lane, Sarah and the children took a footpath that led them away from the village and ran beside fields of ripening barley and wheat that were dotted here and there with the blood-red splashes of poppies. As they meandered along, the children had time to observe and explore. And having come from the city there was so much to see. In the hedgerows, blackberries and elderberries were swelling amid the pink-white trumpets of bindweed, while in the shadows of the foliage rabbits and other small creatures darted, disturbed by the nearness of the four strangers. In the low-growing branches of a hawthorn Joel spotted a small bird's nest. Stretching up on her toes Sarah peeped in and observed that it was abandoned, its occupants having flown.

Keeping to the footpath beside the hedgerow, they came at last to a wood. They entered it and, following one of several worn paths, walked in the cool shade of the trees. After wandering around for some time they emerged onto the side of a hill where they sat down in the grass to rest. Around their feet grew mauve and white clover, daisies and buttercups. Some thirty yards away a starling was feeding her offspring, the chick following her around, repeatedly calling for food. On the far side of the field cows contentedly grazed. On first seeing the animals Lydia and Kitty had expressed alarm, but Sarah had quickly reassured them, telling them they had no need to be afraid.

After resting there for a while Sarah said they had better start back, and they got up and re-entered the wood. They took a different path this time, and when they eventually emerged found themselves in unfamiliar surroundings. Lydia asked a little nervously, 'Are we lost, Nana?'

'No, dear,' Sarah replied. 'We'll soon find our way home again.'

Moments later, breaking through a little thicket of silver birches and brambles, they saw the village lying below them in the valley, the sun shining on the rooftops.

A while later they re-entered the village on its more

southerly side, finding themselves in a narrow lane with small, old houses on either side. Halfway along, Sarah came to a halt before a small, white-walled Victorian house where on the front step a cat lay basking in the sun. At Sarah's side a profusion of cream-coloured rambling roses cascaded over the grey stone wall. Although Sarah found the house attractive, it was the garden that took her attention. With small areas of neat, green lawn, the major part of it was planted with roses in shades of pink, yellow, orange and white.

'Oh,' she said, 'it's absolutely beautiful.'

'Let me see, let me see,' came the voices of the twins, and in turn, with an effort, she hoisted them up to look over the wall. 'Isn't it a picture!' she exclaimed, and in turn they agreed that it was. 'You wait and see,' Sarah said as she set Kitty back on her feet, 'our garden's a mess right now, but in time it'll look just as nice as this one. You wait till I've had a real chance to get to work on it.' Turning her head to the roses that cascaded over the wall, she exclaimed, 'And aren't these lovely?' Putting her face to the blossoms she breathed in the scent. 'Oh, what a lovely smell. I don't think we've got any like these.' She added, 'But give us time and we may well have.'

Taking Lydia and Kitty by the hand she moved on again. As they turned out of the lane at the corner she looked around. 'Where's Joel? Where's he got to?' A moment later he came in view, running towards them, in his fist a small bunch of the cream-coloured rambling roses. As he got to Sarah's side he held them up to her.

'Here you are, Nana. They're for you.'

'Joel,' Sarah said, her eyes widening, 'what have you done?'

His happy expression faltered. 'I picked them,' he said, 'for you.'

'But they're not yours to pick. They belong to the owner of the house. You can't just take them.'

'But—but there's lots and lots of them. And they were all hanging down the wall into the lane.'

'That doesn't matter. It's *stealing*.'

'I thought you'd like them,' he said. 'You said we haven't got any like them at home.'

'I do like them. But that's quite beside the point. It was wrong of you.'

He stood there in silence while Sarah and the girls looked at him.

'Well,' Sarah said with a shrug, 'I suppose it's done now. We can't very well put them back.'

Looking very crestfallen, Joel said, 'What shall I do with them? Shall I throw them away?'

'What for?' Sarah said. 'That won't make it right, will it?'

'No.'

She gave a sharp sigh of exasperation. 'Give them to me.' She took the flowers from him. 'Now that you've picked them we'll have to keep them.' She looked down at him as he stood before her with his head lowered and his eyes downcast. She sighed, reached out and brushed her hand across his fair hair. 'Anyway, cheer up. I don't suppose it's the end of the world. But you mustn't ever do it again, you understand?'

'Yes.'

'Right, come on, then. Let's get home and have some tea. I'm getting thirsty.'

When they got back to the house Sarah made tea and sandwiches, and while the children sat eating in the kitchen she put the roses in water. She was just

70

setting the vase down on a little table in the hall when Connie entered carrying several bags and packages.

'Oh, they're pretty,' she said, seeing the roses. 'From our garden? I didn't know we had any like that.'

'I'm sorry you asked,' Sarah said. She moved to the kitchen door, closed it, and then with lowered voice told what had happened.

'Oh, dear,' Connie said. 'I suppose that's one thing that comes of living in a city. Children just aren't used to seeing so many flowers growing. Though we've hardly got a shortage of them here in our garden.'

'No, I know,' Sarah said. 'He picked them because I happened to remark that we didn't have any like them.'

Connie sighed. 'Anyway, it's done now. And as long as he realizes he did wrong I don't suppose there'll be too much harm done.'

Sarah followed Connie into the kitchen where they joined the children. After a minute or two Jack came in. 'So,' he said to the children, 'did you enjoy your ramble?'

'We found a bird's nest,' said Kitty.

'Yes,' said Lydia, 'and we saw some rabbits, too.'

'Rabbits, eh?'

'Yes, and we got lost and had to come back home a different way.'

'Yes,' said Kitty, 'and Joel picked some roses.'

Lydia nodded: 'Yes, he *pinched* them, and Nana told him off.'

'You girls,' Connie said, 'don't tell tales.'

As she spoke there came a ring at the front doorbell. Connie looked at Jack in surprise then started towards the hall. 'Who can that be?' she said with a frown.

She opened the front door to find herself facing a tall, elderly man, and recognized him at once as the

71

Bernard Taylor

villager whose dog had caused the unpleasant confrontation the day before.

'Oh, it's you,' she said, and then, 'Yes?'

'My name is Callow,' he said. He was glaring at her. 'John Callow. We met yesterday afternoon.'

'I haven't forgotten.' Connie looked down towards his feet but the dog was not in evidence. 'Yes?' she said again.

'Yes, indeed,' he said shortly. 'I've come to find out whether your family makes it a practice to go around stealing other people's property.'

Connie gaped at him with eyes wide. 'What are you talking about?'

Glancing past her shoulder he pointed with his forefinger, and Connie turned and saw the object of his gesture.

'That's what I'm talking about,' he said. 'Those. My roses—stolen by your son. I assume he's your son. I saw him from the window. He was with the old woman, so I knew where he lived.'

As he finished speaking Jack appeared at Connie's side.

'What's the trouble?' he said.

Connie gave a deep sigh. 'This is Mr Callow. It's what the girls were talking about. When they were out on their walk Joel picked four or five roses that were hanging over a wall.' She gestured back to the flowers on the table, and then nodded towards the angry visitor. 'This is the owner, come to complain.'

Jack glanced at the roses, then at the man, then spread his hands in a gesture of helplessness. 'Oh, dear,' he said, shaking his head. 'What can we say? I apologize for my son's action. He was wrong to do it, there's no question of that.'

'And he knows he's done wrong,' Connie added. 'He

72

won't do it again, I can assure you.'

'He'd better not,' said the man. 'Anyway, what are you going to do about it?'

'Do?' Jack frowned. 'I don't know that there's anything we *can* do. We've apologized. Unless you want us to pay for the roses. We'll gladly do that, of course.'

'I don't want payment for them.'

'Well—what more can we do?'

'What are you going to do to him? The boy?'

Jack shook his head. 'I don't get you. What do you mean?'

'What I said. What are you going to *do* to him? Is he going to be punished?'

Before Jack had a chance to reply Connie stepped forward. 'Excuse me,' she said shortly, 'but that's got nothing to do with you. We've apologized and offered to pay for the flowers—and that's it. Whether we punish our son is no concern of yours. As I said, he's been reprimanded. His grandmother's already spoken to him about it and you can rest assured that he won't do anything like it again.'

'Oh, his grandmother's *spoken* to him, has she?' he said with a note of scorn in his voice. 'A lot of good that'll do, I'm sure.'

'What exactly are you saying?' Connie said.

Callow ignored her sharp question. 'Spoken to him about it,' he repeated contemptuously. 'And I suppose that'll be the end of it.' Glaring at Connie and Jack he added, 'The boy should be punished. Severely. And if he were my son he would be.'

'Yes,' said Connie, her anger growing. 'I quite believe it. Well, let's just be glad that he's not your son.'

At her words Jack touched her on the shoulder, urging her not to be provoked. Then, after a moment's hesitation he turned and strode towards the kitchen.

'Joel,' he called. 'Joel—come out here a minute, will you?'

Connie frowned, turning her glance to follow him. 'What are you going to do?'

Jack did not answer. A moment later Joel appeared in the kitchen doorway. Jack held out his hand to him. 'Joel, come here, will you?'

Glancing down the hall at the man standing at the door, Joel moved to his father's side. Jack bent to him and gestured to the visitor.

'This is Mr Callow. Apparently the roses you took belonged to him, and he's rather upset about you taking them.'

Joel shrank back a little. 'I'm sorry,' he said. 'I'm very sorry.'

'*We* know that,' Jack said, 'but I think you'd better apologize to the gentleman, don't you?'

Joel looked up at his father and gave a reluctant nod.

'Right,' Jack said. 'So you come and tell him that you're sorry and that you'll never do it again.'

Joel nodded once more.

'Good.' With a hand on Joel's shoulder, Jack gently urged him to the front door. 'Right—now tell Mr Callow that you're sorry.'

Joel lifted his pale face to the angry face of the older man. 'I'm sorry, sir,' he said. 'I'm very sorry I took the flowers.'

'And you'll never do it again,' prompted Jack.

'I'll never do it again,' Joel said.

'OK,' Jack said, 'now go on back into the kitchen.'

With obvious relief, Joel turned and scuttled back along the hall. Callow, clearly dissatisfied, watched him go.

'Well,' Connie said into the silence when the kitchen

door had closed, 'he's apologized to you, and I hope you'll accept his apology.'

Callow gave a little snort of derision, then looking past her called out, 'It was you who encouraged the boy.'

Turning, Connie and Jack saw Sarah standing at the end of the hall with her back to the kitchen door. At Callow's words she stepped forward.

'I?' she said sharply. 'I did no such thing.'

As Sarah came to stand at her shoulder, Connie said angrily, 'Listen, before you start lecturing people on how to go on you should turn your attention to your own behaviour. What about that filthy animal of yours? I haven't forgotten what happened yesterday—letting him wander in and foul our garden. I suppose you think that's quite acceptable, do you?'

Callow listened to her outburst and shook his head. 'I might have expected something like that,' he said. Turning to Jack he added, 'Having been told who you are, I suppose I shouldn't be surprised at anything you and your people do. Your uncle who lived here—I knew him. Him and his crazy daughter, they made a good pair.'

Jack drew himself up. 'Be careful what you say,' he said stiffly. 'You're going too far.'

'Oh,' the man sneered, 'what is it now—threats? I'm sixty-five. What are you doing—threatening me with violence?'

Jack did not answer.

'Oh, yes,' Callow said, his lip curling, 'they were as mad as each other. It was no surprise to anyone that they ended up as they did.' He raised an eyebrow. 'I only hope for your sake that the family likeness isn't too strong.'

Burning with rage, but feeling impotent to do anything, Jack could only stand there. Connie, less re-strained, opened her mouth to protest. Sarah, though, was quicker.

'Don't you dare say such things!' she cried. 'Don't you dare come here with your insults. We've done nothing to you that could warrant this kind of treat-ment!' Whirling, she stepped towards the roses, snatched them from the vase, spun again and roughly thrust herself forward between Connie and Jack. 'Get out!' she cried to Callow. 'Get out!' Lifting the dripping roses, she drew back her hand and hurled them at him. They struck him in the chest and then fell onto the step at his feet. 'Get out!' she said. 'Get out and take your flowers with you!'

The moment after she had spoken she raised her hands to her face and burst into tears. Then, turning, she fled across the hall and up the stairs.

Connie and Jack watched her go, then turned back to the man. Callow stood there white-faced, trembling with fury. Bending his head slightly, he looked down at the roses that lay scattered at his feet.

'*She* did that to me too,' he said. 'Maddox's daughter. She did the very same thing.'

When he raised his head a second later there was such hatred in his eyes that Connie shrank from him. He glared at her and Jack for a moment and then, without another word, turned and started up the path to the gate. In silence, they watched him until he was out of sight.

When Connie went up to Sarah's room a minute or two later she found her sitting on her bed, bent over, her chin in her hand. As Connie moved across the room, Sarah looked round at her.

'I'm sorry, dear,' she said with a sniff. 'I'm so sorry about that.'

'Don't worry about it,' Connie said. 'He had it coming to him. And more.'

'Yes, but even so I shouldn't have butted in like that. I shouldn't have. I always swore I'd never interfere where you and Jack were concerned—and there I go, charging in like a bull in a china shop. And then throwing those flowers at him just made the whole thing worse.'

'Mum . . .' Connie sat beside her and put an arm around her shoulder. 'Forget it. Don't worry about it. Besides, he dragged you into it, saying that you'd encouraged Joel in the first place. He deserved what he got.'

Sarah shook her head. 'Even so, I went too far. We've hardly been here a fortnight and I've already alienated one of the neighbours.'

'Forget it,' Connie said. 'It'll blow over. It'll all be forgotten in time.'

'D'you think so?'

'Yes. And even if it isn't I can't say that not having that miserable old bastard's friendship will be any great loss.'

Later, after everyone had gone to bed, Connie lay at Jack's side thinking back over the incident.

'Do you think,' she said into the dark, 'that there was any truth in what Callow said? About your uncle?'

'That he was crazy?'

'Yes.'

'No, of course not.'

'Not only him, but he said Mary as well . . .'

Jack sighed, shifting his head on the pillow. 'Listen, if anyone's crazy around here it has to be Callow. And the less I see of him the better.'

Chapter Three

Lying back in the grass, Jack adjusted his rolled sweater beneath his head. 'Don't wake me,' he said as he closed his eyes. 'Just shut the door quietly when you leave.'

Lydia, sitting at his side making a daisy chain, turned to Connie. 'Did you hear what he said?' She looked down at Jack and sniggered. 'You're silly. There isn't any door.'

Through the shifting screen of oak leaves above Jack's head the warm sun dappled his bare arms and legs. He felt very comfortable, very content, and full. It was so good to relax, and to do so without having the guilt generated by a million unfinished jobs gnawing at one's conscience. And he could begin to relax now. They all could. With most of the work in the house just about finished, he and Connie felt able to slow down and give more of their time to the children in what was left of the summer holidays, and leave them less in Sarah's charge.

Bernard Taylor

On three or four occasions over the past days, taking advantage of the fine August weather, Jack had forsaken his word-processor and he and the family had driven out into the countryside for picnics and visits to unfamiliar towns and villages. Today they had packed a picnic lunch and set out in the Citroën. After visiting a small village where they had stopped to browse around a few antique shops, they had set off again along the narrow country roads. On either side the fields were gold with the harvest stubble, with round bales of straw dotted like giant caramels over the hillsides. After a time, finding what looked to be a promising place, they had parked the car well off the road, unloaded their belongings from the boot and set off along a tree-fringed bridle path. Fifteen minutes later they had found a pleasant little spot at the edge of a piece of rough pasture beside a small copse. It was perfect, a place where the children could play in safety and without doing any harm to the environment.

After setting down their things, Jack and the children had gone off to explore their surroundings. At the foot of the hill where dragonflies darted, a narrow, shallow stream ran by, while in the thicket, where the bracken grew higher than the children's heads, pigeons fed on the ripened elderberries. Here, too, the children picked and ate blackberries, their purpled lips smiling with the pleasure of their discoveries.

Later, sitting at the edge of the thicket, they had enjoyed their picnic lunch. Connie and Sarah had outdone themselves in their preparations and they had all eaten well. There had been canteloupe, followed by cold chicken with salads of avocado, lettuce, potatoes and beans. They had finished off with wedges of Sarah's apple pie. To drink there had been, apart from

mineral water, wine and coffee for the adults and
Coca-Cola for the children. Now Jack lay with the
voices of the others around him, their words mur-
muring desultorily against the sweet background of
the birdsong. The food and the two glasses of wine
had made him mellow. On his tongue he could still
taste the lingering flavour of the coffee, and the mint
chocolate that Lydia had put into his mouth.

'I just might,' he said to no one in particular, 'stay
here for ever.'

The others ignored his words. 'Come on, Nana,' he
heard Joel say, 'let's go down and look at the stream.'

'All right,' came Sarah's voice with a sigh. 'If I must.'

Jack continued to lie there as the children's voices
receded into the distance. There was, he reflected,
nothing standing in the way of their continuing happiness and contentment now. With the work on the
house as good as finished and his own work going
well, he had come to realize more strongly each day
that the move from Chiswick to Valley Green had been
the best move they had ever made. How could he have
had doubts? Looking back, the reservations he had
had now seemed very insubstantial. Though granted,
it had been somewhat disturbing to read what Edwin
had written in the journal, and even more so to find
the gun in the drawer of the desk. Later, he had told
Connie of his finding of the weapon, but she had re-
acted far more pragmatically than he. She had not
seen any reason to be unduly disturbed by its discovery. After all, as she had once again pointed out, Edwin was, by his own admission, a little eccentric.
There was no reason to assume that the revolver had
any sinister connotation. Jack had told himself that it
was foolish to set too much store by what he had
found and had put both the weapon and Edwin's writ-

ings out of his mind. So it was that the journals now
remained unopened and largely forgotten on their
shelf in the study, while the revolver was securely
locked away in the desk drawer, safe from the children.

The only real shadow over the happiness of their
occupancy of their new home so far had been the business with Callow. It had been very unpleasant, and
particularly unfortunate that the altercation had happened so soon after their arrival. But it was over now,
and they would take care to avoid the possibility of
any further conflict. To Jack's relief, and that of Connie and Sarah, it appeared that Callow had now chosen a different route for walking his dog, and as a
result they rarely set eyes on him, only occasionally
glimpsing him at a distance around the village. Over
the following days the distress they felt had faded, the
memory of the incident ceasing to bring little more
than mild annoyance and regret.

A little while later, with the realization that he must
have fallen asleep, Jack became aware of Joel tugging
on his hand and urging him to get up. 'Daddy, come
and see. Come on down to the water. There are fishes
there!'

His brief sleep in the sun was over. Yawning, he got
to his feet and followed Joel down to the stream.

They stopped at the little post office/grocery store on
their return to the village just before five. It was owned
by a middle-aged widow by the name of Emma Stocks
who ran it with the occasional help of her married
daughter Jane who lived nearby. The two women had
warmly welcomed Jack and Connie on their arrival in
the village, and Jane had offered her services as babysitter should the need arise.

On this afternoon when Jack and Connie entered the shop they found both Emma Stocks and her daughter behind the counter. Mrs Stocks was a short, rail-like little woman with greying dark hair, and pristine National Health dentures which she showed in a wide smile of greeting. Jane, in her mid-forties, looked nothing like her mother, being blonde, a good head taller and very stoutly built. She was like her mother, however, in her warm, easygoing nature, and in the dry wit that she was not slow to turn upon herself.

As Mrs Stocks served Connie, Jane chatted about this and that. As they talked an old man entered. Jack and Connie had seen him about the village on several occasions, but they had never met. Now, coming to the counter, he asked Jane for an ounce of tobacco. While she got it for him, he nodded a greeting to Jack and Connie. 'You're Mr Maddox's nephew, ain't that right?' he said to Jack. Like Mrs Stocks and her daughter, he spoke with a broad, West Country accent.

Jack replied that he was. It was common knowledge in the village by now that Jack and his family had moved into The Limes and that Edwin Maddox had been Jack's uncle.

The old man took the tobacco from Jane, paid her and then said to Connie, 'You're settling in all right, ma'am, are you?'

'Oh, yes, indeed,' she said, 'thank you.'

'The Limes is a lovely old 'ouse.'

'Well, we think so,' said Jack. 'We love it there. Though it's kept us busy, I don't mind saying. Still, we're getting straight now.'

Jack introduced Connie and himself, and they shook hands. The man gave his name as George Appleton. He looked to be about seventy. He was lean and wiry and grey-haired, with faded blue eyes and a tanned, deeply seamed face. He had, he said, lived in the village for most of his life.

'And I 'ear tell as you're a writer,' he said. 'For the telly, right?'

'Yes—for my sins.'

'And you wrote that programme about the fat girl. Is that right?'

'That's right.' There would be no secrets in Valley Green.

Jane broke in at this, laughing. 'Yes, George. And if you're thinkin' that I was the model for 'is leadin' lady then you're wrong. 'E wrote that before 'e came down 'ere.'

They all laughed, then Jack said to the old man, 'I'm afraid to ask whether you watch it.'

'Oh, ah!' George Appleton nodded. 'I don't miss that one.'

Jack chuckled. 'Well, that's a relief.'

'I s'pose it's only right in a way,' George Appleton said, 'that you should be a writer too. Like your uncle, I mean.'

'Oh, well, my uncle's work was of a more learned nature than mine. A lot more, in fact.'

'I knew your uncle quite well, you know.'

'Oh, really?'

'Yes. I used to 'elp him out on the garden from time to time. After 'is wife died, that was. Oh, it used to be grand then, your garden. Really beautiful.'

Jack nodded. 'I know. I remember it from when I visited the place as a child. I'm afraid no one could call it beautiful now. It's gone haywire since then.'

'Your uncle loved that garden, and no mistake. That and 'is opera.' He gave a little chuckle. 'Though I'm afraid all that opera stuff is a bit over my 'ead.'

Jack smiled. 'Not your cup of tea, huh?'

'Nah, I'm afraid not. All them fat sopranos with 'orns on their 'eads, dyin' of consumption. Nah, give me *Casualty* or *Coronation Street* any day.'

Connie had finished making her purchases and she and Jack said their goodbyes and started out to the car. George Appleton followed them. While Connie moved to put the shopping in the boot, Appleton bent his head and glanced through the open window.

'So these are your kiddies, are they?'

Jack, his hand on the car's passenger doorhandle, gave a nod. 'That's right. Except for the tall one. That's my wife's mother.'

Appleton and Sarah nodded greetings to one another and introduced themselves. Then the old man looked in at the children again and said, 'Three little ones, eh? I should think they keep you on your toes all right.'

'Oh, they do indeed,' Connie responded. 'No doubt about that.'

A pause, then Appleton said to Jack, 'If you used to visit The Limes, I s'pose you knew Mr Maddox's son and daughter, did you?'

Jack nodded. 'Yes, but we were only children. And I didn't see them that often.'

'I 'ear tell as David, the son, died in America.'

'Yes, I'm afraid so. A few years back.'

'A sad business. I remember 'im when 'e was just a little chap—'im and 'is sister Mary. They were lovely children. And o' course I used to see Mary when she was older and come back 'ere to the village.' With a sorrowful shake of his head he added, 'That was a shock, I don't mind telling you, 'earing what 'appened to 'er.'

Jack sighed. 'It was very tragic.'

'It certainly was.'

Connie, getting into the car behind the wheel, turned and wished George Appleton a cheery goodbye. Smiling, he said he was glad to have made her acquaintance, then to Jack he said: 'Anyway, I mustn't keep you. Just let me wish you a very 'appy time in the village. I'm sure as everything'll go just fine for you all.'

'Thank you.'

'And if there's anything I can do to 'elp, let me know.' He gestured with a thumb across the green. 'I live just over there. Third cottage in Green Lane. Hawthorn Cottage. Everybody knows me.'

'Thank you,' Jack said again. 'I'll remember.' He took the old man's weathered hand in his. 'It was very nice to meet you, and I'm sure we'll bump into each other again very soon.'

'Oh, no doubt about that, I'm sure. In a place this size it'd be 'ard to avoid it.'

Jack gave a final nod of goodbye and got into the car. Connie started the engine and they set off for home.

'Oh, dear,' Connie said a minute later as they drove along Princes Lane. 'To what do we owe this pleasure, I wonder?'

Up ahead of them they saw the tall figure of John Callow. He was standing next to the open driveway gates, looking at the house.

'Just ignore him,' Jack said. 'Don't pay him any attention.'

As they drew nearer, Callow turned his head and saw the car coming towards him. For a second he stood eyeing their approach, then he turned and began to walk on along the lane.

'He's going,' Sarah said with relief. 'And good riddance to the rude old so-and-so.'

'Yes,' said Kitty, 'good riddance to the rude old so-and-so.'

Jack turned round in his seat and frowned at her. 'That's enough of that, thank you very much.'

'Well, Nana said it.'

'Yes, I know I did,' Sarah said, 'and I shouldn't have.'

As the car drove up to the gates they saw Callow come to a stop and look around him. A moment later he was turning and hurrying back towards them, shouting and waving his arms.

'Take no notice,' Jack said to Connie.

'I don't intend to,' she said. With her words she turned the wheel and swept the car through the gates onto the drive.

Jack was the first to glimpse the dog as it came out of the shrubbery on the left. The children saw it just a split second later and in unison raised a horrified cry of warning: *The dog! Oh, Mummy, look out for the dog!* Connie, though, did not see the animal until it was too late.

The jolt and the sound of the impact came in the same moment that Connie, with a screeching of brakes, and a spraying of gravel from beneath the locked wheels, brought the car to a shuddering halt. Turning off the motor she put her hands over her face with a moan of anguish. 'Oh, my God,' she said through her fingers, 'I've hit it. I've hit the dog.'

Leaping out of the car, Jack turned and saw the black labrador lying motionless some yards back, near the edge of the drive. As he moved towards it he was aware of Callow entering at the gates and hurrying forward.

'What have you done?' Callow cried. 'What have you done?'

Jack bent over the still form. The dog appeared to

87

be unmarked, but there was blood trickling from its mouth and its open eyes were vacant and dulled. Jack could see at once that it was dead.

'*No!*' The cry came from Callow as he roughly thrust Jack aside. 'You've killed him! You've *killed my dog.*' Falling to his knees on the gravel, he felt the animal's chest for a heartbeat. 'Chip . . . Chip, old boy . . .' Hopelessly he shook his head. 'He's dead.' His voice was distorted by his tears. 'You've killed him.'

Jack felt utterly helpless. 'I'm so sorry,' he said. He felt near to tears himself. 'We couldn't help it. He just came right out in front of us. There was nothing we could do. We couldn't stop in time.' As he spoke he heard the sound of the car doors opening and closing. Turning, he saw Sarah and the three children standing there, watching with horror-stricken gaze. Lydia and Kitty were weeping, making strange little moaning, keening sounds. He waved a hand, urging them all away. 'Sarah, please—for God's sake take them indoors, will you?'

As Sarah and the children went off towards the house, Jack looked at the car and saw that Connie was still sitting behind the wheel, her head bent forward in her hands. Turning back, he saw that Callow was kneeling, cupping the dog's head in his palm and gently stroking him. Tears streamed down his cheeks.

'I'm sorry,' Jack said again. 'Believe me, I'm so sorry.'

'*Sorry,*' the man said, raising angry, tear-filled eyes to him. 'You're sorry. What good is that! That won't bring him back.'

'I know how you feel,' Jack said, 'but it was no one's fault. I told you, he just came out of the shrubbery, right into our path. We couldn't stop in time.'

'You didn't want to,' Callow said. 'I waved for you

to stop, but you didn't take any notice.'

'I'm sorry. Please believe me. We weren't to know what you were waving about.'

'You were going too fast anyway!' Callow looked over at the car, at Connie sitting behind the wheel. 'That wife of yours shouldn't be allowed to drive a car.'

'Come on now,' Jack said. 'There's no need for that.'

'It's true. She's not safe on the road.'

Stung, and unable to keep a faint note of asperity out of his voice, Jack said, 'If it comes to that, Mr Callow, the fact is we were not on the road. We were on our own property.'

'Oh, yes,' Callow said, his lips curling, 'trust you to come up with some smart answer.'

'I'm merely stating a fact.'

'Well, I'm not interested in listening to your facts. You've killed my dog.' His voice broke on a sob. 'That's the only thing I'm concerned about.' He glared over to where Connie sat in the car. 'Damn her!' he said venomously. 'Damn you both. *All* of you!'

'Now listen here—' Jack began.

Callow cut in: 'Don't you realize what you've done? You've killed my dog.'

'I'm sorry,' Jack said again. 'I'm terribly sorry. If I could undo it, believe me I would.' In a gesture of sympathy he reached out a hand towards the dead animal, but Callow roughly smacked his hand away.

'Don't you touch him!'

There came the sound of the car door opening and then the crunch of Connie's shoes on the gravel. As she came towards them Callow raised his eyes to her.

'Well? Are you happy now?' he said.

'Oh, please don't say that,' she cried, her voice breaking on her tears. 'You can't imagine how I feel about this. I'm so sorry. I'm so terribly sorry.'

'Yes,' Callow hissed, 'I'm sure you are.'

'Listen here,' Jack said, getting to his feet, his patience running out like sand through fingers, 'we've told you we're sorry and we are, and there's no need for you to take such a tone. You know very well it was an accident.' He paused then added, 'And if you'd kept your dog on a lead it wouldn't have happened. He shouldn't have been in our garden anyway.'

Callow stood up to face him. 'I don't believe this. Your wife has just killed my dog and you stand there whining about him trespassing on your precious garden.'

'I'm just pointing out,' Jack said, measuring his words in his growing anger, 'that if your dog hadn't been running around on our property in the first place the accident wouldn't have happened.'

Standing at Jack's shoulder Connie grasped his arm in an effort to calm him. Then to Callow she said: 'Really, Mr Callow, I am so sorry. We both are. I don't know what else to say. Please believe me.'

'There's nothing you can say. Nothing can put right what you've done.'

'I'm sorry.'

'You're always sorry.' He almost spat the words at her. 'First of all your son steals from me, and you're sorry for that. And now you kill my dog, and you're sorry for that too.'

Bending low, he awkwardly scooped the lifeless body of the dog into his arms, and then straightened before them, panting slightly from the exertion. The blood leaking from the dog's mouth was staining his sleeve.

'You don't know what sorry means,' he said. 'Maybe one day you will.'

Making a last effort, Jack said: 'Please—at least let me drive you home.'

'No, thank you,' Callow said. 'I want nothing at all from you. You've already done more than enough.'

Jack and Connie stood side by side watching as he walked away. In the gateway he turned and looked back. Silently, he stood for a moment glaring at them, then, turning again, he walked away down the lane.

Chapter Four

Late the following Saturday morning Jack was walking near the green after visiting the village post office when he saw George Appleton coming towards him.

'I've just come past your 'ouse,' the old man said as they drew level. 'I see as you've got the womenfolk busy in the garden.'

'Well,' Jack replied facetiously, 'someone's got to do it.'

'Quite,' Appleton grinned. 'A smart move, that. But you've got a job on there, and no mistake.'

Jack sighed. 'We have indeed.'

Over the past three days, with the weather staying clear and fine, Jack, Connie and Sarah had turned their full attention to the garden. They had spent hours clearing the weeds and cutting the overgrown grass of the lawns, transporting the rubbish to the back garden where, in a little waste patch, it was burned. And gradually their labours were beginning to show results. At the start the children had joined in, but they had soon become bored, eventually abandoning the chore in favour of more pleasurable pursuits of their own choosing.

'Trouble is,' Appleton said, 'once you really let it go it takes ages to get it back in shape again.'

Jack nodded. 'And I bet it's hardly been touched since my uncle died.'

'That's right,' Appleton said. 'It was too much for Mary. She couldn't manage it on her own, and the professor had stopped me working on it not long before 'is death.'

'Why was that?'

Appleton frowned. 'I don't really know. 'E just called an 'alt to it. There I was working on the garden one minute, and without a job the next. That wasn't like 'im at all. I remember I was cuttin' the grass when he comes out and tells me 'e won't need my 'elp any more. I thought maybe 'e meant just for the time bein' and that 'e'd send for me later on. But I never found out. 'E was dead within a few days.'

Jack gave a little shrug of commiseration. There was a brief silence between them, then the old man said, ' 'E was different at the end, you know, the professor.'

'Just before his death, you mean?'

'Yes. On that last day or so that I saw 'im.'

'In what way was he different?'

'It's 'ard to say exactly. I mean for one thing, when 'e come out to tell me to leave off workin'—that would be about four or five days before 'is accident—'e looked kind of—oh, I don't know. 'E wasn't like 'isself, that's for sure. 'E was usually very pleasant and easygoing. But that day 'e was different, there's no two ways about it. 'E didn't like lettin' me go, I could see that. Still—there you are.'

'And you didn't see him again.'

'I saw him just once—though not for any kind of conversation. I 'ad to go round to The Limes to get me money—the money he owed me. This was a day or two later. Mary answered the door to me. She paid me what was owed, and when I asked after her father she said 'e was OK but that 'e wasn't 'aving visitors. I did see 'im there, though, goin' by at the back of the 'all. I called out to 'im sayin' good mornin', but 'e 'ardly answered me. 'E seemed—I don't know—very anxious.'

'Anxious?'

Appleton nodded. 'Oh, I s'pose all manner of things can get a man down, and ge⁺ 'im out of sorts. But it was strange, the way 'e got at the end.'

'What about Mary? Did she seem all right?'

'All right? Oh, yes, she seemed all right—the day I called, I mean. A bit embarrassed, per'aps—a bit awkward because her dad didn't want to see me, I s'pose. But other than that she was OK. At that time, anyway. She was a teacher at the school in Barfield. I s'pose you know that. And very well-liked, I believe. Mind you, I didn't really know 'er that well. She used to be in and out of the 'ouse when I was workin' in the garden, and sometimes she'd come and lend an 'and, but that was really as far as it went. We'd say good morning, and she was very pleasant, but there wasn't a lot more. She was always a tidy-looking girl. Though I don't suppose you'd call her a *girl*, rightly. She must have been near forty when she died. But she was nice-looking for her age. Certainly there were some as thought so. The last one not long before she died.'

'She had a boy friend, did she?'

Appleton gave a snort of derision. 'I don't think boy

friend is the term I'd use! God, no. Callow was old enough to be her father.'

'Callow? You mean John Callow from here in the village?'

'There's only one. And goin' by what I've 'eard, you've made 'is acquaintance all right.'

Jack felt his spirits sink; it had been too much to hope that word of the killing of Callow's dog wouldn't get around. 'Yes,' he said with a sigh, 'we've met him.'

Appleton gave a nod. 'Well, anyway . . .' He shifted his feet, preparing to make his departure. 'I'd better get on, and let you get on too. You've got enough to do without people gettin' in the way and 'oldin' you up.' He paused. 'But remember, if I can 'elp at all I'll be only too glad to. On the garden or anything else. I 'aven't got a lot to do since I retired.'

'I'll remember. And thank you.'

After lunch, leaving Sarah indoors to clear up in the kitchen, Jack and Connie got back to their work in the garden. As Jack fed the bonfire he could hear above the crackle of the flames the voices of the children as they played in the orchard. From the direction of the front garden Connie came pushing a wheelbarrow loaded with detritus. As she approached he straightened and smiled at her, and she came to a stop beside him, sighed and wiped the back of her gardening glove across her brow.

She seemed to be in better spirits today, he thought. Five days had passed since the killing of Callow's dog, and he and Sarah had been very concerned by its effects on Connie. The accident had in no way been her fault, they had told her; she was blameless in the matter, as they all were. The responsibility had been entirely Callow's for allowing his dog to wander into their garden. Connie, however, had remained melancholy and brooding over the affair. It was not only the death of the dog, she had said, but the fact that it had further alienated them from Callow. Before, there had been a chance that the bad feeling between them would blow over. Not now. They would never, now, she said, be regarded by him as anything less than enemies.

As for the children, their reactions had been related directly to the animal's violent end. It was their first contact with death and the incident had shocked them considerably. However, as the days had passed they had, with the resilience of childhood, ceased to think much about it. Only Connie had continued to let the matter prey on her mind.

That morning when Jack had returned from his visit to the post office he had told her of his meeting with George Appleton and related some of their conversation. He had not, however, said anything of Callow's name cropping up in the course of their talk. Although he had wanted to say to her, 'What do you think? Mary and Callow were an item,' he had resisted. It was better, he thought, that Callow's name was not mentioned.

Now, seeing her a little more like her old self, he again reassured himself that in time the incident would be forgotten and be a thing of the past.

'How's it going out the front?' he asked. 'Have you finished?'

'Oh, very witty,' Connie said. 'You're a real caution, and no mistake.'

She stood aside while Jack took the wheelbarrow from her and tipped its contents onto the pile beside the bonfire. As he set the wheelbarrow down, Kitty appeared, running up the path from the orchard.

'We're building a tree-house,' she said excitedly, coming to a halt before them. 'You want to come and see?'

'In a while,' Jack said. 'We're too busy right now.'

Kitty gave a sharp little sigh of impatience. 'You're always busy.' She turned on the spot. 'Where's Nana? Is she working in the front?'

Connie answered her. 'No, she's indoors. But don't go bothering her right now.'

Kitty turned and ran off towards the house. 'I'm not going to *bother* her,' she called back.

After clearing away the lunch dishes Sarah had taken a relaxing bath, washing off the dust accumulated from her morning's work on the garden. She was sitting at her dressing table in her bathrobe drying her hair when she heard over the sound of the drier a knock at her door. She called out, 'Come in,' and turned to see Kitty enter.

'Nana, we've nearly finished building a house in one of the apple trees,' Kitty said. 'Will you come and see it?'

'I will later on, dear,' Sarah said. 'I can't come right now.'

'When you've finished your hair, then.'

'Yes, later on when I'm not busy.'

'Everybody's busy,' Kitty said. 'Busy, busy, busy.'

'Yes, well, we've got work to do. We're not all on holiday from school.' Switching off the drier, she began to brush her hair. It fell way past her shoulders. Kitty, moving to sit on the bed, watched her.

'You've got such lovely long hair, Nana,' she said.

'It used to be nice. It's going grey now, I'm afraid.'

'Oh, but it's so lovely and *long*.' Kitty twisted grubby fingers in her own short, dark hair. 'I wish I had long hair. Mummy always makes us get it cut. It's not fair.'

She watched as Sarah began nimbly to braid her hair and pin it in place. 'Why do you always plait your hair and put it up like that?' she said. 'You should wear it long all the time. It looks much nicer like that.'

'Yes, I'm sure,' Sarah said dryly.

'It would—and you could change the colour so it wouldn't have to be grey.'

'Oh, really.'

'Like that lady who lived opposite us in Chiswick. She went a lovely blonde colour when she got old.'

Sarah nodded. 'Thanks a lot. And while I'm about it, I'll get myself a slit skirt and high heels with ankle straps like Joan Crawford.'

'Joan who?'

Sarah smiled. 'It's all right, sweetheart. I'm just rambling. Take no notice. I should really get my hair cut, that's what I should do. It would be so much easier to manage. Ridiculous, keeping it this length at my age.'

'Well, I don't think so.' Kitty got up from the bed. 'Will you then—come and see our tree-house later on?'

'I will, dear, I promise. Give me half an hour or so.'

'Half an hour. All right.' Kitty skipped to the door, making Sarah's perfume bottles rattle. 'You won't forget, will you?'

'No, I won't forget.'

'If you do you'll get a smack.'

'Oh, dear, I'd better not forget, then, had I?'

'No, you better hadn't.'

'Perhaps when I come out I'll bring you a drink and some sandwiches too. How would you like that?'

'Oh, great! Yes, please.'

Kitty left the room and Sarah listened to her feet as she descended the stairs.

Bernard Taylor

When she had finished arranging her hair, Sarah
got dressed and went down to the kitchen where she
began to prepare a plate of ham and lettuce sandwiches. When it was ready she loaded it on a tray
along with three mugs of tea and three glasses of
Seven-Up and went out into the yard. Connie saw her
approach and gave a little cheer.

'Good! I could do with an excuse to take a break.'
With a nod towards Jack who stood working on the
bonfire, she added, 'With him it's tote that barge and
lift that bale practically nonstop.'

Jack smiled at the comment. Sarah set the tray
down on the old garden bench and glanced over at
him as he stood prodding the fire with a garden fork.
'Look,' she said, 'he's totally absorbed. Absolutely in
his element. I don't want to worry you, Constance, but
I think you might well have married a closet pyro-
maniac.'

Connie laughed and Jack joined in. Then Connie's
laughter abruptly died and she gave a little groan.

'Oh, no,' she breathed. '*No* . . .'

Sarah and Jack turned to follow the direction of her
gaze and saw, coming round the side of the house, the
tall figure of John Callow.

'Good Lord,' Sarah muttered, 'what on earth does
he want?'

As he came nearer, Sarah moved to stand closer to
Jack and Connie, and together, their expressions
wary, they waited as Callow came towards them, a
small brown-paper-wrapped package in his hand. All
three were bracing themselves for some kind of ac-
cusation or complaining to begin. To their surprise,
however, they soon saw that there was no anger in his
face. On the contrary, his expression bore a kind of
rather sheepish good will. A moment later he had

come to a stop before them.

'I rang the bell at the front door,' he said, 'but got no answer. So I took a chance and came round to the back. I hope you don't mind.' His voice held no trace of hostility.

Jack shook his head and said guardedly, 'Not at all.'

'I have to say,' Callow said, 'that I hesitated for a while about coming to see you. I wasn't at all sure what kind of reception I'd get.' A smile touched the corners of his mouth. 'I'm still not sure, come to that.'

Jack and the women remained silent. Callow shifted on his feet and said: 'Well, to get to the point—the fact of it is—I've come to make my peace. If you'll let me, that is.'

They remained silent.

Callow cleared his throat. 'This isn't easy, but—well, I feel I owe you an apology. In fact I *know* I owe you an apology.'

Now Jack's face showed the trace of a smile. 'Well, that's very decent of you . . .'

'It's the least I can do. I'm sorry, but I'm afraid I just over-reacted, as they say. About everything. In the first instance about my old dog coming in and—messing up your garden.' Here he looked from Connie to Sarah and gave a nod. 'You had every right to be angry. You had every reason to be. I don't know what you must have thought of me. What a rude, miserable old so-and-so, eh?' He moved his glance to Jack. 'And then that business with your little boy. I don't know why I carried on like that. Good heavens, what do a few flowers matter? And it's not as if he was being in any way delinquent or anything like that.' He gave a self-deprecating smile. 'I think I must be getting very crotchety in my approaching old age. Comes of living alone for so long, I suppose. Anyway, I do regret what's happened. Very much. And please, tell your little boy that I'm sorry for upsetting him.'

Connie, feeling relief sweeping over her like a wave, took a breath and said, 'Well, he was wrong to take your roses in the first place. But he knows that well enough now and it will never happen again.'

He waved a hand, brushing away her words. 'Yes, but he did it without thinking, and I shouldn't have carried on the way I did.' He paused. 'And then of course there was that sad business with my poor old dog . . .'

'Oh,' Connie said, 'you can't imagine how terrible I feel about that. It's been haunting me. I wouldn't have had it happen for the world.'

'Oh, I'm quite sure of that,' he said. 'But as with the other incidents, I over-reacted. It was such a shock, I suppose, and such a very sad thing for me. He was old, and getting rather deaf, but he was a good friend, and it broke my heart to lose him. But—it's done now. And as you said, if he hadn't been in your garden in the first place the accident wouldn't have happened.'

Jack was aware of feeling slightly embarrassed at the unexpected turn of events. 'We're all very sorry,' he said, 'about everything. When you come to a new place you're naturally anxious to get on with everyone. But things happen and you suddenly find you're stepping on people's toes. Look, we really appreciate your coming here today. It can't have been easy. So—let's let bygones be bygones, shall we? We'd like to, very much. I know I speak for all of us.'

As Connie and Sarah murmured words of agreement Jack put out his hand. Callow grasped it, shook it.

'Bygones are bygones,' he said. As he released Jack's hand he added, 'By the way, I'm very sorry also for what I said about your uncle and his daughter. That's been on my mind too.'

'Oh,' Jack said, 'that.'

'Yes—it was very wrong of me. I didn't mean it either. Your uncle was most respected in the neighbourhood. As was Mary.' He spread his hands. 'Oh, I won't pretend that Edwin and I didn't have our differences from time to time. But they were basically artistic differences, and they never amounted to anything of any great importance.' He turned to Connie, hesitantly smiling. 'And can we be friends now, Mrs Forrest? I'd like it if we could be.'

'Yes, of course.' Connie happily reached out and shook his hand.

He turned then to Sarah. 'I'm afraid I don't know your name, ma'am . . .'

'Harper,' she said. 'Sarah Harper. Connie's my daughter.'

'And are we friends too, Mrs Harper?'

'Yes—yes, of course.' Sarah smiled back at him and gave an awkward, self-conscious little nod.

'Good. I'm very glad.'

They shook hands.

'Your talk of over-reacting,' Sarah said with a nervous little laugh. 'I hope you'll forgive me for mine. Oh, dear, when I think of what I did. That business with the flowers—'

'No, no,' Callow said. 'That's all over and done with. You were provoked. So please, let's say no more about it. It's forgotten. We've all said and done hasty things we didn't really mean, and in this case I've been the worst offender.' He looked down at the package he was holding, hesitated for a second and then held it out to her. 'Will you accept this from me?'

Sarah looked from the package to Callow's contrite

smile. Seeing the puzzlement in her face, Callow said quickly: 'It's nothing much—just a little token.' He smiled. 'A little peace offering, shall we say.'

'Oh—well—thank you.' She coloured slightly. 'Thank you very much indeed.'

'It's no Cartier bracelet, I'm afraid,' he said dismissively as she took the package from his outstretched hand. 'Just a few chocolates, that's all. And I'm afraid there's not that great a selection in Mrs Stocks's little emporium.'

'Oh, I'm sure I shall enjoy them very much,' Sarah said. 'I have to admit that I've got a bit of a weakness for chocolates.'

'Well, that's good,' he said and added with a little chuckle, 'Sweets to the sweet, as Hamlet said.'

Sarah's responding chuckle was touched with embarrassment. With the others watching, she tore away part of the wrapping to expose a box of Cadbury's Milk Tray. 'Thank you,' she said. 'You really shouldn't have done it, but thank you very much.'

'Not at all. It's nothing.' There was a moment of silence then Callow added with a sigh, 'Well, that's done. I've made my peace and I'm very glad.' With a smile that said the subject was now closed he gave a nod and turned, glancing about him. 'So,' he said, 'how are you all settling in? Is everything going all right?'

'Yes, fine, thank you,' Jack said.

'It's such a lovely old place.' Callow turned to look up at the house. 'And looking very smart now, if I may say so, with the new paint on the woodwork.'

'It needed it,' said Connie.

'And you'll soon have your garden in shape too, I'm sure. Though that's a never-ending job, isn't it?'

'It certainly is,' said Jack.

As he finished speaking there came a shout of 'Nana!' and the four turned and saw Kitty standing over by the orchard gate.

'Nana,' Kitty called, 'you said half an hour.'

'We're talking right now,' Jack called to her. 'Can't you see that?'

Sarah added, calling out, 'I'll be there in a minute, Kitty. Just be patient.'

'All right.' With a sigh Kitty turned and vanished from their sight.

'So that's Kitty, is it?' Callow said with an indulgent smile. 'And how old is she?'

'She's six,' Connie said. 'And has no patience whatsoever.'

Callow chuckled then said, 'Well, I'd better not keep you any longer. I've held you up for long enough as it is. But I did so want to come and—well—set matters straight, if I could.'

They thanked him again for calling, Sarah adding further thanks for the gift of the chocolates. He wished the three of them a good afternoon and then turned and started towards the front of the house. Jack went with him. In the drive, Jack put out his hand.

'Thank you again for coming by. It's meant a lot to us. It was very nice of you.'

Shaking Jack's hand, Callow said, 'I'm just so glad I did.' With a smile he added, 'I hope you'll all be very happy here. I'm sure you will be.'

As Callow started off along the lane Jack turned and headed back round the house. He found Connie sitting on the garden bench on the lawn, sipping at a mug of tea.

'Where's your mother?' he asked as he moved to join her.

'In the orchard. Gone to take the children their sandwiches and see their tree-house.' As she handed him a mug of tea she added, 'Wasn't that nice of Callow?' There was relief and happiness in her expression and in her voice.

'Yes, it was,' Jack agreed. 'It can't have been easy for him, coming round and eating humble pie like that.'

'It just goes to show—people have more than one side to them.' She gave a little laugh. 'Oh, I feel so much better now!'

As they talked of Callow's visit they drank the tea and ate the sandwiches that Sarah had left.

When they had finished Jack brushed the crumbs from his lap, got up and moved back to the bonfire. As he did so Sarah appeared from the direction of the orchard carrying the empty tray.

'Well,' she said as she drew near, 'that'll keep them quiet for at least two minutes.'

'What have they done there?' Jack asked. 'They're not doing any harm, are they?'

'No, don't worry. They've just put a couple of bits of wood across a low fork of one of the old apple trees and draped a bit of sacking over it all.' She sat down at Connie's side and took up the remaining mug of tea. 'They're all right.'

'I'll go and have a look in a minute,' Jack said.

'We were talking about Mr Callow,' Connie said, 'and what a surprise it was, his calling like that.'

Sarah nodded. 'It certainly was.'

'And how nice of him to bring you the chocolates.'

'It was a very nice gesture.'

'Could it be, d'you think, that he's taken something of a shine to you? I mean "sweets to the sweet" and all that stuff.'

Sarah gave her a withering look while Jack stepped

back a little from the leaping flames and said dryly: 'I think they were a peace offering, Connie, not a token of affection.'

'Quite,' Sarah agreed.

'Well, we can dream, can't we?' said Connie.

'Oh, my God,' Sarah said, pulling a face. 'If you ever do decide to play matchmaker and try to get me married off again, I hope you'll pick on somebody a little different from him.'

Connie chuckled and took up the half-opened package containing the box of chocolates. 'Hardly what you'd call gift-wrapped,' she observed, 'but it's the thought that counts.' She peeled back the wrapping a little further to reveal the corner of a piece of white paper. 'Is that a note he's put in?' she said.

Sarah put down her mug, took the packet from Connie and drew out a slip of paper. 'It looks like it.'

In the top right-hand corner Callow had scrawled his address. Underneath it he had written: 'Please accept this small token. With very best wishes from John Callow.'

'How very nice of him,' Sarah said. 'How thoughtful.'

As she spoke, a sudden cold wind sprang up, rustling the leaves of the trees, whipping up the twigs and dead leaves and sending the smoke from the fire billowing. Sarah's skirt was flattened against her legs while Connie's hair sprayed out. A moment later the note was torn from Sarah's hand and sent spinning round in the air. The next second, as if drawn by some unseen hand, it straightened its course and went spiralling towards the bonfire, flying right into the heart of the flames where, in a sudden, brief blaze, it was consumed.

As swiftly as it had begun the wind died, and all

about them the garden was as still as it had been only moments before. Jack, Connie and Sarah looked at each other in silent amazement.

'My God,' Jack said, 'what the hell was that?'

'Weird,' said Connie. 'It just seemed to come out of nowhere.'

Rubbing her arms, Sarah said, 'And it was so *cold*. I wouldn't have believed it. A chill wind like that, in August.'

'Mummy? Daddy?'

The three turned to see Joel standing over by the orchard gate.

'Have you got time now?' he called. 'Will you come and see our tree-house now?'

'Come on, Jack,' Connie said, getting up from the bench, 'or we'll never get any peace.'

Chapter Five

With Monday dawning bright and clear, Jack and
Connie decided it was a good opportunity for another
outing and picnic. They left the house after an early
scratch lunch and, as Connie put it, 'a lick and a promise' for the children in the way of a wash. They would
be dirty within an hour, she said, so what was the
point; they'd save their showers till they got back.

They went to the spot they had discovered on their
earlier jaunt, settling on the gentle slope of the hillside
near the thicket. While Jack, Connie and Sarah laid
out rugs on the soft grass, the children—instructed
not to wander too far away—were immediately off,
yelling and whooping among the trees.

With the sounds of the children's happy voices continuing in the distance, the three adults lounged in the
shade, talking of this and that. When three-thirty
came round, Connie and Sarah opened the bags and
baskets, spread out a cloth and began to set out the
picnic things. When everything was ready Jack went

off and called the children, and when all were assembled they sat round and ate. Afterwards, Sarah took from a bag the box of chocolates that Callow had given her, and at her request Joel handed them round. When he brought the box back to her she said teasingly, 'And I suppose you want one too.'

He said he did.

'All right, then,' she said, 'on condition you tell me who your favourite grandmother is.'

He frowned, looking up, as if seeking the answer in the sky. 'That's a hard one, Nana.'

'I thought it might be.' She closed the box. 'Too bad about that. And they were such delicious chocolates.'

'Oh, I've just remembered,' he said. 'It's you.'

Sarah handed him the box. 'What a sweet, honest child. And how well brought up.'

'And you're my *only* grandmother.'

'Now don't go and spoil it.'

When more of the chocolates were gone, the children went off to play again. As Sarah put away the half-empty box Connie smiled at her and said: 'Nearly finished now—your little peace offering?'

Sarah gave her a look. 'Peace offering—huh.'

'You don't like Callow, do you?' Jack said.

Sarah shook her head. 'No, I must confess that I don't. In spite of his apologizing and giving me the chocolates and everything. I certainly don't think I could ever make a friend of the man.'

'Why not?' asked Connie.

'I don't know.' Sarah gave a shrug. 'There's just something about him. Perhaps it's because I've seen that other side of him. I mean, regardless of the fact that he apologized and was very nice about it, there's no getting away from the fact that he was perfectly beastly to us beforehand. His behaviour was really in-excusable, I think.'

'Yes, it was,' Connie agreed. 'Still we *will* excuse it and be very glad that it's all over and done with.'

Later, when it was time to go home, Jack got up to summon the children. Sarah said she would go with him, and together they went off into the thicket. Following the sounds of the children's voices, they made their way, Jack leading, along a narrow, winding path that wove among the shrubbery and trees.

'I keep thinking about him, you know,' Sarah said to Jack's back as she followed him.

'Who?' Jack half turned his head. 'Callow?'

'Yes.' She paused while she navigated a stretch of uneven ground. 'I still don't understand him.'

'What's to understand?'

'Well, how can a man change so much, so completely, in such a short time? It's beyond me. I mean, when he came round to the house on Saturday he was like a different person.'

Jack shrugged. 'He'd seen the light, I suppose. He realized he'd been behaving like an idiot and saw how unreasonable he'd been.'

The path grew wider and Sarah moved forward to walk at Jack's side. 'Unreasonable,' she said. 'I'd put it a little more strongly than that. His behaviour was absolutely monstrous. And then that sudden change. It was so—extreme.'

'What are you saying?'

'I don't know. Take no notice.'

'Listen,' Jack said, 'there's nowt so queer as folk, as they say. Don't search for reasons. Just be thankful it's happened. Just accept it and be glad.'

'Yes, you're right, of course.' She smiled. 'Put it down to my age.'

Crossing an area of open turf and heather, pock-marked here and there with the entrances to rabbit burrows, they entered another patch of sparse woodland. Here in a little clearing the children were playing. Joel had climbed up into the branches of an old oak while, nearby, Kitty and Lydia were in the act of gathering fallen fruit from around the base of a wild-growing apple tree. Kitty had found a magpie's feather and stuck it into her hair.

'Look,' said Lydia to Jack and Sarah as they drew near, 'we've found some apples. They don't belong to anyone, do they?'

'No, I wouldn't think so,' Jack said. 'But what do you want with them? We've got plenty of apples at home.'

'But these are *ours*,' said Kitty, to which Lydia added,

'Yes, these are ours. We found these.'

'I wouldn't bother with them,' said Jack. 'Besides, we're packing up now to get back home.'

There were groans from all three children, but after a little nagging persuasion the girls set off through the trees, their hands full of apples. As they disappeared, Joel scrambled down from the tree and, whooping loudly, set off after them. Jack and Sarah, amused, stood for a moment watching them go, then Jack moved across to look at the apple tree.

'They're crab apples, are they?' Sarah asked.

He bent and picked up one of the apples from the leaf-strewn ground, looked at it and then gingerly bit into the flesh.

'No, I don't think so. It's quite sweet.' Peering at the apple where he had bitten into it he added, 'But full of maggots.' Drawing back his arm, he threw the apple off into the trees. As he did so a bee buzzed past his ear.

'There's another apple tree over there,' Sarah said, starting off across the clearing. As she reached the other side she came to a stop and made a little ducking, dodging movement of her head. 'There are so many bees around. I didn't notice them just now. They're all over the place. There must be a nest here somewhere.' A moment later she pointed to the forked trunk of the apple tree. 'It's there, look, in the tree.'

Jack moved closer and saw the bees moving to and from a fissure in the trunk's fork.

'Somebody's bees must have swarmed and they've ended up here,' Sarah said. She turned to Jack. 'You know, I always thought I'd like to keep bees. They're such fascinating things.'

As she finished speaking a bee alighted on her bare arm. She flinched and jerked her arm, trying to shake the insect off. When it did not move she went to brush it away with her hand. As she did so she felt the sudden, sharp pain of its sting in her flesh. She gave a little cry. 'Oh, it's stung me!' Her words were barely out when she felt another sting, this time on the back of her neck. 'Oh!' she cried out. 'Oh, Jack! *Jack!*' There came another sting, and another. She let out a shriek. Raising her hand to brush one bee away from her cheek, she saw a dozen more clinging to her forearm. Frantic and terrified, she screamed again.

In another moment Jack was at her side. Desperately he brushed and slapped at her body while the bees swarmed in a darkening cloud about them. They were everywhere, and the air became filled with the sounds of their loud, angry buzzing and of Sarah's shrieks as she fought to ward them off. She could feel their agonizing stings stabbing at every inch of her unprotected skin.

'Keep still! Keep still!' Jack yelled as, desperate in

her growing agony, Sarah turned to run. Heedless of his own danger, he ripped off his shirt and tried to throw it over her head as a shield, but her flailing arms knocked it aside. In seconds, it seemed, her face and arms were almost black with bees. A moment later, with her terrified screams renting the air, she was running, dashing blindly away, deeper into the thicket. As she ran, the bees kept pace in a moving cloud about her head and followed in a long, undulating tail behind.

Leaping forward to follow, Jack went sprawling over the root of a tree. Scrambling to his feet again he ran on. He could see Sarah up ahead of him as she rushed blindly forward, stumbling among the trees and shrubs, the bees like a pall of smoke about her.

Jack was within a dozen yards of her when, in a small clearing, she suddenly halted, staggered, spun a full circle and fell backwards onto the earth.

Gasping with horror and exertion, Jack ran to her side. As he reached her the bees began to rise up from her body. A moment later there was not one left upon her. On the rough ground he knelt beside her. She lay on her back, her face turned away from him, her legs twitching spasmodically, while her fingers curled and uncurled. Wherever he looked, her bare flesh was hideously swollen and discoloured.

'Sarah . . . Oh, Sarah . . .'

At the sound of his voice she slowly turned her head towards him. He knew that she could not see him; her eyes were swollen shut, mere slits in the huge swelling of her grotesque, unrecognizable face. She tried to speak, but her mouth and throat were so swollen that she could not form words. As, with difficulty, she parted her lips, a dead bee fell from her tongue. Arching her back, she emitted a hoarse, agonized sound as she tried to draw air into her lungs. With a little moan, Jack bent forward, pinched her nose between his finger and thumb, sucked in air and clamped his mouth down over hers. Desperately he tried to force the oxygen into her. But it was no good. As he worked he felt a sharp shudder go through her body. He straightened, picked up her wrist, feeling for a pulse.

He knew it was useless; he had no doubt at all that she was dead.

Chapter Six

Bending over the grave, Connie set the pot back on the earth, gently pressed it in and made a final, careful adjustment to the roses.

'They're so pretty.' She didn't look at Jack as she spoke, but kept her eyes trained down at the flowers.

She and Jack stood opposite one another in the little graveyard of the village church of St Matthew. Sarah had been buried close to the spreading boughs of an old yew tree, in whose branches mistle thrushes had gathered to eat the scarlet berries. To Jack's right stood Joel, while opposite on either side of Connie stood Kitty and Lydia, beyond their slightly bowed heads a damp, misty backdrop of evergreens and the old churchyard wall. Above them hung a grey October sky.

Jack studied Connie as she bent over the grave in a moment of silent communion. For himself the shock and horror of Sarah's death was beginning to recede now, and he supposed that it must also be so for Connie and the children. Nature's way of protecting her own. The impact of even such unbelievable, indescribable horror must, if dwelt upon and continually faced in all its nakedness, eventually start to lose some of its impact. Nothing could withstand such microscopic examination and remain unchanged. Now Connie could speak of her mother's passing without giving way. More difficult for her to deal with, however, was the manner of Sarah's passing. That was something that she could not face yet—the knowledge that Sarah had died in such terror and agony. In time, though, Jack felt sure, much of the horror of that would pass.

Lifting her head and looking at Jack, Connie sighed and gave him a melancholy little smile.

'OK?' he said.

'OK?'

She straightened, glanced at the children and gave them a reassuring smile. Lydia was in blue today; Kitty in red. 'Right, let's get off and get the shopping. We've got a lot to do today, and your father and I are going out this evening.'

'Can we come with you?' Kitty said. 'We want to come with you.'

'Well, you can't, and you know that. We've been through all this.' She took the girls' hands. 'Come on. It's Saturday afternoon—the supermarket will be like a madhouse.'

'Don't forget,' Lydia said, 'we've got to get our scrapbooks for nature study on Monday.'

'We shan't forget.'

Connie, driving the Renault, dropped Jack and Joel off at the house and then set off with Kitty and Lydia for Pangbourne. While they were gone Joel played in his room and Jack worked in his study.

After a time Jack left his desk and went into the

front room where he had left some notes the previous evening. Nearing the window he glanced out over the front garden. They had done no work on it since Sarah's death, and now, with the coming of autumn, the leaves were beginning to fall so that the whole place was taking on a forlorn and neglected appearance. This was not the way they had planned it, but his work on the TV series was taking up so much time and Connie had more than enough to do about the house and in looking after the children. He had proposed that they take on some home help, but for the present Connie was reluctant to do so. He could only go along with her wishes, and in the meantime hope that as time passed they would get better organized.

As he stood at the window his eye was taken by movement to his left, and he saw the tall figure of John Callow come into view along the lane. Callow had acquired another dog recently, a little wire-haired terrier. Jack's sight of the dog was cut off for the present by the garden wall, but he knew he was there; he could see the lead in Callow's hand.

A moment later Callow was drawing level with the garden gate, glancing over and catching sight of Jack at the window. The older man raised his hand in a cheery salute and a little self-consciously Jack returned the gesture. He watched as Callow moved on along the lane and out of sight.

Callow, along with many other inhabitants of the village, had expressed sympathy at Sarah's death. In the short time of her life in Valley Green Sarah had struck up acquaintance with many of the villagers, and following her death a number had sent flowers and letters of condolence. Callow had written a warm letter expressing deep sympathy for their loss, adding that if there was anything he could do to help them in any way they had only to ask. On the occasion of the funeral he had sent a large wreath of roses. Jack and Connie had been much touched by his gesture.

When Connie and the girls returned from the supermarket, Jack helped to unpack the groceries and put them away. That done, he sat with Connie in the kitchen over a cup of tea.

'I've been thinking about the garden,' he said. 'I think there's only one thing for it. We've got to get some help to get it into shape. I thought I'd ask George Appleton. After all, he offered, and I think he'd be glad of the work. He knows the garden too, so it isn't as if he'd be taking on anything new. It's not going to cost a fortune.'

Connie gave a judicious nod. 'Well, we certainly haven't made much headway on it, what with one thing and another.'

When Jack had finished his tea he went into the hall and put on his jacket. As he did so Joel came to the top of the stairs.

'Where are you going, Dad?' he called down. From behind him came the sound of the twins, their voices raised in their game of domesticity like those of over-the-top actors.

'Just into the village,' Jack said. 'To see Mr Appleton. D'you want to come along?'

'Can I?'

'Come on, then. Get your coat.'

Three minutes later, with Joel at his side, Jack left the house and, eschewing both cars which were parked in the drive, set off for Appleton's house.

As they walked along the lane Joel said, 'They never want to play anything I want to play.'

'Kitty and Lydia?'

'Yes, they just want to play girls' games all the time.'

'Mmm.' Jack considered the problem. 'Well, they *are* girls.'

'I know. But they could play other things sometimes. But most of the time they just want to play with their dolls, or play nurses. Stuff like that.'

A pause and Jack asked, 'Where are your friends from school? Can't you play with any of them? What about the boy who came round after school with you the other day? Daniel, wasn't it?'

'Yes. Daniel Shaw.'

'Can't you play with him today?'

'He's gone away for the weekend.'

'Well, he'll be back soon. You can play with him then.'

'I suppose so.' A sigh and then: 'Dad, why did you have to have two girls? I mean, why *two*?'

'You know very well you don't get a choice in these things.'

'No, I know, but—well, it's just that sometimes I think it would be nice if one of them was a boy.'

'I thought you all got on pretty well together.'

'Yes, we do, but sometimes I wish I had a brother.' He turned and lifted his head, looking up at Jack. 'Couldn't we have one? Is it too late?'

Jack smiled, briefly tightening his hand around Joel's. 'I think it is, now. Besides, if we did have another baby there's no telling whether it would turn out to be a boy or a girl. Anyway, even if it was a boy, you wouldn't be able to play with him, would you? He'd be just a baby.'

Joel's sigh gave evidence of his impatience with his father's obtuseness. 'Of course he'd be just a baby. I know that. But he wouldn't *always* be a baby, would he? Babies grow up, you know.'

'Of course they grow up. But you're nearly nine years old.'

'Yes, so don't forget that he'd get to be the same age as me in time, wouldn't he?'

They had reached the end of the lane and now crossed the road to start along beside the green. Jack looked down at Joel's upturned face and said, 'Oh, Joel, Joel.' He let go of Joel's hand and ran his fingers through the boy's coarse, wiry hair. 'You're forgetting, you won't stay the same age for ever.' He took Joel's hand in his once more. 'If we had a baby next year you'd be ten by then. By the time the baby was ten you'd be grown up. You'd be much too old to play with a little boy.'

A moment of silence then Joel lifted his head and gave a sudden laugh, hooting out into the misty October afternoon. 'Of course! I was forgetting that I'd be growing older as well.' He laughed again. 'That was really stupid.'

They turned left at the entrance to Green Lane, a narrow road with high hedges on either side, the cottages spaced widely apart.

'Daniel's got a dog, you know,' Joel said. He waited a couple of seconds for a response, then: 'Did you hear that, Dad?'

'Yes, Daniel's got a dog. Really.'

'His name's Tigger.'

'Oh, yeh.'

'He's really great. He's a Dalmatian.'

'Really.'

'He's not that big.'

'No?'

'No.' A sigh. 'I wish we had a dog.'

'Do you?'

Evil Intent

'You said one day that if we ever had the space we could get a dog.'

'Did I say that? I don't remember saying that.'

'In Chiswick when I asked you if we could have a dog you said no because we didn't have enough space.'

As Jack pondered on this Joel added: 'Now we have. Got the space, I mean.' He looked up at Jack. 'Haven't we?'

Jack was saved from answering by the fact that they had reached George Appleton's cottage. 'Here we are,' he said, pointing to the sign on the wall beside the front door. 'Hawthorn Cottage.'

The small cottage was of whitewashed stone with a slate roof. Enclosed by a head-high privet hedge, it was fronted by a small, neatly kept flower garden, with a narrow lawn to its right. Jack unlatched the gate and they passed through, Joel closing the gate behind them. They walked up the narrow cement path to the front door where Jack rapped with the knocker. When there was no answer, he knocked again. Still no answer. 'Let's try round the back,' he said.

Together they started round the side of the house to the rear where the narrow garden, planted to vegetables and fruit bushes, stretched away to a small gathering of trees. As they approached the back door they saw that it was ajar. 'Well, somebody's home,' Jack observed. He knocked on the door and waited, but there was no answer. 'Mr Appleton?' he called out. 'George?'

And then from behind them came George Appleton's voice, cheerily hailing them: 'Hello, there. Good afternoon to you,' and turning they saw him coming towards them from the direction of a small shed situated to the right of the rear garden path. With Joel in tow, Jack started towards him.

Bernard Taylor

'Good afternoon, George.'

Jack held out his hand and George Appleton moved the rake from his right hand to his left and shook Jack's hand.

'We tried at the front first,' Jack said, 'and I guessed you might be busy here at the back.'

'Oh, nobody bothers with the front door when they comes 'ere,' the old man said. ''Less 'e's the tax man or some other bill collector.' He stepped to the right and leant the rake against the small lean-to at the side of the cottage. 'Well,' he said, brushing the dust from his palms, 'this is a pleasant surprise. It's not often I gets visitors.' He smiled down at Joel. 'And now not just one visitor but two. And how are you, young man?' He put out his work-hardened hand as he spoke, and Joel shyly took it.

'Very well, thank you,' Joel said.

Appleton nodded. 'D'you know, I did know your name, but now I can't for the life of me remember it.' Then just as Joel opened his mouth to speak, the old man said, 'Joel. It's Joel, isn't it?'

'Yes.' Joel smiled.

Appleton smiled along with him. 'Y'see,' he said, tapping his temple, 'it's not quite gone. Not yet, anyway.' He gave a little sigh of pleasure and spread his hands before them. 'Well, to what do I owe this pleasure? Can I get you a cup o' tea or something?'

'No, thank you, George, that's all right,' Jack said. 'We can't stop long. I came to ask you a favour.'

'Oh, ah. Well, ask away, then.'

'Well, not long after we got here you mentioned that you'd helped my uncle on the garden at The Limes, and you said that if we ever needed any help we should ask you.'

'That I did. I remember.'

124

'So that's what I've come to ask—whether you could see your way to giving us a hand with the garden. I'm afraid it's just too much for us with things as they are, and it's going to rack and ruin.'

'Of course, I'll be glad to 'elp in any way I can. When did you want me to start?'

Jack shrugged. 'Whenever suits you.'

'I should make a start soon, I reckon. Start to get it in shape and tidied up a bit afore the winter comes. Then we can start in the spring with a clean slate. Don't you reckon?'

'Fine,' Jack said, nodding. 'That would suit us fine. At the start we thought we'd be able to manage it on our own. But even so I think it would have proved a bit too much. And now it's all got so overgrown. It hasn't had any real attention for a good while. When Connie's mother was alive we did make a start but I'm afraid it didn't come to very much. And then, of course, with her death . . .' He left the rest of the sentence unspoken.

Appleton gave a sympathetic nod. 'Ah, I'm not surprised. Oh, dear, that was a dreadful business and no mistake. It was such a shock to 'ear of it. Something like that 'appenin'—it's the last thing you expect. And because it's so sudden and so unexpected it must be doubly 'ard to accept.'

'Yes, indeed. But you have to go on, don't you? And anyway, I'm glad to say that things are getting a little easier now.'

At Jack's side Joel, growing bored with the conversation, moved his weight from one foot to the other.

'Such talk's not of much interest to you, is it, young man?' George Appleton said, smiling down at him. Not denying it, Joel smiled and shrugged. Appleton looked at him for a moment longer then turned and glanced down towards the foot of the garden where, just beyond the vegetables, stood the trees. Most of them were fruit trees, but in the forefront stood an ash. From one of its lower branches hung a rope with a car tyre suspended from it.

'You see that, Joel?' the old man said, gesturing with his thumb. Turning, following his glance, Joel saw the swing. His eyes brightened and he looked at Jack.

'I put that up for my grandson a couple of years back,' Appleton said. 'It ain't had much use though, I'm afraid. My daughter lives so far away, and it's not often she gets the chance to visit me.' He nodded at Joel. 'Why don't you go and see if it's still in workin' order? Test it out, as they say.' To Jack he said, 'It's quite secure. He can't come to no 'arm.'

'Oh, I'm sure,' Jack said; then to Joel, 'Go on then, if you want to. But we can't be too long.'

He and George Appleton stood watching as Joel, needing no second invitation, went hurrying off down the narrow path. They watched as he examined the makeshift swing, hoisted himself through the ring and began to propel himself backwards and forwards. 'That'll please him,' Jack said smiling. 'Something new to do. He's feeling a bit lost today. On the way here he was moaning because he doesn't have a brother to play with.'

Appleton laughed. 'Complainin' because 'e doesn't 'ave a brother? Oh, dear me—I 'ad five, and the times I wished I was the only one . . . Ah, well, there's no pleasin' everybody, is there?'

The two men continued to watch Joel for a moment or two in silence, then Appleton said: 'I've no doubt 'e misses 'is grandma, does 'e?'

'Oh, yes, they all do. She doted on them.'

'It's a sad business for children to come up against such a thing in their lives.'

'True. But they're very resilient, thank God.'

'There is that.'

'And fortunately they didn't see her immediately after it happened. For which I'll always be thankful. That was a sight I don't think they'd have got over very well.'

'That's something to be glad of. And like I said, there's nothin' to prepare you for these kind of 'appenings, is there? These things that come out of the blue.'

'True.' Jack looked at Joel as he swung back and forth on the tyre; he was going at it with enthusiasm and had got up considerable momentum. Jack didn't particularly want to dwell on the subject of Sarah's death, but George hadn't finished yet.

'Yes,' the old man said, nodding, 'it's not like when someone's been ill—those 'appenings that just sort of—take place. The sort of thing that 'appened with your uncle. I mean his trippin' on the stairs and fallin' like that. Same kind of thing in a way.'

'I suppose so.'

'Yes, specially with the fact that 'e tripped over a cat.'

'It's easily done, isn't it?' Jack said. 'Don't they say that most accidents happen in the home? And I should think it's quite a common cause of accidents among old people—their pets getting under their feet when they're not aware of it.'

'Yes, except that in your uncle's case it wasn't no pet.'

'What d'you mean? He didn't fall over the cat?'

'Oh, yes, 'e did that right enough. That come out at the inquest. But the cat 'e fell over wasn't no pet. Not

127

'is, anyway, not by a long chalk.'

'I don't understand. You mean it was Mary's? What's the difference?'

'No, it wasn't Mary's. It didn't belong to neither one of 'em. It didn't belong to the 'ouse at all.'

'You mean it was a stray or something they took in?' Jack couldn't see what the old man was getting at, or why he was bothering with such a fine point.

'Nah.' George shook his head. 'They wouldn't 'ave done that, neither of 'em—taken in some stray. Mr Maddox, 'e 'ated cats. Couldn't stand to 'ave 'em anywhere round 'im. I know that from years back. I remember bein' there one day workin' in the yard when young David come in with a kitten somebody'd given 'im. 'Is dad told 'im to take it straight back to where 'e got it from. 'E wouldn't 'ave it in the 'ouse. There was no two bones about it. David was upset, but 'e 'ad no choice but to take it away again. And I remember later Mr Maddox turns to me and says 'ow 'e could never abide the creatures.' He gave a shrug. 'Well, some people can't, can they? Like a lot of folks 'ave an aversion to spiders and such. I know as they kept a dog for a few years, but cats never.'

'But one got into the house somehow. The night my uncle died.'

'That's right. According to what Mary said at the inquest, it was there on the stairs when 'er father come down in the mornin'.' He spread his hands before him. 'Not so surprisin' that he fell, is it? I mean, if you've never kept cats in the 'ouse there's no way you'd expect to find one under your feet, is there?'

'I suppose not.'

'No, you wouldn't. Never.'

'Dad? Dad, look at me!'

The voice came ringing over the garden, and the two

turned and looked over to where Joel was swinging backwards and forwards in wide rhythmic arcs.

'I'm looking,' Jack called back, then to George Appleton: 'You started something there.'

The old man laughed. 'It's good to see kiddies enjoying theirselves.'

'Oh, yes. On our way here Joel was asking if we could get a dog.'

'Oh? And what did you tell 'im?'

'I managed not to give him an answer. Though I don't suppose I'll be able to avoid it for long. Once he gets something in his head . . . He reminded me that in the past I used lack of space as the reason for not getting one. And he hasn't forgotten, of course. The girls, too. They've always been very keen, so I doubt we've heard the last of it. We shall probably end up getting one. But one that's a manageable size and won't turn out to be as big as a St Bernard and develop the temperament of a Rottweiler.'

'You can't be too careful. I see as Callow's got 'isself another dog.'

'Yes.' Jack sucked the breath over his teeth. 'Don't remind me. After the accident with his old labrador, I thought we'd made an enemy for life. Thank God it turned out all right in the end. He was very forgiving, but for a time there it was a very depressing business, I don't mind saying.'

'I'm sure it must 'ave been. He's not a man I'd care to get on the wrong side of.'

'Quite.' Jack was about to let Appleton's remark pass, but then he said, 'Why do you say that?'

Appleton looked down, frowning, his lips drawn back over his teeth. 'Oh, I don't know. It's just that— well, I don't reckon as 'e's the most pleasant piece of work, that's all. I 'aven't 'ad any real dealings with 'im meself, and I don't care to neither but—well, for a start I don't see 'im as a man you could make a friend of. And I'm not alone in thinkin' such a thing.'

'He's not popular in the village?'

'Popular? No, I certainly wouldn't call 'im popular. I don't reckon as 'e's got many friends, if 'e's got any at all. Not 'ere in Valley Green, at any rate. Mind you, I don't think 'e's ever made any great effort to make friends, or to be liked, come to that. By all accounts 'e's not what you'd call neighbourly—not like you find the other villagers to be.'

'He's been very pleasant to us lately. And when Connie's mother died he was one of the first to send his sympathies.'

Appleton nodded. 'Yeah, well, don't take no notice of what I say. You 'ave to speak as you find, ain't that right? And if he's been nice to you, then that's to 'is credit—specially after the business with 'is dog.'

'Yes. Maybe he's one of those people it takes longer to get to know than others. Some people are very reserved. They put up all kinds of barriers.'

'I s'pose that's right.'

'How long has he been here?'

'Oh, I can't rightly say. About seven or eight years, or thereabouts I s'pose. 'E come down from London, I believe. The cottage where he lives used to belong to the Simpsons, an old couple. When they died their son came back and put the place up for sale. There were two parties after it—Callow and a young married couple—but Callow was the lucky one.' He nodded. 'Oh, there's no doubt about it, when John Callow wants something, it seems 'e usually gets it. One way or another 'e gets lucky. Though 'is luck ain't always that lucky for others.'

A keen wind had blown up, rustling the dying leaves

and sending some of them fluttering to the ground. Joel came towards them down the garden path, his cheeks flushed. Jack looked at his watch. 'We must go,' he said to the old man. 'Connie will think we're not coming back. I've taken up enough of your time, anyway.'

'No, it's me,' George Appleton said, then added, 'Trouble is, I don't get that many visitors and once they're 'ere I start makin' up for lost time.'

Joel stepped to Jack's side, took his hand and leaned against him. 'Did you have a good swing?' Jack asked him.

Joel nodded. 'Yes, it was great. Did you watch me?' 'Yes.'

'We both did,' George Appleton said. 'You did very well.'

'Right, young man.' Jack brushed a hand over Joel's hair. 'It's time we started back.' He turned to George Appleton. 'So when shall we see you, George?'

'I'll start on Monday if you like. There's nothing to keep me.'

'Good. We'll see you then.'

'I'll be there, Mr Forrest.'

'*Jack*, please,' said Jack, 'or I shall have to call you Mr Appleton.'

The old man smiled. 'Oh, well, that wouldn't do, would it?'

With Joel at his side and George following, Jack turned and started back round the side of the cottage. There they said their goodbyes and set off back for Princes Lane.

'So you had a good swing, did you?' Jack said as they walked beside the green.

'Yes, it was excellent. He's got chickens too, did you know?'

'Where were they?'

'Over by the swing. D'you think we could keep some chickens, Dad?'

'Chickens as well?'

'I'd look after them.'

'You say that now, but you'd soon get fed up and then it would be left to me and your mother.'

'No, honestly.'

'Honestly, he says. Yes, I'm sure.'

'No, I would. They'd lay eggs for us.'

'Don't you think a dog will be enough to cope with?'

Joel raised his head and looked up at him, unable to stop the smile. 'So we *are* getting a dog, are we?'

'You,' Jack said, unable to suppress his own smile. 'What have you talked me into?'

Joel gave a laugh and whooped out into the autumn air. 'I'm getting a dog!' he said. 'I'm getting a dog!'

Chapter Seven

Connie was in the hall. She had put on her coat and was just finishing getting the girls into theirs when Joel came bursting in at the back door.

'Mum?' he yelled. 'Mum, where are you?'

'I'm in the hall,' she called.

He came hurrying through. 'Mum,' he said breathlessly, 'I'm getting a dog. Dad says I can have a dog.'

'A dog?' Lydia said. 'Can we?'

To which Kitty added at once, 'Really? We can have a dog?'

'No,' Joel said, 'not *we*—*I*. It's going to be for my birthday.'

'Oh,' Lydia said, 'that's not fair. Why should it be just his? Mum, why should it be just his?'

'Because Dad said so,' Joel replied.

The happiness in his tone was not echoed in Connie's. 'And did your father say all this?' she asked.

Joel's expression changed and suddenly he was

looking a little doubtful. 'Yes, he did. It's all right with you, Mum, isn't it?'

'Oh, please, Mummy, please,' Lydia said.

'Did Daddy really say that?' Connie asked.

'Yes, truly,' Joel replied. 'It is all right, isn't it? Oh, Mum, say that it is.'

She sighed. 'Well, if your father's already told you it's all right, then it must be. Though I could have wished he'd spoken to me about it first. Where is he now?'

'He'll be in any second. I ran on ahead to tell you.'

'That was kind of you.'

The happiness in Joel's expression dimmed still further. 'Oh, Mum, you don't want it, do you, a dog? I thought you would.'

Seeing the anxiety in his eyes, the fear that it might not happen after all, Connie nodded and said, 'I told you, if your father says it's OK then it's OK.'

'But I want you to want it, not just put up with it. It'll be great, Mum. It'll be excellent, you'll see.'

'Will it? Will it be *excellent*?'

'Yes, really, I promise you.'

He was gazing at her with his brow furrowed, his eyes full of misgivings. She smiled, stepped to him and gently touched her forefinger to the bridge of his nose where the summer's freckles had still not faded. 'It'll be fine,' she said. 'It was just a bit of a surprise, that's all. On further thought I think perhaps a dog is just what we need.'

'You mean that?'

'Of course I mean it. You want it in writing? No, seriously, I know that for a long time you've wanted a dog, and—' she shrugged, 'so you'll have one.'

'Oh, great! *Great!*'

At this point there was the sound of the kitchen door

opening and closing, and a moment later Jack entered, taking off his coat as he came into the hall.

'We're getting a dog,' Kitty announced at once, to which Connie added with a sideways smile:

'Yes. Something else for me to think about while you're working and the children are at school.'

Jack raised his eyebrows and spread his hands. 'I got manipulated.'

'So it would seem.' She shrugged. 'Oh, well, I'm sure it'll turn out all right.'

'When can we get her?' Lydia said. 'Can we go and buy her today?'

'I told you,' Joel said, 'the dog's going to be mine. And who says we're getting a *her*? I want it to be a *boy* dog.'

Ignoring Joel, Kitty said excitedly, 'Listen, listen, can we have one of those white fluffy ones? Those with the pompons on their tails.'

'That's a *poodle*,' Joel said contemptuously. 'I don't want one of those.' He turned to his father. 'Dad, you said he would be mine, for my birthday.'

'Anyway, we'll discuss it later,' Connie said. 'Right now I have to go out to the shop. I forgot to get lemons.'

'It's starting to rain,' Jack said. 'You want me to go?'

'No, thanks, it's all right. I'm ready now, and I'm sure to think of other things while I'm there.' She turned to the girls. 'Now that your Daddy's home you don't need to come with me.'

'Oh, but we want to,' said Kitty. 'You said we could.'

'But it's going to rain.'

'Oh, Mummy-y-y.'

The rain was falling quite heavily a few minutes later when Connie, with the twins sitting belted up in the rear seat, backed the Renault out into the lane.

'Can we come in with you when we get to the shop?' Lydia said.

'No, you stay in the car. I shall only be a minute.'

'But we want to come in as well.'

'I'm sure you do. You want to come in because last time Jane gave you each a sweet and you're hoping it'll happen again. No, you stay outside.' Connie put the car in first gear and set off along the lane.

'Oh, please,' said Kitty.

'No, I'm sorry.'

'You're a cruel mother.'

'Yes, you are,' Lydia agreed, laughing at the idea. 'You're the cruellest mother ever.'

The rain had stopped by the time they reached the village shop. As Connie pulled the car to a halt the girls began to fumble with their seat belts. Connie leant over to the back seat and undid the buckles. 'But you can't come in,' she said.

'But it's stopped raining now,' Kitty said. 'Why can't we come in?'

Connie said reasonably, 'Well, if you're seen with me people might think you're mine.'

'We *are* yours,' said Lydia.

'Oh, dear, are you?' Connie sighed. 'How is it that a beautiful woman like me could have two such awful-looking daughters?'

In unison the girls shrieked their derision. 'We're not awful-looking,' Lydia said. 'It's *you* that's awful-looking.'

Connie looked crestfallen as she turned and started out of the car.

'Can we come in too?' Kitty said.

Connie looked at her with eyes wide. 'After what you've just said? Certainly not.'

There was an elderly woman being served, and with

only Emma Stocks behind the counter, Connie had to wait a minute or two. As she stood there she glanced back through the door pane and saw that a man had stopped beside the car and was bending, talking to the girls. It was John Callow. When she left the shop with her purchases a little while later he was still there. As she approached the car he turned, saw her and straightened. 'Good afternoon, Mrs Forrest.' He had a rolled umbrella hooked over his arm.

She returned his smile. 'Hello, Mr Callow.' She saw that Kitty had wound down the nearside window.

'I've been having a chat with your two young ladies.' He bent his head briefly to beam a wide smile at the girls. They stared back at him, their expressions rather uncertain.

'I hope they've been behaving themselves,' Connie said.

'As good as gold.'

Widening her eyes at the twins she said, 'Well, that would be something new, wouldn't it, girls?'

Kitty sighed and flicked a long-suffering glance at her sister.

'They were telling me that they wanted to go with you into the shop but that you wouldn't let them.'

'I know. I'm very mean.'

'Oh,' he said, putting his head a little on one side, 'I'm sure that's not true.' His exaggerated expression of concern and sincerity made Connie want to say, 'I'm joking, I'm joking,' but she said nothing.

Turning again, looking down at the girls once more, Callow said, 'They're lovely little girls. And they're so alike. If they weren't dressed differently I wouldn't be able to tell them apart.'

'Well, we want our children to know who they are.' Connie looked down at the twins. 'Isn't that right?'

Kitty and Lydia gave half-hearted nods.

'We dressed them differently from the moment they were born,' Connie said. 'Identical twins have enough problems with identity as it is, without being dressed so that no one's ever sure who they're talking to. At one time we even thought about trying to send them to different schools, but that wasn't practical.'

She smiled at Callow and, preparing to take her leave, took a step away. As she did so he reached out and gently laid a hand on her forearm.

'Let me ask you,' he said,'—how are you feeling now?'

'You mean . . . ? Oh—oh, fine, thank you.'

'What a dreadful, dreadful thing to have happened. Your poor mother.'

Connie nodded. 'Yes, it was.'

'But things are getting back together now, are they?'

'Yes, thank you.' She was very much aware of his touch, and she shifted her arm to adjust her grip on the bag and his hand fell away. 'It gets easier,' she added.

'Nature is a wonderful thing.'

'Oh, yes.'

'Anyway, I should think you've got plenty to keep you occupied. What with your husband and son and these two young ladies.'

'Oh, no doubt about that.'

'And not much time for outside interests, I'd imagine.'

'Well, not really. They'd have to be pretty special.'

He nodded. 'The reason I say that—I was wondering whether you're fond of the opera.'

'Oh, yes. Though I can't recall the last time we went. Ages ago. Why, have you got a new production coming up? I understand you run an amateur operatic society in Reading.'

'That's right. We're working on *Sonnambula* right now.'

'I'm sorry?'

'*Sonnambula*. *La Sonnambula*. Bellini's opera.'

'I don't think I know that one.'

'*The Sleepwalker*. Oh, it's a beautiful work. And I think ours is going to be a very good production. We've got a wonderful Amina—that's the main female character. I think Bellini himself would have approved. But that's not the reason I mentioned it. Of course I'd love it if you and your husband could come and see it when it's ready but, well, I was wondering whether you might like to join us. As a member of the group, I mean. Get involved with the production.'

Connie said with a little laugh, 'Me join an operatic company?' She glanced down at Kitty and Lydia as they sat looking out over the top of the open window. 'Did you hear that, girls?' To Callow she said, 'Mr Callow, you haven't heard me sing. And be thankful for it.'

He laughed, opening his mouth wide. 'I'm sure it can't be that bad.'

'That bad, believe me. Ask my family. Though on second thoughts don't; I'd like to keep a little pride. But truthfully, not only do I not have a halfway decent voice, I can't even sing in tune. When I try to sing the children leave the room.'

He smiled down at the girls. 'Is that true? That can't be true, can it?'

They nodded.

'You see,' said Connie. 'And they wouldn't lie about a thing like that.'

'Oh, dear.' Callow chuckled. 'That doesn't sound so good, does it.'

'It doesn't sound so good. You've got it exactly.'

'Well,' he said after a moment's consideration, 'what about being one of the supers? We always need extra members for the crowd scenes.'

'Oh, no, I couldn't go on stage at all, in any capacity. I'd be terrified.'

With a sigh Callow said to the twins, 'It doesn't look as if we're going to make a star out of your mother, does it? Shame.' Turning back to Connie, he said, 'But we also need people backstage, you know. To look after props and costumes and make-up and such. There's plenty you could do. And we'd be so glad of the help.'

'Listen,' she said, 'if you want someone to help with props and scenery and things you should ask my husband. He spent five years at art school. He's brilliant at all that kind of thing.' Then she added quickly, 'Though he's terribly busy, I know.'

'Perhaps you'd both like to join.'

'Oh, I don't know. But I'll talk to him.'

'Good,' he said. 'Think about it, anyway. And I'll tell you what, I've got some literature on the society—copies of some of the reviews and past programmes. Have a look at them, and see what you think. I'm sure you'd be an asset. You both would.'

'I wish I could be that certain. Speaking for myself, I mean.'

'Oh, I'm sure you would. Anyway, I'll call round and drop it in. You can let me know when you've had a chance to look through it. You don't have to make up your mind right now. We'd be glad to have you join us at any time. But sooner rather than later, of course.' He paused. 'I think this production is going to be a very special one for us in the society.'

'Oh, why d'you say that?'

'Well, we're after the trophy.'

'What trophy's that?'

'The Maddox Plate, of course.'

'The *Maddox* Plate. Maddox as in *Edwin* Maddox?'

'The very same.'

She was silent for a moment, casting her mind back. 'Yes,' she said, 'of course. We saw it mentioned in Mr Maddox's papers, but I didn't take much notice.'

'Oh, it's quite important in the amateur operatic scene. He initiated the award many years ago. Long before I started producing any of the shows.'

'It's a prize, right?'

'That's right. An engraved silver plate, awarded bi-annually for the best amateur operatic production in the south-west of England.'

'Have you ever won it?'

'I'm afraid not. Though the group has won before my time.'

'But you've got your eye on it now.'

'Oh, yes. The finals are to be held at the festival in Chapelton in the spring. Apart from being the greatest possible thrill for me if we should win, it would also be the greatest irony. And I think we've got a very good chance.' He smiled into Connie's face, showing his long, yellowing teeth.

'Why do you say that?' she said. 'That it would be an irony if you won it?'

'Oh—well, for the simple reason that Edwin Maddox and I didn't always see eye to eye over opera.'

Connie smiled. 'Oh, that.'

'I'm afraid our ideas on interpretation varied occasionally. Sometimes we were perfectly in tune, but at other times we were greatly at odds. Not that it bothered me. It would be a dull and boring old world if everyone held the same opinions, wouldn't it?'

'I suppose it would.'

'Oh, indeed. Of course, most people regarded Maddox as the authority on opera, but he wasn't infallible, not by any means. If you don't mind me saying so.'

'Not at all. Well, he was a critic, and no critic's infallible."

Callow smiled. 'Quite.'

At that moment a spattering of raindrops began to fall. Connie seized her excuse. 'Oh, dear,' she said, 'here comes the rain again. I'd better get back.'

'Yes, and I mustn't keep you any longer.' He raised and opened his umbrella and added with a little inclination of his head, 'It's been very nice talking to you, and I'm sorry if I've held you up.'

'Oh, not at all.' Connie opened the car door, saying as she did so: 'Wind up your window, girls.'

'As soon as I get a chance,' Callow said, 'I'll drop off the literature about the group. I think you'll find it interesting.'

'Right, thank you.'

Callow ducked his head beneath his black umbrella and gave a wide smile and a wave to Lydia and Kitty. Then with a further nod and wave to Connie he turned and started away. From the back seat the girls watched his departure and then turned, looked at one another and said in unison, 'Uulllgghhh . . . !'

That evening Jack and Connie were due to meet the TV show's producer and her husband for dinner at a restaurant in Soho. Jack had not been over-keen to make the excursion; for one thing, driving the car would preclude his being able to drink more than a glass of wine. Connie insisted that they go, however;

it had been so long since they had got away from the house and the children, and she would drive on the way home, so he could enjoy a drink without worrying.

Jane Standing arrived just before six to babysit for the evening. The children were glad to see her; to them, a babysitter was still something of a novelty— this would be only the third time Jane had come to look after them. In the past their grandmother had nearly always been there when Jack and Connie went out, and since her death such occasions had been few.

Now Jane settled her considerable bulk on the sofa and at once the girls were at her side, showing her their dolls and their books. She was good with them, and all three children warmed to her. Jack and Connie felt secure in leaving them in her care.

As they drove along the M4 motorway a little later, Connie said, 'I didn't get a chance to tell you before, but I had an encounter this afternoon.'

'Oh, yes? What sort of an encounter?'

'She pursed her lips. 'I can't say for sure.'

'A romantic one?'

'Good God, no. I should hope not. If it was, I wasn't paying attention. I ran into Mr Callow. In the village when I was coming out of the shop.'

'Oh, yes?'

'Yes. He put a proposition to me.'

'The dirty old man. What sort of proposition?'

'I don't know how to put it exactly. But—well, what do you think of this—" Opening her mouth wide, she sang off key, in a cod operatic soprano's voice: 'One fine day dah dah dah . . .'

'Christ! What brought that on?'

'Didn't you like it?'

'And I thought you were fond of me.'

Bernard Taylor

'You can be very hurtful at times, you know. Anyway, to give you the good news, Mr Callow has asked me to star in his next opera production. We're doing *La Sonnambula*. I'm to be the lead soprano and we're going to win the south-west of England competition with it.'

Jack could barely keep his laughter in check. 'That's very nice for you,' he managed to say. 'So when's your debut—and isn't it a pity that I've got to be out of the country at the time.'

'I thought you might.' They laughed together, then she said, 'No, seriously, he has asked me to join his operatic society.'

'Not as a singer.'

'No, not as a singer. And I think you've already made your point there. As one of the backstage crew. Wardrobe or props or something. I suggested that you'd be better at that stuff than I would.'

'Thanks a lot.'

'But I also told him you were very busy.'

'Thank God for that.' He paused. 'You're not really interested, are you?'

'No, but I couldn't tell him straight off. He was so enthusiastic. Where would I find the time to do something like that, anyway?'

Jack shrugged. 'We'd manage—if you wanted to do it.'

'I don't. Anyway, it was just a whim on his part, I'm sure. I doubt I'll hear anything more about it.'

Connie was wrong. When she and Jack got back to The Limes just before midnight, Jane announced that Callow had called at the house in their absence.

'He had something for you,' Jane said to Connie.

'Oh?'

144

'He didn't leave it. He said he'd call back when you were at home.'

Late the following evening Connie sat beside the fire in the sitting room. The children had long since been bathed and settled in bed, Jack was working in his study, and she had put aside her book to watch the television news. She watched with a jaundiced eye. Nothing seemed to change. The government's stock was low, as were the employment figures, the output of manufacturing industry, house prices and general confidence. The only things that seemed to be on the increase were unemployment, the collapse of small businesses, doubts over the European Community and unrest. As for the troubles in the rest of the world, they didn't bear thinking about. Another minute and she switched off the set and took up her book again. She had hardly opened it when there came a ring at the doorbell.

In the hall she peered through the spy hole in the front door and saw John Callow standing in the light of the porch, his dog at his side. She opened the door.

'Mr Callow, hello.'

He touched fingertips to the peak of his cap. 'Excuse me for calling on you so late, but as I was bringing the dog out for a stroll I thought I'd just drop this off.' As he spoke he held out a large brown envelope. 'It's the stuff on the opera society I mentioned. I hope you don't mind. I called yesterday evening but you were out.'

'No, of course not.' She paused, then, hoping that he would decline, said, 'Would you like to come in for a minute?'

'No, no, please,' he protested. 'I wouldn't dream of

it. As it is I feel rather bad about ringing your bell so late. I do apologize.'

'That's quite all right.'

He touched a hand to his cap again. 'Anyway, I won't keep you. I just wanted you to have these things while it was in my mind. There's no hurry to let me have them back. As I said, we'd love to have you in the group. In whatever capacity.' He began to turn away, then, his attention held, stopped and peered past her shoulder. 'Is—is that Malibran?' he said. 'Surely it is.'

'Is what what?' Connie turned to see the object of his focus and saw that he was looking at an ornately framed drawing of a young woman in early nine-teenth-century dress.

'I'm sure it is,' Callow said and, looking at Connie for permission, moved to take a step forward. 'May I? Do you mind?'

'Not at all.'

He came into the hall and moved to the portrait.

'Who did you say it was?' Connie said.

He leaned closer to the picture, studying it closely. 'It's Malibran. Maria Malibran. I'm sure it is.'

Connie shrugged. 'Well, I'll take your word for that. We've no idea who she is. There's nothing on the back to indicate. It was up in the professor's room. Jack took a fancy to it and brought it down here because he liked the drawing. Who was she? An opera singer, I suppose.'

'Maria Malibran? Oh, yes. She was a very celebrated mezzo-soprano, born early last century. She died in her twenties following a horse-riding accident when she was pregnant. Yes, I'm sure that's Malibran.' He shook his head in a little gesture of wonder. 'It's an original, too.' He leaned closer, peering at it in the rather dim light of the hall. 'Who is it by?'

146

'It's signed Buchanan. There's a signature, very faint, in the left-hand corner.'

He nodded. 'Yes, I can see something there.' He drew back a little and shook his head again. 'Well, well, what a find.'

'You look very pleased,' Connie said.

He gave a little laugh. 'I am. It's a beautiful piece. I envy you, owning this.'

'Oh, there are several more, of different women. Professor Maddox was obviously very keen on collecting portraits of the prima donnas.'

'Yes, I know he was. I'm sure this one is quite valuable.'

'Really?'

'Oh, yes. Your husband's right, it looks a very fine drawing, regardless of the subject. But add to that that the subject is Maria Malibran, a famous diva of the past, then it's bound to be of considerable interest to collectors.'

'Well,' Connie said with a smile, 'that'll be good to know if times get hard.'

'Do you think you might sell it?' There was a note of eagerness in his tone.

'Oh, I wouldn't think so. I was only joking.'

'Well, if you do, then please give me first chance at it, will you?'

'Yes, all right. But I can't imagine that Jack would want to get rid of it. We've kept nearly everything that belonged to the professor. His library, all his pictures and everything. We've discussed what should happen to it all, and Jack's rather of the opinion that it should eventually go to one of the theatre museums.'

Callow gave a nod of ironical approval. 'Lucky museum.' He bent and peered at the picture briefly once more, then straightened again and said, 'Well, I won't keep you any longer. Thank you for letting me see this.'

'It's a pleasure. Any time.'

He moved back towards the door. 'And do look at that stuff on the group. As I say, we'd love to have you come and join us.'

'Thank you.' She lifted the envelope before her. 'I'm sure I'll find it very interesting.'

He stepped out onto the porch, they exchanged goodnights, and she closed the door behind him.

Back in the sitting room she resumed her seat and took up her book once more. Half an hour later Jack entered.

'Had enough?' Connie asked as she put down her book.

He closed the door and sat down facing her. 'Yes, I have.' He yawned. 'Was that Callow at the door?'

'Yes, it was.'

He nodded. 'I heard his voice. I'd know those actor's tones anywhere. What on earth did he want at this time of night?'

'He brought some bits and pieces on the operatic society. Wants me to look at them. He hopes he can persuade me to join.' She took up the envelope from the small table at her side; it was quite full. Lifting the flap she half extracted a wad of papers of different sizes. She flicked through the items and shook her head. 'I can't be bothered now. I'll look at it later.' She pushed the papers back into the envelope and laid it on the side table. 'I found out something interesting, by the way,' she said. 'That drawing of the young woman you brought downstairs is of a famous opera singer.'

'Well, that's hardly a surprise, is it?'

'She was a famous diva named Maria Malibran.'

She went on to speak of her conversation with Callow and his appreciation of the portrait. 'So if you ever decide to sell it,' she finished, 'he wants first refusal.'

He nodded. 'We'll bear it in mind.'

A pause, then Connie said, 'He's an odd sort of chap, isn't he?'

'Yes, he is rather.'

'If he really did make a play for your cousin Mary, I can well understand why she didn't want to know about it.'

He nodded towards the envelope on the side table, smilingly narrowed his eyes and said, 'You don't suppose that's just a ploy, do you?'

'A ploy? For what?' She gave a laugh and said, 'Oh, you think there's a chance he fancies me now, is that it? And he's trying to rope me into the opera group just so that he can have his way with me, yes?'

'Stranger things have happened.'

'I'm not sure how to take that.' She shook her head and chuckled. 'No, that's not it. He's just very set on getting the opera prize and I suppose he wants all the support he can get.'

'What prize is that?'

'Oh, I didn't tell you about that. When we met yesterday afternoon he told me he's got his heart set on winning the silver plate with his opera production. Your uncle's plate.'

'What?'

'There, you see. You don't know everything by a long chalk. Your uncle's plate. The Maddox Plate. It's an engraved silver plate that's given every other year for the best amateur operatic production in the south-west of England. Used to be presented by Edwin himself, apparently. It's purely an amateur thing. No national importance. I suppose Edwin did it because he saw it as a way of encouraging a love of opera. And obviously the winning of it is an accolade much sought after. Certainly Callow's very keen. He says he's never won it yet, but he's made up his mind to win it this time.'

'Well, maybe he will.'

'Who knows. I shan't be a part of it, though.'

'You've made up your mind?'

'Yes, of course. It was never a question. I don't really want to have anything to do with him. I just can't manage to like the man. I don't know why. Maybe it's because of what happened at the start—the wrong foot we got off on. I don't know. I'm very glad that all that unpleasant business got sorted out, but I wouldn't want it to go any further. I don't think I'd ever want him as a friend.'

'I know what you mean.'

'While we were talking he referred to the fact that he and Edwin didn't always see eye to eye.'

'Oh?'

'He didn't elaborate. He just mentioned it.'

'Old George Appleton was telling me a bit about him too. Callow usually gets what he's after, George said, so maybe he will win his opera plate.' Jack yawned. 'Look, I'm knackered. I'm going to bed. Would you like some tea or something before I go?'

'No, thanks.'

He got up from his chair. 'OK, then, I'll see you in a while. Don't be long, will you?'

After Jack had gone upstairs Connie sat there for some moments and then idly took up the envelope and pulled out the papers. On the top were several newspaper clippings; some were reviews of the society's operatic productions, while others consisted of interviews with Callow and articles on the society and its works and aims. Next came a number of programmes of actual productions. She took up the top one which was for a production of Mozart's *Don Giovanni*. She opened it and read the producer's note— not written by Callow but by a man named Harold Sanders—and then the biographies of the singers. The names meant nothing to her, and held no interest for her.

She closed the programme and took up the next one. This was for Verdi's *La Traviata*. A photograph on the cover showed the heroine clutching a wine glass and looking soulfully off into the distance. The programme held a piece of paper as a marker, and she opened it at the marked page, moved the slip of paper aside and saw Callow's face smiling out at her. The text below it, from Callow in his role of producer, began by lauding the musical genius of Verdi, the libretto of Francesco Maria Piave, and, finally, that of Alexandre Dumas *fils* whose novel *La Dame aux Camelias* had been adapted for the opera. After that, he spoke of his great love for the work, the pleasures and the problems experienced in producing it and of its high and popular place in the operatic hierarchy. He then went on:

My particular vision of this much-loved piece may cause some members of our audience surprise, as I have chosen to eschew the long-established and familiar staging of the last act in favour of a different interpretation. I make no apologies for this, and only hope that our audiences will appreciate what I have tried to do—to give, in effect, a fresh look at a classic work. *La Traviata*, enjoying the popularity that it has known for most of its life, is subject perhaps more than many other operas to the more banal and prosaic interpretation. By making a change to the plot of the final act—a change at one time considered by Dumas himself—I hope that Verdi's tragic heroine may be regarded in a new light.

Humility, Connie thought, was not one of Callow's strong points.

She moved to turn the page, holding the slip of paper that had been used as a marker beneath the ball of her thumb. As she did so, she felt a sharp blast of cold air come cutting across her breast, stirring the pages of the opera programme and the slip of paper. A moment later the marker was torn free and went fluttering away, gathering speed as it went, in the direction of the fire. In amazement she watched it whirling around in its flight, until finally it came to rest against the fireguard, lying flattened against the mesh. Had the guard not been there the paper would surely have gone into the flames.

Getting up from her chair she stepped over the hearth-rug and retrieved the slip of paper. She could still feel the cold draught and at the same time had the odd sensation that the paper was twitching and moving between her fingers, to such an extent that she felt compelled to hold it more securely. The facing side of the paper was blank, but turning it over she saw that something had been written on the other side. She frowned, squinting at it in an effort to read what was there. It appeared to be a series of words in some unknown language in an alphabet that was quite foreign to her. After a few moments trying to decipher the strange symbols, she put the slip of paper back between the pages of the opera programme and returned everything to the envelope.

Chapter Eight

Soon after Connie had left to take the children to school the next morning, Jack went to his study to start work on a new episode of the series. He had barely sat down at his desk when there came a ring at the back door and George Appleton was there, ready to make a start on the chaos of the overgrown garden. Side by side they stood on the front garden path while George voiced his opinion on what should be done. Jack, with no experience to draw on, concurred with all he said, then left him to get on with it and returned to his study.

Long after Jack had heard Connie return to the house he was still trying to come up with a suitable theme for the *Fat Chance* episode that had to be written. Going into the kitchen to recharge his empty coffee mug, he found her loading dirty laundry into the washing machine.

'I see George is here,' she said. 'And getting down to it. He doesn't waste time, does he?'

'Well, he's one of the old school. Conscientious, with a belief in giving value for money.' Jack flicked the switch on the kettle and spooned out coffee. His mug bore a smiling sun face with the word DAD written in childishly formed letters. A birthday present from Joel.

'How's your work going?' Connie said.

'Don't ask.'

'Like that, huh? Well, you'll get it. You always do.'

'Eventually, I suppose.' He watched as she poured soap powder into a small mesh container and placed it on top of the laundry in the machine. 'You want coffee?'

'Not right now, thanks. A little later.' She closed the washer door, set the dials and turned it on. 'Joel's teacher's leaving at Christmas,' she said. 'Shame. He likes her very much.'

'Which one's that?'

'Mrs Chandler. You remember her. We met her briefly when the children started school.'

'Ah, yes, the reddish-haired woman. She seemed very nice.'

'Yes. It's such a shame she's going. Just when Joel was really beginning to settle in. Still, I'm sure the new teacher will be OK.'

Glancing from the window, Jack saw that George was at work on the rose trees, snipping away with the secateurs, tugging and dragging the cut branches free and dropping them on the ground at his side. Bearing in mind the difficulties he himself was currently having with his own work, the job looked almost enviable.

Back in his study, Jack put down his mug of coffee and pulled his pad towards him. During the early stages of writing an episode he worked only with paper and pencil. It was not until he had worked out the plot and made a couple of drafts of it that he committed it to the word-processor. At the moment such a step still seemed some way off.

On the pad he half-heartedly made a few notes of ideas for themes. 'Medical problems,' he wrote, 'family visits . . . quarrel with neighbours . . . shopping . . . problems with the plumbing . . .' writing the ideas down as they came into his head. When he had made a list he sat and pondered on each idea, trying to stretch his imagination this way and that in the hope that out of one of those words or phrases would come the subject for a viable episode. Each time, however, his thoughts took him onto the same track, like a needle in the groove of a record, so that he always ended up with the same—previously rejected—concepts. An hour later, with a sigh of frustration, he pushed his pad and pencil aside in disgust.

In the hope that he might find inspiration in some quarter other than his own brain, he leaned back in his chair and let his eyes roam over the books on the shelves above the desk. His glance moving to the top shelf, he saw there the row of tall, hardback notebooks that were Edwin's journals. He had not so much as glanced at them since that day when he and Connie had come to look over the house; though exactly why he had not, he could not be sure, unless it was that that first brief examination had left him with a feeling of unease that he had not wanted to renew. Now he got to his feet, reached up and took down the last four volumes.

Sitting in his chair again, he looked at the periods covered by each one. They were arranged in sequence, the last one ending on a date several weeks before the time of Edwin's death. Rising again he took down the rest of the volumes. There were thirty-eight in all and, going by their first and last dates, covered a continuous period of some thirty-five years. Where, though, was the last one? He felt sure there had to be another. Faced with the evidence of Edwin's scrupulous record-keeping, he could not believe that with the completion of one volume he would simply have stopped altogether.

Checking the dates one by one, he carefully went through the volumes again. None was out of sequence. So either Edwin had indeed abruptly ceased keeping his journal, or there was another volume that had been mislaid somewhere.

His problems with the television script for the moment forgotten, Jack opened one of the journals and began to flick through it, stopping here and there at random to read the odd page or paragraph. As with his first cursory examination of the journals, he found that they dealt mostly with opera, occasionally supplemented by observations concerning aspects of Edwin's private and social life. For the most part the entries in the journal appeared regularly, almost daily, as if they had been made as a matter of course, out of habit. Jack saw that it was rare for more than three or four days to have passed without some note or other on the page. When, therefore, he came to a part where the dates of the entries jumped a period of ten days he was struck by its unusualness. Then, looking at the text in his uncle's now familiar hand, he saw the reason for it. The first entry following the gap touched upon the death of his son David.

Reading that brief entry, with the unwritten grief behind it, Jack thought of Connie's words when she had found herself looking at one of Edwin's more personal comments, words to the effect that she felt like a voyeur. He closed the volume and took up another and began to flick through it. He came to a stop, his eye caught by John Callow's name. The entry said:

Harold's funeral took place yesterday. It was a beautiful service, though his dear wife seemed inconsolable. They were so close, and how she'll manage without him I can't imagine. It was so good to see all the members of the operatic society turning out to pay their last respects— the singers, the musicians and all the backstage workers. H was much loved by them all, there's no doubt. It was an especially fine thing to have the singers of the company make their own contribution at the service. They sang beautifully, and with great feeling. The one person conspicuous by his absence was Callow. I'm sure he had his reasons, though one would have expected that as H's assistant his would be the first face in evidence on such an occasion. For a moment I found myself wondering whether there could indeed be anything in what H said. But we live in the real world, I remind myself, where such things cannot happen. I also remind myself of H's state of mind at the end when, not to put too fine a point on it, he was not rational. Anyway, he is at peace now, and there can be no question but that he accomplished so much in forming the society, and making it what it is today. In such a relatively short time to take it from very unpromising beginnings and make it one of the most respected amateur companies in the whole country seems to me little short of miraculous. I'm so happy that he won the Plate on those two occasions. He deserved it. We can only hope that his good work will be continued.

Jack read the piece through again. Parts of it were rather disturbing. After a while he turned the page, and the next one, and then, in an entry dated three days later, Callow's name came up again. Edwin had written:

So, Mr John Callow is to take over the helm of the operatic society, is thrown into the deep end and, not to stop mixing metaphors, is starting by taking over the reins of *Traviata*. Well, he could have a more taxing vehicle for his directorial debut. It's one of Verdi's more simple, compact operas, so if he follows his brief and his text it's hard to see how he could go wrong. We'll see what he makes of it. God knows, if enthusiasm counts for anything, he should do well; I've heard that he's approaching the whole thing with an almost indecent eagerness, and not least by throwing out a great deal of H's ideas. One can only hope that he doesn't throw the baby out with the bathwater. I remember some of H's comments when C first joined the group—not all positive by any means, and if H was right, C's appointment might turn out to be a very mixed blessing. We shall see in time. I suppose I must wish the man well, although I cannot for the life of me bring myself to like him.

Jack leafed through the rest of the volume, his eyes searching the pages for further mention of John Callow. In an entry dated over two months later his name cropped up again. The entry, very brief this time, said simply:

> So at last the proof comes in the pudding. Last night I went to Reading to see Callow's production of *Traviata*. What a fiasco, and how I regret the fact that I agreed to review it. Such things are best not dwelt upon. Oh, H, your friends need you now.

Jack took the journal into the kitchen where Connie was preparing lunch for the two of them. She read the entry where Callow's name was mentioned then handed the journal back. 'You see, it's not just me,' she said. '*Nobody* likes the man.'

Connie and the children met Callow the following Friday afternoon.

First of all, they overtook him in the Renault on their way from school. Joel was telling Connie about some work he had been doing in class that day, saying—his voice raised over his sisters' chatter: 'I wrote a composition today, Mum. Mrs Chandler said it was excellent.'

'Oh, that's good,' Connie replied, catching his eye in the overhead driving mirror. 'What was it about?'

'I'll show it to you when we get in. We had to write on "A Lesson I Learned". After Mrs Chandler had marked it I asked her if I could bring it home and show you, and she said yes.'

'Well, that's very nice. I look forward to reading it.'

It was then, as the car turned the bend in the lane, that they recognized the figure with the dog walking up ahead of them. Immediately from Kitty came a sound of disgust.

'Uulllgghhhh, look. It's Mr Yellow-Teeth!'

'Kitty!' Connie said sharply. 'We'll have no more of that, thank you very much.'

'But he *has* got yellow teeth.'

'Well, he can't help it.'

'He could. If he brushed his teeth properly they'd be nice and white.'

'Brushing won't always do it.'

'That's what you tell us to do.'

'Yes, I know, but it's different if you're older. Your teeth don't stay white all your life.'

Lydia groaned. 'Oh, *no*! I shan't have teeth like Mr Callow when I grow up, shall I? Uullghhh.'

'Be quiet,' Connie said. 'That's enough.'

They were drawing level with Callow now, and Connie eased the car as far to the right as she could in order to give him and his dog plenty of room. As they drove past him she turned and gave him a wave. In response he smiled and waved a hand holding a bunch of flowers. As they all piled out of the car a minute later they saw him appear round the curve of the hedge that fringed part of the southern side of the lane. Catching sight of them he lifted the flowers aloft again and hurried forward.

'I'm glad I caught you, Mrs Forrest,' he said as he stopped before her. 'I was going to leave these on the porch, but now I can give them to you personally.' He held out the flowers, a bunch of beautiful yellow chrysanthemums. 'They're for your mother's grave. I know how much she loved plants and gardening.'

'Oh, that's so kind of you,' Connie said.

'No, it's nothing. I saw them there in my garden as I was about to leave, and thought they might be just the thing.'

'They're beautiful. Mother would have loved them.

I'll take them tomorrow morning when I go to the churchyard. Thank you so much.'

'Don't mention it.' He turned his attention to the three children who stood at Connie's side. 'So,' he said, smiling at them, 'you've all finished school for the day now, have you? Or rather, the week, I should say. Is that right?'

He directed the final part of his question to Joel who nodded and murmured, 'Yes.'

'And you, young gentleman,' Callow added, 'are just the person I wanted to see.' With his words he put a hand into his overcoat pocket, drew out a little paper-wrapped package and held it out. 'Here—I brought you something.'

Joel flicked a questioning glance at Connie and, receiving a nod from her, took the package from Callow's hand. 'Thank you very much.'

'It's nothing much,' Callow said. 'Just a few foreign stamps. You do collect foreign stamps, don't you?'

Joel nodded and said hesitantly, 'Yes.'

'I thought you would. Most boys do. I did when I was your age.' He turned his gaze to the twins. 'So,' he said, smiling at them, 'I see today that one of you is in a red coat and the other is in a green coat. Though it doesn't help me much.' He gave a little laugh. 'I'm afraid I still can't tell one from the other.'

Kitty, wearing red, said, 'I'm Kitty and she's Lydia.'

'Oh, good. Well, that's got that sorted out, hasn't it?' His smile was replaced by a look of mock sorrow. 'I wish I had a little present for you two girls, but I'm afraid I haven't. Perhaps another day, all right?' He smiled broadly at the two of them.

Lydia smiled back uncertainly and Kitty said after a moment, 'Why are your teeth so yellow? Is it because you're old?'

The smile froze on Callow's face, and Connie turned on Kitty and said sharply, 'How dare you say that! Apologize at once.'

Kitty, looking shocked at the effect created by her words, began, 'Oh, but Mummy, I—'

'You heard what I said!' Connie snapped. 'Apologize at once. At *once*.'

Tears welled suddenly in Kitty's eyes. 'I'm sorry,' she said.

'Not to me,' Connie said. 'To Mr. Callow.'

Kitty forced herself to look up at the man. 'I'm sorry.'

Callow stood unmoving, his face set as if cut from stone, a little beating nerve in his left temple the only sign of animation. Then he gave a little nod of acknowledgement, followed by a smile that neither parted his lips nor touched his eyes. 'No, *I'm* sorry, little girl,' he said. 'I'm sorry to have caused offence by smiling at you. Unfortunately, though, as you'll discover, people can't stay looking young. People change as they grow older. Their hair, their teeth, their shape—everything. It all changes. And, sad to say, it doesn't change for the better. Sorry about that, but that's the way life is.'

Although Kitty stood quite still, it was clear that she was inwardly squirming at his words. Connie, turning to the children, said coldly: 'Now go on indoors, all three of you. And don't make a noise and disturb your father's work.' As they turned away she added to Kitty, 'I'll talk to you in a little while, young lady.'

In silence the three children trooped along the drive and round the side of the house. Connie watched them go then turned back to Callow.

'Oh, dear,' she said with a deep sigh, 'I'm terribly

sorry, Mr Callow. I can't apologize enough. I just don't know what to say.'

He raised a hand, palm out. 'Don't worry about it. Children say these things. There's no malice in them.'

'No, I know, but . . .' She shook her head.

'Please, don't give it another thought. Forget it.' He smiled at her, close-mouthed. 'Anyway, you want to get in, so I won't keep you.' He gave a rather formal little bow. 'Good afternoon.'

'Good afternoon,' Connie replied awkwardly. 'And thank you again for the flowers.'

He started to turn away, then stopped and turned back to face her. 'I don't suppose you've had a chance to look at the bits and pieces I left with you last Sunday, have you?'

'Well, no, not really. Nothing more than a brief glance.'

'Not to worry. There's no rush.'

'I'll get to it over the weekend.'

'Fine, fine.' He waved again, turned and walked away up the lane.

In the house, Connie put the flowers in water then got the children a drink and a snack. When they had eaten she sent Lydia upstairs to play and took Kitty into the sitting room and read her the riot act. 'And this isn't over yet,' she finished as Kitty stood tearfully contrite before her. 'I shall tell your father when he's through working, and I shouldn't be at all surprised if he has something to say as well. Now, go on upstairs and don't come down until I call you.'

While Kitty went miserably upstairs Connie went back into the kitchen where Joel was waiting to show her his English essay. When she had cleared away the tea things she sat down and he opened his exercise book. With him standing at her side, leaning against her chair, she read what he had written. Under the heading, 'A Lesson I Learned', he had given an account of his taking Callow's roses, the subsequent confrontation with the man and his apology to him. Connie read it through a couple of times and gave a nod of approval.

'What d'you think?' Joel asked. 'D'you think it's all right?'

'I think it's more than all right. I'm extremely impressed.'

'Really?' He smiled.

'Extremely. I think it's a very good piece—excellent.' She lifted her arm, put it round his shoulders and briefly hugged him to her. 'And I also think you've been quite brave.'

'Brave?' This was something he was not expecting.

'Yes.' She kept her arm lightly around him. 'To talk about it. I know it was a very unpleasant experience for you, when you didn't intend to do any wrong, and I think you've been brave to write about it like this.' She turned and looked into his grey eyes. 'I'm proud of you.'

'Really?'

'Really. And when your dad's finished his work you must show it to him, too.'

'Yes, I'm going to. Mrs Chandler thought it was good, too.'

'She thought it was *excellent*,' Connie said. 'She's written it here.' She read out the teacher's comment: ' "You have given thought to this, Joel, and it shows. It's also very well presented. Excellent work." '

He grinned self-consciously.

'Tell me something, though,' Connie said. 'Why didn't you mention Mr Callow by name?'

He shrugged. 'I don't know. D'you think I should have done?'

'I'm not saying that. I was just curious. No, I think you did the right thing, not mentioning his name. After all, it's all over with now.'

'I did tell Mrs Chandler his name.'

'Did you?'

'Yes, after she'd read it she called me up to her desk and told me she thought it was very good.'

'Did she ask you who he was? The man?'

'No. She asked if he was really that cross with me, and I said yes he was. And then I told her that it was Mr Callow.'

'Did she say anything to that?'

'She just said, "Oh." '

'Just "Oh"?'

'Yes. Later on she read some of the compositions out to the rest of the class.'

'Did she read yours out?'

'No. I thought she was going to, but in the end she didn't.'

A pause, then Connie said, 'By the way, what are the stamps like that Mr Callow gave you? You have looked at them, have you?'

'Well, I just opened the packet. It's a little stamp album.' He sighed. 'I didn't tell the truth, did I?'

'Didn't you?'

'Well, he asked me if I collected foreign stamps, and I said yes. But I don't. But I couldn't tell him that, could I? He'd already given me the album by then. Should I have told him?'

'No, I think you did the right thing. Sometimes we have to tell a little lie in order to make another person feel better. And if that's all it does then there can't be any harm in it. That's what I think, anyway. You couldn't have just handed them back to him and said you weren't interested, could you? That would have seemed very rude when he was trying to be nice. Besides, you might find you like the stamps. It might start you off as a collector.'

When Jack emerged from his study just after five-thirty Joel told him of the present he had received from Mr Callow and then showed him the essay in his exercise book, pointing out his teacher's words of praise. 'You see, Jack?' Connie said when Jack had read Joel's piece and expressed his approval. 'Perhaps you won't be the only writer in the house.'

Later, in the sitting room, when the children were in bed, Connie told Jack about Kitty's rude and tactless question to Callow. 'Oh, my God,' he groaned. 'Just leave it to her.' He shook his head in despair. 'How did Callow take it?'

'How do you think? He wasn't happy. Would you be?'

'And just when we'd all got on an even keel with him. Everything was going so well, too.'

'Still, I don't think it's going to make any difference. He was pretty pissed off with her, but at the same time he does recognize that she's only a child. I don't think he'll take it that seriously. He was a bit stiff afterwards, but I've no doubt he'll get over it.'

'I hope so. I can hardly believe it. And wouldn't you know it would have to come right after he gave Joel the stamp album. It was so nice of him to do that.'

'Yes.'

'I suppose with Joel he was trying to make up to him for the business with the roses.'

'I expect so.'

'You have to admit that after all the unpleasantness he's done everything he can to put matters right.'

166

'It seems that way.'

Jack frowned. 'Why do you say it like that?'

'I don't know.' Connie gave a shrug. 'To me he just seems to be doing a little too much. First the chocolates for Mother and now flowers for Mother's grave and stamps for Joel. What next, I wonder.'

'Oh, come on now. None of us is perfect. Obviously that's the way the man is. His anger was a little over the top and so, it seems, are his efforts to make up for it. But you can't hold that against him.'

'I suppose not. It just makes me feel a bit uncomfortable, that's all. He's said he's sorry and I accept it and now I'd rather he just left it at that.'

'Yes, but you mustn't let it count against him. I know you don't care for him, but we must be fair and give him the benefit of the doubt.' He looked at her expression. 'Oh, Con, come on. The man's doing his best. All right, so he might not be the most popular guy in the village, but you have to speak as you find.'

'That's what I'm doing,' she said.

On Sunday morning Kitty and Lydia, with no concession to their parents' habit of a Sunday lie-in, decided to have a screaming contest. Jack and Connie were very quickly awakened by the noise. Their initial reaction was one of panic, but as they started up from the bed they realized that the high-pitched screams were not manifestations of fear. Jack groaned and sank back on the pillow. Connie, going into the girls' room, found them sitting on their beds facing one another while they calmly shrieked at the tops of their voices. Not only was volume a factor in the contest, it appeared, but also the length of time that each scream could be sustained. At their mother's appearance they stopped screaming.

'For God's sake,' Connie groaned in disbelief, tying the cord of her dressing gown, 'you woke us up. D'you realize what time it is? It's not long past seven.'

'Oh, sorry,' Kitty said. 'We were having a competition.'

'I should think you were. I never heard such a noise.'

'Sorry,' said Lydia.

'When we moved here,' said Kitty, 'you said we wouldn't have to worry about noise any more.'

'We meant noise that might disturb the neighbours. We didn't mean us. If you want to play, then get dressed and play, but play quietly.'

Leaving them to more peaceful amusements, Connie went back onto the landing and softly opened the door to Joel's room. He was just getting dressed.

'They ought to be gagged,' he said.

Connie agreed and went downstairs to the kitchen. Now that she was up she might as well stay up. She was making coffee when Joel came in. 'Breakfast won't be ready for a while yet,' she told him. 'Make yourself some toast for now if you want. Perhaps you'd like to take your dad some coffee and the paper, would you? When I've had a cup I'm going to run a bath.'

When Connie had poured a cup of coffee Joel carried it into the hall, picked up the newspaper from the mat and took both upstairs. Connie poured herself some coffee and sat drinking it at the kitchen table. Joel returned a little while later, announcing, 'Dad says he's getting up,' and set about pouring orange juice and putting bread into the toaster.

Connie was rising from the table a few minutes later when Jack appeared in his dressing gown, carrying the paper and his empty cup. He poured himself more coffee and moved to the table at which Joel sat eating toast loaded with raspberry jam. 'Don't stint yourself,' he said as he sat down.

'Dad, I'm a growing boy,' Joel said.

Jack nodded. 'I'm glad you told me. I'd never have known.'

Connie was moving to the door. 'I'm going up to have my bath. Then I'll come and get breakfast.'

She was in the bathroom turning on the taps a minute later when Joel came to the open door.

'Mum,' he said, 'have you seen the stamp album that Mr Callow gave me?'

'No, I haven't,' she said.

'Dad wants to have a look at it, and I can't remember what I did with it.'

'It's probably in your room.'

'Probably. I'll look again.' Joel went away along the landing and reappeared moments later carrying the book. 'I got it,' he said.

'Good.'

As he went clattering down the stairs, the door of the girls' room opened noisily and Lydia and Kitty came by. They had dressed themselves. To the blue jeans that each wore, Kitty had added a green sweater and Lydia one of dark blue. 'Will you be long, Mummy?' Kitty said, stopping at the bathroom door. 'We're hungry.'

'Well, you'll just have to be patient,' Connie said. 'I'll be down to get your breakfast soon.'

Downstairs, the girls found Joel and their father at the kitchen table. Jack was looking at the little stamp album, Joel standing at his side.

'Is that what Mr Callow gave you?' Kitty asked her brother.

Joel said that it was.

'It's not fair,' she said. 'He gave you a present but

169

not us.' She sniffed. 'I don't care, though. I wouldn't want some silly old foreign stamps, anyway.'

'Well, you've no need to worry,' Jack said, shooting her a stern glance. 'After what you said to Mr Callow yesterday I doubt you'll ever get any kind of present from him.'

Kitty said nothing to this, and Jack gave his attention back to the album. 'It looks as if some of these stamps are quite old,' he said.

Joel nodded. 'Perhaps they were Mr Callow's when he was a boy.'

'They might well be. Are you going to write him a note and thank him?'

'Yes,' Joel didn't sound too enthusiastic.

'Well, it would be polite, and a nice gesture.'

'Yes, all right.'

'Daddy, can we have some orange juice?' Lydia asked.

'Can't you wait ten minutes?' Jack said. 'We'll be having breakfast as soon as your mother gets down.'

'I'm thirsty.'

'All right.' With a sigh Jack closed the album and handed it back to Joel. 'I'll finish looking at it later.' He moved to the fridge while Joel sat down and idly began to leaf through the pages. 'There's a note here, Dad,' Joel said. Between two of the pages at the back he had found a small slip of paper. He took it up and looked at it.

Jack glanced up as he poured juice into two glasses. 'What does it say?'

Joel peered at the paper. 'I don't know. I can't read it. It's just a lot of weird-looking marks.'

Joel had no chance to study the paper further. Suddenly, as if from nowhere, a blast of air came gusting through the room. All the windows were closed and yet abruptly the wind was there, strong and chillingly cold. Jack, standing with the juice carton in his hand, felt it ruffle his hair and snatch at the legs of his pyjamas. It was Joel, though, who took the full force of it. 'Ohhh!' he said, his cry expressing sudden shock.

Jack turned and saw that Joel's hair had blown back from his forehead and the collar of his shirt was flattened against his throat. On the table, the pages of the stamp album were lifted.

'*Oh Dad . . . !*' Joel breathed. In his hand the slip of paper trembled and writhed as if possessed of life. And then all at once it was torn from his grasp and went spinning across the room. The girls had left the door open the merest crack and the four watched as the paper swept up to it on the stream of icy air. It hung there unmoving for a moment and then, in a sudden, swirling movement, whipped around the edge of the door and was gone from sight. The thought flashed through Jack's mind: *This has happened before. It has happened before* . . . He flashed a glance at Joel and then, with the juice carton falling from his hand, strode across the room and flung open the door.

As he dashed into the hall, with Joel only a second behind him, Jack saw the paper hovering at the foot of the stairs, twisting and turning in the current of air. He leapt forward. He was too late, though. The paper was almost in his grasp when the wind seemed to strengthen and he felt himself buffeted by a sudden, strong gust that chilled him to the bone and took his breath away. Next moment, as he reached out, snatching at the paper, it slipped round the newel post and went flying upwards out of his reach.

Jack took a gasping breath and followed, his slippered feet pounding on the stairs. Reaching the top, he swung onto the landing and saw the bathroom door open before him and Connie appear in her dressing gown. In the same moment the slip of paper went spinning towards her. She gave a little cry of surprise as the paper seemed to be flying straight at her, but then at the last moment it skimmed past her head.

'What's happening?' she said as Jack came running forward and pushed past her into the bathroom. He did not answer. Inside the room he stood and looked around him, searching for the piece of paper. Then he saw it, floating on the water in the bathtub. Stepping forward, he bent and scooped it out and stared at it as it lay sodden and limp in his hand. He turned it over. There were no strange marks on it now. Whatever Joel had seen written was no longer there.

A moment later as he turned to face Connie and Joel in the doorway he realized that the wind had also gone.

Chapter Nine

'I can't get over what happened to that piece of paper,' Jack said. 'There's no explaining it.'

It was the afternoon of that same Sunday. The children were in the sitting room watching a film on TV, and in order to talk without disturbing them, Jack and Connie had come into the study. Jack sat in his desk chair and Connie in the armchair at the desk's side.

'I'm sure,' Connie said, though with a note of uncertainty in her voice, 'that there's a reasonable explanation for it.'

'Are you?'

'There has to be.'

'But you felt that wind,' he said. 'You were in the bathroom doorway and you felt it. Can you explain that? I certainly can't. When we were in the kitchen, there was no window open, but suddenly the wind was there—a sudden gale. It was even more strange, though, in that it didn't fill the entire room. It just seemed concentrated in a fairly narrow channel.'

After he had taken the wet slip of paper out of the bath he had gone back downstairs into the kitchen. The signs of the wind's path had been clear. Where it had struck it had disturbed various items. In the kitchen it had thrown the newspaper and Joel's stamp album onto the floor, while in the hall it had overturned a vase of flowers and knocked Jack's cap from the coatstand. Everything else appeared to have remained undisturbed.

Jack thought about it for some seconds then said, 'Did it remind you of what happened with your mother that day in the garden?'

'By the bonfire? Yes.'

He nodded. 'It was exactly like that. That sudden wind springing up, and the piece of paper—Callow's note—going into the fire.'

Connie said after a moment, 'It happened to me, too.'

He frowned. 'It happened to *you*?'

'Yes. I didn't mention it at the time.'

'What are you talking about? What happened? Tell me.'

'It was last Sunday. After Callow had come round bringing that envelope of bits and pieces connected with his opera group. You'd gone up to bed. I opened the envelope and started looking at the various things it contained. There was a piece of paper, quite small, about the same size as the one in Joel's stamp album, between the pages of one of the programmes. And the same thing happened. I was looking at it and suddenly there was this really sharp draught, and the paper blew out of my hand and flew towards the fire.'

'And it got burnt? Like your mother's note?'

'No, the fireguard was up and it got caught on that. It was so odd. The wind. I didn't know how to account

174

for it.' She gave a little laugh. 'Hey, perhaps this place is haunted. If this were a Hollywood film and we were living in the States we'd probably discover that the house had been built on some ancient Indian burial ground or something.'

He nodded. 'Yes. But this is reality.'

'And we don't have Red Indians in Berkshire. How about some English pagan burial ground? The Druids or something? Would they do?'

'I'm trying to be serious, Connie.'

'Yes, I know. But what can I say? I'm as much in the dark as you are.'

Neither spoke for some moments. In the silence they heard through the closed door the faint murmur of the television.

'The odd coincidence,' Jack said after a while, 'is that in each case Callow has been involved. I mean in each case the paper that blew away came from him.'

'I know. And all three pieces of paper had writing on them.'

'There was writing on the paper you had as well?'

'Didn't I say that?'

'No. What did it say?' He paused. 'Go on, you're going to tell me that you couldn't make out what it was.'

'I couldn't. It was some very odd-looking symbols of some kind.'

'I didn't see what was written on the note your mother had,' he said. 'Nor Joel's. They were gone before I had a chance to look. What did you do with the paper you had?'

'I put it back with the rest of Callow's stuff. It's still there.'

As soon as she had spoken, Connie got up and went from the room. She was back a minute later carrying the envelope that had come from John Callow. After closing the door against the sound of the children's TV show, she sat down, extracted the envelope's contents and laid them on the desk. Quickly sorting through the various items she came across the programme for *La Traviata*. She opened it, took up the slip of paper and looked at it.

'No,' she said, shaking her head, 'I still can't make head or tail of it. I've no idea what it means.'

Jack reached out and she put the paper into his hand. He sat back in his chair, studying the strange symbols.

'Any ideas?' Connie said.

'Not a clue.'

The symbols were inscribed in black ink, in a series of five groups. The smallest group was made up of two symbols, the largest of six.

'I've never seen anything like them,' Jack said. 'But they're runes.'

'I remember Edwin mentioning runes in his journal,' Connie said. 'And that's what these are?'

'I can't think what else they could be.'

'I'm not sure I know what runes are.'

'I believe they're some kind of ancient alphabet characters.'

'How ancient? You mean one that nobody uses any more?'

'Not as far as I know.' He got up and reached for a dictionary, riffled through the pages, studied one of the entries then said, 'According to this they're the characters of an ancient German alphabet in use mainly in Scandinavia from the third century AD to the end of the Middle Ages. And each character in the alphabet was believed to have a magical significance.'

'Aha! So perhaps we *are* dealing with some ancient burial site, or something equally weird.'

Jack did not respond. He closed the dictionary and pushed it aside. Then he bent over the paper, studying the runes again. 'Of course, there's no way of knowing now whether the same things were written on the papers that your mother and Joel had. Joel saw them only briefly, and I doubt that he'd remember what they looked like or be able to recognize them again. Besides, I don't want him involved in this.'

Connie frowned. 'Involved in what? Do you know something I don't?' She sounded slightly alarmed.

'No, of course not. It's just that—I don't know—I don't get a good feeling from it, that's all I'm sure of.'

She nodded. 'I know what you mean. I don't either. But why not? I mean, all that's happened is that Joel and Mother and I have received some bits of paper with weird markings on them. Runes, as you call them. If that's what they are.'

'Not only that,' Jack said. 'There's that odd, freaky wind that sprang up in each case. And in both your mother's case and in Joel's the markings on the papers were destroyed as a result of it. And yours—this one—only survived, you tell me, because the fireguard was up.'

Connie nodded. 'You realize something else, don't you?'

'What's that?'

'There's no wind now.'

'No.' He held the paper by a corner. It remained hanging there, unmoving. With a groan he said, 'If we're not careful we could let this drive us crazy.' He laid the piece of paper down on the desk. 'Look, no hands.' He waited but the paper remained there. 'And no wind either.' After a moment he picked up the paper and handed it back to Connie. 'It beats me.'

She put the paper back between the leaves of the

Bernard Taylor

opera programme and returned all the papers to the envelope. 'Forget it,' she said.

'I intend to. I've got more important things to cope with. Not least finishing this blasted series. But I just wish I knew what it all means. It's something to do with Callow, that much is certain.'

'Maybe you should ask him.'

He thought about this. 'No,' he said, 'I don't think I'll do that.' Raising his head he looked up at the row of journals. 'Perhaps the answer's up there somewhere.'

'In Edwin's writings, you mean?'

'Perhaps.' He rose, took down several of the journals, then sat down again and began to look at their dates. He found the one he was looking for and began to look through its pages. He came to a stop at the entry concerning the burial of Edwin's friend, the opera company's former director. He read part of it aloud and then said, 'I wonder why Callow didn't go to the funeral.'

'Who knows? Maybe they didn't get on.'

'Maybe so, but surely you'd bury the hatchet at a time like that.'

'I should have thought so. But Callow's a pretty weird customer, to my mind.'

'Certainly Edwin had no time for him. Or his opera productions either, judging by his entry here after he'd gone to see Callow's *Traviata* production.' He turned to the relevant page. 'He'd agreed to review the production for a local newspaper. It would be interesting to see what he wrote.'

'You want to see what he wrote?'

'I'd love to. Why? Is it possible?'

'It might be.' She got up. 'There's a couple of binders somewhere with a load of his opera reviews and other

178

press items and photographs and stuff in them. Mum and I came across them when we were cleaning the place up. I think I know where they are.'

She went out of the room, and three or four minutes later she was back holding three large, thick blue binders. 'Say no more,' she said. 'All you have to do is ask. They were in the spare room upstairs. I thought I remembered putting them there.'

Jack moved the journals to one side and she set the binders on the desk. He drew the top one in front of him and untied the tape to reveal a large number of glossy photographs. He took them up and laid them aside. The rest of the binder's contents consisted of a loose-leaf scrapbook, the pages of which were covered with newspaper cuttings, all in date order, of various articles and reviews that Edwin had written. After glancing at a few of the pages, Jack turned to the back of the book and checked the date.

'This one's too early,' he said. 'If it's anywhere here it'll be in one of the other binders.' He pushed the first volume away, drew the second one towards him and untied the tape.

As he did so, Connie, who had been looking through the photographs, said: 'You were wondering about the Maddox Plate. Well, here it is.'

The photographs she laid before him looked as if they had been taken by a newspaper photographer. There were two photographs of Edwin posing stiffly with the plate in his hands, holding it up for the camera. He was wearing a dinner jacket and looked very elegant with his silver hair and neat, pointed beard. Another picture had obviously been taken at an awards ceremony and showed him presenting the plate to a tall man of about his own age, also dressed in a dinner jacket. Behind the smiling pair sat others at a white-clothed table. The fourth and fifth photographs were close-up studies of the plate itself, showing it in all its detail, so that the fine engraving of the design and the names written there were clearly shown.

'So this is what Callow's got his heart set on,' Jack observed. 'It's a handsome piece.'

He handed the photographs back to Connie and gave his attention once more to the newspaper cuttings. After leafing through the pages for some seconds he stopped and gave a nod of satisfaction. 'Here we are.' He tapped a newspaper clipping that was pasted to the right-hand side of the page.

Connie moved closer to him and bent her head to read the piece over his shoulder.

The review had come from a local paper named the *Berkshire Advertiser*. Under the heading 'TRAVIATA FAILS TO SATISFY' was written:

Last night the Reading Light Operatic Society presented *La Traviata*, its first offering under the direction of its new producer, John Callow. Well, much was hoped for but, sad to say, very little was delivered. Not that the singers, the orchestra or the conductor sold us short. They did not, and if the production could have been saved they would have done it. Unfortunately the damage was done at the outset, through misconception of the piece, and for this they can in no way be held accountable. This production of Verdi's great masterpiece is the sorriest attempt at entertainment that I have seen in many years.

It was always my belief—and if not my belief, then my hope—that the field of amateur opera could do much to bring the music of the great opera composers to the masses, to those who would not usually consider spending an evening at Covent Garden or the Coliseum.

Reading's *La Traviata* has made me think again, for I cannot imagine any viewer of this lamentable production ever wishing to see an opera again, in any form.

Here we had Mr John Callow, the producer, one-time soap opera performer, one-time bit part film actor, one-time radio actor, deciding in all his great theatrical experience that he could improve upon Verdi, the great master; and Verdi's excellent librettist, Piave. *La Traviata* must be the most beloved of all Verdi's great operas, and the greatest novice should be aware that a man trifles with the idols of others at his peril. Yet that, and seemingly quite blithely, even arrogantly, is just what Mr Callow has done.

The opera tells a tragic, well-known story. Having at last found love and happiness, the Parisian courtesan Violetta feels compelled to renounce her young lover Alfredo for the sake of his family's good name, which she does, though lying to Alfredo, allowing him to believe that she loves another. Then in the final act, when she is destitute and dying of consumption he, having learned the truth of her sacrifice, returns to her. He has learned the truth too late, however, for she is now at the point of death. The ending of Verdi's opera (I say Verdi's opera, to distinguish it from this travesty) is nevertheless almost exultant. '*É strano*,' Violetta murmurs. '*In me rinasce, rinasce. Ma io ritorno a viver*'—'It's strange, I feel reborn . . . I'm coming back to life.' And with her words she dies in Alfredo's arms.

It is one of the most moving moments in all of opera.

Except, that is, in Mr John Callow's production. Here Violetta spends the last act alone. There is no tender Alfredo to return to her, except in her imagination; no whispered words that they will leave Paris and live the rest of their lives in happiness and love together. No. Violetta spends the act beside her bed, singing out into the audience to some imaginary Alfredo, rather as if it is her brain that has been consumed by disease and not her lungs. And when Alfredo and his father appear, they do so as phantoms, standing embarrassedly and ineffectually on the other side of the stage.

Rarely have I seen such incompetence.

Connie gave a low whistle. 'My God. If Callow was pissed off with Edwin it's hardly to be wondered at, is it? Imagine picking up your newspaper and reading that. If somebody wrote something like that about you, you'd feel like killing the bugger.'

When the bell had sounded for mid-morning break the next day, Joel took his exercise book to his teacher. She was sitting at her desk. In a minute she would be leaving to go to the staff room. 'I brought my book back, Mrs Chandler,' he said, putting his English exercise book down on her desk before her.

She thanked him and asked, 'Did your parents read it?'

'Yes, Miss.'

'And did they like it?' she said.

'Yes, Miss. They thought it was very good.'

'And so it is.' Behind him the last of the other children were trooping out into the playground.

'I got some stamps, Miss,' he said after a moment.

'Stamps? You mean foreign stamps?'

'Some are foreign and some are English.'

She glanced at her watch. 'You collect stamps, do you?'

'Well, no, Miss. Not really. They were given to me.'

'Oh, well, that was very nice.'

'Mr Callow gave them to me.'

'Oh?'

'Mr Callow. You remember, miss. I wrote about him in my composition.' He pointed to his exercise book and added, lowering his voice, 'It was his roses I took.'

'Yes, I know, Joel. I remember.' She gave him a bright smile. 'Well, that was very nice of him, wasn't it? I expect that was his way of saying that after what had happened you were friends, yes?'

'Yes, Miss.'

'I should think that's what it was.'

He nodded. 'Yes, Miss. I didn't tell him I didn't collect stamps. He thought I did.'

'Well,' she gave a little shrug, 'that's all right. It's the thought that counts, isn't it?'

'Yes, Miss.'

She pulled some papers towards her, banked them, and replaced them on the desk.

'He sent me a note, too,' Joel said.

'With the stamps, you mean?'

'Yes. The stamps were in an album, and the note was along with them.'

'And what did he have to say?'

'I don't know, Miss.' He gave a little laugh. 'I couldn't read it.'

'You couldn't read it? You? Joel Forrest? Your reading ability is very high.'

'This wasn't written in English. It was in some other language. Some foreign language.'

'Which language? Do you know?'

'No, I don't know.'

'Did your parents know? Did they read it?'

He laughed again. 'They didn't get a chance, Miss.'

She smiled along with him. 'What d'you mean, they didn't get a chance?'

'Well, it *went*. I took it out of the stamp album and I was just looking at it when the wind came up and blew it out of my hand.'

She was silent for a moment, then she said, 'How very strange, Joel. I wonder what caused that.'

'I don't know. You should have seen it, Miss. It was really weird. It went right up the stairs and into the bathroom and into the bath. When my dad took it out the writing had all gone.'

'The writing had gone?'

'Yes, all of it.'

'Couldn't you see at all what had been written there?'

'No, it was just like a plain piece of paper. Like new.' He smiled. 'Except that it was wet.'

Her smile remained. 'I'm not surprised, having fallen into the bath. And what happened to it then?'

He shrugged. 'Nothing. My dad threw it away. It wasn't any good.'

She said nothing to this but sat looking down at her desk, so that Joel wondered after a few moments whether she had forgotten he was there. She had not. Raising her head she gave him a warm smile, looked at her watch again, then sighed and said, 'I must get to the staff room, Joel.' She picked up her bag and stood up. 'And you must go out and get some air.'

'Yes, Miss.' Joel turned towards the door.

As he did so she said, 'When did this happen, Joel? Your getting the stamp album?'

He turned back to her. 'I got it on Friday, Miss. But I found the note yesterday. In the morning. That's when it fell into the bath.'

'I see.' She nodded. 'Right.'

In the doorway he stopped again. 'Miss?'

'Yes, Joel?'

'It's my birthday on Thursday.'

'Is it?'

'I shall be nine.'

'Yes, I know.'

'I'm getting a dog.'

She smiled. 'Are you? What kind?'

'We're not sure yet. One that's not too big, though.'

'Well, whatever you get I'm sure it's going to be just great.'

'Yes, Miss.'

She nodded. 'Good. Off you go, then.'

'Yes, Miss.' He turned to go again.

'And Joel?'

'Yes, Miss?'

'Be careful, won't you?' She gave a little laugh.

After he had left the room she remained standing at her desk, looking at the door through which he had gone.

There was some excitement on Thursday morning for Joel's birthday. He needed no urging to get up, and was dressed and having his breakfast well before the postman arrived. As he ate he unwrapped the little gifts that the girls had given him. From Lydia he had a book on trains, and from Kitty a set of felt-tip pens. He thanked them, and then turned inquiringly to his parents. Reading his look, Connie said, 'You'll just

185

have to be patient a while longer,' and he groaned as if waiting were beyond him. Five minutes later the postman came ringing the bell and Joel opened the door and took the little pile of mail that was held out to him, thanking the postman and also informing him that it was his birthday.

Back at the breakfast table he sorted out the post. Thee were four cards for him, one from each of the girls, one from Jane and Mrs Stocks, and a fourth from his parents. This last was actually two cards— the anticipated birthday card and also a special one that Jack had made himself. Two days previously, while the children were at school, he had used some of the art materials that had been Mary's to make a large, elaborate gift voucher. In elegant script, painted in gold and silver, the beautifully made card announced:

THIS VOUCHER ENTITLES THE BEARER
JOEL MARK FORREST, TO ONE DOG,
OF A BREED TO BE YET DETERMINED.
IT COMES WITH ALL THE LOVE OF HIS
PARENTS AND HIS SISTERS

Jack and Connie had rarely seen such joy, and as Joel whooped and laughed, and proudly passed the card to his sisters, they exchanged self-satisfied glances.

'When can we get him, Dad?' Joel asked. 'When can we go and get my dog?'

'Well,' Jack replied, 'when you come out of school we'll pick up a paper and look through the ads, shall we? See what's available. And if there's something, we might be able to go and look at him over the weekend.'

Joel happily agreed to this, and minutes later he and

the girls, who were almost as excited as he was over the promised pet, were kissing Jack goodbye and setting off with their mother for school.

After they had gone noisily out of the front door, Jack poured himself another cup of coffee and picked up the rest of the mail. There were a couple of letters in connection with his work, a bill, and something in a large brown envelope. He thought at first that it must contain a script, perhaps one of his own, for rewrites, though he was not expecting to receive such a thing. Also, there was nothing on the envelope to indicate that it had come from the BBC. Tearing it open he drew out not a script but a large, hardback notebook. He stood for a few moments looking at the familiar appearance of the object before realization came to him. He opened it and saw the handwriting, the dates of the first and final entries. It was the last of Edwin's journals, the one he had searched for but had been unable to find.

Chapter Ten

There was a typewritten, unsigned letter with the journal. It said:

Dear Mr Forrest,
The accompanying item belongs to you. I am sending it at this time for the simple reason that I think it imperative that you read it without further delay. I have no wish to sound melodramatic, but I believe it holds information that you would do well to heed. Further, and at the risk of sounding like a complete crackpot, I would like to give you some advice—and that is to take Joel and the rest of your family away from here at the earliest opportunity. I do not mean within the next year or years, or even the next month; you should leave now, before it is too late. Rather than that I should waste precious time trying to give you believable reasons for what must seem very strange advice,

189

I urge you to read your uncle's journal. He
became aware of the truth—though his
awareness came too late to help him.

When he had finished reading the letter he sat for a
while as if stunned, just staring at it. One part of his
mind wanted to insist that it was nothing more than
a joke, a sick joke, but at the same time he could not
ignore the sensation of real fear that sat upon him like
a cold sweat. He read the letter again. Who had written it? And why? And what was this unspecified threat
that was apparently so near?

He turned to the journal. Most of the pages were
blank. The first entry was dated Monday, 6 February,
following on from the last entry in the previous journal without a break. He began to read.

As before, Edwin's writings seemed mostly concerned with the opera and, after that, with Mary and
their day-to-day living. He wrote that he had received
some new opera recordings from *The Gramophone*
magazine for the purpose of reviewing them. He
wrote also of a production of *Turandot* that he had
been to see at Covent Garden. It was all very innocu-
ous and anodyne. But then, turning a page, Callow's
name seemed to leap out at him. At the end of a long-
ish entry dated 11 February, Edwin had written:

As fate would have it I bumped into Callow today
in the village. I'd called at the Wheatsheaf's off-
licence for a bottle of whisky and ran into him
outside. I wanted no reprise of my last, and very
unpleasant, encounter with him. That was
almost exactly six years ago and it's still very
vivid in my memory. So today, thinking
discretion the better part of valour, I would have

ignored him and gone on. He stopped me, however (with a smile, yet!), and before I realized what had happened I found myself in conversation with him, if conversation it could be called—he did most of the talking. I could scarcely believe it: Callow apologizing for the things he had said. Clearly, then, notwithstanding the time that has passed, he remembers it as well as I. I really didn't know what to say. I was certainly not about to retract any of my comments on his *Traviata* fiasco, though I have to admit that I regret voicing them publicly, mainly because of their ramifications. I understood that they caused his position as newly elected director of the opera group to be much canvassed by the committee.

But that's all in the past now, according to him, anyway. Now with him it was all a matter of let's let bygones be bygones. We both live in this small community, so let's put our artistic differences aside and try to be friends. Well, friends never, I thought. I loathe the man, and no amount of apparent good will on his part is ever likely to change that. But I went along with it. One has no option, and while it wouldn't bother me if we never spoke again I have to think first of Mary. She's had enough problems with him, and since he also assured me that he regrets being a nuisance where she's concerned, I accepted his apologies.

Callow's name appeared again a few pages on. In the entry for 16 February, Edwin had written:

A ring at the doorbell this afternoon while Mary

was at school. No caller on the step, but a package left in the porch. From Callow, it turned out. An LP set of *I Puritani*. Czech pressing, imported. Anna Moffo and Gianni Raimondi. Callow remembered from long past conversations that I admired Moffo's radiant and agile soprano. I had never heard this recording before (taken from an Italian television production) and I was delighted to get the chance to hear it now. It's only on loan, of course. The accompanying note said merely: 'I know you love La Moffo, so enjoy this with my best wishes. You might care to make a tape of it. Anyway, return it when you wish. There's no hurry for its return.'

I did so enjoy it. A lovely recording, a little truncated—to meet the exigencies of the TV programme's format, I should think—and with Raimondi straining a little at times for the high notes, but nevertheless a fine interpretation. When I'd finished listening to the record set, I found myself actually feeling grateful to Callow and almost began to think of him with some slight degree of warmth. I say almost—but not quite; mustn't get carried away there. Perhaps, though, it was a genuine attempt on his part to bury the hatchet and put the past where it should be. I'm willing to, though my cynical nature does whisper, 'Beware the Greeks when they come bearing gifts.'

I cannot ignore, of course, his almost desperate eagerness to win the Plate. I think he wants this above everything, though he knows well that I no longer sit on the panel, so he can't be hoping to curry favour in that respect. Unless he hopes that I might not be averse to trying to influence the judges. I can't imagine he'd be that crude. He tells me he's now putting together a cast for the company's new production. They're doing Leoncavallo's *La Bohème*—a tricky piece. It's not as good as Puccini's but it has its own very definite attractions and would, I'm sure, were it not for Puccini's work, have a regular place in the popular repertory. I have to admire Callow for opting for such a project when others must be more immediately attractive. But however his production turns out, I have no intention of reviewing it—or of ever again reviewing anything of his. I wouldn't let myself get into such a situation a second time.

Following this there was a brief comment on a new biography of Benjamin Britten, and then the entry came to an end.

The next entry where Callow's name cropped up was dated 27 February:

I called at Callow's house today to return the *Puritani* set, and to thank him for his kindness. I've made a tape-cassette of it to keep. Knowing of my antipathy to cats, he kindly banished his moggy and invited me in for tea. Not altogether an easy tête-à-tête, but at least a step on the road to a better understanding. He once again touched on the matter of his pursuing Mary, and again expressed his regret at having made her unhappy. I told him that Mary had suffered considerable unhappiness in her marriage and only wanted a little peace. As far as he, Callow, was concerned, I added, if his past overtures to

Mary were indeed things of the past, then that
was where they should remain. We left it like
that and got on to other matters. When I
eventually left I think we were on better terms
than we've been for a very long time. That
evening I told Mary about our meeting. She was
sceptical, but naturally anxious for peace
between us all.

The next entry concerning Callow came just over a
week later, on 8 March. A brief one, it said:

Callow telephoned today to ask whether I was
familiar with Moffo's recital with Gerald Moore
at the piano. Songs by Schubert, Schumann,
Brahms and Strauss. I told him I was not aware
that she had even made such a recording. Yes,
he tells me, made towards the end of her career
and, further, if I'm interested, he knows a dealer
who has a copy. Apparently the record was never
issued in Britain. I hesitated on hearing his offer
to help. As much as I'd like the record I have no
wish to be beholden to the man for anything. My
hesitation was sufficient, though, and he at once
said, 'Leave it with me; I'll see what I can do.'

The rest of that day's entry concerned his work on
a biography of Donizetti that he had been engaged on
for a year or so.
Jack continued on through the journal. On 20
March came another mention of Callow's name:

A note through the letter box this morning. From
Callow, saying simply, 'The Moffo/Moore LP still
available, so I hope to have good news for you

soon.' Why is he being so nice?

The entries were drawing towards their end now. Over a period of several days he wrote on a variety of things: a Covent Garden production he had seen, a number of CD sets he had been playing for the purposes of reviewing, and, to a lesser extent, his daily life with Mary. On 31 March he wrote of having met one of the members of the opera society who was in Callow's new *La Bohème* production. Apparently there was much enthusiasm for it in the group.

In the entry for 9 April Callow's name was there again:

Callow brought me the record yesterday evening. Actually brought it round to the house. Mary answered the door to him (poor Mary!) but he would not hand the LP to her and insisted on giving it to me personally. She invited him in and then made herself scarce. It matters not a bit he has voiced regrets over the past where she is concerned; the man is anathema to her, and I don't believe there is anything now that is likely to change her feelings. Anyway, he came in and, with obvious pleasure, gave me the record. 'A rare one this,' he told me. 'And although used, nonetheless perfect.' Of course I was grateful to him; who wouldn't be? I asked him to stay and have a drink, but he wouldn't; said he had to get back. He asked very little for the record. I played it as soon as he had gone. It's beautiful, and although Moffo's voice is obviously mature and has less agility, still it's a very fine performance. There are some passages and instances of phrasing, particularly in the Schumann, where the tone and the interpretation are quite exquisite.

The entry for 10 April was very brief:

We all must die sooner or later, and if H was indeed telling the simple truth then my end is in sight, not within years, nor even months, but in a matter of days. Perhaps this will be the last entry I shall write in this journal.

It was not the last entry. Below it, in an entry dated 11 April, he had written:

I have always regarded myself as a pragmatic man, a realist, and so even now I find it almost impossible to believe that such a thing could happen. Not that the final proof is here, of course—that can only become evident with my death, and whether I shall be aware of that proof remains to be seen. Will there perhaps be a moment when I shall be able to acknowledge it? Some split second before the dark when I shall see that it meant what I now believe it does? I am not ready. And who will take care of my dear Mary?

The following day's entry, dated 12 April, said:

And still I'm here, and on waking this morning I murmured those very words aloud. But for how much longer? I wonder. Was H right? I still ask myself that question over and over. And even while I tell myself, repeatedly, that such things can't happen in this corporeal world, still the signs are all there, just as H said they were for him. The odd thing is that I almost feel I could have prevented it. I saw the runes, and took no steps to prevent it happening. Though maybe I'm just telling myself that; perhaps in reality it was out of my hands in more ways than one. Perhaps I'm doing her no favour by trying to protect her from what I now see as the truth. At the same time, when I awake to the daylight and the sun again each morning I start to believe that this is one time when it will not happen. Yet H said there was no escape once the runes were cast; that death was inevitable. And he mentioned names—names of past victims, he claimed, though at the time I took little notice of more than a couple. But if he was right then he himself was certainly not the first, and neither were the Simoneaus.

One line was left blank here, and then the next entry began:

Thursday, April 13th. It's almost midnight. I couldn't rest today. I've hardly stirred from the house these past five days, and seen no one apart from Mary. George won't be coming round any more; I've told him we shan't be needing him. I wrote just now that I've seen no one. Not true; I've seen *him*, of course. I saw him today. I hoped there might be a way to reverse it and so this morning I made the attempt. I was unsuccessful, however, and when I think back on it I can't really see that I could ever have entertained any great hope of achievement. Not realistically, anyway. And none there was. He laughed in my face. Well, of course he was prepared for such an event, and was ready for the most imaginative of ruses on my part. As must have happened in the past, I should think, for I can't believe that this is a phenomenon of just the last few years. There is ages' old evil in this. And even as I write, the time is going by.

When I got back to the house I sat like some frightened rabbit in the gaze of a stoat. Mary is upset, of course. She wants to know what is happening, why I will not venture out, why I sent George away. I can't tell her, for such a thing is truly incredible. I did not believe H at first, so how can I expect anyone to believe me? Oh, but I am tired—exhausted, rather—but I don't know how I shall sleep. I have taken all the precautions I can think of. I must try to sleep for a while.

It's gone three in the morning now, and some little time has passed since I wrote the above. I slept for a while and then awoke bathed in sweat. I am writing now merely in order to keep myself occupied; anything to make the minutes pass. I feel sure that if I can get through today I shall be safe. I'm sure it's so. But how slowly the minutes pass. I was never in my life before so aware of the slowness of time. Before, it would never go slowly enough, but how different now. When I think of

And here the entry ended, in the middle of a sentence. Jack turned the page, but there was nothing more. Edwin had broken off writing at that point and never gone back to it. But then Jack realized that it had been written in the early hours of 14 April, and on that morning Edwin had died.

* * *

When Connie got back from Barfield she found Jack sitting in the study. She stood in the doorway looking at him as he sat with several of the journals on the desk before him.

'What's so interesting?' she said.

He did not answer.

As she began to take off her coat she said, 'I thought you might have cleared the breakfast table by now.'

Now, still not looking at her, he said quietly, 'This came in the post this morning. It's Edwin's last journal.'

She frowned. 'It came with the post?'

'Yes.'

'Where did it come from?'

'I don't know.' He hesitated for a second then handed her the letter. 'This was in with it. In with the journal.'

She put her coat over the back of the chair, took the letter and sat down. When she had finished reading it she looked at him and said, 'Is this for real?'

He shrugged. 'You tell me.'

She studied his expression for a moment, then said, 'I don't like this at all.'

'No, me neither.'

'It's a joke,' she said. 'Some stupid bastard's idea of a joke. Well, I don't think it's so funny.' She stared at him. 'Say something, Jack. Say something.'

'I think you should read this.'

He held the journal out to her. As she took it she said: 'Where's it been all this time? Why wasn't it here along with the others?'

'I don't know.'

He reached out and took the journal from her, flicked through it and handed it back. 'There,' he said, indicating with his finger, 'April the tenth. "We all must die sooner or later . . ." Read on from there.'

She frowned, then bent her head to the open page and began to read. He sat watching her for some moments, then got up and went out to the kitchen where he cleared away the breakfast things and put on the kettle. Returning to the study he saw that she was reading an entry close to the start of the journal.

'Did you read the last entries?' he asked.

'Yes. Then I went to the beginning.' A little silence, then she added, 'I don't understand what's happening.'

'Neither do I.'

She lowered her gaze, looking unseeing at the desk between them. 'You say to yourself that it's just an old man rambling, letting his imagination run away with him, but then you realize that . . .' She gave a shrug of helplessness. 'Well, you can't escape the fact that he died that day, can you? It was the fourteenth when he died, wasn't it?'

'Yes. Just a little while after he wrote that last part. That unfinished bit.'

Touching fingertips to the letter she said huskily, 'Why does the writer specifically mention Joel? Do you think he's in some—some kind of danger?'

He did not answer.

'Is he?' she said, her tone demanding now, touched with fear.

'Oh, God,' Jack said, spreading his hands before him, 'I don't know. How *can* he be? It doesn't make sense. Nothing of it makes any sense.'

'No,' she said, 'except that here we have a man believing that he's going to die, and within hours—perhaps minutes, for all we know—his fears are realized. And what's at the bottom of it all? What's behind it?'

She slapped the flat of her palm on the open page of the journal. 'Is this whole thing somebody's weird idea of a joke?'

'Do you think it might be?' He watched as her chin quivered and tears glistened in her eyes.

'It's what I want to believe,' she said. 'But I'm afraid it's not. And I'm afraid for Joel.' She looked at the letter again. 'Somebody's telling us that Joel is in danger. And if Edwin's journal is to be relied on then that danger is very real. What are we going to do?' There was desperation in her tone. 'If we believe that letter then we've got to pack up and get away from here. Take the children and go.'

'How can we do that?'

She said nothing for a moment, then she gave a little moan, a plaintive, keening sound. 'No,' she said, 'it can't be true. This isn't happening.' Getting up from the chair she stepped aimlessly to the window. 'We've got to do something. If Joel's in some kind of danger we've got to do something before it's too late.'

Jack got up, moved to her and wrapped her in his arms. After resisting him briefly she gave in and let him hold her.

'Don't worry,' he said, 'it's going to be all right.'

'Don't worry?' She looked into his eyes. 'How can you say that? Somebody's written telling us that our son's life is in danger. How can I not worry?'

'He'll be all right. I promise you. Connie, nothing's going to happen to Joel. Believe me. We won't let anything happen to him.'

She burst into tears at this. 'I couldn't bear it. Not Joel. Not Joel.'

'Please,' he said again, 'don't worry.'

At this she cried out, 'Don't keep saying that! Don't

tell me not to worry! *Do* something! We've got to *do* something!'

He held her closer. 'Connie, please. Let's go over this. I mean it—I promise you that Joel is safe—and he will be safe. I'd never let anything happen to him.'

After a few moments she grew calmer. She pulled herself free and sat down again. Jack sat facing her.

'If there is a threat—against him,' Connie said, 'then where is it coming from? It's got to come from somewhere. But where? And why? He's just a little boy. He's never done harm to a living soul.'

'Listen,' Jack said after a moment, 'I know how people scoff at any idea of—of supernatural evil, but supposing there *is* something . . .'

'Some evil power? Is that what you mean?'

He nodded. 'That's what Edwin says, more or less. And he says that his friend Harold Sanders was a victim of it.'

'Does he?'

'He might not say it in so many words, but that's what he means. And if we read his journal correctly, then the same thing happened to Edwin himself.'

'But this power,' Connie said, 'where does it come from? If both Edwin and his friend were destroyed, then who was responsible? Who wanted them dead? Was—was it Callow?'

Jack said nothing. The whole thing was like a nightmare. How could a man exert power to cause the death of another? But that, in effect, was what the journals were saying.

From the kitchen came the sound of the kettle switching off. Jack stepped to the door. 'I'll make the coffee.' As he got into the kitchen the telephone began to ring. He called out, 'I'll get it,' and lifted the receiver. It was Rachel Barlow, the producer of *Fat Chance*.

Was it possible, she wanted to know, for him to get to the Television Centre in Wood Lane for a production meeting on Tuesday next? One of the scenes in the seventh episode threatened to pose a few problems, and they were anxious to get it sorted out at an early stage. He made a note of the date and time of the meeting and said he would be there.

'How's the rest of the series coming on?' Rachel asked.

'Fine,' he replied. 'Fine.'

'Do you reckon you'll have them finished soon, the remaining episodes?'

'Soon, yes. A few more weeks.'

'Good.' There was relief in her voice. 'That's good, because we're running pretty tight on this one.'

'I know. Don't worry, though. I'll have it done. I've had a few disturbances, but things are looking a little easier now . . .'

When he had replaced the receiver he made two mugs of instant coffee and then just stood there, looking out over the rear garden. Dully he observed the signs of George's work. He had already done a considerable amount on the shrubs, pruning them and getting rid of the dead wood. Over to the right in the distance Jack could just see the top of the bonfire that George had been laying. He suddenly thought of Sarah reading Callow's note and then having it torn from her hands by the wind and getting burnt in the bonfire. He thought of her death from the attack of the bees. How terrible that had been. And how very odd, too, the fact that he himself had not sustained one single sting.

Returning to the study he placed the mugs of coffee on the desk. Connie was reading the journal. As he sat down she said, 'When Edwin speaks of H, he means

203

Harold Sanders, doesn't he?'

'Yes.'

She nodded, then looked back at the open pages before her. 'He says that Harold was not the first victim. He also mentions some people called Simoneau. Do you know who they are?'

'No. I've never heard of them.'

'He says that Harold spoke of other people too, mentioned other names, though he couldn't remember who they all were. I suppose he didn't take it that seriously at the time.'

'I guess not. But who would?'

'And it's connected with these runes, isn't it? That's what Harold believed, anyway. And Edwin too, eventually, even though he was so sceptical at the start.' She fell silent for a moment, then took up the letter. 'Who do you think sent this?'

'I've no idea. If we knew that we might be able to find out a bit more. Find out what's behind it all.'

'It's Callow,' she said with a confirming nod. 'It's Callow who's behind it.'

'So it would seem.'

She nodded again. 'It is. Edwin doesn't say so, but there's no doubt that that's who he's talking about. Do you know what happened between Edwin and Callow? After Edwin slated Callow's opera production of *La Traviata*, he refers to a "very unpleasant" encounter.'

'Yes. Edwin said it happened almost exactly six years earlier, so I looked in his journals for that time. There's a reference to a confrontation he had with Callow in the village one day. Apparently Callow told him he didn't know as much about opera as he liked to think, and that he'd get even with him for what he'd written about him.'

Connie said after a moment, 'You don't think Callow could have sent us this letter, do you?'

'Why should he do that? If he's responsible for these terrible things, it seems hardly likely he'd write to us like this. This letter's from someone who wants to help us, not harm us.'

'And do you think that Callow's out to do us harm?'

'God, I don't know.'

'Well, I think so. Look at what happened with Edwin. Callow had very good reason not to like him after that scathing review in the paper, and you say now that he even said he'd get his own back, but then suddenly Callow's whole attitude towards him changes, and he starts being very friendly—bringing the records for him and all that business. And Edwin was suspicious, too.' She leaned forward in her chair, shoulders hunched. 'What are we going to do, Jack?'

He couldn't meet her eyes. He could think of nothing to say. He had promised that all would be well, but he had not the slightest idea of what to do to ensure that it would be so.

Chapter Eleven

After lunch, which neither felt much like eating, they decided they had better do something about Joel's promised puppy. From Mrs Stocks's shop they picked up copies of some of the regional papers and scanned the classified ads. There was not a great deal of choice in the various breeds of puppies available, but they eventually found an ad offering yellow labrador pups for sale in Eversham. Jack at once telephoned the number and made arrangements for Connie and himself to drive over that afternoon.

Eversham was on the far side of Pangbourne, and following directions they arrived some forty minutes later at a small house on the outskirts of the village. Whatever reservations they had felt as to the breed of the puppies vanished at the sight of the appealing little animals, and twenty minutes later they were driving away with one of the male puppies lying on a rug in Connie's lap.

In Pangbourne they stopped off at the supermarket

to buy pet food and a collar and lead and a few other accessories, and then drove on back to the house. Ten minutes later they were starting off in the car again, this time heading for Barfield and the children's school.

Five minutes after their arrival at the gates they saw Lydia and Kitty coming across the playground towards them.

'Are we going to phone up about Joel's puppy?' Lydia said as she came to their side.

'We'll see when we get home,' Connie replied. As she spoke, another cluster of children came out onto the playground and she saw Joel emerge from a crowd of boys and come dashing eagerly across the playground.

'Dad,' he said as soon as he reached them, 'did you get the papers?'

'That's nice,' Jack said. 'Whatever happened to hello, nice to see you? Anyway, what are these papers you're talking about?'

Joel groaned. 'Oh, Dad, you know. With the ads for the puppies.'

'Oh, those papers. Yes, we'll get them.'

'I'm not so sure,' Connie said as she turned, heading for the car. 'You've got to have a voucher. You don't get anywhere without a voucher.'

'I've got one.' Joel dipped into his pocket and brought out the now much battered and thumbed card that he had received that morning.

'Let me see that.'

With a sigh Joel handed it to her. She looked at it with a jaundiced eye, said, 'Hmm,' and handed it on to Jack. He looked at it as if he had never seen it before, and read aloud what was written on it: 'This voucher entitles the bearer, Joel Mark Forrest, to one dog, of a breed to be yet determined.' He turned to Connie. 'It seems to be in order.'

Joel groaned and grinned. It had all happened before.

'OK,' Connie said. 'Let's go, then.'

A little while later as they neared Princes Lane Joel said, 'I thought we were going to stop somewhere and get the papers—to look at the ads.'

'We'll try to do it later,' Connie said. 'We have to call in at home first.'

At The Limes, Jack halted the car and he and Connie got out. 'You stay here for a minute,' Connie said to the girls; then to Joel: 'Just give us a hand for a minute, will you? Then we can go off to get your newspapers if you still want to.'

Willingly, Joel followed Connie and Jack into the house. In the hall Connie said to him, 'You can do me a favour before we go out, Joel. There's a cardboard box up in our room. Will you go and get it, please.'

Joel ran up the stairs as fast as he could, while Connie and Jack watched him go. They waited, listening, as he opened the door to the main bedroom where the puppy waited, and then a moment later heard his voice: 'Oh, *Mum! Dad!*'

While Jack laid down house rules over the care and training of the dog, Connie prepared sandwiches. The children ate distractedly; it was one of the few times when they were so caught up in something else that they were without their usual appetites. Joel made so much fuss of the puppy that in the end Connie suggested that for its own sake it should be left alone for a while. He complied for a time, but then the temptation was too great and once again he was taking the puppy up into his arms.

Jack left them to it and carried a mug of tea into his study. He sat down at his desk while the thoughts came pouring into his mind, tumbling over and over. What was he going to do? Was Joel truly in danger? And if so, how could he be protected from that danger? Jack felt totally impotent. Without more knowledge it was like trying to fight whilst wearing a blindfold. Where did he begin? Where, in Joel's defence, was he to strike the first blow?

Voices came to him and he looked from the window and saw that Joel had taken the puppy into the back yard. With Lydia and Kitty looking on, he had set him down in the grass, moved some distance away and was calling him. 'Goldie, Goldie—here, boy.' He had named him too. Jack turned from the sight, his feeling of ineffectuality like a bitter taste in his mouth.

From a drawer he took the letter that had come with the journal. He read it again, but there was no clue as to its source. As he put it back in the drawer he saw there the envelope in which the letter and the journal had come. He drew it out, and looked at it. There was something about the handwriting that was familiar . . .

Later on when the children were having their supper, Jack went into the kitchen to join them. The puppy lay in a cardboard box beside the washing machine. And no, Connie was telling Joel, Goldie would not be allowed to sleep in his room; he must stay downstairs in the kitchen. And at the weekend, she added, they would go out and buy him a basket to sleep in.

'Shall we get a puppy too when we're nine?' Kitty asked. 'One each?'

'And have three dogs running around the house?'

Jack said. 'I'm afraid we'll have to think of something else.'

Kitty nodded and glanced at her sister, as if to say this was the answer she had expected. 'It's not fair,' she said. 'I don't think it's fair.'

Changing the subject, Connie said to Joel, 'So, how was school today? What did you do today?'

He shrugged. 'Oh, nothing much. We did nature study. I got a gold star.'

'Oh, that's good,' said Connie.

He nodded, pleased. 'I brought my book home for you to see. We did a thing about how seeds from flowers and trees get carried away and get planted in different places. D'you want to see it?'

'Please.'

He went into the hall and came back a few moments later carrying a blue exercise book. As he handed it to Connie, Lydia said, 'Everybody knows all about seeds and stuff.'

'Of course they do,' agreed Kitty. 'They get blown on the wind, like with dandelions. The seeds float about.'

'They don't *all* do it like that,' said Joel. 'Some seeds are carried by birds.'

Kitty snorted. 'Everybody knows that, too.'

'You didn't,' said Joel.

'I did. Of course I did.'

'Well, how do they do it, then?'

'Well,' she gave a shrug, 'they carry them in their beaks, of course.'

'Well, there you're wrong.' Joel's expression was all superiority. 'Because they don't. If you want to know, they swallow them.'

'They *swallow* them?'

'Yes, when they eat the berries and other fruits.'

'Well, of course. We all know that,' Lydia said.

'Everybody knows that birds eat berries.'

'Yes, well, that's how they carry the seeds from one place to another. In their stomachs.'

Kitty: 'In their *stomachs*?'

'Yes.'

'The seeds?'

'Yes.'

'Well, that's silly. If the seeds are in their stomachs how do they get them out again?'

'The seeds come out in their poo.'

'They don't!' Lydia looked shocked.

'Yes, they do. Mrs Chandler told us.'

'She didn't. She wouldn't say that.'

'She did.'

'That the seeds are in their poo? She didn't! She didn't, did she, Daddy?'

'I don't know,' Jack said. 'I wasn't there. But that's what happens.'

The girls' eyes were wide with disbelief.

'She didn't say poo, though,' Joel said. 'She said the seeds are in their droppings when they go to the toilet.'

Lydia shook her head. 'I think that's awful.'

'Well,' Joel said, 'it's true.' He pointed to the exercise book in Connie's hands. 'And we had to write about it and draw pictures.'

Kitty hooted. 'You drew a picture! Of a bird having a poo?'

'Of course not.' Joel flicked glances to Jack and Connie and raised his eyes to the ceiling.

'Of course he didn't,' Connie said. She nodded to Joel. 'Take no notice, Joel. It's very good work. Very good.' She handed the book to Jack. 'And what else did you do today?'

'The usual things. Sums and writing. I did some extra work at playtime, too.'

'What sort of extra work?'

'Oh, sorting out papers and things.'

'What d'you mean?'

'Mrs Chandler kept me in.'

'Kept you in?'

'Yes.'

'Why? Had you misbehaved?'

'No, she wanted me to help her in the classroom, she said. I helped her sort out some papers and books and things. I helped her all day. In the morning break and the afternoon one, and also after lunch. I helped her yesterday too. She had a lot she wanted to get done.'

Frowning, Connie said, 'That's all very well but you should have been out in the fresh air, not staying cooped up in the classroom all day.'

'I didn't mind; I liked doing it. It wasn't only me, anyway. In the afternoon she let Daniel stay in with me. We did it together.'

'That's all very well,' Connie said again. 'But surely a teacher can get her work done without having the pupils stay in to help. After all, what are they paid for? I think they—' She broke off as Jack laid a hand on her arm, and frowned at him, wondering why he had stopped her in mid-flow.

Disregarding her glance, Jack said, 'Your teacher Mrs Chandler wrote these comments in your exercise book, did she?'

Joel nodded. 'Yes, of course.'

'You like her, don't you?'

'Yes. She's leaving soon. We don't want her to go.'

A pause then Jack asked, his tone studiedly casual, 'Do you know where she lives, Joel?'

'In Ashampstead, I believe. Why?'

'Yes,' Connie added, 'why do you ask?'

'It's all right.' Still holding Joel's exercise book, Jack got up from his chair, left the room and went into the study. There he laid the open book on the desk and took the journal's envelope from the drawer. After studying them for a few seconds he reached for the local telephone directory. A minute later he was in the hall putting on his overcoat. Connie came out just as he was taking up the Citroën's keys from the hall table.

'Where are you going?' she said.

'To Ashampstead.' He kept his voice low. 'I think I know now who sent us Edwin's journal.'

'You know?'

'I think so.'

'But who?' Then she nodded as realization came. 'You think it was Joel's teacher?'

'Yes. And I'm going to talk to her if I can.'

'What makes you think she was the one?'

'The handwriting on the envelope the journal came in. I felt sure I'd seen it before. I had. It's the same as in his exercise book. But don't ask me anything else, because I don't know.' He turned, moving to the door. 'I'll be back as soon as I can.'

Chapter Twelve

The telephone directory had listed an R. Chandler in Ashampstead, at an address given as 4 Rupert Lane. Jack had driven through the village before, but had never had occasion to stop. The drive on this October evening took him some thirty-five minutes. He could see little of the place in the dark, but he remembered it as being a typical Cotswold village, with its few streets set round the green and the church. It was towards the church that he now made his way.

Rupert Lane, he discovered, ran close to the southern edge of the churchyard, and he pulled up outside number four and opened the front gate. The cottage was of Cotswold stone with a red-tiled roof and a neat, small front garden. He rang the bell. There was no response. He knocked and rang again, and then after standing there for a while got back into the car. He drove to the first junction where he turned the car round and headed back, bringing the car to a halt at a distance where he could see the entrance to number four. There he turned off the motor and settled down to wait, trying not to look conspicuous but feeling that he must stand out like a sore thumb.

Several cars went by as he sat there but none stopped, until some twenty-five minutes had passed and then a dark green Ford Fiesta drove past and turned in at the entrance to the short driveway to number four. He waited a few minutes, then got out of the car and walked to the cottage.

This time when he rang the bell the door was opened almost immediately by a tall woman with reddish hair. He recognized her at once from their brief meeting when Joel had begun as a pupil in her class.

'Yes?' There was no trace of a smile, and she glanced at him a little warily, while at the same time frowning in half-recognition.

'Mrs Chandler,' Jack said. 'Good evening.'

She nodded. 'Good evening.'

'Excuse me for just calling on you unannounced like this, but I had to see you.'

'Oh, yes? What about?'

Now that he was here and facing her he did not know how to begin. After a moment he said, 'We've met before, briefly. When my son joined your class. I'm Joel Forrest's father.'

She stiffened, and her eyes widened slightly. The change in her expression was small, but it was enough; he knew at once that he had not been mistaken.

'Please,' he said, 'I need to talk to you.'

'What about?' On the surface, at any rate, she seemed to be regaining her former composure.

He could feel his heart thumping. 'May I come in and talk to you? It's very important.'

'Well—what do you want to talk about? I haven't

got a lot of time. Usually the parents of my pupils come to the school to see me.'

'Yes, I know, but . . . Please—may I come in?'

She hesitated, then stepped aside. 'All right.'

'I'll try not to keep you.'

He moved past her into the hall with its low ceiling, and stone flags polished by decades of feet. Ill at ease, but trying not to show it, she led the way into the front room on the left, a pleasantly furnished sitting room with overstuffed chairs and sofa, and shelves lined with books. 'I'm sorry it's not too warm,' she said, 'but I've only just got in.'

They stood facing one another for a moment, then she said, 'Please, sit down.' He sat on the sofa, sure from her manner that she did not expect the conversation to be about Joel's grades. She remained standing there for a moment, then bent before the fireplace and set a match to the paper and wood that had been laid. That done, she sat in a chair facing him and lit a cigarette.

'I believe you wrote to me, Mrs Chandler,' Jack said.

She drew on her cigarette, avoiding his eyes. 'Did I? I don't recall doing so. When, exactly? Was it to do with Joel's work?'

'No, nothing to do with that.' He paused. 'Just this morning, in the post, we received a package. It contained a journal, one of a series of journals written by my late uncle. And a letter, unsigned—from you.'

She did not protest or deny his charge.

He went on, 'The letter we received warned us of danger to Joel and the rest of my family. It urged us to get away. The letter was typewritten, but not the envelope. I thought I'd seen the handwriting before, and then I realized where. It was yours. I'd seen it in Joel's exercise books.'

Bernard Taylor

For a moment she looked at him with opening mouth, as if about to protest, but she said nothing, only lowered her gaze to the smoke that curled up from her cigarette. In the silence Jack heard the crackle of the fire as it caught the wood, and then the sudden flurrying patter of rain on the window.

'It all fitted together,' he said. 'The first hint I got was when Joel came back today saying that you had kept him in class during break-time. You were keeping an eye on him, weren't you? Trying to look after him. Isn't that it? Making sure, as far as you were able, that he came to no harm.'

She studied her action as she tapped ash from her cigarette, then raised her eyes to his. 'It was the only practical thing I could think of doing. Once I'd written the letter, that is. You probably think I'm stark raving mad. I wouldn't blame you if you did.'

'No, I don't.' He shook his head. 'We've been worried sick. My wife—she's got herself into such a state. But if it's some kind of joke just tell us now. It would be a relief.'

'Do you think I could play that kind of sick joke?'

'No.'

'It's no joke, believe me. I wish to God it were. But you've read the journal. You either believe it or not.'

'I don't know what to believe.'

'At first I didn't believe it—when I heard about it from Mary, Edwin Maddox's daughter. But later I had to. I had no choice. I can't explain it. I don't pretend to understand what's been happening.' With a sharp little stabbing movement she stubbed out her cigarette in the ashtray, then got to her feet. 'I wish you hadn't come,' she said, and there was deep anxiety in her expression. 'I don't want to become involved in all this. That's why I sent the journal and the letter

218

anonymously. I thought that once you'd read the journal you could take it from there. I wanted nothing to do with it. It's not my concern, anyway.'

'But you've become concerned,' he said.

'No, no.' She shook her head. 'This whole thing—it's nothing to do with me. I've never had anything to do with John Callow and that's the way I want to keep it.'

'So,' he said, 'you believe it's Callow who's responsible for this whole business.'

She nodded. 'Yes, I think so.' She stepped to the fireplace and in silence laid a couple of logs on top of the crackling kindling. She remained staring into the flames for a moment or two, then said, 'I really would be glad if you'd go. I'm sorry, but this whole thing makes me so uneasy.'

He said nothing.

'Please,' she said, 'don't drag me into this.'

'Mrs Chandler,' he said, 'I don't want to drag you into anything, but you can't expect me to leave it like this. What is it you know? I have to find out as much as I can.'

'I don't really know anything,' she said. 'I'm just—guessing at things.' She sat down and lit another cigarette. After a moment she went on, 'I was with Mary on the day she died. I saw everything that happened. Later I was called to give evidence at the inquest, but I couldn't tell what I saw as the truth. It would have seemed so bizarre. No one would have believed me, anyway.'

He frowned. 'I don't understand.'

She shook her head, briefly closing her eyes as the memories came back. 'Her death was put down to an accident, but it was not that. It wasn't that at all.'

'She was run down by a car or a lorry or something, wasn't she?'

'Yes, but it wasn't an accident.'

'It wasn't?'

She said nothing.

'Are you suggesting that it might have been suicide?'

'No. No way.'

'How can you be so sure?'

'I knew her well. We were good friends, and we'd just spent some time arranging a trip to Italy. She had a few preoccupations, but she wasn't in any way suicidal. On the contrary, she was very positive. She was more positive than I'd seen her for some time. She was making so many plans, looking forward to the future with real optimism. No, Mary didn't want to kill herself.'

'Well, if it wasn't that, and it wasn't an accident, what was it?'

'I don't know. I can't explain it. One moment she's standing beside me, laughing and talking enthusiastically about our trip to Italy, and the next thing I know she's calmly walking out into the path of a lorry. She didn't have a chance. There was no way the driver could stop in time.' She spread her hands before her. 'You tell me how I could have told something like that at the inquest. So her death was given as an accident. But it wasn't. I'll never believe that it was.'

'But if she knowingly walked out in front of the lorry, then—'

'Then she meant to do it? No. Listen, I was there. It was almost as if she had no control over herself at that moment. As if she was—was being compelled to do it. I don't know.'

After a moment Jack said, 'How did you come to have my uncle's journal?'

'Mary had brought it with her to show me. I didn't read it, but afterwards, after the—accident I picked up her belongings and took them home. Later, going through her things, I found it and—I read it then.'

'And?'

'I said just now that she'd been preoccupied to a degree. Well, she was. For one thing she was still fretting over her father's death. It had been a year since he'd died, and although she seemed to be getting over the fact of his loss, and adjusting well, still she was concerned over the way it had happened. I didn't pay it a lot of attention, really— her fretting, I mean. I think I just put it down to some kind of rather irrational worry. It was only later that I came to realize that there was more to it than that.'

'When you'd read the journal, you mean.'

'Yes. That, added to some of the things she said to me that day.'

'What did she say?'

'Well, she'd had this very unpleasant confrontation with Callow a week earlier and I suppose it was that that got her back to worrying about her father's death. She'd also found her father's last journal, and that set her off too. It had made her think of certain odd things that had happened shortly before he died.'

'Such as?'

'I remember when we were sitting in the restaurant she got the journal out of her bag. It was obviously very much on her mind. She spoke about her father having written about some runes—whatever they were; I didn't really know. But she said they had been destroyed, and that their destruction had brought about her father's death. I asked her what she was talking about and she said Callow had suddenly become very friendly with her father, getting him rare records and things like that. She said Callow sent her father this paper with runes written on it. And they were destroyed.'

'How were they destroyed?' Jack was aware of the quickening of his heartbeat as the thought came to him that everything was following a pattern, a pattern that was beginning to seem inescapable, inevitable.

'She said the paper was burnt. Which was what her father said in his journal.' She sat in silence for a moment or two as if preoccupied, then said, 'Can I get you a drink? A Scotch or some tea or coffee or something?'

'No, thank you. Go on, please.'

'I don't know that there's any more to tell you.'

'About Mary. What about Mary?'

'There's nothing more to tell. Callow pursued her. Did you know that?'

'I was told something.'

'She wouldn't have anything to do with him, though. Who would? He's such a creep.'

'You said—well, you think Mary's death was strange . . .'

'It was. To say the least.'

'Are you saying that—that you think Callow had something to do with it?'

She drew on her cigarette as she gazed past him, her eyes focused on some distant point. 'It sounds insane, doesn't it? I mean, Callow was nowhere around when Mary died. But it all fitted in.'

'She received something from him too? A paper with symbols on it? Runes?'

'Well, I don't know about that. She never said so. But I realized afterwards that she could have done.'

'What makes you say that?'

'On that last day in the restaurant she told me that

222

Callow had been to her house to see her a week before. He gave her a letter, she said. But she didn't read it. She said she'd told him she'd burn any further correspondence from him. And apparently that's what she did. He gave her this letter and she put a match to it there and then, right in front of him. So I suppose it's quite possible that he could have put a paper with the runes on it with the letter or—' She broke off, shook her head then added, 'Jesus Christ, I can't believe we're having this conversation. I mean, look at us, sitting here talking about—well, I don't know what. All I know is that if we're to believe Mary and her father, there's someone in Valley Green—Callow—who has the power to bring about a person's death. And he does it by sending some weird coded messages or something. And that he's done it to both Mary and her father.'

'And to Harold Sanders, the man who ran the opera company before Callow.'

'Three people, then.'

Jack nodded, then said quickly, 'No, four.'

'Four?' She peered at him, frowning.

'If such a thing could truly happen, then it's possible that my wife's mother was also one of his victims.'

Her eyes widened. 'Really? Are you serious?'

'I'm afraid so.'

He told her then of the incident when Callow had brought the chocolates for Sarah, of the note going spinning into the bonfire.

'And within a week she was dead,' he finished.

'I remember it happening,' she said. 'Her being attacked by the bees. Everyone in the area was talking about it. It was such a terrible thing.'

'It was the same pattern,' he said. 'A note from Callow that got destroyed. And then death for her, the

223

recipient of the note. But like an accident, of course, with Callow nowhere around.'

'But what could he have against your wife's mother? I mean, his antipathy towards Edwin Maddox was an accepted fact according to Mary, and also towards Mary herself when she rejected him. But he didn't even know your mother-in-law, did he? If he—' She broke off, then added: 'Was it to do with that business with the roses—with Joel taking his roses? I know about that. Joel wrote about it in one of his English compositions.'

'I know,' he said. 'Yes, she was involved in that business. She was with him when it happened, and she got very angry with Callow when he came to the house complaining and demanding that Joel be punished. But there was another incident as well, an earlier one when Callow's dog came into our garden and left his calling card. That made for a certain amount of bad feeling too. It was my wife and her mother who had a scene with him at that time.'

'I see.' She stubbed out her cigarette. 'And then his dog was killed, isn't that right? I remember hearing about that.'

'Yes. Where Callow's concerned I'm afraid it's been a catalogue of difficulties and catastrophes.'

'And then you say he became friendly, bringing chocolates to your mother-in-law.'

'Yes.'

'That's part of the pattern, isn't it? Or it would seem to be.'

'Yes.'

'Are you sure you won't have a drink? I'm going to have one.'

'No, really, thank you.'

She got up, went out of the room and came back a

minute later carrying a glass of Scotch and water. As she sat down the ice clinked in the glass.

'I find it so hard to accept that there's anything in this strange business,' Jack said. 'I mean, this isn't the dark ages. In no time at all we shall be hitting 2001, the first year of a new millennium. Sorcery, magic, witchcraft—no one believes in that stuff any more. The problems facing man today are all too tangible, with wars and famines devastating one country after another, and the rest of the world being destroyed by man's greed. If this is really happening, this business with Callow, then the irony is unbelievable. I mean, our lives are governed by science now, not by belief in charms and evil spells and ancient curses.' He shook his head. 'I just can't take it in.'

She took a swallow from her glass and said, 'I have the same problem. And I've told myself the same thing over and over again. But in the end you're faced with what's happening—or what seems to be happening, and you have to deal with that.'

Rain was falling quite heavily now, lashing at the window, driven on the wind. A particularly heavy flurry rattled the pane and they both turned and glanced towards the window. As they did so there came from the distance a low growl of thunder.

'Perhaps,' she said, turning back to face him, 'the thing to do is not to keep denying it, but to accept it, try to find some way to fight it.'

'That's what I find so hard—accepting it. And if it's true, if it really is happening, what can one do about it? There's nothing to go on. It's so far outside our experience.'

She nodded. 'It is. Where does one start?'

'It would be no good going to the police, would it . . .' He presented this as half statement, half question, as if hoping for some affirmation from her that would make the whole matter easily solved. In reply she gave a snort of derision.

'What would you say to them? "I believe there's someone who's intent on harming my family. He does it by using some kind of spell." That would go down well, wouldn't it?'

'I know. The idea's ridiculous. The only way is to put a stop to it myself. But how? If I don't know what I'm fighting, how can I begin to fight?'

On the horizon, lightning flashed, lighting up the room, followed seconds later by a crack of thunder. The storm was coming nearer. In the silence that followed the thunder's roll Jack said dully: 'I didn't tell you, but my wife also received a note from Callow.'

She paused with her glass halfway to her mouth and remained like that, waiting for him to go on.

He said, 'It was in with some opera programmes and newspaper clippings that he brought round to the house for her.'

'And what happened to it, the note?'

'She said she was looking at it, and in just the same way a wind came and tore it out of her hand. It got caught on the fireguard—otherwise it would have gone into the fire.'

'Where is it now?'

'In the envelope with the programmes and other papers. She put it back.'

'Did you get a chance to look at it?'

'Yes, we've examined it since then. Strangely, though, nothing happened.'

'What do you mean, nothing happened?'

'Nothing happened to it. I think perhaps it was different in some way from the others. When we studied it it didn't get blown away or anything. It was just like any other piece of paper. It didn't seem special in any way. Except for what was written on it.'

'What was that?'

'Hieroglyphics. Runes. We could make no sense of them. Though obviously they must have meaning to somebody.'

'To Callow.'

'Perhaps. Yes, perhaps.' He paused then said sharply, 'I've just thought of something. As I said, the paper that Connie received was caught on the fireguard. Perhaps that's the reason nothing happened to it when we looked at it together.'

'I don't get you.'

'Well, if there's some strange kind of power in the paper, or what is written on it, perhaps it has to be destroyed the first time round. But with Connie's it wasn't.' He shrugged. 'So perhaps—I mean, perhaps it's possible that having escaped destruction it has no power any longer.'

'I don't know,' she said helplessly.

'It's possible.' He said nothing more for a moment or two, then feeling his throat suddenly tighten and tears prick at his eyes, he said hoarsely, 'But with Joel it wasn't like that. The marks on the note he received were destroyed.' He leaned forward and put his head in his hands. 'I don't know what to do. Oh, God, I just don't know what to do. If anything should happen to Joel . . .'

He heard her get up and go out of the room again. He sat there while the thunder growled and the rain lashed at the window.

'Here, drink this.'

He lowered his hands to see that she had put a drink on the coffee table before him. He nodded his thanks. As he reached out for the glass he saw that his hand was shaking. She had brought him Scotch with ice and water. As he swallowed he felt the welcome warming of the liquid. 'I must be careful,' he said, his words sounding pathetic in his ears. 'I've got to drive.'

'That's not going to hurt you.' As he set the glass back on the table she added, 'When Joel told me what had happened I knew that somehow or other I had to try to warn you. I know it must have seemed very melodramatic, but I felt I had no choice.' She gave a faint smile, affectionate and melancholy. 'He's the nicest little boy, your son. You must be very proud of him.'

'Of course,' he said gruffly. He wanted to add, He's all I ever wanted in a son; he's one of the greatest joys of my life, but he kept the words to himself.

Ruth Chandler went on, 'When he joined my class after you'd moved here I knew, of course, that he lived at The Limes. And I suppose, knowing that, and the history of the place—what had happened to Mary and her father—I suppose I took a special interest in him. And then in his English composition he wrote the piece about taking the roses. He told me later whose roses they were. I don't know, perhaps then some little warning bells rang. And then he told me about Callow giving him a stamp album and of a note being inside with odd markings on it. When he told me that I went cold. Not that he was bothered by it. I think he found it rather amusing. I didn't know what to do for the best, though I knew I had to warn you. So as soon as I got home I wrote you the letter and packed it up with the journal and sent it off.' She picked up her cigarettes, lit one and then went on, 'I meant it, Mr Forrest. What I said in my letter. You've got to take your family away from here.'

He nodded. 'Yes.'

'That's why I'm going,' she said after a moment. 'I'm going up to York. I just don't want to be anywhere near Callow. He's evil. And I don't mind admitting that I'm afraid of him.'

'There's got to be a way to fight him, a way to combat this,' Jack said. 'There's *got* to be.' A thought occurred to him. 'Do you know of anyone named Simoneau?'

'Ah, yes, Simoneau,' she said. 'Your uncle mentioned the Simoneaus in his journal, didn't he?' She shook her head. 'I'm afraid I don't. The name rang a bell, but I couldn't say why.'

'My uncle believed the same thing happened to them, whoever they were. Maybe if I could find out something about them I might also find an answer to it all.'

'I can't help you there. As I say, the name rang a bell, but no more. And I didn't want to start digging, either. I didn't want to find out any more than I already knew.'

'Harold Sanders, too. The man my uncle wrote about, who ran the opera group before Callow came on the scene. My uncle was convinced that he was a victim. Do you know anything about him?'

'No, I don't. I came here after Mary returned to live with her dad, and by that time Callow had long been running the society.'

Jack nodded, took up his glass and drank from it. 'The thing is,' he said, not meeting her eyes, 'if Joel is under any kind of threat I don't know what factor time plays in it all. I mean, if this isn't all some nightmare, and it is real, then how—how long have we got?'

'It was a week with Mary,' she said. 'From the time of her burning Callow's letter to her death it was a week almost to the minute. And I believe with your uncle it was only a matter of days, too, wasn't it?'

'Yes. And the same with my wife's mother.' Quickly he put his glass down. Fear was rising in him like a flood. Perhaps there was not much time left for Joel. 'I must go,' he said. 'I've got to go.' Hardly pausing in his stride as he thanked her, he was crossing the room into the hall, moving towards the front door and running out into the storm.

Kitty flinched, cowering as another clap of thunder cracked nearby. 'Mummy, I'm frightened,' she said.

She and Lydia sat on either side of Connie on the sofa, pressing against her for comfort and reassurance. Joel lay in his stockinged feet on the rug before the fire, the puppy burrowing into the warmth of his arms. At any normal time they would all three have been in bed, but because of the storm Connie had said they might stay up for a while longer.

'There's no need to be afraid,' Connie said. 'We're quite safe.' She had drawn the curtains against the lightning, but there was no cutting out the sound of the thunder. 'Joel's not afraid, look. You're not, are you, Joel?'

'No,' Joel replied untruthfully, putting on a brave face in front of his sisters. He drew the puppy even closer. 'But Goldie is.' In his arms the puppy whimpered while his small body shook.

'The storm will soon pass,' Connie said. 'It'll soon be over.'

'When's Daddy coming back?' asked Lydia. 'I want Daddy to come home.'

'He'll be back soon,' Connie said. She thought for a moment then said, 'Let's play a game, shall we?'

'What shall we play?' This, without enthusiasm, from Kitty.

'We can play whatever you want.'

This led to an argument between the girls as to what game they should play. Kitty wanted to get out the Snakes and Ladders, while Lydia favoured a quiz game. Connie let them argue it out; at least while they were arguing their minds were off the storm.

Wriggling free of Joel's arms, Goldie moved to the door and stood there. Joel looked at him in amazement. 'Look, Mum!' he said. 'He's learning already— about going outside.' He got to his feet and went to the door.

Connie said, 'Well, even if he does want to go out now he'll feel differently when he sees what the weather's like. You'd better take him out to the kitchen and put him down on the newspaper.'

Joel opened the door to the hall, then bent and picked up the puppy. 'Come on, Goldie.' Holding the puppy in his arms, he carried him out to the kitchen and placed him on the newspaper that had been laid on the floor. The puppy stayed there for a moment then trotted off the paper and towards the kitchen door. Sitting before it he looked up and gave a whine. Joel looked down at him approvingly for a moment then murmured proudly, 'No, Mum, you're wrong. He doesn't want to go on the paper, he wants to go outside.'

Joel opened the door and the driving rain struck at his bare face and arms like cold needles. Goldie whined, and Joel gave a sympathetic nod. 'Yes, you're having second thoughts now, aren't you?' Then, as the puppy shrank back against his legs: 'It's all right, you don't have to go out in weather like this. I told you, you can go on the paper.' The storm seemed to be overhead now. There came a terrifying crack of thunder, so loud that Joel involuntarily stepped back, while at his feet Goldie whimpered again, though showing no signs of retreating.

'Make up your mind, Goldie,' Joel said. 'I'm getting wet standing here.'

And then, suddenly, giving a whimpering little whine, the puppy was off, leaping out over the threshold, down the step and onto the cement of the back yard. In a brilliant flash of lightning that lit up the scene Joel saw the little dog go darting away along the path, seconds later to be lost from his sight. He stood there for some moments, peering into the rain-lashed dark, but could see no sign of the puppy. 'Goldie!' he called. 'Goldie, come here, boy!'

Thunder clapped again and after another moment Joel, heedless of his unshod feet, was leaping over the step and dashing off in pursuit.

Jack's car had reached the house and was slowing, turning onto the drive when the beam of the headlamps caught a movement at the side of the house and he saw Joel come dashing through the rain.

Immediately Jack brought the car to a halt, tyres protesting on the gravel. Joel, eyes trained on the ground ahead, seemed to be running after something. And then Jack saw another figure, and there was Connie following round the side of the house. He saw then the object of Joel's pursuit as the puppy came running, a moment later coming to an abrupt halt in the middle of the lawn. In seconds Joel was on him, bending to scoop him up in his arms.

It was as he straightened and began to turn that the shaft of lightning struck, coming snaking down, forking down out of the sky. It took only a moment; less than a second. Jack saw it all. Connie, still some dozen yards away, was thrown violently to the ground. For a moment Joel, holding the puppy, seemed to be lit up, bathed in a blinding light that transfixed him. And then it was over. For a brief second Joel remained standing there, caught in the beam of the car's near-side lamp. Then, the dog still clasped in his arms, he toppled forward and fell face down into the wet grass.

Chapter Thirteen

As the days followed one after the other, the newspapers continued to give their reports of the agonies and problems afflicting the world at large and, domestically, of the government's struggle to keep its footing on the perilous slopes of the economic recession. The world did not stop with Joel's death. Outside The Limes it continued as usual, barely touched by the tragedy.

To Jack and Connie, though, it seemed that nothing would ever be the same again. And nor would it. Life had to go on but life would be different, would be as they had never known it, never conceived of it before.

Through the depths of his own misery Jack watched Connie going about her daily work, caring for them and for the house. For much of the time she was like an automaton, seemingly untouched by the little things of living. She cooked, she cleaned, she took the girls to and from school, but Jack knew, as with himself, that it was with only a part of her consciousness.

For the rest she seemed numb and detached.

Aware of the depths of her grief, Jack felt himself somehow constrained. If anyone had to be strong, he told himself, then it must be he, for if he gave way to the terrible all-consuming misery that threatened to overwhelm him he did not know what would happen.

The twins were coping far better with Joel's death than he and Connie. Their salvation lay in their youth, in which was an inherent resilience coupled with a lack of comprehension over the finality and reality of death. 'Where is Joel?' they had asked at the start. 'Daddy, when is Joel coming home?' And he would tell them again, as well as he could, that Joel would not come home again. And as the days passed they ceased to ask for him, becoming gradually used to his absence. In time children grew accustomed to any change.

For Connie and himself, Jack was sure, there would never be a time when such knowledge could be truly accepted. When he awoke in the morning there would be a brief blessed moment before memory and reality came to him, but then it would return, and once again his world would be destroyed. And if he awoke before Connie he would watch her awaken and see her go through the same process, seeing the moment of not knowing and then that split second when memory touched and held her, when reality came flooding in like light into a darkened room, bringing with it all the horror and misery that the hours of oblivion had kept at bay. And she would weep, as often beforehand he, silently, had wept. And seeing her eyes fill with tears he would hold her, while knowing that no comfort he tried to give could ever really help.

Whatever they did, their waking hours continued to be tormented by visions of Joel's last moments. For

Jack it was always the same. Always he sees Joel, caught in the car's beams, come dashing around the side of the house in pursuit of the puppy. And then a second later the lightning strikes, missing the house and the tall lime trees, seeming to seek out Joel alone as he straightens with the dog in his arms. Time and again Jack would run through the brief sequence of events, and as if watching a film he sees himself leaping out of the car and dashing across the grass. He watches himself bending to cradle Joel in his arms, sees the dead puppy falling onto the wet grass. He feels Joel's body, so hot, so hot, so terribly burnt, while at the same time he is dimly aware of Connie getting to her feet, stunned and winded from the blow of the lightning, staggering to him as he holds Joel to him, throwing herself upon them, pressing herself to the child: 'Oh, Joel, Joel, Joel . . .' No one had been able to help. A doctor had been summoned, but Joel had died within minutes.

Connie tried not to weep before the girls, doing all she could to spare them. And observing her grief when they were alone, Jack remembered the promise he had made her, that whatever happened Joel would be safe. He would let nothing happen to him, he had said. And he had failed. 'I know,' Connie once said to him, 'that you did all you could. If there had been any way to save him you would have found it.' And she had wrapped her arms around him, offering him comfort, trying to assure him that he was in no way to blame.

They supported one another. They had always been close, but Joel's death brought them closer, and they needed each other more than ever in the days that followed. First came the inquest, held in the coroner's court in Reading. The verdict, a foregone conclusion, put Joel's death down to an accident—in the coroner's

words: to an 'act of God'. To Jack, this was a great
irony, for if God existed, Joel's death was in no way
the result of any act of His.

Further stress came in the shape of the press, both
local and national, whose members came with their
cameras, notebooks, tape recorders and microphones,
besieging the house and intruding on the privacy of
the family. With Jack having gained a certain fame
through the award-winning TV series, the tragedy—
and such a dramatic one—promised excellent copy.
First the mother-in-law, then the son, both dying
within weeks, and in the most spectacular ways. The
tabloid papers made the most of it all.

The people of Valley Green, however, were a different matter. Their sympathy and good will were evident at every turn. So many flowers were sent for Joel
at his funeral and letters offering sympathy and help.
The little church of St Matthew was full at the service
on that late October morning, and many other sym-
pathizers stood watching from beyond the churchyard wall while Joel was laid to rest beside his
grandmother. Jack, raising his head from the grave-
side, saw the villagers standing there, their faces set
with sorrow and sympathy, and recognized among
them George Appleton, Ruth Chandler, Emma Stocks
and her daughter Jane. John Callow was nowhere in
sight, though he had written to them of his sorrow at
their loss, and sent flowers. Seeing Callow's wreath
and accompanying card, Jack had wanted to snatch
them up and throw them into the wastebin, but pro-
tocol forbade what would appear such an irrational
act. Instead, he had to content himself with removing
the card so that Connie would not see it.

He and Connie had no doubt now that Callow had
been responsible for Joel's end, regardless of the fact

that they were still no nearer to understanding it. Connie, having learned from Jack of all that had passed at his meeting with Ruth Chandler, was now as convinced as he that Callow was able to use some malign power to get what he wanted and to avenge himself for old grudges.

Gradually, as the days grew into weeks, the impact of the sensation lessened around them, while at its centre Jack, Connie and the girls were left to try to pick up the pieces and rebuild for themselves new lives with new patterns. Lives without Joel.

After school broke up for the Christmas holidays, Ruth Chandler packed the last of her bags and moved away from Ashampstead—though Jack discovered that she had ceased teaching at the school the week after Joel's death. Before she left she wrote to Jack and Connie, once again expressing her sorrow, along with her hopes that they would eventually begin to come to terms with their loss. Her letter carried with it a note of finality, for she was getting out, away from the scene of such inexplicable tragedy. Whether she intended to resume her teaching career in York, she did not say, but it was clear to Jack that they would neither see her nor hear from her again.

For Jack, the matter of his work had become the sourest thing. Before the tragedy, the series was still unfinished. Afterwards, he was quite unable to continue writing it. The very last thing he felt like doing was sitting for hours in his study trying to dream up amusing situations and snappy one-liners for his frustrated, overweight heroine, and the crunch came with the producer suggesting that they employ another writer to complete the remaining episodes in the series. Jack agreed readily and gave the replacement his blessing. Later, if a new series was required—and there was every indication that it would be—he hoped he would be able to give his mind to it again.

For Kitty and Lydia's sake, he and Connie tried to prepare a Christmas that was as near normality as they could make it. Jack got through some of the heavy hours by making little pieces of furniture for their dolls' house. Working in Mary's studio, he fashioned several of the pieces from papier-mâché, patiently adding layer upon layer of newspaper with glue, the whole hardened on the stove and then carefully sanded, polished and lacquered. The act of working with his hands had always been a pleasure for him, and he had often used it as a refuge in difficult times, even as a child, spending days designing and making intricate models out of papier-mâché, cardboard, wood and anything else that came to hand. On this occasion, while the work did not exactly bring him comfort, still it was something in which he could become involved, and which helped to pass the slow, leaden time.

A few days before Christmas they got a tree. Hiding their absence of enthusiasm, he and Connie helped the girls to dress it with tinsel and brightly coloured baubles and a silver-winged fairy for its top. On the night of Christmas Eve the girls hung their stockings (Connie's cut-down tights) over the end of their beds. While they slept Jack crept in and took them away to fill them and then replace them along with the brightly wrapped packages that he and Connie had prepared.

On Christmas morning they sang carols and in the evening played parlour games, and throughout it all the spirit of Joel remained, challenging Connie and himself, forbidding anything but a mere lip-service to enjoyment. Often Joel's name would be mentioned by

one of the girls, or there would be some other re-
minder of him, and when it happened Jack would
watch Connie stopped in her tracks as memory and
grief took hold, and would see her make the attempt,
for the sake of the girls, to put on a brave face and
carry on. It was the same for himself.

It was with a certain feeling of irony and not some
little bitterness that he observed how John Callow
continued to thrive. Looking through the local paper
one evening he saw an article on the Reading Operatic
Society and Callow's forthcoming production of Bellini's opera *La Sonnambula*, due to open in early
spring at the repertory theatre in Reading before going on to performance in the Chapelton Festival.
While his own and Connie's lives lay in pieces, Callow
continued on, letting nothing get in his way.

And always, overshadowing their attempts to rebuild their lives, was the knowledge that Connie had
herself received from Callow a paper bearing the
runes—a paper that had survived destruction in the
fire only by dint of the fireguard. It lay among the papers in the envelope, in the dark of the locked drawer,
seemingly safe for the moment, yet at the same time
like an unexploded bomb whose time-setting for det-
onation was unknown.

One Monday morning in January, Jack brought up
the subject. For weeks neither he nor Connie had
mentioned it, but they could not continue to ignore it
like a problem that would in time go away. Connie
had remained safe, but for how long would she continue to do so?

'Con,' he said, 'we have to talk.'

The twins were at school, and he and Connie were
sitting in the kitchen. The radio was giving out some
phone-in programme on juvenile crime.

'What about'? She was wary. The shield of normality they had built around themselves was transparent and eggshell thin.

'The paper you got from Callow.'

She shook her head. 'I don't want to talk about it.'

'Con, we *must*. We can't just go on from day to day pretending it doesn't exist. That paper's *there*. It's just lying there. We've got to *do* something.'

'What do you suggest we do?' Her voice had a brittle note, defensive.

'I've been thinking about this whole thing. Trying to see whether there are any patterns. If Callow isn't stopped there's no knowing where it will end. We've got to find a way.'

'You think we can?' There was doubt in her tone and in her eyes. 'I still can't believe it—the way he's able to make it happen. And every time it has all the appearance of an accident. Your uncle tripping over the cat and falling downstairs. It's so *banal*. Mary being run down. My mother . . . Joel . . .'

Jack nodded. 'And there have been others, according to Edwin. God knows how they died, but whichever way it was it must have been put down to an accident in each case.'

A little silence, then she said: 'And me next, right?'

'Con, don't.'

'Why not? It's what he's got in mind. And after me, who then?'

'Nothing's going to happen to you.'

'We said that about Joel.'

'I know. I know.' He reached over and switched off the radio. 'We've got to find some way of getting the whole thing stopped. There's got to be a way.' He paused. 'In each case where the runes were destroyed, the recipient died within a week of their destruction.'

'But the note he gave to me with the programmes didn't get burnt or go into the bath or anything.' She gave a little laugh that was touched with hysteria. 'And I'm still here. So as far as Callow's concerned, something's gone wrong, right?'

Ignoring this, he said, 'As the runes you got were not destroyed, perhaps they've lost their potency. But we don't know that, do we?'

'I think they could have,' she said. 'I mean, when we looked at the paper in your study there was not a breath of air to disturb it. It didn't move. It had no power.'

'But we can't depend on it.'

'So what are we going to do?'

He did not answer. Connie continued to look at him in silence for some moments, but still he said nothing. After a while, her lips compressed, she got to her feet. 'I know what to do,' she said.

'What's that?'

She was already turning, moving across the room. 'The obvious thing. What I should have done at the start.'

The winter sky was heavy with cloud, making the light even poorer than it usually was at such a time. Connie leaned forward slightly as she drove, hands gripping the wheel, her heart thudding in her breast. On the passenger seat beside her lay the envelope holding Callow's bits and pieces on the operatic company— and the paper bearing the runes. She didn't know what she was going to say to him; she only knew that she could not continue to do nothing.

In Gorse Way she parked the car near Callow's house, looked out and saw to her great relief that there was a light on in one of his windows. She got out, walked up the path to the front door and rang the bell. After a few moments she heard footsteps and then the door opened and he was standing there smiling his yellow smile. He wore cords and a white fisherman's sweater.

'Well, Mrs Forrest,' he said, beaming at her, 'this is a very pleasant surprise.'

Nervously she greeted him in return, and then waited, expecting, hoping, that he would invite her in. He did not, however, but remained facing her on the threshold. For a brief moment she saw his sweeping, curious gaze take in the manila envelope she held in her hand. Did he guess? Could she detect a slight unease behind his smile?

She held up the envelope. 'I had to drive by your house, and I thought it was high time I returned your opera papers to you.'

'Oh,' he said, 'that's very nice of you, but you shouldn't have troubled yourself.'

'It was no trouble. And I've had it for months now. I'm afraid I forgot all about it.'

He made no attempt to take the envelope from her outstretched hand, and she held it a little nearer to him. Still he made no attempt to take it. On the contrary, he took a small step back.

'I gather,' he said, 'that you've decided against joining our happy little band.'

'I'm afraid so, yes. For the time being, anyway.' She lowered the envelope back to her side. 'I'd love to have come along, but I'm afraid I just don't have the time. I think it'll have to wait for two or three years—till the girls are a little older. Maybe I can think about it again then.'

'Yes, indeed. But I'm very sorry it's not possible now. It would have been so nice to have you with us.

244

But, as I say, I do understand your situation. So perhaps at a later time.'

'Yes, perhaps.' She raised the envelope again and took a step forward. 'Anyway, while I'm here I'll let you have these things back.'

His hand moved; not towards the envelope, however, but towards the edge of the door. 'It's all right,' he said, 'you keep them.'

'Oh, but—'

'I've got plenty of copies. And besides, you might want to look at them again. You did look at them, did you?'

'Oh, yes, of course. They're very interesting.'

Under his hand the door moved, preparatory to closing. 'You won't think me rude, will you?' he said. 'But when you called I was just in the middle of cooking something, and if I don't give it some attention very soon I'm going to have a disaster on my hands.'

She held the envelope up again, closer still, but now he behaved as if it were not even there, looking only into her face, his smile as wide as before.

'Well,' he said, 'if you'll excuse me . . .'

A moment later the door had shut and Connie was left standing there, the envelope still in her grasp. After a second she turned and made her way back up the path towards the car.

The next morning Jack went to talk to George Appleton where he was working in the orchard pruning the apple trees. The day was crisp and cold and as Jack moved across the grass his breath vapoured in the chill air.

'Good morning, George.'

'Good morning to you, Jack.' The old man gave him a warm smile as he approached. Following the period immediately after Joel's death he had shown his kind-

Bernard Taylor

ness and sympathy in the ways he had known best. After first expressing his sorrow he had worked longer hours on the garden, and put into his work even more care and conscientiousness, if that were possible. Jack and Connie had been touched by it. To Connie herself he had shown his thoughtfulness by bringing her some choice fresh vegetables that he thought she might like. He brought gifts for the girls, too—sweet Blenheim apples from his own garden, that he had kept and stored. He had shown his thoughtfulness in a dozen ways.

'So,' said George now, 'what can I do for you?'

'What do you know about some people called Simoneau?' Jack asked.

'Simoneau?' George frowned. 'Oh, dear me,' he said, 'that name's familiar, but I couldn't for the life of me tell you exactly why. I know I've 'eard it, but in what way, that's the question. No,' he shook his head, 'I'm sorry but I can't 'elp you there.'

Jack sighed. 'I thought if anyone knew it would be you.'

'I wish I could 'elp. Is it important?'

'It might be.' He paused. 'I have another question.'

'Oh, ah. Fire away, then.'

'Can you tell me how Harold Sanders died?'

'Sanders? Who used to run the opera set-up?'

'Yes.'

'Well, that ain't a difficult one. 'E was killed in 'is garden. Usin' one of them chainsaws. By all accounts it went out of control and cut his leg. Sliced through a main artery and 'e bled to death afore the ambulance could get there. There was an inquest. It was in all the papers. One of them freak accidents, as they say. I don't trust them saws meself.' It was clear from his expression that he was curious as to the reason behind Jack's inquiry, but he asked no questions. 'The wife,

246

Mrs Sanders, she left the village soon afterwards. Sold up, lock, stock and barrel, and went. Well, you can understand such a thing, can't you?'

'Where is she now? D'you know?'

The old man cast his gaze to the side as he pondered the question. 'I think she went off to Bristol or Bath or somewhere. I'll tell you who might know—Emma Stocks at the shop.'

There was a customer in the shop when he got there, an elderly woman whom he had occasionally seen about the village. She was buying a little and talking a lot, and obviously in no great hurry to get away. Turning to Jack as he hovered, she said kindly, 'You go ahead, please,' and prepared to wait while he was served. Jack thanked her, but said that he had himself come to have a word with Mrs Stocks.

'Oh, well, then,' the woman said, smiling, 'in that case I'd better get on.' She bade Jack and Mrs Stocks goodbye and went out into the street.

'Yes, Mr Forrest,' Mrs Stocks said, as the door closed behind the woman, 'what can I do for you?'

'I'm sorry to bother you,' Jack said, 'but I'm hoping to get some information, and it occurred to me that you might be able to help.'

'Well, certainly I'll help if I can. What's it about?'

'I'm wondering whether you know where I can find Mrs Sanders.'

'Mrs Sanders who used to live here?'

'Yes. I believe her husband died a few years ago.'

'That's right. Terrible accident that was. He was such a nice man. Everyone liked him. His wife, too. She just couldn't get over it. He ran the opera society, though I suppose you know that.'

'Yes.'

She nodded. 'I s'pose it's because of that that you want to see his wife.'

Jack didn't contradict her and she went on: 'She moved to Bath. But I haven't got an address for her, I'm sorry to say. It's been a few years now since it all happened.' She put a hand to her mouth, narrowed her eyes in thought, then added, 'I tell you what I could do, though. If you like I'll phone the Adamses and ask them.'

'The Adamses? Who are they?'

'Mr and Mrs Adams. They're the couple who moved into the house when Mrs Sanders sold up and left. Mrs Adams might still have a forwarding address, and I'm sure she wouldn't mind letting you have it. Just hang on a minute.' She turned and moved away through the door into a room at the rear and came back a few seconds later carrying a telephone directory. She put it on the counter and opened it. As she began to go through the pages she said, 'I suppose you could always try the Bath phone directory for Mrs Sanders' address, though there'd probably be quite a few by the name of Sanders.' She had come to a stop in her page-turning and now began to run her fingers down the names. 'Here it is.' She looked up at him 'D'you mind if I tell her why you want to know?' She looked a little apologetic. 'I should think she's bound to ask.'

'Not at all,' Jack said, while his brain desperately sought for some acceptable reason. 'It's about the opera company, as you said.' He paused then added, 'Amongst my uncle's things we've come across a couple of books that belonged to Mr Sanders.' He shrugged. 'I'd like to return them, that's all.'

'Right. Well, you just wait here and I'll give her a call.' She went away again into the rear room, and he heard the faint ting of the telephone and then her voice. She came back saying, 'She's out right now, but her husband's expecting her back any moment. That was him who answered. He doesn't know where any address might be, but he's sure his wife'll know. He'll get her to phone as soon as she gets in.'

'That's very nice of you. I'm interrupting your work, too.'

She gave a little snort at this. 'Interrupting my work, he says. Chance would be a fine thing. I'm afraid there's not that much business for places like this nowadays. People all go to the supermarkets today, don't they? Can't blame them, of course. Get everything you want practically under one roof. And cheaper too.' She shook her head. 'When I'm ready to retire I'm afraid there won't be anyone interested in taking over here. Times have changed, I'm sorry to say. In some ways, anyway. The village shop is almost a thing of the past. People only use it for a stopgap nowadays, when they've forgotten to buy something at the supermarket. Natural, I s'pose.'

He nodded sympathetically. He understood only too well what she meant. Both he and Connie used the shop in just that way.

'And the village itself is changing,' Mrs Stocks went on. 'Some of the cottages here are only used at weekends and holidays. Rich people's second homes. They buy up the cottages and fit them up with all the mod cons. And they were only built for the farmhands in the first place, as likely as not. We don't get many young people coming into the village to live. They can't afford the prices of the houses for one thing, not when others with money are determined to move in. No, it's not the same. That's one reason it was so nice when you and your young family moved in.'

249

Jack said, 'It's a lovely spot in which to bring up children.'

The bell on the door rang and he turned to see Jane enter, her tall, broad frame momentarily blocking out the light as she closed the door behind her. 'Oh, dear,' Mrs Stocks said, 'there go the profits on the chocolate.'

Jane laughed, said, 'Oh, very funny,' and then greeted Jack and her mother. As Jane moved behind the counter, Mrs Stocks said to her, 'Mr Forrest was asking after Mrs Sanders. I'm trying to get her address for him from the Adamses.'

A thought occurred to Jack and he asked, his glance moving from one woman to the other, 'Does the name Simoneau mean anything to either of you?'

Jane paused in the act of taking off her coat. 'Simoneau? Oh, indeed it does. They were a young couple who were coming to live here at one time. He was French. Worked at Heathrow Airport as I recall. They were coming to live here in the village.'

'And they didn't?'

'No. They were all set to do so, but they were killed in a road accident.'

Mrs Stocks said, 'Oh, that was terribly sad.' Then, fearing that the topic might be a little insensitive in view of Jack's recent loss, added quickly, 'Still, Mr Forrest doesn't want to hear about that, I'm sure.'

Jack said, 'No, please—I'd be grateful to know anything about them that you can tell me.'

'As a matter of fact,' Mrs Stocks said, 'I introduced Mrs Simoneau to Harold Sanders. They met here in the shop and she showed interest in his opera group.' She gave a little shrug. 'Apart from that I can't say that I really know anything about them.'

Jack turned his glance to Jane as she stood in the

inner doorway. 'Jane, what connection did they have with Mr Callow, do you know?'

She frowned. 'They didn't have any connection at all, as far as I'm aware. Do you know of anything, Mum?'

Mrs Stocks shook her head. 'No, I don't.'

'No,' Jane said, 'they had nothing to do with him. I don't think they even knew the man. Oh, unless of course you're thinking of the house. That's just occurred to me. Is that what you mean?'

'What house? What about it?'

'Well, they were after Callow's house.'

'I don't understand.'

'It wasn't his house then, of course. No, before he bought it, they were after it, the Simoneaus. And just beat him to it, so I gather. Which he wasn't too pleased about. Though he got the place in the end anyway. Strange how these things happen. It had been on the market for quite a while, and then suddenly there were two people after it at the same time. But that's always the way, isn't it. But as I say, the Simoneaus got in first. Just pipped Callow at the post, so to speak. But then there was the car crash so he got the place after all.'

'They *both* died?'

'All three of them. They had a little girl. She was killed too. Apparently their car skidded on the motorway one night and ran into a bridge support. The husband and his wife were killed outright and the little girl died later in hospital.'

As she finished speaking, the telephone rang in the other room.

'That might be Mrs Adams,' Mrs Stocks said, and turned and went to answer it.

'They were such a nice young family,' Jane said.

'Such a tragedy, their deaths.'

After a minute Mrs Stocks came bustling through from the rear room. 'I've got Mrs Sanders's address and phone number,' she said, handing him a piece of paper. 'Though whether she's still at the same place, Mrs Adams couldn't say. They haven't had any post for her for a good long while.'

Anxious now to get away, Jack thanked her and Jane, wished them goodbye and left the shop. Outside, in the street beside the green, he stood and looked at the paper. It gave a telephone number and address in Bath. He knew he had no choice but to try to see the woman, to talk to her. The thought went through his mind that he could just drive to Bath and try to see her unannounced. After all, it had worked with Ruth Chandler. But on thinking it over, he realized that in this case it would probably not be the best course. After all, Ruth Chandler had been the one to make contact with him in the first place, whereas Mrs Sanders did not even know of his existence. She might panic at his appearance, or on the other hand she might not even be there. After a moment's hesitation he went to the nearby phone box, inserted a phone card into the slot and dialled her number.

The telephone was answered after its fourth ring. 'Hello?'

'Hello, is that Mrs Sanders?'

'Yes.'

He took a breath, aware of the strengthened beat of his heart. 'Mrs Sanders,' he said, 'you don't know me. My name is Forrest. Jack Forrest. I'm the nephew of Edwin Maddox.'

'Yes?' A slight wariness in her tone.

'My family and I have come to live in Valley Green,

at The Limes and . . .' He hesitated. 'I understand that my uncle and your late husband were good friends.'

'Yes, that's right. They were very good friends. Why?'

'Mrs Sanders,' he paused, trying to find the right words, 'd'you think I might come and see you for a few minutes? Talk to you?'

'Talk to me? What—what about?'

'Well, it's difficult to explain over the phone, but I'll try not to take up much of your time. And it is rather important.'

'Well, I . . . Look, what is this about? What do you want to talk to me about?'

He would have to tell her something, he realized. After a moment he said, 'Mrs Sanders, I'm looking for some information. I need to talk to you. It's imperative that I talk to you.'

'I don't know . . .' The wariness in her voice was much stronger now. 'I don't think there's anything I know that could possibly be of help to anyone.'

'There is. Believe me, there is.'

'But you still haven't told me what this is all about.'

'There are some things—things that only you can tell me,' he said. Then he added, jumping in with both feet, 'It's about your late husband's death.'

There was a little silence, and then she said, her voice now sounding tight, suspicious, 'I'm sorry, Mr Forrest, but I have no wish to discuss my husband, and least of all his death, so I'm afraid you're wasting your time. Now, if you'll excuse me I—'

He broke in. 'Oh, please don't hang up on me, Mrs Sanders. This is a matter of great urgency. I swear to you, I don't ask such a thing lightly. Please, just let me come and talk to you for a few minutes.'

He heard a little sound of despair, half sigh, half

groan, then she said, with obvious reluctance, 'Well, what is it that I can tell you?'

He took a breath while thoughts, words and phrases tumbled over in his mind. 'Since we came here,' he said, 'in only six months I've lost two members of my family. First my wife's mother, and now recently my son.' His voice cracked on the last words, and as he steadied himself to continue the woman's voice came:

'Oh . . . I'm terribly sorry to hear that, Mr Forrest. Believe me, I'm so sorry.' Yet along with the sympathy in her voice there was that wariness, stronger now, and touched with what sounded like fear.

'Thank you,' he said, then added, 'And I'm afraid. I'm afraid that something else is going to happen—to another member of my family.'

For a moment there was only silence on the other end of the line, then she said, carefully, choosing her words, 'Is there someone else involved in this—this thing?'

'I believe so, yes.'

A pause. 'Go on.'

'I think you know who it is, Mrs Sanders. His name is John Callow.'

There was no sharp intake of breath, no sound at all of surprise. She had known; she had expected the name to be spoken. After a moment she gave a soft little keening sound, and when she spoke he could hear that she was crying.

'I'm sorry,' she said. 'But I just can't get involved. I can't. I'm sorry.'

'But Mrs Sanders—'

'No. Please.' And now her voice had taken on a slightly hysterical note. 'I can't help you. I wish I could, but I can't. And please, I beg you, don't ask me again.'

As he opened his mouth to speak, to plead with her once more, he heard the click of the receiver going down.

Chapter Fourteen

That night Jack lay sleepless in bed, aware that Connie at his side was also awake.

The rebuff from Mrs Sanders had put him back to square one, and he had no idea at all what to do next. He could, of course, knowing her address, just drive to Bath to see her, but that wouldn't do any good, he was sure. He'd just end up having the door slammed in his face.

So where to go from here? They could move away, as Ruth Chandler had urged, and that they would do, eventually, but at present such a move would solve nothing. The runes that Connie had received from Callow hung like a sword of Damocles over her head. For how long would she remain safe? With every passing second her time could well be running out. If only he knew of some way to fight back. But perhaps there was no way. Perhaps it was inevitable that Callow, having set out on his course of destruction, would win. As far as Jack knew, no one in the past had survived; all who had received the paper bearing the runes had, sooner or later, died.

Why did Callow do what he did? Was it just for satisfaction? A pleasure that came from exercising his strange power? No amount of rationalizing and insisting that such things could not happen could deny the fact that they *were* happening. Where would it finish? *Would* it finish?

Breaking abruptly into Jack's thoughts came the ringing of the telephone on the bedside table on his right. As he shifted and lifted his arm, Connie stirred, turning towards him. The time on the clock-radio said 11.50. He switched on the lamp and lifted the receiver. 'Hello?'

'Is that Mr Forrest?' A woman's voice, familiar.

'Yes.'

'Mr Forrest, I'm sorry to call you at such a late hour but—'

'Mrs Sanders?' he broke in. 'Is that Mrs Sanders?'

'Yes, it is. I've been thinking about you ever since you phoned today. You've been on my mind all the time. And I realized that I—I can't just turn my back on you like this. So, if you still wish to come and see me . . .' She let the question hang in the air.

'Yes, I do. Very much.'

'Fine. I called now because, well, I thought you might be leaving early for work in the morning or something. I wanted to be sure of catching you.'

'I'm so grateful you called. When can I come?'

'Whenever you like.'

'Tomorrow?'

'Fine.'

'Good. In the morning? Say late morning?'

'Yes, that's fine. About eleven o'clock?'

'I'll be there.'

'I'll give you my address.'

'I think I've got it, but just in case . . . Let me get a pencil.' He opened the chest drawer, fumbled around and found an old ball-point pen and a paperback book. 'OK.'

The address he wrote on the book's inside cover was the one he had been given by Mrs Stocks. 'I'll be there at eleven,' he said. 'And, Mrs Sanders?'

'Yes?'

'Thank you. Thank you so much.' He replaced the receiver, turned off the light again and sat there, leaning against the headboard.

Connie said into the dark: 'Who was that?'

'Mrs Sanders, who used to live here in the village.'

'Whose husband ran the opera group.'

'Yes. I'm going to see her tomorrow morning.'

'What for?' The tension was clear in her voice.

'I want to talk to her about Callow and her husband—and whatever else.' He turned, put his arm around her. 'We're going to beat this, Con. There's got to be a way, and we're going to find out what it is.'

'But—'

'Go back to sleep now,' he said softly. 'Try not to worry. Go to sleep.'

She took a breath as if to speak, then sighed and turned away. He moved down in the bed, turned towards her and cupped her body in the curve of his own, his arm around her waist. After a moment her hand moved and touched his, pressing it to her, holding it tight. After a long time he felt the pressure of her hand relax as she drifted off into sleep.

He was up early for the trip to Bath. Snow had fallen in the night, carpeting the garden and the drive and muffling all sound. The girls were still in bed when he set off. He kissed Connie goodbye and crept out, eased the Citroën out of the snow-covered drive and into the lane, and set off for Bath.

By ten-thirty he was in the street where Mrs Sanders had her home. She lived in a narrow terrace house a little distance from the town centre. When he rang the bell she answered it almost at once.

'Mr Forrest?'

'Yes. Hello, Mrs Sanders. I'm a little early, I hope you don't mind.'

'Not at all. Come in, please.'

He followed her into the hall and gave her his coat, and she ushered him into a sitting room on the left, where an old gas fire hissed warmly and comfortingly into the quiet. He took a seat in the armchair she indicated.

'I'm just making some coffee,' she said. 'Would you like some?'

'I would indeed, thank you very much.'

She left the room, and he sat looking around him, taking in the polished bureaux, the bookcases, the Morris chairs, the too-large gilt mirror over the fireplace and the pictures on the walls. It all looked a little too crowded, as if its owner had moved her possessions from larger premises and had been reluctant to part with too many treasures.

After a few minutes Mrs Sanders returned with a tray. Jack said he would take his coffee with just a little milk and she poured and handed him a cup, took her own and sat down in the chair opposite. She was a small, slim woman, with greying hair, small features and bright blue eyes. She wore grey slacks and a blue sweater. Jack put her age in the mid-sixties. Added to her obvious nervousness she had a rather shy manner about her. Facing him from her chair she took a sip from her cup and said in her soft voice: 'I'm so glad I could get you on the phone. Thank goodness you'd mentioned you were living at The Limes. That's how I was able to get your number from the operator.'

He nodded. 'Yes, I'm so glad.'

'I must have sounded so uncooperative, to say the least. But you see, well, all that business, it's something I've been trying to forget. That's why I moved here after Harold's death.' She glanced around her at the room. 'It's not what I would have chosen if I'd had more time to look around. But I didn't. I was anxious to leave. I just wanted to get away.' She studied him in silence for a moment. 'I left because of John Callow.' She gave a little shrug and added, 'We might just as well get to the point straightaway, don't you think? There's no sense in our skirting round it. That's not what you've come for.'

Jack nodded. 'Thank you.'

'Yes,' she said, her voice little more than a whisper, 'it was because of Callow that I came away. I could have come to terms with Harold's death eventually. Generally one does. It's in the nature of things that we recover from the deaths of those we love. If we didn't then life would come to a stop.' She did not look at him now as she spoke, but kept her eyes cast down at the carpet at some point between them, as if looking into the past. 'Callow was the reason I had to leave.' She raised her head at this and added with a bitter little smile, 'Quite simply, I was afraid. Of him and of all he stands for. He's evil.'

'Yes. That's what I believe, too.'

She nodded. 'You mentioned your little boy. I already knew. I'd read about it in the papers. Are you saying that Callow had something to do with his death?'

'Everything to do with it. He—killed him.'

'Spoken so badly, the statement sounded so outrageous in his ears that he found himself watching her face for some expression of incredulity. It was not there. She merely nodded her sympathy and her understanding, and then said: 'I read in the papers that there was a storm, and lightning, if I remember correctly.'

He bent his head. 'Yes.'

'You mentioned your wife's mother, too.'

'Yes.'

'I remember reading of her death also. Please, tell me what happened. If you don't mind. Tell me everything.'

As the coffee grew cold in his cup he told her all of it, starting with the confrontation over Callow's dog fouling the garden and finally of the deaths of Sarah and Joel. 'They both received from Callow slips of paper with the runes,' he ended. 'And through it he destroyed them.'

She nodded; it came as no surprise to her.

Jack said with a little laugh, 'My God. If anyone were listening right now they'd think I was mad. I'm sitting here talking about a man using some evil power in order to kill—to get rid of people who have displeased him in some way. It sounds insane.'

'Not to me. That's how he works. I've seen it with my own eyes. I don't need any convincing.' She paused. 'Do you know what happened with him and my husband?'

'Not much. I was told that your husband died after using a chainsaw. That he fatally injured himself.'

She gave a sigh, lowering her glance again to take in the pictures from the past. 'He bled to death, and there was nothing I could do to stop it. I tied a tour-

niquet round his leg and hoped that that would keep
him until the ambulance arrived. But when I tried to
phone for the ambulance I couldn't get through.'

'They didn't answer?'

'The phone wouldn't work. It was dead. I was frantic. I didn't know what to do. We lived on the very
outskirts of the village, and our nearest neighbour was
a hundred yards away. I ran to their house to use their
phone, but they were out. So I had to go into the village to phone from there. I ran to the phone box at
the end of Flax Street, only to find that that phone was
dead too. I couldn't believe it. I ran to a house nearby
then, and eventually, but only after several minutes,
was I able to get through. The people there kindly
drove me back home. By that time Harold had lost a
great deal of blood and I knew that if the ambulance
didn't arrive at once it was going to be too late.' She
shook her head. 'They didn't get there in time, of
course. I couldn't stop the bleeding and he was dead
by the time the ambulance arrived.'

Her expression was calm when she looked up at
him, but he could see the suffering behind her glance.

'I can talk about it now,' she said, then added pa-
thetically, 'My husband was a good man, Mr Forrest.
He was a truly good man. We had no children, but we
had one another, and he was everything to me. The
trouble was, he was in Callow's way.'

'With the opera, you mean?'

'Yes. It was Harold who began the society. He built
it from scratch. And he made it a wonderful thing considering that he had only amateur talent to draw on.
But he knew it could be done.

'We'd gone to the amateur festival in Chapelton a
number of times to watch the various societies compete for the plate. And he wanted to be a part of it. He

was determined, and he *became* a part of it. Because he and Edwin Maddox were friends, Edwin refused to take part in the judging once Harold had got his production entered, in case there should be cries of nepotism, you understand. But Harold's production still won. He did a production of *Don Giovanni*. And it was marvellous, it really was. The next production was of Massenet's *Manon*. We didn't win with that one, but we came very close. And he went on to do other productions—and I helped him wherever I could. Oh, it meant everything to him—to both of us. And it was all going so well.

'Then Callow joined the group. After that it was never the same. He caused so much dissension, thinking he knew better how things should be done. Harold just hoped and prayed that he would get fed up and leave. Callow wasn't living in the village at that time. He was still living in London. Hammersmith or Chiswick or somewhere. We kept hoping he'd find the journey too much to cope with, especially in the winter months. But he didn't. He kept on coming. And then he moved into the village. From that moment he was right on the doorstep and a real thorn in Harold's side. Callow seemed to think that just because he'd been in a few soap operas and played a couple of supporting roles in the West End he was the expert, that everyone, Harold included, should defer to him. After all, he'd been a *professional*. He'd been "in the business", as he never stopped reminding us all, never missing a chance to tell some tired old anecdote about when he'd worked with Richard Attenborough or John Mills or Maggie Smith or whoever. Always the famous names, of course.' She nodded. 'He was really sickening. But what we didn't know at the time was that he was also so very dangerous. Only later on did we find that out. And by then it was too late.' She gave a little shrug. 'He wanted to run the society, of course. And to run it the way he thought it should be run. I don't know why it was so important to him. Perhaps because he'd never had the success he felt he deserved—in his professional career, I mean. And perhaps he saw a way of getting the glory he wanted by being a big fish in a little pond. I don't know. But that's what he got. Eventually. Eventually he got it all.'

She gazed off into the distance for a second, then turned back to Jack and gestured to his cup. 'Your coffee's gone cold. Let me get you some more.'

'No, it's fine, thank you.' He took up the cup and drank the rest of the coffee. As he replaced the cup in the saucer he said, 'What makes you so sure that Callow was responsible for your husband's death? Not that I have any doubt—knowing as much as I know—but how did you know?'

'It wasn't me, it was Harold. He knew. He somehow knew what was going to happen to him. And he was right. I didn't believe that such a thing could happen, that anyone could have such a—a power. I thought it was all myth and superstition. I was wrong. You see, Harold knew about the young couple who planned to buy the house that Callow also wanted.'

'The Simoneaus.'

'You've heard about them?'

'I was told that they were just in front of him putting in an offer for his house but that they were killed in a road accident.'

'That's right. They came down to look at the house, decided that it was just what they wanted, and put in an offer which was accepted. But then Callow came along, and he also wanted it. Too late, though. The Simoneaus had got in first. So he got rid of them and the house was his.'

'He got rid of them?'

'Yes. It came about through a poster in the village shop, advertising the opera group's latest production. Mrs Simoneau saw it and was interested. I think she had it in mind to join the company once she and her husband had moved into the village. Anyway, Harold happened to call in at the shop while the Simoneaus were there, and they met. Harold told me that when they were outside afterwards they had quite a conversation about it. He said they seemed a very nice young couple. They had their little girl with them, I believe. Well, as they stood there talking, Callow appeared, having driven down from London. He said hello and Harold introduced him to the young couple. On learning who they were, Callow said to them something like, "Oh, so you're the lucky ones, are you?" And something to the effect that if he'd been a bit quicker off the mark the luck would have gone his way. Apparently he was very pleasant about it, and the Simoneaus were sympathetic towards him, and it was all very civilized. Then, Harold said, Callow went into the shop and came out a few minutes later—they were still talking—and handed Mrs Simoneau—Angela her name was—an envelope. He said something like, "Just to show there're no hard feelings, I want to be the first one to wish you happiness in your new home." Something like that. Then as she went to open the envelope he said, "Don't open it now; open it later." Then he wished them all goodbye and went away. When he'd gone Mrs Simoneau opened the envelope and there was a card inside. Just a simple greeting

card, I understand, with a few words from Callow—
and something else.'

'A slip of paper with the runes on it.'

'What else? She couldn't make it out, of course,
and neither could her husband. Harold took a look
at it and was very shocked. He knew they were
runes. He'd made something of a study of them
over the years. He didn't know what these particular ones meant, but he said he was immediately
afraid. And suddenly he was seeing Callow in a new
light. But there was nothing he could say at the
time, and he didn't know enough to be absolutely
sure. Then the young woman took the paper back
to look at it again. And then it happened.'

'It was blown out of her hand.'

'Yes. Into the pond. Her husband went and fished it
out, but there were no marks left on it. It was completely blank. I'm sure they thought no more of it—
no more than that it was a bit odd. Harold did,
though, and he worried about it terribly. He began to
consult various books over the next few days, even
going up to London on two occasions to do so. He got
obsessional about it. Not that he told me about his
fears. That came later.' She paused. 'But he couldn't
help the Simoneaus. They all three died. A little less
than a week later. They'd been to Valley Green to sort
out a few things concerning the house and they were
killed on the motorway while driving back that night.
Mrs Simoneau was at the wheel.'

A little silence fell in the room, then Mrs Sanders
went on: 'Harold was different from that time. He'd
been a happy man until then, really quite carefree. But
I could see the change that came over him. I didn't
know the cause of it. I was only aware that he had
something on his mind. He wouldn't say what it was.

When I asked him he'd just tell me, "It's nothing; it's nothing." But I knew that wasn't the truth. I knew him too well to accept that. Of course later I realized what it was. Basically it was his—his discovery, his realization, that there was this terrible evil. And that it was so close and there was nothing he could do about it. Well, I mean, if somebody is ill you can call a doctor, or if someone's robbing a bank you can call the police. But what do you do with something like this? If you went running to the law with this you'd end up being certified.'

Jack said, 'What exactly happened to your husband? How did Callow get the runes to him?'

'By being very friendly, very pleasant, and altogether very agreeable, which wasn't really like him at all. But I suppose he was just preparing the ground, so to speak, getting himself in the right situation. When it happened it was in the easiest way. With their working together as they did, Harold didn't really have a chance. At one of the rehearsals Callow slipped a paper with the runes among the pages of Harold's libretto—*Traviata*, they were doing—and then handed it to him. That's how it must have happened. The following evening Harold set about doing some work on the production and sat down in front of the fire with his libretto and his notes. He picked up the libretto and opened it and saw there this little slip of paper with runes written on it. I was with him at the time. I remember how he gasped and went white. I can see him now, sitting there with the book open on his knee. And then almost at the same second the wind came. I'd never known anything like it. It was so sudden, so extraordinary. And so violent. The next thing the paper was caught up in the draught and went straight into the fire. It was burnt at once, of course. And if I'd

detected a change in Harold earlier, I really saw one
in him then. He changed completely after that. He became totally paranoid, it seemed to me. I couldn't understand it. It was so unlike him, and I had no idea
what was causing it. For one thing, he hardly ventured
out again. The only person he saw was Edwin Maddox. He phoned him and asked him to come over. I
don't know what they talked about, but they sat for a
good while together in Harold's study. I remember
that when Edwin left he was very grave. Obviously he
was concerned about Harold, though he didn't say as
much to me.

'Later on, Harold said that if anything should happen to him I should leave the village. I asked him what
he was talking about. "Nothing's going to happen to
you," I said, but he would have none of it. He made
me promise. Eventually he told me what was happening. I insisted. Well, we'd shared everything from the
moment we first met, and I said if there was some
awful problem, we would face it as we'd faced every
other difficulty in our lives together. And then he
told me,' She paused. 'That he was going to die. And
not only that, but that he was going to die within a
week.'

Silence in the room. In the quiet, Jack could hear
the sound of some distant wailing police siren. It had
a strangely muffled sound, deadened by the snowfall.
As the sound faded away Mrs Sanders said: 'You can
imagine the shock, hearing someone you love say such
a thing. I couldn't believe I was hearing right. I
thought at first he was talking about some illness, that
perhaps he'd had some terrible diagnosis from the
doctor that he'd been keeping to himself. And then he
told me about the runes. Their power, what they could

do, what they *would* do. It was a great revelation to me, as you can imagine.'

'Did you believe it?'

She cast her gaze to the side. 'Did I believe it? I really don't know. No, I don't think I could have done. After all, it's not within our experience, is it? All our teachings go against belief in such a thing. What I had to believe in, though, was his fear. Oh, God, that was real enough. He was so afraid. As I said, he was so afraid that he wouldn't set foot outside the door.'

'How—how did it happen, the accident with the saw?'

'There'd been a gale during the night. Very high winds, rattling the windows and bending the trees. When I got up in the morning I saw that one of our trees had come down. A little ornamental cherry tree in the front garden. It had fallen across the drive. The problem was I had to drive into Pangbourne to keep a doctor's appointment, and there was no way of getting the car out. It wasn't a big tree, but it was too big for us to move between us so Harold got out the chainsaw to cut the tree up so that we could get it out of the way.' She compressed her lips briefly, then went on, 'I don't know how it happened. I was there, helping him, but I was looking elsewhere at that particular moment. I heard a cry and looked round and—the saw had gone right into his thigh. In seconds there was blood everywhere. I'd never seen such bleeding. He was still holding the saw, and as he sort of staggered he caught himself with it again, in his calf. Oh, God . . .' She shut her eyes, put her hands to her face and bent forward. Seconds passed then she lowered her hands and said dully, 'He was so careful when dealing with any kind of electrical thing, any potentially dangerous tools. And he was used to working with that saw. It was nothing new to him.' She gave a little shrug. 'You know the rest of the story.'

'I don't know what to say,' Jack said, feeling very ineffectual. 'I'm so sorry.'

She nodded acknowledgement of his words. 'I don't know if there's anything else I can tell you. I did what Harold wanted, of course—I left the village as soon as I could. Not only because I'd promised, but because, well, because I'd realized that it was all true, what he'd said.' She gave a little nod. 'And if I still harboured any doubts at all, they disappeared when Edwin Maddox and then Mary died.' She gazed at Jack. 'And now he's turned his attention to you and your family.'

'Yes.'

'What are you going to do about it?'

He gave a deep sigh. 'I don't know. I don't know what to do?'

She leaned forward, giving her words greater emphasis. 'You must leave, of course.' Her tone brooked no possible question. 'You can't stay where you are. You must take your family away at once. Get as far away from him as possible.'

'I know, but it's just not—not as simple as that.'

'Of course it is. And if it's not that simple then you must make it so. What can be more important? You must just pack up and leave. It doesn't matter where, just so long as you go. The safety of your family is all that matters.'

'I know that. And that's why it's not so simple.'

'What do you mean?'

He had been putting off telling her, and now that

Bernard Taylor

the moment had come he realized that it was because he was afraid of her response.

'My wife,' he said, 'Connie. She's received the runes from Callow too.'

Mrs Sanders looked at him, frowning, then she gave a nod. 'Well, that does change things.'

'Yes.'

'Tell me what happened.'

He told her, and related how nothing had happened when they had taken the slip of paper out of the envelope to examine it. 'We thought,' he said, 'that perhaps it had lost its potency with its having failed the first time to go into the fire.'

She shook her head. 'I don't know, but I would doubt that. Where were you when you looked at it the second time?"

'In my study.'

'And did you have a fire burning there?'

'No.'

'Any body of water?'

'No.'

'Then I should think that there you have your answer. It didn't move because there was no immediate means of its being destroyed.' She shook her head. 'Mr Forrest, you mustn't start to relax. You can't afford to. Not for a moment.'

'No. I realize that.'

'How long ago did your wife receive the runes from Callow?'

'Three months. That's another reason we were hoping that somehow she'd be safe—because of the time that's elapsed.' He shook his head. 'I do realize now, though, that the time might not be significant.'

'No, I'm sure it's not. Not going by what Harold told me, and what I've read.'

'I don't know how to fight this,' he said after a moment. 'Oh, God . . . Connie. If anything should happen to her as well . . .' He leaned forward. 'That's why I've come to see you. I've got to find out as much about it as possible. I thought you might know if there's a way out. There's got to be one.'

'There is, just one—as far as I know.'

'What's that?'

'You've got to return the runes to him. The receiver of the runes has to get them back to the giver.'

'My wife took them to him just two days ago,' he said. 'They were still in the envelope they came in. He wouldn't accept the envelope even though he had no way of knowing that the runes were inside.'

'There you are,' she said. 'He couldn't take the risk. He dare not.'

'Why not?'

'Because if he did, the curse would transfer to him— or so I understand. If the runes are returned to the giver, then the curse goes with it. But with greater power than ever. Harold said that once the runes are returned to the giver then his death would be indescribable. Unimaginably horrible, he said. But that's what you've got to do—get them back to Callow. Or rather your wife has to.'

'How is she supposed to do that if he won't accept them? As I said, she's already tried.'

'Well, she'll have to do it somehow, and without his being aware of it. For he'll never take them willingly.'

'But how can she do that? He'll be so wary.'

273

Bernard Taylor

'He's bound to be. He can't afford to take any chances. And he won't.'

'Supposing there is a way to get them back to him, does it have to be Connie who does it? Couldn't *I* try?'

'Well, if you did then you'd first have to accept the runes from your wife. She'd have to give them to you. They have to be willingly given. Either openly or covertly. And with them would go the power that they hold.'

'So if Connie gives the runes to me then the curse or whatever it is would come with them.'

'So I understand.'

'And it would be removed from her.'

'And be on you.'

'But she would be safe.'

'Yes. But then of course you would be the one in danger.'

He nodded. 'What if I took them from Connie and sent them to Callow in a letter or something?'

'No, they have to be handed over in person— passed from hand to hand. And it has to be the original paper. I don't think it would work making a copy of the runes and trying to get that to him.'

A thought occurred to Jack. 'What if we just kept the paper with the runes locked up? The way we're doing now? So that nothing could happen to them?'

'Keep them locked up indefinitely, you mean?'

'Yes.'

'No, that wouldn't work. As I said, Harold did a considerable amount of study on it, particularly towards the end, and I learned a lot from him, and from the notes he made. In all the cases I know about, the runes have been destroyed by fire or water. But they can also be destroyed by air. By *all* the elements, you see.'

'By air as well?'

'Air, fire and water. Perhaps the runes would be safe if they were never exposed to the air. But they already have been, haven't they? I don't know. Perhaps if you could immediately seal the paper in some airtight container or in a vacuum. But Harold said that air will destroy them.' She shook her head. 'You dare not just lock them away and trust to luck. There's only one thing to do, and that's to get them back to Callow. I don't know how you can do it, but that's your only chance.'

Chapter Fifteen

After leaving Mrs Sanders, Jack stopped in the town and bought a sandwich. Eager to get back home, he ate it as he drove, not tasting it but using it merely to stem his hunger. The roads were a mess from the snow, but he hardly noticed the conditions, and in spite of not being familiar with the route back to Valley Green he drove almost on automatic pilot. As he drove he thought over what Mrs Sanders had told him. At least now he knew what had to be done. And somehow he would do it.

It was almost two o'clock by the time he got back to the house. On the kitchen table was a note from Connie saying that she'd gone to the supermarket in Pangbourne. The house was silent. He stood at the kitchen window, drinking coffee and looking out into the back yard. The temperature had fallen further and the rear garden looked bleak and cold. Snow lay on the toolshed roof and the trees, from whose branches icicles hung, palely shining in the dull afternoon light. Near his hand lay a plate bearing a cold slice of toast—left over from Connie's breakfast. He opened the window, broke the bread into pieces and tossed them out into the cold air. Immediately the sparrows were there, pecking at the crumbs in the snow.

He finished his coffee, set down his empty mug and then began obsessively to move about, going from room to room, unable to settle anywhere, and all the while thinking over the question of what had to be done. Eventually, after much thought, he came up with a strategy that he thought might work.

He was standing in the main sitting room when he heard the sound of the Renault, and then Connie came in carrying some shopping. She greeted him with a half-smile but said nothing of his trip to Bath, and he realized that, ostrich-like, she was simply hiding from the situation. When she had put the shopping away, she asked if he had eaten lunch. He'd had a sandwich, he replied; he'd get something for himself a little later. She nodded, and silently got out vegetables and began to make preparations for dinner.

'Con,' he said, 'leave that for a minute.'

'I must get it done,' she said. 'I've got to go and pick up the girls from school in a few minutes.'

'I'll do the vegetables while you're gone—or I'll go and get the girls.'

'It's all right, I'll go.'

She went on with her task. He watched her for a moment then moved to her side.

'Listen,' he said, 'I had a long talk with Mrs Sanders.'

Connie put down the paring knife, wiped her hands on a cloth and turned to him. 'I'm being silly,' she said. 'I suppose I'm still trying to pretend that this whole thing isn't happening.' She gave a deep sigh. 'I can't just keep shutting it out, can I? It's got to be faced.

278

We've got no choice. Tell me what happened.'

He told her all that had passed between himself and Mrs Sanders, all the while doing his best to keep a positive tone. No matter how hard he tried, however, there was no way he could diminish the gravity of the situation. When he had finished, Connie briefly, wearily closed her eyes and said: 'Jack, what did we do to deserve this?'

He wrapped his arms around her. 'Oh Con . . .'

'What did we ever do to Callow that was so terrible? Why is he doing this to us?'

He did not know what to say, and merely held her closer.

'First Mum,' she said dully, 'and then Joel. And now it's me.'

'No,' he said firmly. 'It's not going to be you. It's not.'

She pulled back from him a little and looked into his face. 'I don't see how you can stop it. We couldn't stop it happening before, and I don't see how we can stop it happening now.'

'We will.'

She opened her mouth to speak again, but no words came. Her chin quivered, the corners of her mouth turned down, and she burst out on a sob, 'I'm afraid! Oh, Jack, I'm afraid.'

He held her to him again. 'I know you are. And I am too. But we're not going to let him beat us. We're not.'

'How are we going to stop him?' There was a note of hysteria in her voice. 'He's going to kill me. He'll find some way.'

'No, he won't. I shall stop him.'

'How can you?'

'I shall.'

Pulling out of his grasp, she shook her head. 'There's no way you can. All that Mrs Sanders said about returning the runes to him—it's not going to work. I've already tried, and he'll be so much more on his guard now. He'd never let it happen.'

'I have a plan. Of sorts.'

'A plan?'

'To return the runes to him.'

'How? How am I to do it?'

'Not you, me.'

'But they weren't given to you. They were given to *me*. They were meant for *me*. *I'm* his target this time.'

'Yes, I know, but—'

'*I'm* the one who has to return them.'

'Not if you give them to me first.'

Her eyes widened. 'But if what Mrs Sanders said is true, I'll be passing this curse thing on to you.'

He nodded.

'No,' she said. 'I can't take that chance. Why should you put yourself in jeopardy? No. There must be another way of doing it.'

'Connie, there is no other way. The runes have got to be returned to him, and I'm the one to do it. For one thing, he won't necessarily be expecting me to try.'

She did not speak for a moment or two, then she said quietly, 'Tell me, then. How do you propose to go about it?'

'Well—he'll be rehearsing his opera in Reading some of the evenings this week. I'll find out when and where, and I'll go and see him.'

'Yes?'

'He'll have scripts and notes and things lying around. Bound to have.'

'Go on.'

'Well, I'll find some way to return the runes to him there. Perhaps among his own papers, as he did to

Harold Sanders. That would be poetic justice, that would.'

'But don't you see? As soon as he sets eyes on you he'll be suspicious.'

'But he won't see that I'm carrying anything. I'll have the paper safely in my pocket out of sight. Then, when the right moment comes, I'll find some way to put it in with something of his. I'll get it to him somehow.'

Connie shook her head, unconvinced. 'What's he going to think you're there for? He'll know you're there with a purpose. He'll be on his guard.'

'That might not be so. After all, he can't know that we're aware that the runes have to be returned to him. He can't know that I've been to see Mrs Sanders. For God's sake, he can't even know that we suspect him or are even aware that there's anything sinister going on. You didn't give anything away when you called at his house with the envelope. He still thinks we trust him. He must do.'

'Well, if you think it'll work . . .' The doubt was still in her voice.

'I do.' He put his hands on her shoulders. 'Now, go into the study, unlock the bottom drawer—you know where the key's hidden—and bring me the envelope with the paper inside.'

'But—'

'Please, Connie.' He lowered his hands. 'Please do as I ask.'

She remained standing there.

'Connie, trust me. Go on now. Get the envelope. And don't open it, whatever you do. Just bring it here to me. Please.'

She gazed at him for a moment longer then turned and went from the room. She was back two minutes

281

later with the envelope in her hand.

'Now,' he said as she stopped before him, 'give it to me.'

She looked from the envelope to him.

'Give it to me,' he said. 'I can't take it against your will. It's got to be willingly given.' He paused. 'Come on now.'

She gave a little sigh then held the envelope out to him. He nodded and took it, holding it firmly.

'Good.' He forced a smile. 'Now try to relax, all right?'

Lips compressed, she gave a little nod. He leaned closer and kissed her lightly on the mouth. 'I love you, Con. I never loved anyone in my life the way I love you.'

Her eyes filled with tears that spilled over and ran down her cheeks. 'I love you. And, oh, God, if I've done something dreadful in passing this on to you I'll never forgive myself.'

'You haven't,' he said, smiling. 'You've done the right thing. The only thing.' He kissed her again and they held one another. As he released her he saw, past her shoulder, the kitchen clock. He raised his free hand and wiped the tears from her cheek. 'You'd better get off,' he said, 'or you'll be late to school to meet the girls.'

She nodded, turned away and went into the hall to get her coat.

He remained standing there until he had heard the sound of the Renault pulling out of the drive and then, still holding the envelope, he went into the study. It would be safe in here without access to water or fire. Sitting down, he laid the envelope on the desk before him. He sat without moving for several minutes and then, after one more check to ensure that the door was closed, he switched on the desk lamp, lifted the flap of the envelope and drew out its contents.

He placed the pile of papers before him. He could not recall where among them lay the runes. One by one he took up the items, carefully opening the opera programmes and leafing through the press cuttings. He found the slip of paper near the bottom of the pile, lying between the leaves of a programme for *La Traviata*. He recognized the paper at once by its size and proportions. Gingerly he picked it up and turned it over.

He frowned, gazing at it in bewilderment, and turned it over again. He moved it nearer to the lamp, and then held it up so that the light shone through it. The runes were gone. There was not the slightest trace left of their ever having been there.

Realization dawned and he felt his heart leap in his chest and sudden sweat break out on his palms. Pausing only long enough to stuff the blank slip of paper back into the envelope he got up from the chair and hurried for the door. Seconds later he was dashing out of the house and running for the car.

By the time Connie arrived at the school, the children were trooping out to join the adults who were waiting in the cold air. Some children, whose parents had not yet arrived to meet them, were taking a last opportunity to play together before going home. Connie moved among them as she made her way across the asphalt playground, dodging the boys who chased one another or kicked a football about.

Outside the main door of the school building she came to a stop and stood waiting, her breath clouding in the chill air while the children straggled out in ones, twos and threes, laughing and chattering together.

God, but it was so cold. She had not known such cold-
ness for a long time, and in her hurry to get to the
school she had come out without her scarf and gloves.
She would be relieved to get back home again and into
the warm.

Added to the growing cold as she stood there she
was aware of a great feeling of tension. Although Jack
had taken the paper from her, it had in no way lifted
her anxiety. That would remain, she knew, until the
whole desperate business was finished with and they
knew they were safe. And that could not happen as
long as they remained in Callow's orbit. As things
were, everything would depend upon what happened
when Jack drove to Reading to see Callow at his opera
rehearsal. Jack had been so convinced that he would
be able to return the runes to him, but she knew that
it would not, could not be an easy matter. And if he
did not succeed? No. She thrust the notion away. He
would succeed. He had said he would, somehow, and
she must have faith.

There was a loud yell from nearby and one of the
boys came dashing towards her in pursuit of the ball,
yelling out and skidding on the icy surface. She
stepped back out of his way, and he went whizzing
past. As he did so he snatched up the ball with a
Yeahhh! of triumph, tossed it into the air, caught it
and then threw it again. Connie turned back to the
door in time to see Lydia coming towards her, smiling
at her as she pulled on her woollen hat.

Connie bent and kissed her. 'Where's Kitty?' she
asked.

'She's just coming. She's talking to Miss Sherill.'

'Well, I hope she won't be long. I'm getting cold
standing here.' She bent and put her arms around Lydia's shoulders, drawing her in close. 'Keep me warm,

Lydia,' she said. 'Keep me warm.'

'Yes, I'll keep you warm.' Lydia pressed against Connie's body, her arms around her. Connie shivered and pulled the collar of her coat closer about her throat. Raising her head she looked up and saw icicles suspended from a leaking gutter, hanging like huge crystal stilettos in the fading light, while high, high above, the sky was a dull, slatey yellow. So much snow up there still. Not ready to fall yet, however; it was surely too cold right now.

A yell of warning rang in the crisp air, and the ball thudded against the wall only a yard from her shoulder. She turned and gave a reprimanding glance at the group of boys. 'Sorry,' one of them called to her, and she waved a hand in acknowledgement of the apology.

'Mummy, here's Kitty now,' Lydia said.

Turning, Connie saw Kitty coming through the lighted lobby towards them. A moment later she was at their side and Connie was bending to kiss her on the cheek. It was just as she straightened that there came a ringing thud as the boys' ball struck the guttering overhead. It was followed a split second later by a loud warning yell from one of them: *'Look out!'*

As Connie tipped back her head to look above her, the largest of the icicles, knocked free of the gutter by the ball, was already in mid-air, falling. She had no time to move out of the way; she hardly had time to register it in her sight. One moment she was glimpsing the huge icicle coming straight down towards her, and the next moment it had struck, plunging through the socket of her right eye and into her brain.

She gave a little cry and staggered, raising her hands to her face, while at her side Lydia and Kitty shrieked out in horror. As their small, mittened hands reached towards her, she staggered again and spun, sending blood spraying out in a wide arc. Then, to a chorus of horrified screams, she took three drunken, weaving steps and fell backwards onto the hard ground. As Lydia and Kitty and others gathered about her, she lay with her limbs involuntarily twitching and jerking, while the blood bubbled from her nostrils and poured from her mouth.

Chapter Sixteen

Pt . . . pt . . . pt . . . pt . . . pt . . .

The fly was persisting in trying to find a way out through the glass, and through the fog of his unhappiness Jack wondered how it was that the creature could sustain such a battering and survive. One would think that by now it would have learned from experience and given up the attempt. As he watched the fly throwing itself against the pane there came to him the memory of Joel coming out with a joke he had heard in school; sitting at the dinner table and saying, barely able to contain his laughter; 'What's the last thing to go through a fly's brain when it hits the windscreen of a car?' 'I don't know,' Jack had said, 'tell us.' Joel, laughing, 'Its arse, of course.' Connie, unable to suppress a smile, had said, 'Oh, very funny,' to which Kitty had added, clicking her tongue, 'That's rude.' Daddy, that's rude.' Jack had said yes, it was, and Connie had joined in with his laughter.

There was no laughter now, and he could not imagine that he would ever know a cause for laughter again. How was it possible, he asked himself, for the thousandth time, that what had begun with such happiness and hope could have ended in such bitter tragedy?

While Lydia and Kitty had come to terms with the death of their grandmother, and had begun to do so with that of Joel, Jack knew that it would take them a good deal longer to deal with the death of Connie. It was not only the loss of their mother that profoundly affected them, but the added factor of their having been present when it happened. They had witnessed it with their own eyes, had seen her struck down, had been a part of the horror.

He himself had arrived at the scene only minutes after it had happened. When he had seen that Callow's slip of paper was quite blank, he had realized that the runes had already been cast. His accepting the paper from Connie had made no difference; the runes had gone, destroyed by the third element—air.

By the time he had arrived at the school Connie had been carried inside and an ambulance had been called. It had not been possible to save her, though, and she had died on the way to the hospital.

Now only he and Kitty and Lydia were left.

Pt . . . pt . . . pt . . . The fly wasn't giving up. The insistent little sound irritated him. Looking around, he saw the morning paper, lying unread where he had dropped it. He took it up, folded it into a weapon and raised it in his right hand. He leaned forward, waiting for the fly to settle on the glass. When it did, however, the blow did not come. Instead he dropped the paper onto the table, reached out and slipped the catch off the window and pushed it open. Alarmed, the fly buzzed away into the room behind him, but then seconds later it was back, heading again for the light, and Jack watched as it found its freedom and zinged out into the sweet-scented April air.

At the foot of the front garden, near the gate, stood the 'For Sale' sign erected by the estate agent. Within a fortnight of Connie's death he had put the house on the market. Several prospective purchasers had come to view the property, but there were no takers so far. Jack was not too surprised; he was convinced that of those who had called, many had come just out of morbid curiosity. Connie's death had been widely reported in the newspapers; following so soon after the sudden deaths of Sarah and Joel, it had given the tabloids another field day. Reporters and photographers had again besieged the house and crowded into the Reading coroner's court. A couple of the papers had spoken of the house being jinxed, which might well have put off those who in normal circumstances would have jumped at the chance of living in such a place.

He had no intention, however, of waiting for a sale to be made before leaving Valley Green. In two weeks he and the girls would be off, back to London. Back to Chiswick, in fact, where he had taken out a mortgage on a small house not that far from where they had been living before. They had come full circle. And when the move was accomplished they must start their lives over again. They had no choice; their old lives were finished now, broken, and there was nothing to do but pick up what pieces remained and do what they could with them to build a new existence. Experience told Jack that in time the girls would recover even from the death of their mother, but for himself he could see only a kind of dull, day-to-day existence, conscious always of what he had lost, of what could never again be his.

He continued to gaze out onto the garden for a few minutes longer then closed the window and turned away. A couple of half-packed tea chests stood against the far wall. The house they were going to was a good deal smaller than The Limes and there was much in the way of furniture and other possessions that would have to be disposed of when the time came. It would be no hardship for him. The things he had once so treasured had no meaning any more. All he was concerned about was the welfare of Lydia and Kitty; what was enough for them would be enough for him.

And once they were settled in Chiswick, he told himself, he would get back to his writing. He had to. The new series of *Fat Chance* had been running for several weeks now. He had not watched any of the episodes, though he had heard from the producers that the viewing figures were excellent. The news had touched him with only a passing, academic interest, however. For the present the whole business seemed far-removed and foreign. Hopefully, this would pass. It would have to if he was to build on his past success and continue making a living for himself and the girls. If he did not, could not, then it would be back to the classroom. But that was something that he could not deal with at present, and he didn't need to. For the time being he had sufficient funds to see them through into the near future; anything beyond could wait. For the moment the only thing on his mind was getting away from the village, away from Callow and his evil.

Lost, aimless, he wandered slowly from room to room. Signs of their impending exodus were everywhere, and the whole place seemed unutterably dismal and uninviting. In the study he sat at the desk.

Ranged before him were the bookshelves, some already empty, their contents packed into the chests and boxes that stood against the wall.

With a deep sigh, he put his head in his hands and leaned forward over the desk. His eyes were dry. He had wept so much over the past weeks. Now he was left with only a kind of numbness. Steeped in unhappiness, he seemed to go through the days in a stupor. Yet life had to go on, and like an automaton he did what was necessary for himself and the girls—the shopping, the cooking, the cleaning, the laundry. He did it mechanically, and in a hit-and-miss kind of way, learning as he went along, having the girls correct him: 'Daddy, we don't do it *that* way. Mummy always does it like *this*.' He would learn it all in time, and he would get by; they would all get by. He thought of the words written to him by his producer at the Television Centre immediately following Connie's death: 'One day at a time, Jack. One day at a time.' It was good advice, and it was only with the heeding of that advice that he could get through the time.

Near his elbow on the desk lay a stack of mail, some of it still unopened. Among it lay letters of condolence he had received from friends and colleagues at the BBC and from the villagers.

Callow had sent expressions of sympathy and regret. And had he smiled as he had put pen to paper to write his warm tributes? Had he taken pleasure in searching for the right words and the florid little embellishments? Jack felt sure that he had taken pleasure in the whole exercise.

He began to go through the mail, putting on one side letters that required answers and throwing into the wastebin those that did not. One letter, received some weeks back, had come from the organizers of the Chapelton festival, asking him, as the only surviving relative of Edwin Maddox, if he would consent to present the Maddox Plate at the festival's end. He had not responded, and seeing the letter again now he was touched once more by the bitter irony of it. If he accepted the invitation, and if Callow won the award, then he, Jack, would be giving him all that he had worked for.

Nothing had got in the way of Callow's happiness; he had continued with the staging of his opera production. In one of the local papers some days before, there had been a photograph of him, taken at one of his recent rehearsals. In the accompanying interview he had expressed cautious optimism about the festival, now so close. And he had reason for his optimism, it appeared; the few reports that had come to Jack had all been very positive. Callow had apparently assembled an excellent cast and had found the best available musicians. He was taking no chances with the text this time, remaining faithful to the original. It was clear that he was eschewing anything that smacked of the avant-garde, anything that might alienate the panel of judges. At the same time, however, it appeared that within the scope of his frame he had been as adventurous as he could safely be. If these reports that had reached Jack's ears were to be relied upon, then perhaps at last Callow was about to achieve his goal.

And now Jack was being invited to play a part in what might turn out to be Callow's greatest moment. He took up the letter, held it over the wastebasket and let it fall. He wanted nothing to do with Callow in any way, least of all to give him further cause for celebration.

He looked at his watch. It was ten past three, time to go and pick up the twins.

He got to the school five minutes before classes ended and stood near the gate with the waiting mothers whose faces he had come to recognize. There was no conversation between himself and them, and he made no attempt to initiate any. After all that had happened they were keeping their distance, but whether from sympathy or suspicion he did not know, though the occasional sidelong glance indicated the latter.

At last the doors opened and the children came bustling out onto the playground. And then Lydia and Kitty were there too, their bags slung over their arms, their little faces lighting up as they saw him; their steps quickening as they ran to his arms.

Back home he made them each a sandwich and poured them glasses of milk. They chattered as they ate, telling him of the work they had done during the day and of various events that had taken place. Listening with only half an ear, he did his best to join in and show interest while he began to prepare the chicken pieces he had bought for their evening meal. It would have been so much simpler to take the easy way and rely on frozen, pre-cooked meals and other convenience foods but he fought against this temptation—at least where the girls' meals were concerned. Connie, he knew, would not have approved, so, in the main, he cooked for them the things that she would have cooked.

He had finished preparing the chicken and the sauce and was washing his hands at the sink when Lydia, in the course of saying something to Kitty, mentioned Callow's name. He froze for a moment, then turned off the tap and faced them.

'What was that?' he said into their chatter.

They fell silent, looking at him.

'Lydia,' he said, 'what were you saying? Tell me.'

293

She gave an awkward little laugh and then said brightly, colouring at the same time, 'Mrs Browning said today that she'll be sorry to see us go. She said she'd like us to write to her and tell her how we're getting on. She said—'

'That's not what I meant,' Jack broke in. 'That's not what you were talking about.'

They said nothing, merely exchanged glances and then looked down at their half-eaten sandwiches.

'I heard you mention Mr Callow's name,' Jack said.

Kitty raised her head at this and looked at him. He could see guilt in her face.

'I told you,' he said, 'that you are not to speak to him.' He became aware that water was dripping from his hands and he took up a towel and dried them. 'Have you been speaking to him?' He looked from one to the other.

A little pause and Kitty gave a nod. Then she turned to Lydia and said accusingly, 'That's your fault. Tattle-tale, tattle-tale.'

'Never mind all that,' Jack said. 'Tell me what happened.'

'*We* didn't talk to *him*, Daddy,' Lydia said, her expression slightly pleading. '*He* talked to *us*.'

'When was this?'

'At school today.'

'He was at your school?'

'When we were out in the playground at lunchtime. He came to the playground and talked to us over the wall.'

Jack could feel his heart beating. 'What did he say?'

Kitty said: 'He said hello to us, and he asked us which was which. And I said I was Kitty and Lydia was Lydia.'

'Go on. What else?'

'He laughed and said he'd never be able to tell the difference, and that we ought to wear signs round our necks with our names on them.'

Lydia laughed at this. 'Yes, but then he said we'd probably switch the signs round so nobody would know who was who.' She laughed again and Kitty joined in with her.

'Is that all?'

Kitty: 'He said he'd learned that we were leaving Valley Green and going back to London, and I said yes, and he asked whether we were looking forward to it, and I said no, and he said that was a shame.'

'He asked when we were going,' Lydia added, 'and we said we were going in two weeks.'

'Go on.'

'He said he'd miss seeing us around the village.' She turned then to Kitty and said, 'Shall we go upstairs and play?' Then to Jack, 'Daddy, can we go upstairs and play?' As she spoke she took her worn old hessian bag from the back of the chair and started down from her seat.

'Not for a minute,' Jack said. 'Stay where you are.'

They looked concerned at his words and his expression, their spirits a little dampened. They hoisted themselves back onto their chairs and sat waiting.

'And he said something else, obviously,' Jack said. 'That wasn't all.'

They did not speak.

He took a breath and asked: 'Did he—give you any-thing?'

Neither one answered, and in their silence Jack had his answer.

'Did he? Did he give you something?'

They looked at one another, confirming his fear.

'*Did* he?'

Bernard Taylor

For a second or two they looked at him in silence, then Lydia said sheepishly, 'Oh, Daddy, you *know*, don't you?'

Jack's heart was hammering. 'Tell me. What did he give you?'

'Oh, Daddy, please don't be angry,' Kitty said. 'We didn't mean to.'

'*Tell* me. What did he give you?'

'It was just a little going-away present, that's all. That's what he said it was. Daddy, please don't get mad.'

'I'm not mad at you. What was the going-away present?'

'You promise you won't be mad?'

'*What did he give you?*'

She looked at him for a moment, then dipped into her hessian bag, brought out a cardboard box and held it up for him to see.

'He gave you a doll?'

'Yes.' She put the box on the table. 'She's got my name too.'

Jack stepped forward and looked at the doll lying in her little nest of tissue paper behind the clear window. She was a small, charmless, plastic re-creation of an adult figure, with red lips, round, long-lashed blue eyes and a head of shiny gold nylon hair. She was dressed in a cheaply made little cocktail dress and high heels. In the corner of the box was set a little plastic hatbox with 'Kitty' written upon it in black ballpoint.

He stood looking down at it. It was useless now to reiterate his admonitions not to take any gifts from Callow's hands; it was done. After a moment he raised his head to Lydia and said: 'And what about you, Lydia? Did you get one as well?'

Evil Intent

'Yes.' With a reluctant nod she gestured to her bag which lay on another chair.

Jack's mouth was dry. He licked his lips, then said, looking from one to the other: 'Have you played with them yet?'

'Not yet,' Lydia said. 'Mr Callow said to wait till we got home. He made us promise.'

'So you haven't opened the boxes yet?'

'No.'

He nodded. 'Lydia, let me see your doll, too.'

She got her bag, took out the box and set it down on the table. The doll inside was identical apart from the name on the hatbox.

'Now,' Jack said after a moment, 'I want you to give me the dolls and then go upstairs to play for a while.'

'What d'you mean,' Kitty said, 'give you the dolls?'

'Just give them to me, please. They won't come to any harm.'

'But—but why?' Her face fell. 'Can't we keep them?'

'You can have them later. But for now I want you to give them to me. Will you do that?'

Kitty nodded and pushed the box towards him.

'No,' he said, 'I want you to give it to me—put it into my hands.'

She gave a little laugh, then with a shrug said, 'All right,' then took up the box and placed it in his open hands.

'Thank you.' Carefully he placed the box back on the table. Then he turned to Lydia. 'Now you, please.'

She looked at him doubtfully for a moment then picked up the box, came around the table and gave it to him. He nodded, forcing a smile. 'Thank you.'

He placed the second box beside Kitty's. 'Now,' he said, 'you go upstairs and change and then you can

297

play in your room or watch television for a while. I'll call you later on.'

They moved reluctantly, not wanting to leave their dolls behind. 'Go on now,' Jack prompted. 'I'll give you a yell in a while.'

He stood there while they left the room and their feet sounded on the stairs. After a while he took up the two boxes and went out into the hall. At the foot of the stairs he stood listening. From above came the murmur of the girls' voices. Satisfied, he turned, walked along the hall and opened the study door.

Inside, he pushed the pile of letters to one side, set the boxes on the desk, and then checked the window to make sure that it was tightly closed. That done, he turned to the door and checked that too, making sure that the doormat was pushed up flush against the door's foot. Satisfied at last, he drew up his chair and sat down at the desk.

First he picked up the box containing Kitty's doll. He turned it over in his hands and then carefully pulled out the securing flap. The doll was laid in a little polystyrene base. He drew it out and set it before him. Gingerly he picked up the doll and examined it. There was no slip of paper concealed anywhere among her clothes. He laid the doll back in its base and then took from its nest the little plastic hatbox, suddenly quite certain that this was where the paper would be. He took off the lid. There was no paper inside. He realized that he had been so keyed up that he had been holding his breath, and he let it out on a long sigh. The fact that the box was empty meant nothing; if the paper was not there then it was somewhere else, for there had to be a paper, of that he was certain. He could not imagine for a moment that Callow would present the girls with gifts merely to give them pleasure. He lifted out the tissue paper from the polystyrene base. There was nothing there, and neither was there anything behind the base itself. Had he been mistaken . . . ? He picked up the box and upended it. A little slip of paper fell out onto the desk.

Very quickly, his fingers trembling, he picked it up and turned it over. And saw the runes that were written there.

There was no wind to disturb the paper as he held it in his grasp, but he was not fooled by its absence. He knew it would have been there immediately had there been access to water or fire. Even so, he took no chances, and when he laid the paper down on the desk he secured it beneath a heavy paperweight.

He turned then to the box that had been given to Lydia. And moments later the second slip of paper was in his grasp. He placed it under the paperweight along with the other, and sat staring at them.

Lydia and Kitty were safe now—for the time being, anyway, for he had taken the runes to himself. And not one set, but two. In time the runes would be destroyed, and then—he had no doubt of it now—his death would follow soon after.

Chapter Seventeen

That night when the girls were in bed Jack sat alone in the sitting room while the questions churned round in his brain. For the moment the runes were safe. He had sealed both papers in an airtight plastic bag and locked them away in the desk drawer. They could not, however, remain there indefinitely. Where they lay at present they were not likely to come to harm from fire or water, but in time they would succumb to the air to which they had already been exposed. Eventually it would have its effect and the runes would fade to nothing. How long that would take he did not know. With Connie it had taken three months. But in the end it had happened.

How foolish, how complacent he had been, thinking that the evil was behind them. After all, why should Callow stop with Connie? It was clear now that he would not stop until all the family had gone. And it was his intention, obviously, after dealing with Lydia and Kitty, to turn his attention on Jack himself. Why was he leaving him until last? To see and enjoy his suffering? Probably. Except that with Jack having taken the runes to himself, Callow's plan would not work as he had intended. But even so, that did not mean that Lydia and Kitty would remain safe. Once the runes were destroyed, he, Jack, would die, and the girls would be totally unprotected and at Callow's mercy.

After a disturbed and restless sleep Jack awoke early, got the girls up and washed and dressed, gave them their breakfast and then set off with them to Barfield. This was not only the girls' last day of term before breaking up for the Easter holidays, it was also their last day at the Barfield school. When they began the new term they would do so at their old school in Chiswick.

Sitting in the car with them on their arrival outside the school he impressed upon them the absolute necessity of accepting no more gifts from Callow. 'No matter what it is,' he said. 'Not so much as a sweet, not so much as a piece of paper. You mustn't even talk to him. If you see him you must pay no attention to him. Don't listen to anything he has to say.' He told them that he was still angry with them and added very sternly that he would never forgive them if they disobeyed him again. Their faces set and solemn, and much subdued by the severity of his tone and his words, they promised him that they would not. He got out of the car with them then and escorted them to the school yard. At the entrance he crouched before them. Fighting the impulse to crush them to him, he hugged them briefly and kissed their cheeks.

'Daddy, we'll be good,' Lydia assured him, to which Kitty at once added her own assurance.

'Oh, I hope you will,' he said. 'I'm trusting you to.'

Reluctantly he released them and watched as they joined the other schoolchildren on their way towards the school building, pausing and turning at the entrance to wave to him. He waved back and remained watching until they were out of sight.

Returning to the car, he got back in and just sat there bent over the steering wheel. And all the while the seconds, the minutes, the hours, were running out. The sword was now hanging over his own head. Something had to be done. But what? He remained for some time pondering on the situation and then, with a decision made, straightened, turned the key in the ignition, revved the motor and started away for Valley Green.

When he emerged from The Limes a while later he carried a brown paper-wrapped package under his arm. He got into the car, backed out into the lane and headed off in the direction of the village.

Driving along Gorse Way, he saw with relief that there was smoke issuing from Callow's chimney. He pulled the car to a halt outside the house, took the package from the seat beside him and got out. He opened the gate, walked up the path to the front door and rang the bell. A few moments later the door was opened and Callow was standing there, his cat in his arms and his little dog standing next to his feet. Callow smiled at Jack over the cat's head, his yellow teeth gleaming in the morning light.

'Mr Forrest, hello!'

On the surface his tone was warm and friendly, but Jack thought that he could detect behind the greeting a certain wariness, an air of nervousness that he had not known before.

'Mr Callow.' Jack forced a smile in return.

'And to what do I owe this unexpected pleasure?'

Jack sighed and gave a little shrug. 'You know we're leaving, of course.'

'Yes, I do indeed. And very sorry I was to hear it. When are you going?'

'In two weeks.'

'Well, that's a great shame. Though I do understand why you'd—why you'd want a change of scene.' He took a step back. 'It's cold out here. Would you like to come in for a minute?'

'Thank you.'

As Callow closed the front door behind him, Jack said, 'Are you sure I'm not calling at a bad time?'

'Not at all. You're calling at a very good time. I'm so tied up with the production for the festival that I'm hardly here these days. You were lucky to find me in. Life's very hectic right now.' He stopped at the open door to the sitting room. 'Anyway, come on in.' He led the way into a smallish room with a flower-patterned wallpaper that made it appear even smaller, an effect added to by the rather low ceiling. The walls were hung with pictures and framed posters connected with the opera, rather in the way that Edwin's had been, though with far less style and authority.

'Please, do sit down.' Callow gestured to an arm-chair beside the fire. 'Would you like some tea?'

'No, thank you,' Jack said as he sat. 'I can't stop that long. I know you're busy, and I'm running around too.' He placed the package on the carpet near his feet, leaning against the chair. 'It's just that while I've got the chance I thought I'd call in and—and thank you for your kindness to us while we've been here.'

Callow raised a protesting hand. 'Oh, please, there's nothing to thank me for.' Still holding the cat, he sat down in the chair facing Jack. 'I've done nothing.'

'Oh, but you have,' Jack said. 'You've been very sympathetic and kind.' He gave a sad little smile. 'And I know we didn't get off on the right foot.'

Callow's hand waved the words away. 'Oh, that's all in the past. All that business—it was so trivial. We mustn't let those minor things assume importance.'

'No, you're right, of course.' Jack looked off and gave a sigh. 'Everybody in the village has been so kind. I've had such marvellous support.'

'Well, no more than you deserve, I'm sure. But how could one fail to be touched by what has happened? You've been through a terrible time. And I'm sure that if people could have done more to help you they would have done. There's very little we can do, really, except perhaps let you know that we care, and that you have our good wishes. Beyond that . . .' He spread his hands and shrugged, letting the rest of the sentence go unspoken. Looking fondly down at the cat he gently rubbed a finger behind her ear. She stretched and purred under his touch. 'Well,' Callow said after a moment, 'how are your little girls getting on? How are they coping with it all? Poor little things.'

Feeling his heartbeat quicken, Jack was aware at the same time of a brief sense of relief. Callow was curious about the girls after giving them the runes. He had to know; he wasn't able to just sit back and wait to see what happened.

'They're all right,' Jack said. 'They're bewildered and they're somewhat stunned by it all, but they're all right.'

Callow gave a little sigh, for all the world one of sympathy and compassion. 'Poor little things,' he said again. 'Did they like their little dolls?'

Jack put a hand to his forehead. 'Oh, Mr Callow, I'm *so* sorry. Whatever must you think. I should have

305

thanked you at once. Do forgive me.'

'Don't mention it, please.'

'That was one of the reasons I called, to thank you on the girls' behalf. That was such a nice gesture. But you really shouldn't have done it.'

'Oh, it was nothing,' Callow said. 'I saw the dolls in a shop in Reading, lying there in their boxes like a pair of little twins, and I thought at once of your two girls. And I thought, too, of all they'd gone through lately and what they were still going through. So I went in and bought them. I should have asked your permission, I know, but I didn't think you'd mind.'

'Of course not.' Jack found that his mouth had gone dry. 'It was very nice of you.'

After a couple of seconds Callow said, quite casually: 'And did they get the notes I sent?'

'Notes? You sent them notes? You wrote them letters?'

Callow gave a deprecatory smile. 'I'd hardly call them letters.'

'When did you send them?' Jack asked. 'There was nothing for them in this morning's post. Though they might come by the second delivery, of course.'

'I didn't post them,' Callow said. He paused. 'I put them in with the dolls.'

Jack looked a little nonplussed. 'You put them in with the dolls?'

'Yes. In the boxes.'

Jack sighed. 'Oh, dear, then I'm afraid they didn't get them.'

'They didn't get them?'

'No, they didn't. And it's too late now, I'm afraid.'

'Why? What happened to them, the notes?'

'I'm afraid they've gone up in smoke. They must have done.'

'Oh?'

'Along with the rest of the packaging. It all went into the kitchen boiler. I'm sorry; they didn't say anything about finding any notes there.'

'It's all right. They weren't important.' Callow gave a little sigh and, hearing it, Jack couldn't miss the faint tone of pleasure it contained. Callow gently stroked the cat. 'Are you sure you won't have some tea?' he said.

'No, honestly, thank you.' Jack looked at his watch. 'I'd better go in a minute, anyway. Let you get on. Are you rehearsing this evening?'

'Oh, yes, indeed. Rehearsing every evening right now. Well, we open at the Playhouse in Reading a week Monday.'

'So soon?'

'Yes. You'll be very busy, I'm sure, it being your last week in Valley Green. But if you should find you have a spare evening, do come along and see the production. I'm sure you'll enjoy it. We'll be playing there all week, getting ready for our one vital performance at the festival in Chapelton the week after.'

'And how is it going, your production? Are you optimistic? I'm sure you are.'

Callow smiled. 'Well, let's say I'm *cautiously* optimistic. We have a very fine production. Do you know *Sonnambula?*'

'I saw it once, years ago. It's Bellini, right?'

'Yes. Oh, it's a lovely piece. And I'm so pleased with our production of it.'

'According to what I've been told, and what I've read in the paper, you've got every reason to be pleased.'

Callow inclined his head. 'As far as I can tell we've only got one real rival. That's the Bristol company. They're doing a production of *Lucia di Lammermoor*.

But I wouldn't think we've got too much to worry about. Like ours, so much depends on the soprano, and if they haven't got a halfway decent Lucia then they might as well forget it.' He shook his head. 'No, I'm not overly worried. Anyway, I shall get a better picture once I've seen the other productions for myself. Then I'll find out what the competition is really like.'

'Well, I wish you good luck.' Jack got to his feet. Callow bent to allow the cat to hop down onto the carpet and then stood up. 'Listen,' Jack said, putting out his hand, 'you're going to be very tied up over the next two weeks, so it's possible we shan't meet again. So let me thank you once more for your kindness and your—your thoughtfulness.'

Callow briefly took his hand, shook it. 'Please, don't thank me. There's nothing to thank me for. I haven't been able to do anything. You look after your little girls now. And I do hope you'll find some happiness, eventually, in your new home.'

'Thank you.' Jack paused a moment. 'Just one other thing before I go . . .' Bending, he took up the package. 'A little something for you. We can't take everything with us; there's just too much. And Connie told me how much you liked this.' He untied the string and took off the paper. 'So . . .' He held out the framed drawing that had hung in the hall at The Limes. 'Madame Malibran for you. I know she'll be going to a good home.'

Smiling, Callow reached out to take the picture, and then stopped, his fingers inches from the frame. Jack felt that he could almost read his thoughts, the questions that were going through his mind. Would he dare to accept the gift? Jack had just said that the runes had been destroyed, burnt in the kitchen boiler, and if that were true then there could be nothing now to cause Callow any harm.

Over the pencilled study of the diva's face the two men smiled at one another, Jack holding the picture and Callow's hands poised, ready to accept it. Although the two remained like this for only three or four seconds, the time seemed to Jack never-ending. And then Callow lowered his hands.

'Dear me,' he said with a rueful smile and a little shake of his head, 'that is such a kind gesture, and I'd love to accept it, but I really can't. It's just too much.'

'Not at all,' Jack said. 'Please, do take it. I know that Connie, too, would have wanted you to have it.'

Callow shook his head, a little more firmly now, even taking a step back, away from temptation and possible danger. 'I couldn't, honestly. But thank you again.'

Seeing the chance slipping away, Jack, growing desperate, said quickly, 'Ah, but just look at her. How can you resist her?' He held the portrait closer to Callow. 'Look at that capricious little face.'

He knew, though, that it would do no good. Briefly the chance had been there, but now it had gone and it would not come back. Callow had taken a further, but very definite, step back; there was no longer even the slightest question of his accepting the gift. All the well-chosen words in the world would not now persuade him to take the picture into his hands. Looking into his eyes, Jack could see that he knew. Tiny beads of sweat had broken out on Callow's brow, and there was fear in his eyes. He knew that the papers bearing the runes were behind the backing of the portrait, and he had come so close, so very close to accepting them.

'Ah, well,' Jack said, as he lowered the picture. 'If you won't accept it, then you won't. Never mind.' He

picked up the brown paper from the chair and
wrapped it around the picture once more.

Callow nodded approval of the action. 'Yes, you'd
best take care of that picture. You wouldn't want it to
come to any harm.'

The cat wove about Callow's ankles and he stooped
and took the creature up. Jack hitched the picture under his arm, turned for the door and walked out into
the hall, Callow following a yard behind. At the front
door, Jack stopped. He was leaving with nothing re-
solved, and in a situation that was worse than when
he had arrived. An hour ago there had been the chance
that he might somehow be able to return the runes to
Callow. But Callow had not been taken in and from
now on would be wary as never before.

Turning to him, his mouth dry, Jack said, 'This has
got to stop. Now.'

Callow frowned, an over-the-top expression, as
from some bad amateur actor. 'What are you talking
about? What's got to stop?'

'Please,' Jack's mouth was so dry that his upper lip
adhered briefly to his teeth, 'I didn't come here to play
games.'

'I'm pleased to hear that.'

'I mean it. It's got to stop. And you know what I'm
talking about.'

'I'm afraid I don't.'

Jack looked at him steadily for a moment. 'You
killed my wife, you killed my son, you killed my wife's
mother.'

Callow opened his eyes wide in another ham-actor's
stock expression. Then in a tone of wonder he said,
'As they say in the best melodramas, Mr Forrest, have
you taken leave of your senses?'

Jack's breath poured out in a long sigh. He had no

weapons to fight with; he could only ask for mercy. 'Oh, God,' he said, 'please, leave us alone. Let us be.'

Callow shook his head in a gesture of bewilderment. 'What do you mean? I don't understand you.'

Jack felt that he could weep with despair and frustration. 'I beg you,' he said, 'please, put an end to it. Let us alone.'

'Put an end to what?'

Jack groaned. 'You know.'

'My dear man, I do not. If I knew, I wouldn't be asking you.' He scratched the cat's head and it purred loudly at his touch. 'We don't know, do we, Miss Puss?' Raising his head to Jack again he said, 'The only thing I'm aware of is that you're rather overwrought after all that's happened.'

Callow was just playing with him, Jack thought, and was immensely enjoying the game. 'For God's sake,' Jack said, 'what had my boy ever done to you?' He could feel a tightening in his throat as he spoke, and he forced back the threatening tears. 'He took a few of your flowers, that's all. He was just a child. He'd never harmed anyone in his life. He paused to get a hold on his fading control. 'And my wife, too, and her mother. How could they have hurt you? You had a falling out with them over your dog and then with Joel over your flowers, but how could that be reason enough?'

Callow asked with wide-eyed curiosity, 'Reason enough for what?'

'For killing them.'

'My dear fellow,' Callow said, 'these are terrible accusations you're making. I hope you've got something to back them up with.'

'I don't begin to pretend to know how you do it.' Jack said. 'I just know that somehow you are able to do it. You send those bits of paper with the runes on them and you're able to destroy people.'

'Bits of paper? Runes?' Callow sighed. 'I'm afraid this has got beyond me. And I'm afraid also that my patience is running out. I think you'd better leave. I mean, I enjoy a rational discussion as much as the next man, but I really can't stand here listening to such nonsense. If you want my advice, I'd suggest you go and see a good psychiatrist.'

'You bastard,' Jack said, 'you're just making fun of me!'

'I'm not accustomed to having people talk to me in that way,' Callow said stiffly, 'and I only excuse it now because I know you're going through a bad time. But I mean it, I do think you need help. You need to go to see someone—get some counselling.'

'Listen to you,' Jack said, 'and even as you speak you're making more plans.'

'Plans? What plans?'

'You know what I'm talking about. Your plans to destroy my daughters.'

'I'm planning to kill your *daughters*?' Callow exhaled loudly, then looked down at the cat. 'Did you hear that, Miss Puss? Did you hear what he said? The plot sickens.'

'You sent papers to them, too. In with the dolls you gave them.'

Keeping his eyes on Jack, Callow's hand moved rhythmically over the soft, tabby-coloured fur. 'I thought you said just now that the notes I put in with the dolls had got burnt.'

'Please,' Jack said. 'Please, I beg you. Leave us alone. My son and my wife and my wife's mother are dead. You don't need to do any more if you want to destroy me; you've already succeeded.'

Callow gazed at him in silence for a second, then gently set the cat down on the carpet. 'Listen, old chap,' he said as he straightened, 'I know that you've suffered, and still are suffering. But you've got to get rid of these wild, fantastic notions, otherwise you'll never start to come to terms with what's happened.' He reached out for the door catch, signifying that the meeting was over. 'Now go on back home and try to pull yourself together. Your little girls need you to be strong at a time like this. You're not helping by taking refuge in this weird supernatural fairy-tale. And the sooner you realize that, the sooner you can begin to come to terms with your—with the tragedies that have happened.'

Jack stood there, helpless. He had tried. Everything. He turned and stepped through the open door onto the porch. As he did so, Callow said: 'And give my best wishes to your little girls. Tell them I hope they enjoy their dolls.' He smiled. 'And tell them I'm sorry about the teeth—mine, that is—but tell them I'm an old man. And tell them too that it's a pity their parents didn't bring them up to be a little more tactful, a little more polite to their elders.'

Jack turned back to face him, horrified disbelief in his expression. 'So that's the reason. God help me, I—'

'I shouldn't think there's much point in calling on your dear God for help,' Callow said. 'And if he's in a position to help, you might ask yourself why, if he's so powerful, he let you get into this mess in the first place.' He inclined his head. 'I don't wish to sound harsh or unsympathetic, but I'd rather you didn't call again. It does no good. And I've got important things of my own to think about. The festival's only a week away, and believe me, I need to give it all my concentration. So, if you'll excuse me . . .'

Jack watched the door close in his face. Then, like one in a dream, he stepped down from the porch and set off along the garden path.

When he got to the gate he turned and looked back at the house. The front door was closed now, but he could see Callow at the window of the sitting room. For a moment the two stood looking at one another, and then Callow lifted a hand and, his eyes fixed on Jack, drew a finger across his throat. Throwing back his head, he bared his yellow teeth and began to laugh. Jack could hear no sound from where he stood, but sound was not necessary; Callow's whole body was shaking with his laughter.

Chapter Eighteen

Jack drove home with his mind in a daze. When he got there he made a mug of instant coffee and carried it into the study. He sat at his desk, sipping at the coffee and staring unseeingly ahead. He could not think of anything now that could be done. He had tried to best Callow and had failed. There would not be another opportunity—at least not one that could be engineered in the short time that was left. Pushing the coffee aside, he folded his arms before him on the desk, laid his head upon them and closed his eyes.

He remained like that for some time, until he felt the muscles in his neck growing stiff. He opened his eyes; the room had grown cold, and he realized that the central heating had not been turned on. It didn't matter; nothing mattered. Now it was all over but the shouting. Callow had won.

As he straightened, massaging the back of his neck, his glance fell upon the correspondence that he had earlier pushed aside. And he remembered the letter

that had come from the committee of the music festival. He bent down and rummaged through the waste
basket until he found it. He placed it before him on
the desk and read it through. Afterwards he sat deep
in thought for several minutes, and then turned to the
telephone. He dialled a number and waited.

'Hello?'

'Hello, is this Mrs Charlotte Wilding?'

'Yes, it is.'

'Mrs Wilding, this is Jack Forrest.'

'I was so pleased to get your phone call, Mr Forrest.
I'm delighted that you're going to be able to present
the opera award.'

Charlotte Wilding, in her mid-fifties, was able to
look elegant in a simple sweater and blue jeans. In the
private bar of a pub in the older part of Swindon, she
sat facing Jack across a small corner table. She drank
white wine while Jack nursed a half-pint of bitter.

'It will be a great honour,' Jack said, then added,
'You must have thought me very rude, not getting
back to you before today.'

'Not at all. We've all been very much aware that—
that you're going through difficult times. In fact, we
debated whether to approach you in the first place.'

'I'm very glad you did.'

'I am too.' She gave a little nod of pleasure. 'The rest
of the committee are going to be so pleased when I
tell them. Not having heard from you we'd rather assumed that you were unable to accept our invitation,
and we'd just about resigned ourselves to your not being available, and to the festival's president, Sir Brian
Harwich, presenting the opera award as well as the
others.'

'I hope I'm not giving you problems, am I?'

316

'Oh, not at all,' she assured him.

'The award is to be given in three weeks, on Sunday, May the third, isn't it?'

'That's right. Three weeks this Sunday. The festival is on for a fortnight, finishing on the Sunday with the presentation of the awards. There are six competing opera productions, and they'll be presented at the theatre each evening, Monday to Saturday, over the second week. There are also concerts of orchestral works, chamber music, choral works, and poetry and drama too. It'll be a very crowded two weeks, both as regards the time and place. Every possible venue in Chapelton is being used. It'll be a splendid two weeks. Very, very exciting.'

'There is one thing . . .' Jack said.

'Yes?'

'My uncle, Edwin Maddox, also left a monetary prize in his will, to be presented along with the plate.'

'Really?' She looked at him in surprise. 'Well, that's wonderful.'

Somehow he was surprised that she had accepted this without question. 'I should have informed the festival committee before,' he said. 'I do apologize for that. I'm afraid it went out of my head.' He smiled. 'Anyway, it's good news, isn't it?'

'It is indeed.'

'It's not a fortune, mind. A matter of five hundred pounds. A token. And it's just a one-off, for this particular year. It's to be used by the winning opera company in the development of a future production. Not a great deal, I'm afraid. I wish it were more, but there you are.'

'Mr Forrest, it'll be a wonderful addition to the honour of winning the award. And it will be extremely useful. This is really excellent news.' She took a sip from her wine glass. 'And of course, you'd like to present the cheque along with the plate, I imagine.'

'That's what my uncle had in mind, yes.'

'Fine. Then it shall be done. I'll get an announcement off to the local papers at once, telling them about the cheque and the fact that you'll be making the presentation.'

'No,' Jack said quickly, 'I'd rather you didn't do that.'

'Oh?'

'At present,' he said, 'I'd rather only the committee knew that I'm going to present the award. Just in case at the last moment I'm not able to do it.'

'I see. Do you think there's some doubt that you'll be able to?'

'Oh, not at all. It's just that . . .' He let the sentence go unfinished, allowing her to come to her own conclusions.

She said with a sympathetic nod, 'I understand. We'll leave it as it is for the time being, with the general understanding that Sir Brian Harwich will give the award.'

'Thank you.'

They went on then to speak of the competing opera companies. Jack learned that all six would be presenting their productions in the week prior to the competition in theatres in their home towns in final preparation for the performances that would be presented over the second and last week of the festival.

From her bag Charlotte Wilding took a sheet of paper which she handed to Jack. It gave, she said, details of the competing companies and their productions, and the venues where they could be seen in the week before the competition. Jack folded the paper and put it in his pocket.

They chatted for a few more minutes, and then, saying that he would have to go and meet his daughters from school, Jack took his leave of her.

On the way back from Barfield later that afternoon Lydia spoke of one of their schoolfriends who was going away during the holidays. The idea lodged in Jack's mind, and he decided that if it was possible he would take the girls somewhere for a few days. It would be good to get away from Valley Green, the scene of so much recent horror and heartache.

Over that weekend he scanned the holiday pages in the newspapers and eventually, after several telephone calls, was able to make a booking at a holiday cottage on the outskirts of the Somerset coastal resort of Burnham-on-Sea. They would be there, he told the owner, on Monday afternoon.

By Monday morning their bags and cases were all packed, and they were ready to go. There remained just one job to do before their departure. In his study Jack sat down at his desk with the list of opera productions that Charlotte Wilding had given him. Then he telephoned the box office of each of the theatre companies, reserving a seat for himself for one of the performances during the following week. The first production he would see—next Monday evening—was Callow's, in Reading.

Now he was ready to go. When he had loaded the luggage into the Citroën, he saw Kitty and Lydia strapped into the rear seats and then locked up the house. That done he backed the car out into the lane and they set off.

They arrived in Burnham-on-Sea in the mid-afternoon under grey skies, with clouds driven by a cold east wind. The cottage, situated within a fairly short distance of the sea, was semi-detached, the adjoining dwelling being at present unoccupied. Although small, the little house looked comfortable enough, and Jack told himself that they would have all that they required for their short stay.

That evening he made supper for the three of them and after the girls had had their baths he said he would read them a story. On the sofa, in the glow of the electric fire, the girls, in their pyjamas and dressing gowns, pressed against him while he read aloud. Afterwards he led them upstairs to the larger of the two bedrooms and saw them both into one of the twin beds. There he covered them up, tucked them in and then sat on the side of the bed. They both held on to his right hand. 'What shall we do tomorrow, Daddy?' Kitty asked, and he replied that they would go down to the beach, to the seaside.

'But we won't go *in* the sea, will we? I don't want to go in the sea.' She sounded a little afraid.

'You don't have to go in the sea. Of course you don't. It's much too cold for that, anyway.'

'What shall we do, then?' Lydia asked.

'Well . . . we'll walk by the sea. On the sand. Maybe you can find some nice shells or something.'

'I thought it would be sunny,' Kitty said. 'Isn't it usually sunny at the seaside?'

'Well, it usually has been in the past,' Jack said. 'But that's because it's been in the summer when we've gone on holiday in the past.'

'Won't there be any sun this time?' asked Lydia.

'I don't know, sweetheart.' This wasn't turning out at all the right way. But what had he expected? He had seen no further than the fact of getting away from Valley Green. 'We'll have to wait and see.'

He bent and kissed them goodnight. As he straightened, he moved to withdraw his hand, but Lydia held on to it. 'Don't go yet,' she said.

He remained with them until they were asleep and then crept downstairs. There he poured himself a Scotch and water and sat steeped in misery in the little sitting room, sipping mechanically at his drink and gazing off unseeingly into space.

It rained during the night, and in the morning the clouds remained. 'But it will brighten up, you'll see,' Jack said encouragingly as he got the girls into their coats and hats. They had brought with them their buckets and spades, and at his suggestion they carried them into the car. Reaching the long, sweeping stretch of beach, they walked on the sands for a while until Jack found a relatively sheltered spot where they came to a stop. Here, in the lee of the esplanade wall he spread out a rug and sat hunched over his knees watching as the girls dug in the damp sand and did their best to fashion a castle. There were few other people about, and he remarked to himself that everybody else had more sense than to be sitting out in such unwelcoming conditions. Some twenty yards away Lydia in blue and Kitty in red crouched over the sand, their hair blowing out from beneath the rims of their woollen hats. Beyond their bending forms the swollen, windswept waters of the Bristol Channel looked grey and dark. After a while the girls left their tottering castles and came back to his side, their faces a little reddened by the wind. What should they do now? they wanted to know. He asked them whether they had had enough of the beach for the time being, and they replied that they had. He nodded and got up and shook the sand from the rug, folded it up and put it back in the bag. 'Let's go and find somewhere nice to have lunch,' he said.

They ate hamburgers, and afterwards went to a cinema to catch a matinée showing of Disney's film of *The Little Mermaid*. In the dark of the half-empty cinema he was disappointed but unsurprised to find that neither of the girls appeared to be involved in what was happening up on the screen. What a slick and utterly charmless piece of work it was, he thought; how far removed from the magical animated classics of the past. It was no wonder that the girls fidgeted in their seats and were so easily distracted. When it was over they got in the car and drove back to the house.

That night Jack bent over them as they lay in bed and kissed each of them on the forehead. 'What would you like to do tomorrow?' he asked. 'We could drive to Weston-Super-Mare and go on the pier. There's a wonderful pier there, and perhaps on the beach there'll be donkey rides and a Punch and Judy show. Would you like to go there?'

'Daddy,' Kitty said, 'I want to go home.'

'Yes, I do too,' said Lydia.

The following morning they packed up and left.

Back in Valley Green Jack did his best to keep the girls amused while he waited for the days to pass until Monday, when he would begin to view the competing opera productions. The question of the care of the girls while he was out each evening was solved by Jane, who readily agreed to come and look after them in his absence. She did not question his desire to see the competing opera productions; with his being Edwin's nephew she took it as a matter of course that he would have a strong interest in the festival.

The weather on Monday was fine and Jack took the girls into Reading to do some shopping, and then, by their choice when it came to lunch, to eat pizzas and ice cream.

Jane arrived at the house promptly that evening. Jack was ready to leave when she appeared, and with admonitions to the girls to be good, he kissed them and set off for Reading and the Playhouse.

He had only once before seen a production of *La Sonnambula*, and that had been performed in its original Italian. He could remember little of its story apart from the fact that it was about a young village girl, Amina, whose sleep-walking compromises her honour but who nevertheless ends up with her intended sweetheart; this and the fact that towards the end of the opera came a famous and fiendishly difficult coloratura aria. This aria, he had read somewhere, was something of a test piece for a soprano, and many found it beyond their abilities. That Callow should have chosen such a taxing opera for entry in the festival either showed great and foolish bravery or indicated that he had managed to find an amateur soprano capable of meeting Bellini's exacting demands.

The auditorium was not full, though Jack doubted that this would bother Callow or his company unduly; they would be using these early performances merely as rehearsals, to polish and hone the production ready for the all-important festival performance that would take place the following week.

From his seat near the back of the theatre, Jack saw Callow, holding a clipboard, walk down the aisle and sit in one of the side seats. Shortly afterwards the orchestra's conductor took up his position, the brief overture began and then the curtain rose to reveal an Alpine village scene with the villagers gathering to celebrate the betrothal of Amina to her young lover El-vino.

Charlotte Wilding had told him that each of the six competing companies had two sets of principal singers. This was deemed necessary to avoid over-taxing the voices of the main soloists, and to ensure that there would be a replacement readily available should the need arise. Jack was seeing Callow's first cast this evening—which was important; he wanted to get the best possible idea of Callow's chances in the coming competition.

Now, as the opera unfolded before him, he knew that those chances had to be excellent. Preoccupied as he was with the oppressive fear that hung upon him at all times, and hating Callow as he did, Jack never-theless could not help but be impressed. Callow might have made misjudgements in the past in the produc-tions he had mounted, but this time he had made no mistake. Jack found himself thinking—irony of iro-nies—that even Edwin would have approved.

In spite of the excellence of Callow's production, it was with some trepidation that Jack set out the following evening to see the Oxford company's pro-duction of *La Bohème*. This was the company that had won the plate at the last competition, and their reputation was high. Before going into the audito-rium, he stood for some time in the foyer in front of the glass display case holding the Maddox Plate and read there the engraved names of the past win-ners. Eventually came the bell giving notice of the raising of the curtain, and he turned and joined the crowd going inside.

When he emerged and made his way onto the street following the final curtain some while later, it was with a feeling of relief. All his fears had been unjustified. The production would not, he was sure, offer Callow's *Sonnambula* any serious competition. It was a plodding, heavy-handed offering, full of wasted opportunities and unsubtle characterizations. The chorus had seemed ragged and unprepared, and the general staging had been awkward and amateurish in the worst way. Although he had seen the second cast of principal singers, he was sure that even with a topnotch cast in place, it could not at its best be that much better.

He felt much the same the next evening in Chapelton where he went to see that town's production of *Carmen*. To his relief he found that Carmen herself came over as a rather lacklustre character, presented by a singer who seemed to find the whole thing beyond her capabilities. The rest of the cast seemed not much happier.

The Swindon Opera Guild's presentation of *Rigoletto*, which he saw on the Thursday evening, offered to give Callow a run for his money, but it nevertheless lacked much of the spirit of the Reading group's production. Massenet's *Thaïs*, presented by the Bath company, also proved to be a fine piece. Even so, in Jack's view it still came way behind Callow's offering.

By Saturday, having seen all but one of the competing opera productions, Jack could not help but feel a certain sanguinity. Callow would have to win. He must.

And then, in Bristol on Saturday night, he saw that city's production of *Lucia di Lammermoor*.

When the final bows had been taken and the curtain had fallen for the last time, he remained in his seat while the other members of the audience made their way towards the exits. While they were animated and lively in their satisfaction, he was filled with despair. No matter how he tried to view it otherwise, he could not but admit that the production had been one of the most memorable that he had ever seen, and one which, he felt sure, any professional company would have been proud to own. The playing of the orchestra had been vibrant and exciting and the staging excellent, with fetching designs and very fine singing and acting. He could not see how such a production could lose.

As he sat there he saw the figure of John Callow moving up one of the far aisles. For a moment he was surprised at the man's presence, but then he realized that it was only to be expected. Like all the competing producers, Callow would be anxious to check out the competition. Although he was too far away to make out Callow's expression, Jack was sure that he could no longer be optimistic about his chances of winning.

Jack remained in his seat and watched as Callow left the auditorium. Only when he felt sure that he must be safely out of the way did he get up to leave.

He was almost the last to go out, following the final stragglers out into the foyer where little knots of people stood around talking. And there again was Callow, standing talking to two men, one of whom Jack recognized as the orchestra's conductor. Quickly, before Callow had a chance to see him, Jack turned to the right and slipped into the bar.

It was quite crowded and Jack made his way with difficulty to the bar itself where eventually he managed to get a half-pint of beer. As he stood drinking it, some of the cast of the opera appeared, to be met by friends who greeted them with warm praise and handshakes and kisses. The young soprano who had sung the part of Lucia came in, followed immediately by the tenor who had sung Edgardo. They came close to where Jack was standing and were at once surrounded by friends and admirers. One of those who greeted them was a very pretty, dark-haired young woman, and overhearing some of the remarks that passed between them Jack concluded that she was the alternative Lucia from the second cast of principals. He looked at the two young women as they stood facing one another. They were the barrier between Callow and the prize he so coveted—and also, Jack told himself, the barrier between himself and any final chance of salvation. He turned away from the animated little group, took another swallow from his beer glass, set it down on the bar and moved towards the door.

He had only gone two or three yards when Callow appeared in his path. They stood there facing one another for a moment in silence, then Callow's lips parted in a semblance of a smile.

'So, Mr Forrest, you're an opera-lover too. I'm delighted to see it.'

Jack said nothing, merely nodded.

'And what,' Callow asked, 'did you think of tonight's performance?'

'I thought it was excellent—the whole thing.'

Callow nodded. 'It was. It was indeed.'

Observing him, Jack half expected to see some trace of resentment or envy on his face. But there was nothing there other than an acknowledgement of the production's obvious merits.

'Have you seen any of the other productions in the area?' Callow asked.

'A couple. I saw yours.'

'Oh, really. I won't ask what you think of it.'

'I thought it was an extremely fine piece of work. I loved every minute of it.'

Callow looked a little taken aback at this, as if he had been unprepared for a compliment. He gave a little nod. 'Thank you.' A pause. 'And will you be going to Chapelton next week, for the last part of the festival?' Before Jack could answer, he added, 'Oh no, you're leaving to return to London, aren't you?'

Jack said nothing to this. They remained without speaking for a few seconds, then Callow said: 'Well, you must excuse me. I want to congratulate the members of the company on their splendid work.'

With a little nod he moved on and made his way towards the crowd near the bar. Jack saw him smilingly approach them, hand outstretched. He remained watching for a few moments longer as Callow launched into warm congratulations, then turned away, left the theatre, and went out into the street.

He knew now with certainty that to hope for success where the opera competition was concerned was not realistic. Furthermore, even if Callow should, against the odds, win, there would still remain the feat of getting the runes back to him without his being aware. He couldn't rely only on desperate hope and the very slimmest chance of success; he would have to have an alternative, back-up, plan.

By the time he got back to Valley Green he had made a decision; if the worst came to the worst he knew what he would have to do. After Jane had left, he went to the study, took the key from its hiding place and unlocked the drawer. Before him lay the padded envelope holding the papers with the runes. He ignored this and, reaching past it, grasped the cloth-wrapped shape there and drew it out. Sitting at the desk he placed the small bundle before him and pulled aside the wrapping of oil-impregnated cloth to reveal Edwin's pistol and the little box of ammunition.

Chapter Nineteen

Monday, 27 April. The start of the festival's second and final week also marked the beginning of the new school term after the Easter holidays. On this day Kitty and Lydia should have been starting school in Chiswick. Instead, they were still living in Valley Green, and Jack had driven them to school in Barfield. There he explained to the headmistress that their plans for moving back to London had been postponed for a week or two and for the time being the girls would have to continue their schooling where they were.

During that week he drove them to Barfield every morning and picked them up again in the afternoon when classes were over for the day. Most of the time of their absence he spent alone in his study or upstairs in Mary's studio, preparing for the awards ceremony. He was convinced that Callow must eventually win the game that he was playing but he had to do what he could. He prayed that Callow's production would be voted the best in the opera competition. Only then would his plan have a chance of working. If the worst should happen and Callow's production failed, then he had the gun.

Sitting at his desk, he took the weapon from the drawer and turned it over in his hands. It was a revolver bearing the inscription Smith and Wesson. Opening the small accompanying box he found that it held seven .38 calibre shells. Holding the weapon very carefully he pushed the cylinder out into his hand. It was empty. He replaced the cylinder, laid the gun before him on the desk and sat looking at it. Would he be able to use it? Unless he could return the runes to Callow very soon, he would have to. He himself might be doomed but he was determined to save the lives of his daughters. If he died leaving Callow still living, then Lydia and Kitty would have no chance whatsoever against his evil; he had no doubt that Callow would destroy them eventually.

He couldn't take his eyes from the revolver. If the time came to use it he would need to carry out the action swiftly and surely. Yet he had never in his life fired such a weapon. The closest he had ever come to such an act was as a youth when taking potshots at targets at a fairground rifle range.

He picked up the gun again, slipped one of the shells into the chamber, then closed the gun and secured the safety catch. He sat there for a moment or two longer then, with the revolver in his hand, got up and left the room. From the hall he went into the kitchen where he took a large apple and put it in his pocket. That done, he made his way down to the bottom of the orchard. It was a warm day, and the setting was one of great peace and tranquillity. The cherry trees and some of the apple and pear trees were in full bloom, with the bees busy among the blossoms. The air was full of the varied sounds of birdsong. Around his feet the sweet green grass was starred with the flowers of dandelions and daisies.

He took the apple from his pocket and placed it in the grass at the foot of a cherry tree. Then he released the revolver's safety catch, levelled the muzzle up close to the fruit and squeezed the trigger. There was a click; nothing more. He tried again with the same result. He pulled the trigger a third time, and the deafening shot shattered the apple and stilled the sounds of the birds.

He did not go near the festival that week; did not go to see any of the competing operas. Instead he chose to spend the time with the girls. On Friday evening Charlotte Wilding telephoned to get confirmation that he would be able to present the award for the winning operatic entry. He assured her that he would, and that he would be at the dinner at the Chapelton Corn Exchange on Sunday.

Early on Sunday evening, as he was getting ready for the journey to Chapelton, Jane telephoned to say that her mother had had a slight fall and could not be left alone; she was very sorry but she would not be able to sit with Lydia and Kitty after all. Jack replaced the receiver in a daze. There was so little time left to make other arrangements. Then, taking up the phone again, he dialled George Appleton's number. The old man was at home and, to Jack's great relief, agreed at once to come and help out. He would be round in half an hour, he said. Within twenty-five minutes he was there and receiving from Jack the necessary instructions with regard to the girls' supper and bedtime.

A while later, wearing his dinner jacket, Jack went

into the sitting room where George and the girls were sitting on the sofa in front of the television. The girls looked up at him approvingly. 'Oh, Daddy,' Lydia said, 'you look so smart.'

'Thank you.'

'Can we come with you?'

'Oh, yes, please,' added Kitty. 'Can we?'

'I'm sorry, but no. Not tonight.'

'Why not?' Lydia asked.

'Because it's going to be a meeting only for adults.'

Kitty: We wouldn't talk. We wouldn't make a noise.'

'No, I'm sorry. It's just not possible. But I'll be back as soon as I can.' He turned to George. 'I don't think I'll be too late, George. No later than eleven, I hope.'

'You take as long as you like,' George said. 'We shall be fine.'

'I'm sure you will.' Jack paused, then took from his pocket a sealed envelope which he placed on the mantelpiece. 'I've been thinking,' he said, his tone casual, 'now that it's just me and the girls, it makes sense for a person to know who to contact in the event of—of some accident or something happening to me. I'm not being melodramatic; it's just a simple precaution.' The envelope held the name, address and telephone number of his solicitor, whom he had telephoned and written to earlier that week with regard to his wishes for the girls in the event of his death.

'Ah, I reckon it is sensible,' George said, glancing up at the envelope. Then he added, 'Anyway, you have a nice evenin'. And don't worry about nothin'. Me and the girls'll be all right.'

In the study, Jack finished packing his holdall, fastened it, and then carried it out to the Citroën and locked it in the boot. Returning to the house, he looked into the sitting room. 'Come on,' he said to the girls. 'Come and see me off, will you?'

They got up from the sofa and went out to him in the hall. There he bent and put his arms around them, pressed his lips to their cheeks and held them close.

'I'm depending on you to be good girls now. I know you will.'

Kitty nodded, while Lydia assured him, yes, they would.

'You said you won't be back till eleven,' Kitty said.

'Maybe not. But I'll try to get here sooner.'

'Eleven o'clock is so late. We'll be in bed.'

'And asleep, I hope.'

Lydia said, 'I want to see you before I got to sleep.'

'Yes,' Kitty added, 'I do too.' There was a little note of panic in her voice, and he thought again of the co-lossal upheavals that she and Lydia had known in the last months of their short lives. No one could know to what degree they had been affected by their losses; they themselves could not have verbalized it. Jack could only begin to sense it at times like these.

'Can we wait up for you?' Kitty said.

'I don't think so. You'll be much better off in bed. You need your sleep. And you've got school in the morning.'

'I don't want to go to school,' Lydia said.

Kitty immediately added, 'No, neither do I.'

Before Connie's death they had never objected to going to school. 'Of course you must go to school,' Jack said.

'Listen,' Kitty said, 'if we wait up for you we'll stay on the sofa. And if we're tired we'll sleep there.'

'Yes,' Lydia said, 'we'll sleep there.'

'Yes, then you can carry us up to bed.'

He smiled. 'Can I?'

'I shan't go to sleep till after you get in,' said Kitty.

'No, neither shall I,' said Lydia. She put her arms around his neck so tightly that she affected his breathing. He loosened her hold on him, looked into her face and then Kitty's. 'Are you my girls?' he said.

Of course, they assured him, matter-of-fact, having no idea of the peril that lay so close, the danger of further loss and separation.

'Good. Now you go on back in with Mr Appleton. I'll be home again as soon as I can. And you're to go to bed when he tells you, all right?'

'All right,' Kitty said reluctantly, 'but you won't forget to come up and see us when you get back, will you?'

'Of course I shan't forget.' Was he merely whistling in the dark? 'And listen, we'll do something special at the end of the week, shall we?'

Lydia: 'Oh, yes! What shall we do?'

'We'll think about it.' He hugged them again, loath to let them go. 'Now—you go on back into the warm.'

A minute later he was in the car and backing out into the lane.

He arrived at the old building in Chapelton, known as the Corn Exchange, a little later than he had anticipated but luckily found a parking space not too far away. He entered the building to find that the guests had finished their cocktails and were filing into the banqueting room to take their places for dinner.

As he went past the cloakroom, the young assistant asked if he wanted to leave his bag. He thanked her, but said no, he would keep it with him. Joining the throng, he made his way into the spacious hall which was laid out with white-clothed dining tables. The scene was illuminated by glowing candelabra supplemented by soft, subtle, concealed lighting. He was

336

shown onto a low platform at the far end on which stood the tables designated for the festival officials and those who were to present the awards. At the place marked with his name he sat down and placed the bag, still securely zipped, beneath the table. As he did so he was relieved to observe that the tablecloth hung to the floor at the front, so forming a screen against view from the assembly in the main body of the hall. He straightened to find Charlotte Wilding coming to sit at his side, and he rose again and took the welcoming hand she offered. 'I've been looking out for you,' she said. 'I was beginning to think perhaps you couldn't come.'

She introduced him to their nearest neighbours at the table—another member of the committee and one of the judges—and then the wine was being poured and the first course served.

As he picked at the food on his plate, Jack glanced over the assembly before them. Among those seated at the various tables were faces he recognized from the competing opera productions. There were the tenor, the baritone and the soprano from the Swindon production of *Rigoletto*; there was the mezzo-soprano from the *Carmen* production, the principals from Oxford's *La Bohème*.

And there, too, was Callow at a table some distance away, sitting at right angles to him, looking distinguished in his dinner jacket. A moment later, as if he had felt Jack's eyes upon him, Callow turned in his chair, briefly frowned at seeing him there, then smiled. Jack ignored the smile and turned again to Charlotte Wilding.

As he talked with her he gradually became aware that there was an air of constraint in the room. What should have been a bright, convivial gathering seemed strangely subdued; there was very little laughter to be heard, and what there was occurred only sporadically and sounded somewhat out of place.

He did not dwell upon the phenomenon. He could not. Caught up in his own preoccupations he needed all his concentration just to appear at ease while he talked and tried to eat. In the end he gave up on the latter, and when the waiter brought the pudding, Jack thanked him and waved it away. His palms were wet and his stomach seemed to be tying itself in knots. Against his right foot he could feel the holdall. The time was drawing near for the awards to be announced, and he had little doubt that the Bristol company's production would be announced the winner. If that happened, then his first plan would count for nothing, and he would be forced to use the gun. He would await his chance and take it when he could, either by following Callow out to his car and shooting him there, or following him back to Valley Green. What became of himself afterwards was not important; it would be academic, anyway, for the runes would soon bring about his destruction.

At last dinner was over and the last coffee cup had been cleared away. At the centre table on the platform a microphone was connected and set in place, while on another table nearby the prizes were being arranged. Among them Jack saw the Maddox Plate.

The mayor was introduced by the festival's president, and he got up to address the assembly, saying what a successful fortnight it had been, and how well the festival had been attended. After that the presentation of the awards began. Prizes were given for poetry, for the production of a play, for painting, for singing, both solo and ensemble. One by one the winners were applauded up onto the platform to receive their awards. In many cases these were presented by the festival's president, Sir Brian Harwich, but in others various celebrities had been asked to present them, among them a well-known musician and an actress from a popular soap opera.

As the time drew closer to the presentation of the opera award Jack was aware of Callow sitting up straighter in his chair in anticipation of what was to come. Surely Callow could not, in the light of Bristol's fine production, be expecting to win. When there came a little break in the proceedings Jack took advantage of the hiatus and, turning to Charlotte Wilding at his side, silently mouthed, '*Lucia*, yes?' He expected either a nod or a shake of the head in response, but instead she frowned and looked at him in surprise. Leaning closer to him she whispered, 'Haven't you heard?'

'Heard? Heard what?'

She leaned in closer still and whispered into his ear, 'Bristol's production of *Lucia* was withdrawn.'

'Withdrawn?'

She nodded. 'Last night.'

'Why?'

She shook her head. 'I can't believe you haven't heard about it. It was in the papers this morning and on the radio.'

'I haven't been listening to the radio or reading the papers over the past few days. What's happened?'

'Two principal members· of the *Lucia* cast were killed yesterday evening.'

'*What?*'

'They were due to compete last night. But they were killed on their way to give their performance.' There were tears shining in her eyes. 'Both sopranos, the Lucias from both casts, died. And one of the tenors and one of the leading baritones are critically injured.'

He stared at her, stunned. 'How—how did it happen?'

'One of the girls was driving. I believe she swerved to avoid a dog.'

Jack looked at Callow again. No wonder he appeared so sanguine. He knew that with the Bristol production no longer in the running he stood a better chance than anyone of carrying off the prize. And as he gazed at him, Jack knew what had happened. He had a picture of Callow as he had last seen him—in the bar at the theatre where he had gone to see the production of *Lucia*. He could see him going up to the singers, smiling at them, congratulating them upon their performances. It would have been the perfect opportunity to pass them the runes. Jack had no doubt whatever that it had happened; he was only surprised that he had not before considered the fact that Callow might intervene to ensure that the prize would at last be his.

At the centre table on the platform, the president rose again and, confirming Charlotte Wilding's words, spoke of the tragedy that had touched the festival. There had, he said, been some discussion as to whether to cancel the operatic competition, but it had been decided to go ahead with it and select the winning production from the remaining five. This, he said, had been done, and the choice of the judges had been unanimous. He looked around him at this, taking in the anticipatory faces turned towards him.

'Before the Maddox Plate is awarded,' he went on, 'let me say that, following the death of Professor Maddox, it was decided that I should present the award, but we were then fortunate enough to have the nephew of Edwin Maddox agree to present it. This is a gentleman known not in the field of opera but in the field of television, in which he has won awards for his writing. Ladies and gentlemen, may I present Mr Jack Forrest.'

His mind spinning, Jack got to his feet and to a wave of warm applause gave a little bow of acknowledgement. As he straightened he glanced at Callow's face and saw shock in his expression; that he, Jack, would be presenting the plate was something Callow had clearly not anticipated.

Stepping to the centre table, Jack shook hands with Sir Brian and then briefly addressed the audience, speaking of the honour it was for him to present the prize, and of how much he had enjoyed seeing the various productions. That done he turned to Sir Brian who handed him a large, white, sealed envelope. From the back of the envelope Jack read out the names of the competing companies and their productions.

When he had finished he paused briefly then opened the envelope, looked at what was written there and said in the manner of one announcing the winner of a Hollywood Oscar: 'And the winner is—Reading Light Operatic Society for *La Sonnambula*.' Loud applause. Jack waited until it had begun to subside then added: 'The award to be presented to Mr John Callow, producer of the winning production.' He looked out into the assembly, smiling expectantly, then set the paper down on the table before him.

On the far side of the room Callow got to his feet. Across the tables he and Jack looked at one another. Callow was hesitating, as if uncertain as to what to do. Even across the distance between them, Jack could see the wariness in his eyes.

At Jack's side Sir Brian took up the Maddox Plate and held it out. Jack thanked him, took it, and turned back to the front. 'Mr Callow?'

Callow hesitated only another moment and then stepped forward. To waves of applause he moved to the platform and stepped up onto it. Jack watched as, smiling, he came to a halt before him, and then addressed the assembly again.

'Sir Brian, ladies and gentlemen, it gives me enormous pleasure to be able to present this award, the plate donated by my uncle, Edwin Maddox, and it gives me further pleasure to tell you that this year there is to be an additional prize awarded to the winning amateur opera company. My uncle stipulated in his will that along with the plate there should go a monetary award, a cheque for five hundred pounds, to be used by the winning company for their next production. I have the cheque here.' At this he turned and, still holding the silver plate, bent to his bag beneath the table. When he straightened, he smiled at Callow and held up the cheque for everyone to see.

As befitted a presentation cheque, it was larger than the norm. Measuring some twelve inches by six, on heavy white card, it was little less than a work of art. Jack had spent many hours making it. Set out on the general pattern of an ordinary Lloyds Bank cheque, he had rendered the lettering in an ornate Gothic script and decorated the whole with colourful and elegant flourishes and curlicues and scrolls.

'Mr John Callow,' Jack stood with the plate held under his left arm and the cheque in his right hand, 'it gives me great pleasure to present you with your awards.'

As he finished speaking, he and Callow locked glances, and he saw a little gleam of understanding appear in Callow's eyes. Then, slowly, Callow smiled back at him, and then looked at the cheque.

Evil Intent

'Presented to Mr John Callow,' Jack announced, 'the sum of five hundred pounds for the Reading Light Operatic Society.' He moved his hand slightly, holding the cheque out to Callow, silently urging him to accept it. And as he did so there came a gust of wind from one of the partly opened windows, a wind that swept through the room, so sharp and acute that on the nearest table two of the candles flared and went out. In the hall the members of the assembly muttered and looked about them, while in Jack's hand the cheque trembled in the sudden gust. Staring at the cheque, as if mesmerized, Callow caught the briefest glimpse of what appeared to be two pieces of paper stuck onto its back, papers bearing markings. The wind came again, as keen and strong as before, lasting for several seconds, snuffing out more of the candle flames and ruffling the hair and clothes of those who sat in its path. And as swiftly it died. Still Callow made no move to take the cheque. Instead, he gave Jack a thin, sagacious smile and then turned to the assembly.

He swallowed, took a breath. 'My Lord, ladies and gentlemen,' he said, 'let me say first of all that it has been a great honour for me to have led the company that has won the award this year. It's been something I have wanted for a very, very long time.' Briefly he turned to take in Jack at his side. 'But Mr Forrest, I feel that we cannot also accept the award of the money.' As he said this he was pleased to see a look of not-quite-hidden disappointment flash across Jack's face. Feeling his strength and his power growing by the second, he went on, 'Our winning today, however, brings a pleasure mixed with great sadness, for very much on our minds is the dreadful tragedy that has so recently struck the festival, and in particular the opera competition that is so important to myself, my colleagues and many others here tonight. I would like to thank Mr Forrest with all my heart—and I know I speak also for the others in the group—for the offer of the cheque, but I would like him instead to give it to the Bristol company who have suffered so much over the past two days. And may I say also on behalf of my own company that I wish the money to be used by the Bristol group in the furtherance of rebuilding their strength so that very soon they may reach again the very high standards we witnessed in the lead up to the festival.'

Applause broke out again at this, applause which Callow quickly silenced with a little wave of his hand. Then, smiling at Jack who still held out the cheque to him, he said, 'However, Mr Forrest, on behalf of my company I shall be most honoured to accept from you the award of the Maddox Plate.'

Then, before Jack had a chance to say or do anything further, Callow reached out a hand and took the plate from his grasp.

And the moment he had done so his smile became fixed and died, and a look of horror and disbelief flashed across his face.

Now the smile was on Jack's face.

While the applause drummed in his ears Callow stood without moving, holding his prize, the plate that was almost weightless in his hands. It was not made of metal at all. Then what was it? Cardboard? Papier mâcheé? A papier mâché plate covered with burnished silver leaf or tin-foil? Whatever it was it was not the Maddox Plate. But how could that be? He had seen the plate, the real plate, placed in Forrest's hands just before he had bent to get the cheque. Of *course*, that must have been when Forrest had made the switch. The genuine plate must be lying now in Forrest's bag or on the floor beneath the table.

Lifting the plate a little higher, Callow saw the two strips of paper that had been glued onto the back of its base, and in a wave of saturating fear—but without surprise—saw that they bore the runes.

How could he have allowed such a thing to happen? On closer examination the plate didn't even *look* like the real thing. It was too thick, and the sheen of its silver covering was too dull. But he had not truly looked at it before; all his attention had been on the cheque that had been held out to him. And now, looking at Jack Forrest's smile, Callow knew that the cheque was nothing more than what it appeared to be: a harmless presentation cheque with slips of paper bearing meaningless scribbles stuck on the back.

As if in endorsement of Callow's realization, Jack turned and, still smiling, let the cheque fall onto the table. It lay there, unmoving.

The applause had begun to die away, but still Callow stood there holding the plate, the look of stunned disbelief fixed on his face. After all his care, after all his vigilance, he had been tricked.

And then, suddenly, the wind was back. It came gusting through the room again, more strongly than ever, lifting the corners of the tablecloths and snuffing out more of the candles. In the narrow path of the gale the plate in Callow's hands bent and bucked like a living thing. He held on, but the wind's power increased even further, until in a final, violent blast the plate was snatched from his grasp. He lurched, reaching out to retrieve it, but it was too late, and he could only watch as it went spinning away on the current, its gleaming surface reflecting the points of the remaining candle flames. He watched as it hurtled towards one of the open windows, and then a second later it was gone, flying out into the night.

Jack, standing at Callow's side, also watched, and like Callow he knew there would be no point in rushing to see what became of the plate. Bearing both sets of runes, it would fly straight towards the nearest fire or body of water.

There was no stopping it now.

The runes were being cast.

Had been cast.

All at once in the room came a darkness that had nothing to do with the lack of candlelight. It was like a creeping shade which, like moisture being soaked up by paper, crept higher and higher up the walls. At the same time there came a sound like that of a strange, stertorous breathing. Jack looked out over the people who sat at the tables. Not one of them spoke or moved; they seemed transfixed. He looked back at John Callow.

He had never in his life seen such fear as that which he saw now. Callow stood on the platform gazing off, eyes wide, his lips drawn back over his teeth, the ugly rictus of his mouth fixed in abject terror. Jack peered off in the direction of the man's horrified gaze but could see nothing but the rising shadows. Turning to observe Callow's terror-stricken face, he remembered what Mrs Sanders had said: *If the runes are returned to the giver, then the curse goes with it. But with greater power than ever . . . His death would be indescribable.* Was this what Callow now feared?

The sound of the breathing, hoarse and rasping, grew louder, while over on the far wall the creeping shadow had become a huge, writhing mass which, even as Jack gazed, grew taller and broader. It appeared to be taking on the form of some strange beast. It continued to grow, stretching upwards towards the ceiling, reaching it and beginning to spread along its length in the direction of the platform on which he and Callow stood.

It drew closer, closer still, and then suddenly Callow's mouth was opening in a silent scream and he was turning, running along the platform behind the tables. Reaching the end, he stepped down onto the floor and turned again, now in the direction of the door. There he stopped, afraid to go further.

The shadow of the beast, now covering almost half the ceiling, seemed to have come to a halt. It remained hovering for some moments, its trembling form shifting and changing as if seen through water, and then began to move again. As its darkness crept forward Callow gave a gasping cry and turned and darted away, back onto the platform and behind the tables once more.

There was no escape. Trapped behind the centre table, just feet from where Jack stood, Callow turned and gazed out over the heads of the stricken assembly. They, not aware of the creeping shadow above them, saw only the strange behaviour of the man. And as they looked at him they saw him cast his eyes wildly about, as if searching for something. He found it, and took it up, and in his right hand they saw the glint of a blade. He stood there for a moment, staring out in terror, and then, with a swift, sure move he grasped the knife with both hands and pushed the point of the blade into the left side of his neck. Crimson blood spouted in a powerful, propelled stream. His hands moved again,

Bernard Taylor

and drew the deepburied blade across the width of
his throat. Then, while the blood continued to pulse
out of the gaping wound, his hands dropped to his
sides and the knife clattered to the floor. He remained standing there for a second or two longer,
and then fell forward over the blood-spattered table.

Chapter Twenty

Delayed like everyone else at the gathering while the police took statements, Jack didn't get back to Valley Green till almost one o'clock. Reaching The Limes, he pulled into the drive and brought the car to a halt. His bag now held only the gun; as far as he knew the Maddox Plate still lay on the floor beneath the table where he had placed it when making the switch.

Inside the house he found George dozing in a chair in front of the flickering television, an open book in his lap. He awoke at Jack's entrance, surprised at the lateness of the hour. The girls had been in bed for ages, he said. Back in the hall, Jack went up the stairs two steps at a time. Reaching the girls' room, he quietly opened the door and then just stood there in the doorway.

His heart was so full he could have wept. In the faint light that spilled from the landing he saw them lying in bed. He moved forward and crouched beside the two small sleeping figures. They lay with their heads only inches apart. The sound of their combined breathing was the sweetest sound he had ever heard. Briefly he closed his eyes in silent thanks and then leaned over and softly kissed each of them on the cheek. As he straightened, Kitty stirred and opened her eyes.

'Hello, Daddy.' Her voice was soft, sleepy, like warm velvet.

'Hello, sweetheart.' He could hardly speak.

Lydia awoke too. 'Hello, Daddy.'

'Hello, my baby.' Tears stung his eyes as he touched his fingers to her cheek.

Her hand came out and held him. 'We stayed awake for you,' she said, her eyelids flickering. 'We said we would.'

'Yes, you did indeed.'

Kitty said, 'Have we still got to go to school in the morning?'

'You know you have.'

'All right, then.' She nodded her tousled head on the pillow. 'What about afterwards?' She was beginning to drift off again.

'Afterwards?'

'You said we're going to do something special. What are we going to do?'

'What would you like to do?'

'I don't know. Something nice.'

'Yes,' Lydia murmured, 'something nice.'

'Well, you think about it, OK?' He leaned down and kissed them again. 'But you don't have to decide at this moment. You can think about it tomorrow.' The tears ran down his cheeks. 'There's plenty of time. We've got all the time in the world.'

In the doorway he turned and looked back at them as they lay in the soft and gentle dark. 'Good night,' he whispered. They did not answer; they were already asleep.